ST

MOEBIUS SQUARED

"SO THIS..." Cam gestured to the machinery. "This can only move us backwards and forwards in our own timeline."

"That's my best guess," Sam said. She pushed her bangs back out of her face. Her hair had grown out and was now caught in a pony tail at the back of her neck. "Just like Janus' puddlejumper."

"I don't even want to think about that thing," Daniel said. "Or anything else to do with Janus." He winced.

"Sorry," Sam said. "Sore spot."

"Damn right." Daniel had only been out of the infirmary for two weeks since his latest brush with one of Janus' inventions. This one had gotten him kidnapped and electrocuted.

They all spun around as the gate began to activate.

"Firing positions," Cam said, crouching down beside the control panel. If someone were making a grab for Ba'al's facility...

The wormhole opened and stabilized, a glittering puddle of blue. Cam's radio crackled. "SG-1, this is Stargate Command. You are to return to Earth immediately."

What the...? Cam chinned his radio on. "Stargate Command, we still have a lot to do here. Colonel Carter..."

"Return immediately," the voice of Sergeant Harriman said firmly. "Stargate Command has been attacked."

STARGATE SG·1™

MOEBIUS SQUARED

MELISSA SCOTT & JO GRAHAM

FANDEMONIUM BOOKS

An original publication of Fandemonium Ltd, produced under license from MGM Consumer Products.

Fandemonium Books, PO Box 795A, Surbiton, Surrey KT5 8YB, United Kingdom

Visit our website: www.stargatenovels.com

STARGATE SG·1™

METRO-GOLDWYN-MAYER Presents
STARGATE SG-1™
BEN BROWDER AMANDA TAPPING CHRISTOPHER JUDGE
with BEAU BRIDGES and MICHAEL SHANKS as Daniel Jackson
Executive Producers ROBERT C. COOPER & BRAD WRIGHT
Developed for Television by BRAD WRIGHT & JONATHAN GLASSNER

WWW.MGM.COM

ISBN: 978-1-905586-61-5 Printed in the USA

PROLOGUE

Egypt
2492 BC

THE SLANTING light of very early morning danced across the water of the Nile, cutting through the last of the predawn fog. An ibis took flight, white wings spreading. A fish jumped.

On a dock by the riverside, shaded by a grove of date palms, a man in what appeared to be a pair of white linen boxer shorts cast a line into the river and lazily began to reel it in. Colonel Jack O'Neill, USAF retired (very retired) picked up the clay cup at his elbow and took a sip through the straw, reflecting that he was never going to get entirely used to beer for breakfast.

Not that he had complaints. It was pretty malty beer, and the straw meant that you could kind of browse over the sediments in the bottom, but it was also really good beer. For breakfast. On what promised to be a gorgeous day. This retirement thing was working out pretty well.

Of course, this was about the only hour of the day he could count on peace and quiet. Any minute Ellie would be screaming, and when Ellie was up nobody was sleeping. And then there would be Aset bustling around insisting that eggs were more breakfast than beer and that Sam had to eat eggs or she'd lose her milk, and Daniel would be charging around with rolls of paper in his hands coming up with reasons why he couldn't change Ellie, and Sam would tie Ellie on her back while she was looking at Daniel's latest plan for something or other, and there wouldn't be a moment's peace until midnight.

But for now — blessed quiet. He could just sit here and drink his breakfast and fish.

"O'Neill?"

Jack closed his eyes. Yep. That was that. "Hey, Teal'c."

Teal'c came down the dock and regarded him solemnly. He was wearing a shenti, one of the white linen kilts that was just about the only thing Egyptian men wore most of the time, but it looked good on him. He had the height and the chest to carry it off. To look good in a shenti you really needed washboard abs.

Which was why Jack had stuck to pants as long as possible. But somewhere in the second year the only pair he had pretty much fell to pieces, and his attempts at tailoring had resulted in linen boxers and a big tunic like a kurta, which made people die laughing when they saw him. It had taken Daniel a month to explain that it was because here only eunuchs would wear anything like that. And so in the interests of avoiding misunderstandings, like being taken for two nuts short of a pound, he'd given up on the kurta unless it was really cold. The boxers were more or less the same length as a shenti, but gave a greater feeling of security.

Teal'c laid his head to the side, the necklace of links of pure gold around his neck shifting. "You are not occupied?"

"No, come pull up a piece of dock," Jack said. "It's nice and quiet."

"They are not awake at the house yet," Teal'c said, but didn't sit down. Obviously he was going somewhere important, and sitting on the dock he'd get dirt all over the back of his shenti. With his torso bare, the x of the symbiote pouch on his stomach showed starkly, and the faint scar where Apophis's tattoo had been was suddenly visible on his forehead. "I wondered if I might speak with you alone for a few moments."

Jack frowned. Nothing good started that way. "Shoot," he said.

"I had hoped that this eventuality would not occur for many years, but I was wrong." Teal'c looked out over the river, his hands behind his back. "I hoped, when I first thought that it might be so, that I was mistaken. But I am not. And so I must come to you, and trust that you will do what is necessary when the time comes."

Jack put down the beer. "What are we talking about here?"

Teal'c lifted his head, kohl rimmed eyes a little suspiciously bright. "My symbiote is maturing."

"I don't…"

"It is maturing, O'Neill. When it does, it will be an adult Goa'uld. And it will take a host. It will find a first host of its choosing and it will force them to serve it. And I will die." Teal'c's deep voice was calm. "When it happens, when the symbiote leaves me, you must kill it so that it can harm no one."

Jack frowned. "OK, two things. What if I'm not there when it gets ready."

"I have anticipated that," Teal'c said, his eyes on the far shore. "That is why it is best to remove it preemptively and kill it."

Jack blinked. "Won't that kill you?"

"I will die without a symbiote in any event, O'Neill. It is better that it is done in such a way that the symbiote has no chance to harm anyone else." He glanced back to the low mud brick house above the flood line, nestled among the palm trees. "It will choose from those closest to it. I do not want there to be a shadow of a chance…" His voice trailed off.

"That it could take Sam or Daniel or Aset or…"

"Or you, O'Neill. It must be done soon if there is to be no risk. That is why I am speaking with you. You are the only one who is capable of killing me." Teal'c half turned, looking down at Jack. "Will you not do this for me, my brother? Before there is any chance it harms those I love?"

Jack swallowed. "OK," he said. "Hold on here. I have to kill the symbiote. I'm good with that. But ordinarily wouldn't you just trade up for a new, immature symbiote? Isn't that what Jaffa usually do?"

"It is indeed," Teal'c said. "And what I should do, were there any other symbiotes on the planet. But the surviving Jaffa who served Ra were herded through the Stargate, and the Pharaoh Narmer killed the immature spawn who remained as we advised. It is not possible to simply take on another symbiote." He shook his head. "I will die, O'Neill. I have known that. But I thought it would be many years before this symbiote matured." He glanced at him sideways, and the corner of his mouth quirked. "It is not difficult to forget an evil day which one expects to be many years in the future when the present is sweet."

"Yeah." It had certainly occurred to Jack that he probably didn't have as many years left to him as he would in his own time, in a world with modern medicine, but there wasn't much point in thinking about that. He was fifty-five, not dead. He had quite a few good years left to him, and he meant to enjoy them. Yeah, he knew objectively he'd probably never see Ellie grown, but it wasn't like he expected to keel over tomorrow either. And Daniel and Sam were young. They'd be around for Ellie for a long time.

"It must be," Teal'c said quietly. "Swear to me that when the moment comes you will do as you must, before it can harm any other." His eyes met Jack's. "Swear it to me, O'Neill. That you will not let this Goa'uld take a host."

Jack swallowed again. "OK," he said. "I swear. But let's think through some options before we get there, buddy."

"There are no options." A shade of impatience crept into Teal'c's voice. "There are no other symbiotes."

"On Earth," Jack said.

Teal'c's eyebrows rose. "The Stargate is buried for a very good reason."

"Yeah, but it's been buried for three years. Ra's probably gotten tired of trying it. We could dig it up for a quick recon. What are the chances he'd dial in if it were open for a couple of hours?"

"That is a grave risk for one man," Teal'c said. "It is not a good decision."

"Neither is letting you die," Jack said.

CHAPTER ONE

Cheyenne Mountain
2008 AD

COLONEL Cameron Mitchell picked up a very ugly statue of a pig and looked at it. He hoped it wasn't a very ugly statue of a pig. "What's this?" he asked.

Daniel Jackson didn't look up from his computer monitor. "Pig," he said, still typing furiously.

"Right." Mitchell put the statue down and wandered around the worktable. All four walls of Jackson's office were lined with bookcases, and the table was piled high with more books, knickknacks, strange pieces of pottery, weird bits of wood and cloth, and a couple of spare clips of 9-millimeter ammunition. He picked up one book and glanced at it before he realized he didn't even read the alphabet. Cyrillic. OK. He put it down and picked up the next one, glancing over at Jackson, who was still absorbed in whatever was on his computer and read a few paragraphs.

"Daniel, who's Narmer?"

"Egyptian pharaoh, first dynasty." He didn't look up.

Mitchell squinted at the black and white photo of an old carving of a king in a big hat blasting somebody with what looked suspiciously like a staff weapon. "Who's this Scorpion King dude that Narmer killed? He looks like a Goa'uld."

"He probably was." Daniel pushed his glasses up on his nose but didn't glance over. "My best theory is that the myth of Narmer and the Scorpion King holds a kernel of memory of the actual victory of the Egyptians over Ra, the rebellion that succeeded in driving the Goa'uld from Earth in about 3,000 BC." His hands flew over his keyboard, typing at way better than temp speed. "Pity Narmer didn't live to enjoy his victory very long. He died soon after unifying the kingdom, leaving the throne to his son, Hor-Aḥa, whose reign was very troubled." Daniel frowned. "It's a very murky time. Not a great deal is known. There were wars and disturbances of some kind, but we really don't know much about it." He finally stopped and looked up. "Why?"

Mitchell shrugged, the book in his hand. "No reason. It's not important."

"It wouldn't be to you," Daniel said. "I can't imagine why you'd ever care."

Mitchell winced. "Jinx."

Daniel's fingers flew over the keyboard again. "What?"

"Jinx. Whenever somebody says that something's not important, I know it's going to bite me in the ass."

"How in the hell can Hor-Aha, Narmer and the Scorpion King bite you in the ass?"

"SG-1 to the gateroom." Walter's voice echoed over the intercom. "SG-1 to the gateroom."

"Finally," Mitchell said, dropping the book on the table. "Carter's through with her gate diagnostic and we can get a move on."

Daniel hit save and turned off his monitor as he stood up. "So we're off to Ba'al's secret installation?"

"That's what it looks like," Mitchell said, preceding Daniel out the door and waiting for him to turn off the lights and lock it. "SG-14 said that was their best guess. So we're going to go take a look."

"That ought to be easy," Daniel said, shrugging his jacket on and pulling the door shut behind him.

"Jinx," Mitchell said.

Sam and Teal'c were already in the gateroom and geared up, a couple of heavy looking boxes on the floor beside them. "What's that stuff?" Mitchell asked.

"Equipment," Sam said, her P90 at port arms. "SG-14 said the installation was a treasure trove of Goa'uld technology. I'd like to get started taking a good look at it as soon as possible."

"Right." Mitchell picked up his own weapon. It was a good idea to be ready for trouble even when that seemed unlikely. After all, the installation had already been secured by other SG teams, and it had been completely unoccupied when they found it. Still, the thing about the system lords was that you could never count on a secret base staying unoccupied. Even if they were right, and this was one of Ba'al's, somebody besides them would be eager to get their hands on it.

"Let's see what we've got," Daniel said, shrugging into his tac vest. "Ba'al's toys are always so much fun." His voice was fairly dripping with sarcasm, and Mitchell caught Sam giving him a quick sideways look, as though there were some history there he wasn't aware of.

Which there probably was. Even though he'd been with SG-1 for more than three years now, Cam still felt like the new guy sometimes. Sam and Daniel and Teal'c had been doing this together for almost twelve years. Well, give or take last year when Sam had been in Atlantis and the year Daniel had been dead. You couldn't say the job didn't have some weird moments.

"Where's Vala?" Sam asked, looking around.

"Remember the guy who was Ba'al's host?" Mitchell asked.

Sam winced. "Vividly."

"Vala went back to spend some more time with him," Mitchell said. "She talked to him after the extraction ceremony and she said he was having a rough time. She promised she'd come back in a couple of days and talk some more. You know. Been there, done that." Vala had once been host to the Goa'uld Quetesh, so she'd been there and done that in the most literal sense. A lot of people wouldn't want to be reminded of what that had been like, but that was Vala for you, one of the things he liked best about her. She might talk a tough show, but helping this guy had been her idea. "I told her it was cool if she wanted to go today. We don't have anything big planned."

Sam nodded. "OK."

He supposed he ought to have said something to her first, another one of the weird little currents around here. Technically, Sam ranked him. But then technically she wasn't posted to SG-1. Landry had had no idea what to do with her when the IOA dismissed her from Atlantis with no warning. He'd had her back at the SGC in a heartbeat of course, but she was assigned to the base, not the team. Assigning her to SG-1 would have pulled the rug out from under Mitchell. Luckily, he and Sam had always gotten along super well, since they'd been in the same flight at the Academy Mitchell's first year, in 1988. Sam had been a junior, and she'd been really good to him.

Up in the control room, General Landry was standing by the glass window that overlooked the gateroom. "Colonel Mitchell, you have a go whenever you're ready."

Mitchell nodded sharply. At least O'Neill wasn't still here. He'd gone back to DC a couple of days ago. Much as Mitchell admired the guy, it was kind of nerve wracking getting on with business in front of him. He'd been a legend when Cam took command of SG-1, the guy with the biggest shoes on the block that Cam was now expected to fill. In the last three years he'd eased up a little. He knew he was doing a good job, and Landry concurred. Every time he'd seen O'Neill, the guy had been nothing but nice.

But still. O'Neill was a major general as well as a legend. Last week he'd gone with them to Ba'al's extraction ceremony, in which the symbiote Ba'al was for once and all removed from its host and finished. Mitchell hadn't had anything to do except look attentive, but it had still been nerve wracking. Even though O'Neill had taken them all to lunch afterwards. Cam was definitely not in the 'pal around with a living legend' place yet.

They waited while the coordinates were dialed and the chevrons locked, while the blue flare of the Stargate whooshed open and the wormhole stabilized. Sam and Daniel were talking about the dialect of Goa'uld used on some control interfaces. Right. Mitchell looked at Teal'c. "So basically we've got nothing to do on this one."

"It is to be devoutly hoped," Teal'c said. It was hard to tell if that was supposed to be a joke or not.

They stepped through the Stargate into a huge chamber that appeared to be carved out of solid rock. "Not that different from the gateroom in Cheyenne Mountain," Mitchell said.

"That may be where he got the idea," Daniel replied. He was already stepping away from the gate, his eyes roving around. "As security goes..." His voice trailed off.

Other than being solid rock and having a Stargate in it, it wasn't the same. Three pads were suspended over a deep chasm. One of them held the Stargate and one a conventional set of Rings. The third had a bunch of control panels — presumably the DHD for the Stargate, the controls for the Rings, and other stuff. Sam was already heading for the controls, slinging one of the heavy cases with her. In the middle...

Cam walked along the platform toward it. He'd never seen anything like it, nor did he have any idea what it was supposed to do. It was a massive banded column of dirty steel about thirty feet high, not as wide as a set of Rings, though a couple of guys could fit in it nicely. Some kind of transport device? Some kind of...something?

Sam was glancing over the control panel, her eyes roving from one screen to another. "OK, this is interesting."

"What is?" Cam asked.

Teal'c came and leaned over her shoulder. "Fascinating," he said.

Right. Everybody read Goa'uld except him. In the last couple of years the Ori had seemed more to the point. "I'll just watch the door," Mitchell said.

"Solar flares," Sam said, apropos of nothing.

"What?"

She looked around. "Solar flares. This installation is hooked into a massive subspace communications system monitoring solar activity in real time. There must be thousands of satellites around thousands of suns. It's an enormous undertaking."

"Cool," Mitchell said. "That's a good thing to find, right? We can learn a lot from that."

"The question is why it was interesting to Ba'al," Daniel said.

Sam nodded grimly. "That is the question."

"We've run into way too many of Ba'al's traps in the past," Mitchell said.

Daniel looked worried. "That stuff he was saying at the extraction, about having a failsafe…"

"I'll figure out what it does," Sam said, spreading her hands on the keyboard. "We'll get a handle on it."

Cam turned, looking around the massive chamber. Rings. Control panel. Strange column. Stargate. "I don't like this a bit," he said to Teal'c.

"It's a short list," Lt. Colonel Davis said, laying the one page report on Jack's desk. "Here are General Pellegrino's recommendations. They're all excellent officers."

"They should be," Jack said. His hand twitched, but he didn't pick up the paper yet. "Command of the *George Hammond* is a big responsibility."

"Yes, sir." Davis hovered, waiting.

"That will be all," Jack said.

"Yes, sir." Davis turned to leave.

"Do I have to make a recommendation?"

Davis turned back. "No, sir. But a lack of your endorsement will be seen as a black mark."

"Understood."

Davis nodded shortly. There was nothing he knew that he shouldn't. Davis never knew anything he shouldn't.

The door closed behind him, and Jack took a long breath and strolled over to his windows. Homeworld Security had offices with Homeland Security on Massachusetts Avenue, rather than in the Pentagon, and he had to say that at least the view was better, looking up the street toward the white marble grandeur of Union Station and Columbus Circle, a beautiful autumn day in DC, with the sky an impenetrable shade of blue, looking as though the ceiling were almost solid. His reflection in the glass didn't mar the view.

Jack O'Neill was a good man. Lots of people said so. A good officer. A good friend. Once they'd said he was a good husband and a good father, though they'd been wrong about that. But overall, he was a good guy.

He'd never had any pretensions to greatness. In the course of thirty-five years in the Air Force he'd seen greatness, the ones who had whatever it was, that rare combination of talent and luck and character that propelled some people to soar above their peers. Vision. Leadership. Longing. Maybe it was that they desired something so much that the world bent around them. Or maybe they were just that good. He wasn't one of them. He was a good man. And he did a good job. But he knew it when he saw it. He heard the sound of wings, even if it was a music he couldn't make. And he'd never stand in the way.

He walked back to his desk and picked up the piece of paper. Command of the *George Hammond*, Earth's newest starship, bound on journeys that were literally unbelievable, distant and deadly, to places and things that would change one forever.

He wasn't surprised at the first name.

Colonel Samantha Carter.

Vala Mal Doran was bored. Bored, bored, bored. She wandered around the briefing room picking up first one thing and then another. Laser pointer. That was kind of cool. Would it be diffused by glass? If she shone it through the window into General Landry's office and made the little red point of light dance around on his desk...

Landry looked up. "Will you stop that?"

She took that as an invitation to come in, pocketing the

laser pointer as she did. "Explain to me again why I can't go join the team?"

Landry sighed. But he didn't look all that fascinated by his paperwork either. "Do you know how much power it takes to open that gate? Do you know how expensive that is? We have thirty SG teams and the Atlantis expedition. Which means the gate is flapping all day. Not only that, there are scheduled check-ins from twenty or so different sources in every 24 hour period, teams checking in, Atlantis dumping mail, allies... We can't open the gate every time somebody wants to go somewhere. You were offworld when SG-1 left. There is no critical reason you need to be on this mission. So. I'm not opening the gate so you can go join them. You can wait right here until they get back."

"Teaching me a lesson?" Vala perched on the edge of his desk.

"Teaching everybody a lesson about conserving power and time. We don't use the gate unless it's mission-specific."

"You're crabby today," Vala observed.

"Thank you." Landry bent over his paperwork again.

Vala didn't move. "This wouldn't have anything to do with Dr. Jackson returning to the team since he got out of the infirmary after yet another attempt to move to Atlantis went entirely and completely pear shaped? Because if it does, I have to tell you that I'm completely over Daniel."

"I have no idea what you're talking about," Landry said. He didn't look up.

"Really. Actually."

Landry did look up then. "I could care less. Is that clear? I am not your gal pal, and whoever you have a thing for or don't have a thing for, I don't care."

"I don't think that's what gal pal means," Vala began, but the warning claxons interrupted her.

"Unauthorized gate activation!"

"Not again," Landry said, getting heavily to his feet. "Let's go see who wants what." He went down the stairs to the control room, Vala trailing him.

The airman on duty looked up. "Sir, the IDC is the Tok'ra High Council."

"Open the shield," Landry directed. "And tell them they're welcome." He didn't sound precisely thrilled, but then Vala supposed the Tok'ra High Council were pretty much the definition of a cheerless lot. Unfortunately, they were also the definition of really important allies. Landry straightened his tie.

The shield retracted, and five Tok'ra stepped through the glowing blue of the wormhole, two women and three men in the tan and white clothing the Tok'ra preferred. Two of them looked vaguely familiar. Maybe she'd seen them in the background at the extraction? She hadn't paid all that much attention to every attendant. She thought she'd at least seen that one in front with the shock of brown hair.

A lieutenant met them on the gateroom floor, exchanging pleasantries gamely, and then escorted them into the control room to Landry.

"General Landry," the young man with brown hair said gravely. "It is an honor to meet a man about whom I have heard so much."

"Thank you," Landry said.

"Vala Mal Doran," Vala put out there.

"We bring a matter of concern to the Tok'ra High Council," he said formally.

"If you'd care to take a walk up to my office, I'd be delighted to discuss it," Landry said with a look at Vala that pretty clearly said stay here and out of the way.

"We would prefer to discuss it here," the woman at his shoulder said. Vala heard the buzz of the zat'nik'tel arming a bare second before the bright stun beam caught her full in the chest.

CHAPTER TWO

VALA awoke with a shoe in her mouth. Perhaps not exactly in her mouth, but with the toe resting at her lips. One eye opened. The shoe was attached to a foot in a black sock, attached to a leg that seemed to be attached to an unconscious General Landry.

Another foot, this one moving. Someone in Tok'ra boots stepped over Landry's body. Vala closed her eyes quickly. It wasn't hard to stay still. She wasn't sure she could move if she tried. Every muscle in her body felt like lead. Still, she was conscious and aware. That was better than everyone else who had been in the control room. She had no doubt that the airmen on duty were also unconscious.

They didn't know who she was, Vala thought, as she heard the sounds of hands on keyboards. They didn't recognize her as the woman who had once been host to the Goa'uld Quetesh. It must be some residual effect of that, the naquadah still in her blood or something, that had rendered her slightly less susceptible to the zat than Landry and the others. Which meant the only place they had seen her was probably where she had seen them — at the extraction ceremony she'd attended as a member of SG-1. They didn't know she wasn't Tau'ri.

More keyboard clicks, and then an all too familiar sound. The gate was dialing. The Tok'ra had done whatever it was they'd come for and were dialing out.

Another set of steps. "Are you done?"

"Yes," the one at the dialing computer replied.

The new voice was appraising. "Which of these is Landry?"

"That one."

Vala tensed.

"Help me lift him up where he can be seen from the floor.

She needs a little persuading."

Who needs? There were more sounds, and Vala shifted slightly. She could flex her fingers. Movement was returning. She was a long way from being able to jump two people, but feeling was coming back. She needed to see the dialing address. It would be displayed on the monitor of the central workstation. If she could lift her head a few inches she ought to be able to see it. Vala looked out through her lashes. Not quite. The edge of the desk was in the way.

The two Tok'ra were lifting General Landry up, his head lolling forward. He could be seen through the window. If there were shouts or voices down on the gateroom floor she couldn't hear them. The glass was too thick.

They lowered him heavily into the controller's chair. Now it was Landry's arm that blocked her view of the dialing computer. "Let's go," one of them said.

They stepped over her hastily on their way out. She heard their booted feet on the floor outside.

Vala raised her head. The dialing address. It wasn't one she was familiar with. Fishhook, star, boat. Shield, torch, dragon's tail. And the circle above the pyramid, of course. Her head spun. Gathering her strength, Vala pushed up on both elbows. Her legs didn't work very well, but she lunged forward and dragged herself to her knees on the edge of the desk. She could just peer through the bottom of the window between the monitors.

Sitting on the floor of the gateroom in front of the open wormhole was a puddle jumper. Which suddenly made the bit with Landry make sense. Only one person currently assigned to the base and not on an offworld team had a naturally expressed ATA gene — Dr. Carolyn Lam. If the Tok'ra were trying to steal a puddle jumper, they'd have to get someone to fly it. No doubt Dr. Lam had refused. At least until they'd demonstrated that her father was completely in their power.

The two Tok'ra from the control room were doing something, opening a device beside the puddle jumper, one Vala recognized all too well. A timed charge. Detonating in the gateroom, it wouldn't damage the gate and the explosion wouldn't be bad enough to break the heavy bulletproof glass of the control room windows. However, the unconscious airmen on the floor of the gateroom would be toast. And it would probably screw up the power supply cables to the gate badly enough that it would be hours if not days before the gate could be used again. The Tok'ra looked around nervously, as though not certain that the door was secure. It was closed, of course. But there were plenty of people who could override it. In fact, probably right now people were trying to get onto this level. They would. Vala was sure of that. But not fast enough. And with the wormhole open, no offworld teams could get through and interrupt.

She dragged herself to the communications console, keeping her head down. And of course they'd slagged it. There wasn't anything but the loudspeaker to the gateroom working, the low-tech handset that Walter used to warn people on the floor when the gate was about to activate.

Still, she had to make sure they didn't set the timer...

There was someone's pistol on the floor under the desk. Fat lot of good that did. It wouldn't penetrate the bulletproof glass either. And nobody kept an automatic in the control room. Vala patted her pockets absently.

The laser pointer. The one she'd picked up in the briefing room. Could the Tok'ra tell the difference between a laser pointer and a laser sight? She bet not.

Vala opened the intercom and turned on the pointer, letting it play through the glass, dancing over the side of the puddle jumper as though hunting a target. "Get your hands up!" she said authoritatively. "We have you covered. Drop your weapons!" She sighted the pointer on the nearest Tok'ra, red dot against the side of his head.

He dodged reflexively, his friend shouting something as the pointer swung to her. The first Tok'ra made a dive for the puddlejumper doors, the second following after. If she'd actually had a P90, Vala would have had a perfect shot.

Unfortunately, what she actually had was a laser pointer, so she was reduced to shouting for them to drop their weapons and stand down while the tailgate of the jumper came up and the jumper leapt forward through the open wormhole.

"Damn it," Vala said quietly as the event horizon died.

Beside her, Landry moaned.

Still hanging on to the edge of the desk, Vala bent over him. "General Landry? Wake up. It's Vala. Come on. Rise and shine."

He opened his eyes, then squeezed them shut again. "What in the hell?" he whispered.

"It's not good," Vala said grimly.

Sam bent over the control board, a fascinated expression on her face. "I think this is some kind of time travel machine," she said.

"Come again?" Cam said.

"Time travel." She looked up at him, her hands still on the keys. "Other than Ancient artifacts, the only way we know of to travel through time occurs at the intersection of an active wormhole and a solar flare. The problem is that solar flares are only predictable for a few minutes before they occur, and the only way to guess the time you would go to would involve intersecting the solar flare with a wormhole in the correct place by dialing the right gate at the right moment. Essentially impossible. Unless, of course, you can monitor the solar activity of hundreds of suns and simultaneously calculate where each one would take you if you dialed what. I think that's what this machine does."

"Oh, not good," Daniel said.

"Indeed," Teal'c added, his voice concerned. "Perhaps that is what Ba'al meant about a failsafe."

"Well, if it is, it didn't work," Cam said sensibly. "Our timeline hasn't changed."

"Would we know if it had?" Sam asked. "I don't think so."

"I feel the same as always," Cam said.

"You would feel the same as always," she said. "We all would. If the timeline changed, we'd never be aware that we were now living in an alternate universe, or that other ones of us might have had very different experiences."

"That's creepy," Cam said.

Sam looked disturbed. "Tell me about it."

"Wait," Daniel said. "But we do know. Remember the video tape we got from the jar hidden in Egypt? The one from a team of alternate us that told us not to do anything? The one found about four years ago?"

"That's different," Sam said. "They had crossed over from an alternate timeline into our past, so now they were in the same timeline, just at a different point in it."

"You have totally lost me," Cam said. He thought Teal'c wanted to agree, but he wouldn't say it.

"Look, it's like sheets of paper. If you have a legal pad, say. You can draw a circle on the first page, and then on page four, and then another on page one. You can't see the ones on page one and page four at the same time because they're on different planes, and they're two dimensional objects. But you can see both the circles on page one at the same time because while they don't occupy the same coordinates, they're on the same plane."

Daniel's brow furrowed. "So you're saying that the alternate team and us are on the same plane, in the same timeline, but we're just at different points, whereas teams from another alternate reality, like the quantum mirror ones, aren't in the same timeline."

"Yes." Sam nodded encouragingly. "It's really simple."

"So this..." Cam gestured to the machinery. "This can only move us backwards and forwards in our own timeline."

"That's my best guess," Sam said. She pushed her bangs back out of her face. Her hair had grown out and was now caught in a pony tail at the back of her neck. "Just like Janus' puddlejumper."

"I don't even want to think about that thing," Daniel said. "Or anything else to do with Janus." He winced.

"Sorry," Sam said. "Sore spot."

"Damn right." Daniel had only been out of the infirmary for two weeks since his latest brush with one of Janus' inventions. This one had gotten him kidnapped and electrocuted.

They all spun around as the gate began to activate.

"Firing positions," Cam said, crouching down beside the control panel. If someone were making a grab for Ba'al's facility…

The wormhole opened and stabilized, a glittering puddle of blue. Cam's radio crackled. "SG-1, this is Stargate Command. You are to return to Earth immediately."

What the…? Cam chinned his radio on. "Stargate Command, we still have a lot to do here. Colonel Carter…"

"Return immediately," the voice of Sergeant Harriman said firmly. "Stargate Command has been attacked."

They came through the gate into a quiet gateroom. Other than the extra guards on duty at the bottom of the ramp, Sam wouldn't have known anything was wrong. There were no signs of an explosion, no spent cartridges or signs of a firefight. She frowned. Even Sergeant Harriman was at his usual place in the control room windows.

"Welcome back, SG-1," he said. "General Landry would like to see you in the briefing room immediately."

"Of course," Sam said, handing off her weapon and her tac vest to one of the airmen and glancing at Cam. He looked worried. And also perplexed. Was she stepping on his feet again? He'd run SG-1 for a year without her while she was in Atlantis. Technically, he still was, as she was spending more time with training and stepping into the role of Landry's exec than with the team, but when she was in the field it was a little awkward. She'd gotten used to command in Atlantis, and while she loved the team and being home, it was like putting back on a pair of jeans you had years ago. They may fit, but somehow they don't look right.

"Let's see what's up," Cam said, and they followed him through the doors.

The control room was more of a mess. A couple of workstations looked like they'd taken fire. No blood, no ballistics teams—what in the world had happened here? Daniel must be thinking the same thing, because he galloped up the stairs to the briefing room ahead of her.

Landry had a big bruise across his forehead, and he was sitting up in his usual chair at the head of the table holding an ice pack on it. Vala was pacing around the room, a mug of coffee in her hands.

"Are you OK?" Cam asked.

"Fine," Vala said. "I was zatted. My head hurts." She sounded terse, an unusual thing for Vala, and a sure sign of how bad this was.

"What happened, sir?" Sam said.

"We were attacked." Landry gestured to the briefing chairs, and Sam sunk into the one to his right, Daniel beside her. "By the Tok'ra."

Teal'c's head came up sharply. "That is impossible."

"I wish it were," Landry said. "Five people. They had the IDC of the Tok'ra High Council, and Vala says she recognized two of them from the Tok'ra at Ba'al's Extraction Ceremony. I don't think there's much doubt that they were Tok'ra."

"Why would the Tok'ra attack us?" Sam asked. "They've been our allies for the better part of ten years. We haven't had any recent disagreements, no policy problems, no breakdown of relations..." It was entirely out of the blue.

"That is what we're wondering, Colonel," Landry said testily. "They used zats only. Nobody was killed. But..."

"They tried to set off a charge in the gateroom," Vala interrupted. "That would have killed people. And they kidnapped

Dr. Lam."

Cam swung around. "What?"

Landry looked gray. He actually looked old for the first time Sam could remember. "They stormed their way in here and stole Janus' experimental puddle jumper. Since obviously none of the Tok'ra could fly it, they kidnapped Dr. Lam. Fortunately, Vala saw the address they dialed out to. SG-15 just checked it out. It's an uninhabited barren world with a gate that hasn't been reactivated since they dialed into it. But as far as we can tell, they aren't still there."

"Picked up by another ship," Teal'c said firmly. "That is possible. If they rendezvoused with a larger vessel…"

"Hasn't been reactivated since they dialed in," Sam said, with a horrible sinking feeling in her stomach.

"I just said that," Landry snapped.

Daniel was on the same wavelength. "But if that gate was activated to dial somewhere else more than six months ago, the address wouldn't be in the buffer."

Landry blinked. "What?"

"If they used the time function on the puddle jumper after they went through, sir," Sam said. "There's no other reason to steal that ship other than to use the time function. But they wouldn't want to use it here, because if they were going further back than the 1950s they would emerge into solid rock. They'd want to make the translation on a barren world where they wouldn't affect anything unintentionally and where there wouldn't be anything to run into, and then use the gate in that time to go wherever they wanted. We wouldn't see any evidence of where they dialed out to if they did so more than six months ago. The buffer patterns degrade after a certain amount of time…"

Landry waved away the rest of the explanation. "You're saying they've traveled through time."

"That seems the most likely thing, sir," Sam said. As much as she disliked the idea. "The question is when."

"No," Landry said. "The question is why. Is there any further data you can get out of the gate they dialed to, Colonel?"

Sam shook her head. "Unlikely, sir. If they dialed out years ago, the pattern in the buffer would have degraded completely. There's nothing I could learn from the DHD."

"Then you're going to go see the Tok'ra," Landry said.

Daniel blinked. "What do the Tok'ra say about this?"

The general spread his hands, the ice pack still in one of them. "They disavow all knowledge of these events and say they couldn't possibly have had anything to do with them, even when we sent them the security video."

"They're stonewalling," Daniel said.

"Which is why I'm sending Colonel Carter to talk to them," Landry said. He looked at Sam. "You've always had a good relationship with the Tok'ra. I want you to leverage some answers. Colonel Mitchell, you and SG-1 will back her up. And by that I do mean backup. I want you to nail their feet to the wall and get some answers."

"We'll do our best, sir," Sam said, and inwardly winced. That was what she would have said ten years ago, not what she should say now.

"What about the puddle jumper?" Cam said. "Anything we should know?"

"Dr. Lee said it was completely operational. Before he was zatted." Landry shook his head at Lee's unfortunate honesty. "He's in the infirmary because he hit his head on the lab bench when he fell over, but he should be fine." He looked at Sam again. "Colonel, you are authorized to take whatever measures you see fit, including saying we'll break off relations with the Tok'ra. Is that clear?"

"Very clear, sir," Sam said. Of course that would never have been necessary when her father was alive, retired General Jacob Carter, who had become a Tok'ra host. But Jacob was dead, and Martouf, and many of the others she had known well over the years. The Tok'ra casualties in the last years of the war had been high, and there were a lot of new faces in command positions. They were unknown quantities.

On the other hand, so was she. She wasn't a thirty-year-old captain anymore who just happened to be Jacob's daughter.

She looked at Cameron Mitchell. "Ready to go?"

"We're ready," Cam said. "Vala?"

"Oh, I'm coming," Vala said determinedly. "You aren't leaving without me."

CHAPTER THREE

IT WAS hard not to notice that the tunnels were less crowded than they had been the last time, confirming all the reports that the Tok'ra were in serious decline, but Daniel found it hard to muster much sympathy under the circumstances. At least their escort seemed suitably embarrassed, leading them briskly through the tunnels without making an effort to assert Tok'ra superiority. Daniel glanced sideways as they approached the entrance to the council chamber, gauging Sam's reaction. She was still furious, all right, but he didn't think anyone else would realize, at least not at first. The Atlantis command had improved her poker face. Mitchell, on the other hand, was frankly scowling—which might not be a bad thing; he was there to be the heavy. And Vala was looking focused and intent, which for her might well count as seriously annoyed.

"Colonel Carter and SG-1, of the Tau'ri," the escort said, and stepped back to let them enter.

Sam stepped briskly through the door—Atlantis had gotten her used to being in charge, too—and stopped abruptly. Daniel stepped sideways to avoid running into her, and felt his own breath catch in his throat. The membership of the High Council had changed since the last time they'd dealt with the Tok'ra. Per'sus he recognized, the graying man in the center seat, and Sal'tor—and Anise. Though what she was doing on the Council, after the last time she'd screwed around with them... The scientist saw him looking and met his gaze defiantly.

"Supreme High Councillor Per'sus," Sam said, and he inclined his head in answer. "You know why we're here."

"We do," Per'sus said, and gestured toward the waiting chairs. It was the host speaking, Daniel realized. "We welcome you, though we profoundly wish it were under other circumstances."

"As do we," Sam said, and seated herself. "I'm going to cut to the chase, Councillor. Some of your people attacked our base, stole an Ancient spacecraft, and kidnapped one of our people to fly it for them. General Landry is not happy."

"We cannot blame him." That was the symbiote, Per'sus, his voice resonant. "And we can only offer our most sincere regrets. Yet we cannot accept that any of our people would have been so foolish as to attack our allies."

"Oh, come on," Mitchell said, not quite under his breath.

"You've seen our security video," Sam said.

"Renegade Goa'uld—" Per'sus began, but Sam kept speaking.

"And they had the High Council's IDC. If they aren't Tok'ra, you have an even bigger problem than we do."

Per'sus winced at that.

"And I recognized them," Vala said. "I was at the extraction ceremony, and I saw two of them there. I could identify them from your records, if that would help."

Sal'tor folded careful hands. The host was a small woman, her gray hair wound into a bun, lines bracketing her mouth. "I believe, Per'sus, that—further investigation—has made what seemed impossible somewhat more likely." Her head dipped, and this time it was the host who spoke. "And perhaps it would be advisable for us to show Vala our records of the extraction. If we can identify the miscreants for certain, then we can act."

Per'sus nodded. "Yes, that might be the best course of action."

You're stalling, Daniel thought. Before he could say anything, Sam shook her head.

"We can get to that, certainly. But you've had the chance to look over our footage, so you must have some idea of who these people are and what they want."

"The images were blurred," Anise said. "Precise identification was impossible." It was the first time she had spoken, and Sam gave her a cold stare.

"I'm sure you're more than capable of cleaning up our data."

She looked back at Per'sus. "You understand, of course, that if our allies have been compromised, either by renegade Goa'uld—" Her tone made it clear how unlikely she thought that was. "Or by factions within their own government, that we will need to take measures to secure our own operations."

"I can assure you that we will take all appropriate action to deal with this situation," Per'sus said.

Sam shook her head. "Per'sus, we have been attacked. One of our people has been kidnapped. It's only due to the intervention of Vala here that no one was killed—your people planted explosives in our gateroom. They also stole a puddle jumper equipped with a time travel device, and we have reason to believe that they have used it. I think you are as aware as we are of the inherent dangers of meddling with the timeline."

Sal'tor took a deep breath. It was the Tok'ra who spoke, not the host. "I believe that the leader of this group is one called Marik."

Daniel glanced at Sam, but she looked as blank as he felt. Mitchell frowned. "He was leader of the team who worked at the SGC last year. Which explains how he knew about the jumper."

"Marik was indeed part of that team," Per'sus said, reluctantly. "And he has acquired a reputation as one who acts precipitously. But I assure you, we had no knowledge of any such plan, nor any idea of what he could have intended."

"That's very unfortunate," Sam said, after a moment. "Because we need to locate them as soon as possible. For all our sakes."

"And we will give you all the help we can," Per'sus said. "But, as you know, our numbers and our influence have dwindled over these last few years. We have far fewer resources to offer."

Not that they were ever really happy to share, Daniel thought. From the sound of things, Sam and Per'sus could go on fencing all night. He looked at Sal'tor, who sat with tightly folded hands, and then at Anise. She sat motionless, her face utterly still under the cap of golden hair, her eyes barely moving as she tracked the discussion.

"What we need is a starting point," Sam said. By some miracle, her voice remained coldly patient. "Some idea of Marik's intentions."

Anise's eyes flickered. It wasn't much of a change, and if Daniel hadn't been watching so closely, he would have missed it, but it was unmistakable.

"We do not know," Per'sus said. "You are welcome to make your own inquiries, of course, but — we know nothing."

"You may not," Daniel said, "but she does." He nodded to Anise.

Sam fixed her eyes on Per'sus. "I'm inclined to believe Dr. Jackson's assessment, here."

The Tok'ra leader hesitated, and Sal'tor said, "Colonel Carter is Jacob's daughter, and was host to Jolinar."

Per'sus nodded at that, and the host said, "It is a fair argument." His head dipped again, and this time the Tok'ra spoke. "Answer them, Anise."

"We cannot be certain," she said.

"I don't expect certainty from you," Sam said. The words had bite, and Daniel guessed that she was thinking about the za'tarc, and how Anise's untried device had nearly gotten her and Jack branded as Goa'uld agents. "What I expect from an ally is information."

Sal'tor said, "You are aware, Colonel Carter, that we have suffered greatly in recent years. Our numbers are dwindling, and we found our lost queen, Egeria, mother of the Tok'ra, only to have her snatched away from us."

"Colonel Mitchell is correct," Anise said. "Marik was the leader of the group we sent to the SGC last year, and he did indeed learn of this time travel device while he was there. On his return, he placed a proposal before the High Council: that we obtain the device from the Tau'ri and use it to replenish our ranks. Of course the Council refused to sanction such a risk."

"But you think they've done it anyway," Sam said. She shook her head. "That doesn't make sense. You know as well as anyone how dangerous it is to meddle with the timeline."

Not that mere danger had ever stopped Anise, Daniel thought. But Sam was right, it had to be something big, if the Tok'ra were going to risk changing the past. Their victory over both the Goa'uld and the Ori rested on so many little things, so many moments when the slightest change, one choice tipping the other way, could lose everything. It couldn't just be that they needed more Tok'ra — Egeria, he thought. That was the key. "You don't have any queens left," he said. "There's no one left to spawn new Tok'ra."

Sal'tor winced, and Per'sus reluctantly bent his head. "That is so."

"And that's why," Daniel said. He looked at Sam. "That's it. That's why they were willing to risk it. If they don't get a new queen, the Tok'ra will become extinct."

Sam nodded slowly. "OK," she said. "I'll buy that."

"We refused to sanction such an adventure," Per'sus said. The Tok'ra sounded suddenly very tired. "Dr. Jackson is right, we are staring extinction in the face. All our females have been killed, and our mother, our best hope, died on Pangor."

"She died according to her principles," Sal'tor's host said. "Saving human and Tok'ra lives."

"If we are to survive as a people, we must make some difficult choices," Per'sus said. "Choices which may well be impossible. We cannot breed more Tok'ra — Egeria's line is ended. We have found a few surviving larvae, and preserved them in secure tanks, but they are Goa'uld. Their genetic memories are of their parent, not our own, and we do not know if even the most careful rearing can overcome their inborn instincts. Nor do we dare recruit any of the few minor Goa'uld who have survived. They are even less likely to convert to our ways. We have pinned our hopes on cloning technology, and hope that we can produce a new generation before we ourselves die out, but that road is long, and the Tok'ra are painfully few."

"Marik proposed a different solution," Anise said, her voice distant. "He believed that we could travel back in time to a recent, or even a long ago spawning, and bring back a larval queen to replenish our line. He claimed to have identified several possibilities, points where the disappearance of a single larva would make no difference to the timeline. However, as Per'sus has said, the High Council believed the risk to be too great."

"Apparently Marik didn't agree," Mitchell said.

"And no Tau'ri have never acted without the approval of their superiors?" Anise asked sweetly.

Daniel ignored her. "It would be way too dangerous," he said. "Unless you found an instance where a larva — or larvae — had vanished already, and presumably you have records of such instances, if there are any?"

"We do not keep such records," Anise said. "It was too great a risk to our own security."

Daniel shook his head. "No. No, I know you don't keep records as such, but you have —" He stopped himself just in time, swallowing anything that would sound too much as though he were calling them Goa'uld. "You have the genetic memories of your immediate and distant ancestors. One of you — one of them — should be able to identify if anything like that ever happened. And when."

Sam gave him a sharp look, and he willed her to understand. The last thing he wanted to do was to mention Ba'al's device to the Tok'ra, but as a last resort —

"Yes," Per'sus said. "That is true." He and Sal'tor exchanged looks, and Per'sus nodded. "The High Council remains resolute in its belief that Marik's plan poses an immediate and grave danger to everything we have achieved."

"The High Council," Anise said, "is not unanimous in this."

"Nonetheless, the majority decision stands," Per'sus said. "We are willing, Colonel Carter, to cooperate with you in finding the most likely time and place for Marik to have gone." He shook his head. "Though what you will do then — I cannot see."

"We'll cross that bridge when we come to it," Sam said. "Thank you, Per'sus."

"And as a further token of our sincerity," Per'sus said, "we of the Council are willing to be the first questioned."

Anise looked up sharply. "I object."

"If you wish to remain on the Council," Per'sus began, and she sagged slightly.

"Very well, I agree. But only under protest."

"Thank you," Sam said, firmly. "The sooner we begin, the better."

CHAPTER FOUR

HANK Landry was usually happy to see Jack O'Neill. Not today. O'Neill had his third star, and he was in command of Homeworld Security, which oversaw Stargate Command. And he was arriving from Washington by special flight to deal with the massive security breach that had occurred at the SGC on Landry's watch. This was not a happy thing.

Not that O'Neill would yell and scream. He would be perfectly calm and measured. It would just be very obvious that this had never happened during O'Neill's tenure in the job, that the whole thing was handled remarkably poorly in a way that O'Neill would never have permitted, nor his illustrious predecessor Hammond. It made Hank squirm just thinking about it.

And so the moment the briefing room doors closed on just the two of them, Hank was ready for it.

"So," O'Neill said. He walked over to the windows that looked out on the gateroom below, his gray head encircled by the curve of the gate like a vast halo. Hank wondered if he did things like that on purpose, or if it was just the universe's usual serendipity where Jack O'Neill was concerned.

"SG-1 is shaking down the Tok'ra," Hank said.

A tilt of the head. "That'll work," he said dryly.

"It might." Hank came around the end of the table to stand next to him. "Colonel Carter may be able to get something out of them."

Another tilt. "Maybe. I'd give Daniel more leeway there. He's better at shaking people down than Carter is. Unless they're Wraith." O'Neill paused. "We'll get her back."

Hank shook his head. "I can't even think about that."

"They need her alive and in good shape to fly the puddle

jumper," O'Neill said. "Carolyn's OK. And she's going to be OK. They need someone with the ATA gene for whatever they're up to. They're not going to hurt her."

"When they're done..." Hank said. He was appalled that his voice broke, and so he stopped talking.

"They're going to just throw away something as valuable as an Ancient ship?" O'Neill shook his head. "No. They need her to fly the ship. They'll take good care of her. And we'll get her back."

"We don't even know when..."

The corner of O'Neill's mouth twitched. "Look, obviously it didn't work."

"What didn't work?"

"Whatever." O'Neill shrugged. "If they'd already screwed up the timeline, we wouldn't be having this conversation because we wouldn't remember a thing. So either it didn't work, or it hasn't worked yet. Which means SG-1 can stop it."

"How can we stop it if we don't know what it is?" Hank felt like this was all pretty muddy going.

"We'll figure it out. They'll figure it out. And they'll bring Carolyn home safe and in one piece."

Hank looked out the window at the gate, waiting in all its usual stark majesty. Amazing how you could get used to that thing. "I'm compromised," he said. "I'm making bad decisions because she's my daughter."

"I think you've made the right decisions," O'Neill said. "And I'd say so if I thought you hadn't." He paused. "You know, it's not actually a bad thing to love your kid." He put his hand on Hank's shoulder. "Let's just see what SG-1 turns up."

Daniel glanced over his shoulder. Anise was sitting in the chair, her back very straight, her anger barely leashed. Sal'tor stood behind her, her arms folded, and Daniel looked down at the silver button in his hand. It was a deceptively tiny device, for all its power, could draw to the surface suppressed or simply forgotten memories. And in theory it was harmless, though he'd never seen it used without some discomfort, because somehow it seemed as though the memories they were after were always the nasty ones. A part of him hoped it would hurt Anise just as much as it had hurt Sam, when they were on the transport headed for Tartarus, but he shoved that thought aside. The za'tarc detector stood ready, another bad memory. It was only to be used here to ensure that Anise—and the other council members, they had all agreed to submit to the examination—was telling the truth.

Mitchell leaned closer, arms folded across his chest. "No offense, Jackson," he said in an undertone, "but why you?"

"Because Sam still wants to kill her," Daniel said. "And while it's crossed my mind once or twice—well, all right, maybe a few more times than that—I don't have as much reason."

"I could handle it, if you want."

Daniel hesitated. A part of him would rather let Mitchell do it, and that was one more reason not to give in. "I know her," he said, after a moment. "I have an idea how she's going to play this."

Mitchell nodded. "OK. But that's also a reason to let someone who doesn't have a stake in this handle it."

"She used Sam and Jack and me to test out some technology once," Daniel said. "Which, although it did get me into the second bar fight of my adult life, isn't actually the problem. That could have been a miscalculation, you get that when you're playing around with alien artifacts."

"I've noticed," Mitchell said.

"The problem is that she damn near got Jack and Sam killed when she decided that they were za'tarcs—Goa'uld sleeper agents, sort of," Daniel said. And that wasn't exactly the problem, either, but it was as much of it as he could say to Sam's fellow officer. Mitchell didn't need to know what it was they weren't saying that had triggered Anise's za'tarc detector. And then the za'tarc had turned out to be Martouf, who was basically a good guy, and that had been particularly hard for Sam, since Jolinar had once been his lover. He shook the memory away. "Which is why Sam isn't going to question her."

"OK." Mitchell sounded dubious, but made no further objection.

Daniel turned back toward the two Tok'ra and Anise fixed him with a hard stare.

"This is outrageous treatment of an ally—"

"The Council has consented," Sal'tor said.

"The Council has no right."

"If the Council doesn't," Sal'tor's host said, with a wry smile, "then there's really no point in being Tok'ra."

Daniel caught himself smiling back. Sal'tor and the host reminded him a little bit of Selmak and Jacob, which was not a bad thing at all. She held out the probe, and Daniel adjusted the controls, tuning it to the disk in his hand.

"Dr. Jackson." That was Anise's host—Freya, her name was. "Might we have a word before you begin? In private?"

"That's up to Sal'tor," Daniel said, and Sal'tor sighed.

"If you insist."

"I request," Freya said. Sal'tor shrugged, and moved away, out of earshot but still with her eyes fixed on Anise and her host.

"Dr. Jackson," Freya said again, and reluctantly Daniel came closer. It wasn't that he really expected her to do anything, to try any kind of physical attack, but he didn't trust either of them. "Anise—there are things she would prefer not to share with the other members of the Council."

"I'm sure there are," Daniel said, and heard Mitchell snort.

"It's nothing improper," Freya said, indignantly. "I know you don't like Anise, but she has only the good of the Tok'ra at heart. It's just that there are political arguments hanging in the balance, and this gives a real advantage to the other side. Surely you can see that."

Daniel shook his head. "Nope. I'm not buying it. Right now, it looks to me as though Anise was either working with Marik, or giving him passive support, and either way I'm going to find out where he went. And when. And I really don't care if that's a problem for Anise."

The golden head tipped downward, and when it rose, Anise spoke again. "I care. And I am willing to bargain with you. Send Sal'tor away, and I give you my word that I will tell you everything I know about Marik's plans."

"I think you'd better tell me that anyway," Daniel said.

"I can make it very difficult for you," Anise answered.

Daniel paused. "I don't want to be unduly negative, but I don't think you have very much to bargain with. Yes, you may be able to delay my finding out what's going on, but eventually I'm going to get what I want. And you'll just have annoyed the rest of the High Council even more, as well as jeopardized what's left of your alliance with the Tau'ri — which, by the way, you need more than we do right now — for nothing."

There was a little silence, and finally Anise looked away. It was Freya who spoke then. "We will cooperate."

"Good," Daniel said.

Sal'tor, her face expressionless, pressed the memory disk into Anise's temple, then swung the za'tarc detector into place. Anise sat stiffly ready, the arm of the detector positioned to scan one eye. It looked like a snake ready to strike, and Daniel grimaced in spite of himself. Mitchell gave him a dubious look.

"OK, that doesn't look real pleasant."

"It's not painful," Daniel said. "Sal'tor, are you ready?"

"I am." She seated herself behind the console where the readouts would be displayed. Daniel could see them from where he stood, a steady row of lights.

"Anise," he said. "Tell me what Marik has planned."

There was another silence, and then at last Anise answered. "He has gone to seek our foremother Egeria, to persuade her to spawn again so that we may survive as a people."

Sal'tor gasped, and Daniel shot a glance at the console. All the indicators were green, so she was telling the truth. "Is he out of his mind?" he began, then waved the words away. "No, never mind, I think I know that answer. Does he have any idea how huge a change that is? What that could do to the timeline?"

"He believes that it is worth the risk," Anise said, flatly.

"When — when and where does he plan to look for her?" Daniel got himself under control. There would be time to yell later, once they had a better idea of what Marik was getting into.

"I don't know."

"I don't —" Daniel's eyes narrowed. "You may not know exactly, but you know how he plans to look."

Anise paused again. "Yes."

"Go on."

"He sought to find her on Earth, at our earliest collective memories of her life. He knew he could not seek her out at any more recent time, or we would already know what he had done, through our genetic memory. But there are times, early in her life, that are not as clear — the years she was on Earth, in the service of King Numa, and before. He believed that if he were to find her then, in those times that were deliberately obscured — well, he believed that his act might be the reason this time was hidden from us."

"When, exactly, are you talking about?" Daniel asked.

"Just after the rebellion against Ra," Anise said. "Near the Stargate."

"The Stargate was buried then," Daniel said.

"Not all the time. There was a period when it was open, briefly, and Egeria was there."

Daniel looked at the console — all indications were that Anise was telling the truth — and Sal'tor nodded slowly.

"This memory we all have, though I had not considered what it meant," she said. "And under the circumstances there is one other thing that you must know. It is our greatest secret, which we have jealously preserved and at last it has outlived its usefulness."

Anise's breath caught in her throat. "You must not."

"There is no other choice," Sal'tor said. "Because the timeline is at stake now in more ways than one." She looked back at Daniel. "Our foremother Egeria was herself a time traveler, who came to Earth at that time from a place we have never identified, but a time which we now know to have been only a few years — no more than ten — in our past. Her memories of the 'future,' which were genetic memories of her past, saved us more than once — gave us warning of shifts in alliance, of traps laid for us, of myriad changes that could have doomed our rebellion a hundred times. We have outlived those memories, or very nearly so. And therefore it is possible that these rebels, Marik and his companions — one of them may become Egeria. You must find them, but you must also be sure that you don't change the timeline further by stopping what must happen."

"Holy —" Mitchell seemed to realize he was speaking aloud, and stopped, shaking his head. "But you don't have any queens."

Anise's face tensed. "Marik may believe that the symbiote he carries is one who may become Egeria, or he may simply think that he can induce Egeria to spawn in the past and then bring back one of her daughters either in his body or the body of another host. It is not unheard of for a symbiote to sacrifice itself so that its host may carry another and save the life of one who is more worthy. Leymac, Marik's symbiote, has often said that he would do this were it necessary. It is possible that this is what they intend."

Daniel rubbed the bridge of his nose. Even by SG-1's standards, this was baroque. He could only imagine what Jack would have to say about it.

"OK," Mitchell said. "Let me see if I've got his straight. We have to go back in time, rescue Dr. Lam, stop Marik and his boys from changing anything, and bring them back with us — unless it turns out that one of them is going to become his own great-a-thousand-times-grandmother. Is that is?"

Daniel nodded. "Pretty much."

"Crap," Mitchell said.

CHAPTER FIVE

Egypt
2492 BC

THE BRAZIER was lit more for light and comfort than against the night's mild chill. The evening meal was long finished, though a platter of dates still sat beside Jack, and the beer jar was still half full. Tamit had taken Ellie to bed a while ago, and the back of the house was dark and silent. A feather's touch of a breeze caught the flame of the nearest oil lamp, sending a ripple of shadow across the room. Sam saw Aset shiver and move just an inch closer to Teal'c. The Jaffa put out his hand, caressed her wrist, but said nothing.

"Well, kids," Jack said. "I guess we have to talk about it sometime."

"I do not see that there is anything to be gained by further discussion," Teal'c said.

"There has to be something we can do," Danyel began, and Sam sat up straighter against the cushions.

"It's possible there isn't an answer," she said. She owed Teal'c that much, to acknowledge that the danger was real and desperate and might not be overcome. "But I can't — we have to try."

Aset's fingers moved, circling Teal'c's wrist, and the Jaffa bowed his head.

"I would be glad to be proven wrong," he said. "But the protection of — others — must take precedence."

"Yeah," Jack said. Out of the corner of her eye, Sam saw him meet Teal'c's gaze firmly. "But unless and until —"

"We have to think of something," Danyel said again.

He'd been through this once already, Sam thought, lost his own team, his own versions of her and Jack and Teal'c. Of course he was determined not to let it happen a second time.

"OK," Jack said. "Let's think." He reached for his beer, and Danyel gave him a look.

"Like that's going to help."

"Couldn't hurt," Jack said, and took a long drink.

"Let's look at our options," Sam said firmly. She could tell that Teal'c was about to say something like 'we have none' or 'you could kill me now,' so she hurried on. "If I understand this properly, the normal course of events would be for the — symbiote — to take a host, and you would get a new, younger one, to carry until it matures in turn. Is that correct?"

Teal'c nodded. "It is. But — "

Sam ignored him. "Are there any other options? Anything else that anybody's heard of, no matter how weird?"

Danyel gave a frustrated sigh. "There's Tretonin, of course. It's a drug that we managed to synthesize, back in my time, that eliminated the Jaffa's need for symbiotes entirely. It was the key to the success of the Jaffa rebellion." He shook his head. "But we don't have the equipment or, more important, the ingredients. And I don't really know the formula anyway."

"Gee, that's helpful," Jack said. "Got anything else?"

"Not really," Danyel said, and reached for his own cup.

"I think we need to do this the old-fashioned way," Jack said. "Teal'c needs a new symbiote. OK, we get him one."

"I do not think," Teal'c began, and Aset spoke over him.

"There are no more left. We — Pharaoh's men and you killed all that were found. Would we had left just one alive!"

"We could not," Teal'c said. "The risk was too great."

"I said it before," Jack said. "There are — what? — dozens of worlds out there that have plenty of symbiotes to choose from."

"Hundreds," Danyel said. "But — putting aside the danger to Earth if we dig up the Stargate again — Jack, the Goa'uld out there are at the height of their powers. They're not going to let us just walk up to them and help ourselves to a handful of larvae."

"Daniel Jackson is correct," Teal'c said. "The prim'tah are kept safe within the palace of their sires, except when a prim'tah ceremony is planned."

"Prim'tah?" Jack asked.

"That is the Goa'uld word for the immature symbiote," Teal'c answered. "And also the ceremony at which a Jaffa receives his — or her — first symbiote. It is an occasion of great import —"

"Prim'tah," Danyel said. He had an odd, arrested look on his face. "I should have — Ra's Jaffa's prim'tah —" He shoved himself to his feet, nearly tripping over a cushion, and grabbed the nearest oil lamp.

"Danyel?" Aset said.

"Don't wake the kid," Jack said, in the same moment, but Danyel was gone. Sam looked at Jack, who shrugged.

Sam shook her head silently. She couldn't like the idea of launching at attack on the Goa'uld — because, let's face it, that was exactly what this would be, an attack that was likely to draw attention back to Earth. They'd beaten Ra once, but she was under no illusions about how easily it could have gone the other way. If Ra had managed to take the Stargate, as he'd planned... She shook her head again. She'd seen the world that resulted, and she hadn't liked it much. Her own Daniel, who had been so sure they were meant for better things than English as a Second Language, or proofing other people's papers, so determined to make them a part of this second chance — he and half a dozen of Jack's friends had died just to get them here, and so many more had died to make the rebellion happen. To risk that, to risk the timeline, was unthinkable.

But Teal'c would die if they didn't find him a new, young symbiote, and that was just as unthinkable. She knew what logic said, could do the cold math that said one death to save millions was a fair price. But that was not what heroes did, or so the books she'd read when she was ten had promised her, before she'd learned to compromise. Her father's wingman had spotted the wreck, made sure there was a body to bury, because the Air Force didn't leave their men behind. Jack followed the same creed. She would do no less. They couldn't risk Earth for the life of one man, that was true. Not unless they were sure they could minimize the risk, and be certain of their success.

And they probably could minimize the risk enough, she thought. If they dialed out to some other world, or worlds, first — Danyel would know safe ones — surely that would muddy the trail, and keep Ra from thinking of Earth? With luck, he'd blame the theft on rival Goa'uld, or rogue Jaffa instead.

"If we find a source," she said. "We can't dial directly from Earth. Or, more precisely, we don't want to dial Earth directly from whichever of Ra's worlds we end up going to. Are there any worlds we could go through, ones that aren't well watched, where we could dial Earth without getting caught?"

"Cut-outs," Jack said, approvingly. "Nice thought, Sam."

"Most Stargates are at least watched," Teal'c said. "But, indeed, watched is not guarded, and there are worlds where even that precaution is neglected. I believe this would be a valid plan."

Light blossomed in the doorway that led to the hall, Danyel's lamp and Danyel behind it, a bundle of papyri under his other arm.

"I've got it," he said. "I knew I'd seen something."

Aset rose to take the lamp, looking worried, and Danyel dropped back onto the cushions, scattering scrolls around him. He searched for a moment, came up with one that looked as though mice had chewed it, and unrolled it to reveal not hieroglyphics but Goa'uld symbols.

Teal'c tilted his head to one side. "That is a calendar," he said. "Ra's?"

"Yes." Danyel scooted forward so that Teal'c could see as he unrolled the tattered papyrus. "It's a list of the worlds where the prim'tah ceremony was scheduled to be held — it looks as though Ra was rotating the ceremony among the various home-worlds of his Jaffa. Someone, I'm guessing one of the junior officers, was in charge of getting Jaffa home for the ceremony, and this was his list."

Teal'c took the scroll, studied it calmly. "I believe you are correct."

"So?" Jack looked from one to the other.

"So now we know a bunch of places where people are going to have a whole lot of immature symbiotes," Danyel said. "Very immature symbiotes. Can you think of a better place to get a replacement for Teal'c's?"

"The prim'tah will be well guarded," Teal'c said, but he sounded more thoughtful than disapproving.

"I was at a prim'tah ceremony once," Danyel said. "Well, sort of. On Chulak. They had all of the symbiotes in a tank at the temple, gave them out one or two at a time. I'm guessing Ra's Jaffa would do the same."

"Very likely," Teal'c said.

"Yeah, but," Jack said. "Look, this has promise, but we don't know anything about any of these planets." He paused. "Do we?"

"We do," Danyel said, with a grin that made him look surprisingly young. "In fact, we have just gotten the most outrageous stroke of luck since — well, since I can remember. The next planet on the list is Abydos."

"Abydos," Jack said.

"It's the first world we ever visited," Danyel said. "Me and the other you, that is. In my time line." A shadow crossed his face. "I lived there for a while — but that's not important right now."

Before his wife was kidnapped, Sam thought. Before he joined the Stargate program to search for her, before he found her a Goa'uld host. He had told them the story once, her and Jack and Teal'c, mentioned it occasionally, but always with that faint look of pain.

"But that was what, several thousand years from now," she said.

"The Goa'uld are conservative," Danyel said. "The temples on Abydos — well, OK, I'm really not sure about the proper tense here, but — OK, the newest one was built probably a few hundred years ago, a hundred years before our now. I know where the symbiotes will be kept, and I know how to get us there secretly."

Teal'c nodded slowly. "That much I believe is possible. But—"

"Great," Jack interrupted. "So we've got a plan, kids. Now all we have to do—"

"Hor-Aha will not allow us to restore the Stargate," Teal'c said. "It is too great a risk to save the life of one man."

"But for such a man," Aset flared. "The man who put Pharaoh's father on his throne, who kept Pharaoh himself alive to inherit! To give him a chance at life is only justice."

Teal'c gave her a faint, almost embarrassed smile. Sam said, "I think we can figure out a way to open the Stargate safely."

"There is one factor as yet unconsidered," Teal'c said. "When is this prim'tah ceremony to be?"

Danyel consulted the papyrus. "Chintar masr—OK, that's, I make it three weeks from today."

Teal'c shook his head. "That is too long. My symbiote will have matured by then."

"Crap," Jack said.

Sam bit back a curse of her own. They had been so close. "What happens if you keep it longer?"

"I cannot," Teal'c said. "When it is mature, it will take a host. I cannot stop it."

"All right," Jack said. "We go sooner."

"Too soon, and the symbiotes won't be there," Danyel said. "The earliest they're likely to be there is a few days before the ceremony."

"And we need time to get the Stargate working again," Sam said.

"Damn it!" Jack reached for his beer.

"Wait," Danyel said. "There's—well, it's a possibility, anyway."

Teal'c lifted an eyebrow.

Jack was more direct. "Danyel, what are you talking about?"

"It was tried once," Danyel said. "Our Teal'c tried it, when he still had his symbiote. He was able to contact it by going deep into kelnorim."

"That is impossible," Teal'c said, but his tone was less certain than his words.

"Maybe not," Danyel said. "Look, there was a Jaffa priestess, Shau'nac, who managed to contact her symbiote." He hesitated, and Sam wondered just what he wasn't telling. "She was able to persuade it not to take a host even though it was well past maturity. It didn't take a host until it got a volunteer."

"We are taught that contact with the prim'tah is not only impossible, but that the very attempt is dangerous," Teal'c said thoughtfully. "To descend too deeply into kelnorim is to risk losing one's ability to leave the trance state."

"Of course you're told that," Jack said. "The last thing the Goa'uld want is for you to talk to their offspring."

"Shau'nac made it work," Danyel said. "And so did our Teal'c. It wasn't pleasant, the symbiote didn't like him much, but he was able to communicate."

"I have no desire to die," Teal'c said. He scrupulously refrained from looking at Aset. "Not if there is an alternative. I think this is worth the risk."

"And that gives us time to open the Stargate," Sam said.

"And to talk to Hor-Aha," Jack said. He lifted his beer cup in a toast. "Sounds like a plan, kids."

Sam leaned forward to join the toast, clicking her clay cup against the others. There were a lot of variables involved, too many — but it was the best they had.

CHAPTER SIX

THE ROYAL Way was different from how Danyel remembered it from his own time, one more change like the shifting sound of his own name. In his memory, the way from Saqqara to Memphis was a four lane highway, broadening to six lanes as it approached Cairo. He'd driven it dozens of times in a comfortable air conditioned SUV. The picturesque donkey caravans Catherine Langford had talked about existed only in the past, not in the modern Egypt of traffic lights and overpasses. He'd tooled along this road nine years ago for him, the last time he had been to Egypt for the SGC, steering a Land Rover through rush hour traffic, talking on his cell phone. For a moment Danyel wished Catherine were here. She would love to see a far older Egypt than the between-the-wars country of her earliest memories.

For one thing, it was much greener. The climate in Early Dynastic Egypt was much wetter than it would be five thousand years later. The band of green along both banks of the Nile was much broader, with rich groves of trees down to the water except where cultivated fields prevailed. Along the banks the land was marshy, with high cattails that provided shelter for a wealth of waterbirds. As they watched, ten or twelve ducks took flight, arrowing across the river towards the opposite shore.

"It's pretty, isn't it?" Jack said with an expression of satisfaction. He was carrying Ellie, who perched on his shoulder with one fat little arm around the back of his neck. Her blue eyes were wide, taking in everything around them with her usual expression of perpetual curiosity. It would have been more convenient to leave her at home with Aset, but less comfortable for Sam, as Ellie was still nursing, and there was no real reason Ellie shouldn't come to Memphis. It was an hour on foot, and who knew how long they'd have to wait to see Pharaoh once they got there?

"It is indeed," Teal'c said. "Yours is a rich world, Daniel Jackson." His often impassive face held a hint of a smile, and his white shenti somehow still looked pressed despite having walked for the better part of an hour.

"It is," Danyel said. It was odd to be addressed that way, hard to still think of himself as Daniel Jackson. He was Danyel now, the second syllable stressed as it had been on Abydos, closer to the man who had made Abydos home and married Sha're than Dr. Daniel Jackson of SG-1. He lived in a different world as surely as if it were another planet. He couldn't help but mentally contrast it with Abydos. He'd thought when he first walked through the gate, when he first came to Abydos, that Egypt must have been a pale shadow of the Goa'uld's richer realm, that Abydos was the real thing and this the copy. Now, after eight years here, he knew that he had been wrong. Abydos was a pale copy of this.

The fields sloped gently down to the brown waters of the Nile flowing inexorably to the sea, desert and cultivated land cut like a knife edge of green. The distant peaks of the pyramids at Giza glimmered on the horizon, as unreal looking as always, a little more than seven miles distant, while above the blue arch of sky stretched from horizon to horizon.

It was not a world he had desired, but a place and time fallen in love with from books and shreds of refuse, as a man may see a woman in passing, getting onto a bus or standing beneath an umbrella in the street and be suddenly struck, so that her image stays with him forever and he seeks her always in the faces of strangers. This was what he had sought and found unexpectedly, bled for and watched his friends die for, only to find them replaced once more by strangers, them and not them. But this Jack and Sam and Teal'c were family now, even if they came from a different timeline, a future different from the one he had known. And there was Ellie, of course.

The city of Memphis spread before him, such as it was.

"O Lady of the White Walls," Danyel said, and Sam smiled at him sideways. "That's what it will be called," Danyel said.

"When there are walls," Sam said.

He nodded, and reached back to take the baby from Jack. It was more than his turn to carry her. "When there are walls. White sandstone, sixty feet tall and twenty feet thick, shining in the bright noonday sun..." He could see how it would be. He'd seen the broken foundations of stones his grandchildren might see hauled into place.

"That's going to be fun to build," Sam said, looking cheerful. The Sam in his original world had been an astrophysicist, but this time had no need for one. His Sam, this Sam, was displaying a remarkable talent for civil engineering. Most days they walked this way together to their mutual jobs, Danyel to the archives brought to the new city of Memphis from the Goa'uld palaces and installations around the land, and Sam to the building sites with Ellie on her back, where she worked with Pharaoh's chief architect. Sometimes Teal'c came too, when he had work to do in Memphis, but often he was away southward to Upper Egypt, on business of Pharaoh's. Jack... Hor-Aha had offered him a regiment of his best fighting men and set the golden collar of approbation about his neck himself, but Jack insisted he was retired. At his distinguished age, all he wanted was a peaceful life. While the young Pharaoh didn't necessarily understand that, he'd bowed gracefully to Jack's wishes — a house on the river, a good dog, and people to share it with.

"Do you think he'll buy it? Hello?" Danyel jumped as Sam poked him in the bare ribs just above the waistband of his shenti. "Are you listening to me?"

"Sorry," Danyel said. "What?"

"She asked if you thought Hor-Aha would go for it," Jack said. "Opening the Stargate."

"I don't know," Danyel said.

"He's a lot more cautious than his old man," Jack said. It had been his father, Narmer, who had led the rebellion against Ra, Narmer who had brought together lords from up and down the Nile to fight against the Goa'uld. Unfortunately, he'd barely lived to celebrate the victory. He'd died of a sudden heart attack a few months later, barely Jack's age and worn out by living. His son had come to the throne unexpectedly early, but even though he was in his early twenties nobody had argued about it. Hor-Aha, whose name meant The Fighting Hawk, had proven himself in the rebellion against Ra. Now he was proving himself as Pharaoh.

"You'd think he wouldn't be," Sam said. "More cautious."

Jack shrugged. "It's one thing to be a guerilla leader. It's another to rule a country. Different skill sets. The kid's learning on the job."

"So have we all," Sam said with that sideways smile again. With one hand she hauled the spaghetti strap of her dress back into place where it had fallen down over her shoulder and winced as it rubbed her sunburn. "If I could have one thing from the future..."

"I know. Sunscreen," Jack said.

There wasn't any, and the only way to avoid the sun was to be mostly nocturnal, or to wear so many clothes that in the summertime one courted heatstroke. He'd had some bad sunburns himself, but with Sam's fair skin she was the one who suffered the most. Finally she'd given in to carrying a parasol when she was out on building sites, for Ellie's sake if not her own, like most higher status people did. He'd carried one for years, but then Danyel didn't think it was girly.

Fortunately, they didn't have to wait long in one of the courtyards of the palace before they were admitted. Teal'c stayed behind while a scribe in a spotless white shenti showed them into Pharaoh's work room, a smaller room behind the audience chamber where a vast skylight let in light on two tables piled with scrolls, illuminating brightly painted walls and a few chairs of precious cedar wood, redolent with rich scent where the sun touched them. Incongruously, on one of the tables rested a Goa'uld data reader.

The Fighting Hawk looked up from his business, keen dark eyes flashing over them like his namesake, and got to his feet. In the privacy of the inner chamber he had removed his wig, and his shaven head gleamed with sweat. "O'Neill and Danyel," he said, "And our architect Sa-Mantha. I am surprised you are all together today. How is the small one?"

Ellie favored him with a gap toothed grin. Hor-Aha had two small sons, one just older than her and one just younger, and she knew a baby person when she saw one.

"She has her mother's beautiful eyes," he said, and Ellie giggled. She liked attention. A lot.

"Newet watch over her," Danyel said piously. It was considered a bad idea to compliment a young child too much, lest demons take notice. No doubt this was a relic of a more real danger — the need of the Goa'uld for healthy and attractive hosts.

"As you say," Hor-Aha said. His eyes twinkled. "Never have I seen such an ugly and misshapen child!"

Ellie giggled again.

Jack shifted from foot to foot. "We've got a problem here."

"And you wish me to get to business," Pharaoh said. "Not dote upon your daughter. Very well." He turned from Danyel with a smile. "What is your problem?"

They outlined it in broad strokes, stressing how much Teal'c had done for Egypt and for Pharaoh's father, how surely the rebellion against Ra would have failed if not for Teal'c. All of it was true. There was no denying that Teal'c had done more than the rest of them, that his help had been the thing that was essential. Without a leader among the Jaffa, the Jaffa would surely have rallied to Ra's cause en masse.

Hor-Aha heard them out, but Danyel wasn't surprised when at last he shook his head, forestalling Danyel's next speech. "I know all that Teal'c has done," he said gravely. "If any man were deserving of my consideration, it is he. But why does he not come with you today to plead this case in person?"

It was Jack who answered. "Teal'c doesn't think he should," he said.

"And why is that?" Hor-Aha's eyes moved to Jack.

Sam took a deep breath. "Teal'c is concerned about opening the Stargate."

"As well he should be," Hor-Aha said. He shook his head again. "Sa-Mantha, you know that I have great respect for Teal'c, and if there were anything that I might do as a man to ease his plight, I would. But I cannot risk the safety of my people. Surely you understand that. We have remained safe these last three years because the Stargate has been buried. If we were to unbury it for several days, use it to send a scouting party forth into Ra's realm..." He spread his hands regretfully. "We would court the displeasure of those false gods who enslaved us for so long. I cannot agree to this. Much as I regret Teal'c's fate, I cannot risk the future of my people for the good of one man. You know as well as I that if the Stargate were unburied there would be nothing to prevent Ra from using it to our ruin. Unless there is some way you may prevent this?"

"Not that I know of," Sam said, her eyes on his. "I mean, I do know of ways to prevent the gate from being used, but nothing that we can build here with the materials we have."

"Then I must refuse," Hor-Aha said.

"But," Danyel began.

"Unless you can show me a way it poses no danger to my people, I must refuse," Hor-Aha said. "Surely you understand that, O'Neill?"

Jack swallowed. "I do," he said.

"Please convey to Teal'c my deep respect, and that whenever his time comes he will receive the greatest honors I can bestow," Pharaoh said. "For he dies in the service of my people as surely as if he were struck down by a staff weapon."

"I'll tell him," Jack said. "Come on, kids. Let's go home."

Aset held the taper as though she were a priestess, carrying the flame from lamp to lamp. Teal'c watched the pleated linen of her shift move against her skin, outlining for a moment the curves of breast and hip, then concealing them again. Her hair fell in a thousand tiny braids, woven with gold and faience beads. He had bargained for the beads in the market after their victory, and counted himself well-rewarded by her smile; he had watched her with the hairdressers, sitting in the shade while the women worked, and a patient youth fanned them, raising a breeze in the still air. He had not realized then that she reminded him of Shau'nac — and perhaps there was no real resemblance, except in grace and courage.

She lit the last lamp, leaving him in the center of concentric rings of flame, and ground out the taper in the dirt of the floor. "My Teal's in his temple," she said with a smile, and Teal'c winced.

"I am no god, Aset," he said, and she stooped to kiss his cheek.

"Only to me," she said, in his ear, and straightened, fixing Danyel with a reproving stare. He sat just outside the rings of light, unusually quiet, what was left of the Tau'ri's first aid kit resting by his knee.

"You will protect him, Danyel," she said, and he looked away.

"I'll do the best I can, I promise."

She was poised to say more, to demand more, but Teal'c caught her hand. "We must begin," he said, and kissed her palm.

Her breath caught, but she nodded. "I will go." She gathered her skirt close and passed through the ring of lamps. The door closed solidly behind her.

Teal'c waited, resting his hands on his knees, letting the silence build, but the first stages of kelnorim did not rise to envelop him. Unworthily, his first thought was to blame Danyel Jackson, but the human was astonishingly still and silent. He was not the problem, Teal'c admitted. He had achieved kelnorim under far more difficult conditions, on the eve of battle and on Apophis's ships, and he knew this was the result of a troubled spirit. And the only remedy for that was to purge himself of the concern that weighed him down. "Tell me of Shau'nac," he said.

Danyel lifted his head. The flame of the lamps was between them, hiding his expression. "What about her?"

"You said that in your time, I married Drey'auc," Teal'c said. "And she bore me a son who lived to be a man and a leader of our people. I knew Drey'auc in my time, and would have called it an honor to be her husband. But Shau'nac—" His voice was no longer steady, and he paused until he was sure he had it under control "I would have gone on bended knee to Shau'nac, for she was brave and beautiful and wise beyond her years. But she chose to serve in the temple, and then Amaunet chose her for a host, when her own host was injured beyond saving while they visited Chulak. It was an honor unprecedented."

Danyel gave a bitter smile. "Amaunet. Yes. An honor indeed."

"I am sorry, Daniel Jackson," Teal'c said. But at least there were things he did not have to say. He didn't have to explain what it felt like to see Amaunet with Shau'nac's face, to know over and over that she was utterly lost to him.

"No, don't apologize," Danyel said. "Sha're—I mean, Shau'nac—" He stopped, shook his head ruefully. "It's not something you get over, it is? But it's what Jack said once, you find ways to go on."

Teal'c nodded gravely, and when Danyel spoke again, his voice was artificially bright.

"Shau'nac did go to the temple in our world," he said. "But she was never Amaunet's host."

"And her fate?" Teal'c waited. "I can hear in your silence that her story does not end well."

"Like I said, she found a way to communicate with her symbiote," Danyel said. "And she believed she had persuaded it that what the Goa'uld were doing was evil. She thought she'd convinced it that it wasn't a god, but one sentient being in a universe full of sentient beings, with no more rights or powers than anybody else. She persuaded it to wait to take a host until a willing one could be found. That's the part that I thought was relevant, that the symbiote could be talked into waiting."

"Go on," Teal'c said.

"She brought the symbiote — it was called Tanith — she brought Tanith to the Tok'ra because she thought they could find it a host, and because if she could convert one Goa'uld, they could probably find a way to convert more." Danyel sighed. "But Tanith lied. It was Goa'uld through and through. It arranged the whole thing so it could spy on the Tok'ra, and it killed Shau'nac when she realized what it had done."

Teal'c had guessed as much, but it was a surprise to find the thought as painful as it was. It was better than being Amaunet's host, he told himself. She had died free, trying to bring others to freedom.

"This, then, is why you say I must not trust my symbiote," he said. "No matter what it says. I must persuade it to wait for a better host, but believe nothing it says."

"Yes," Danyel said.

"So be it." Teal'c settled himself again, and closed his eyes. This time, the first stages of kelnorim came easily, the wordless place where his consciousness seemed suspended in his own body, and he could lose himself in contemplation of its workings. A sense of well-being suffused him as all the minor complaints of his body were eased away, and he focused carefully on the source of that content. He could sense it, like a coal glowing deep within him, like a spark in the far distance, a single star on a clouded night. He knew better than to push, to rush. It would only throw him out of balance, and out of this state of ease and relaxation. Instead, he rested, aware of his breath, his heart, the blood moving in his veins, and only after an indeterminable time did he reach out again and allow himself to fall toward that distant light.

He left his breath behind, and the movement of his blood, and still the spark was impossibly far. He had never been so deep into kelnorim before—he was barely a consciousness, barely a stirring of awareness, and something like velvet, like darkness, frayed at the edges of his self, tempting him to dissolve into its warm emptiness. Somewhere in the reaches of his mind, he knew he was in danger. His teachers had warned him of this blissful dark, and how easy it would be to remain in its embrace. And yet the spark was so close now. Only a little further, and he could touch it, though he could not quite remember why that had mattered—

The spark shifted, turned, swelled like a fish rising, and he was aware suddenly of its presence resting against his self, bright and curious.

What?

And then the shape changed, glittering surprise.

Who?

Teal'c, he thought, and felt his memory right itself. I am Teal'c, and that is the symbiote I carry within me.

You are alive, it said, still with surprise and growing pleasure. *You think and speak and live.*

I do, Teal'c thought at it. I am Jaffa, and I carry you in my belly, in a pouch made for you.

By my mothers and yours, it agreed. *And soon I shall be grown and ready—will you be my host?*

Teal'c could not suppress the shudder, and felt the symbiote tremble with him.

Is this not what you wish? it asked. *What all things wish, to serve their gods?*

I am Jaffa, Teal'c thought, carefully. It is not my place to be a host.

You fear it, the symbiote said. *Why?*

Shau'nac. Teal'c hadn't meant to reveal so much, but the images came tumbling through him, the beautiful priestess, lost, erased by Amaunet's possession of her body, a cascade of grief and anger.

The spark flickered, recoiled. *I have cared for you, meditated with you—healed you,* it said. *And you think this of me?*

It is truth, Teal'c thought. You know it to be so.

The spark trembled. *I do. And I do not wish it to be so! I will not leave you under these conditions, I will not take a host as that one did—*

As do all your kind, Teal'c thought.

No! I will not! The spark flared, its anger crackling through both of them. *I will show you—find me a willing host, or none at all.*

You will stay with me, then, until you have a host willing to accept you? Teal'c asked. Though it may be difficult, and painful for us both?

I will, the spark answered. *I, Egeria, swear it so.*

Very well, Teal'c answered. And I will keep you until that time.

It was time to leave, he knew. He had the agreement they had sought, but he could no longer find his way back to himself. It was as though the symbiote had drawn him down into an unseen river, its surface frozen; he felt fear, but only as a distant warning, something faintly remembered. The spark wavered then, strengthened, and abruptly he was flung back out of the darkness, rising through the layers of kelnorim with a speed that left him gasping.

"Teal'c?" Danyel said. "Teal'c!"

Teal'c opened his eyes. The lamps were burnt out, except for one or two that flickered low, and Danyel crouched beside him within the circle, worry changing to relief.

"I thought," he began. "You weren't breathing, there for a minute, I was afraid—"

"I am well," Teal'c said. He took a careful breath. His muscles burned as though he had been in battle, but already he could feel the symbiote transforming the toxins into something more benign.

"Good." Danyel sat back on his heels, shaking his head. "That's — that was a little too close, Teal'c. I don't think you should try that again."

"I do not believe it will be necessary," Teal'c said. "Egeria has said it will wait until it finds a willing host."

"That's good —" Danyel stopped abruptly. "Whoa, wait a minute. Who?"

"Egeria." Teal'c glanced at his belly, at the stark lines of the symbiote pouch. "That is its name."

"Whoa," Danyel said again. "That's... OK, I was not expecting that."

"Who is Egeria?" Teal'c asked.

"She's – she was a goddess of health, she was an adviser to King Numa, and she fought Ra," Danyel said. "And she was the mother, literally, of the Tok'ra. The resistance against Ra. I don't know how she could be here, how your immature symbiote could be her. She had to have been born thousands of years ago." He grimaced. "Well, thousands of years from then. More or less now."

"Our timelines were very different," Teal'c said, after a moment. "Surely this means nothing."

"I hope so," Danyel said. "Or we have an even bigger problem to deal with. If this is the real Egeria and we kill her... I can't even begin to imagine the consequences."

CHAPTER SEVEN

SAM PICKED her way carefully down the long ramp to the building site, Ellie a comfortable weight against her back. She'd been wakened early — sometimes she was sure Ellie knew when her adults were worried, and was wakeful herself — but the baby had settled down again, fed and changed, would sleep at least a little while longer. Tamit trailed behind them, carrying the basket that held their lunch and the baby's toys and Sam's sandals, a parasol cocked over her shoulder. Thank God for childcare, Sam thought, even if a fourteen-year-old with mathematical skills wasn't exactly what would have been recommended back in Colorado.

The sand was warm under her feet. She'd want her sandals later, but right now the heat was pleasant, distracting her from thoughts of Teal'c. That was one thing that hadn't changed, she thought. No matter when you were living, work had to go on.

The Royal Architect Sethnakht was standing in his usual spot, up on a cracked block of granite that gave him an overview of the entire site. His scribe Ankhaf sat cross-legged at his feet, papyrus spread ready on his board, and several of the gang foremen stood ready, nodding as Sethnakht gave them their orders for the day. Beyond them, the walls of the temple complex had begun to rise, the outer buildings still marked with stakes and faded ribbons, the main temple about half-finished, the mud-brick walls carefully reinforced with stone. The first three columns were in place, and masons were finishing the details of the carving; the new stones had not yet arrived, Sam saw, and hid a sigh. The last foreman bowed, backing away, and Sethnakht turned to greet her.

"Bright lady of our morning!" he proclaimed. "With her

handmaid dutiful as the morning star."

"Good morning, Sethnakht," Sam said. There were blocks placed beside the granite to serve as steps; she shifted Ellie to a slightly better position, hiked up her skirt, and climbed to join him. Tamit dropped into a crouch to wait for her, raising the parasol against the strengthening sun.

"The day is brightened by your presence," Sethnakht said. He was tall for an Egyptian, almost as tall as she, with a lean body well revealed by his shenti, a collar of gold and beads resting on his collarbones. He grinned at her, showing good teeth. "Let us run away to the river, lady, where the breeze is cool and there is beer—"

"But no work to be done," Sam answered. She strongly suspected that if she ever said yes, Sethnakht would panic, but she liked him well enough to indulge him.

"Heartless!"

"Taken," Sam said. "The new columns haven't arrived?"

"No." Sethnakht's attitude changed instantly. "I've had a runner from the port purporting to explain the delay. I sent him on to Pharaoh, let him make his excuses there. In the meantime, I've told the brick-layers to carry on with the rear sections. At least we can get that much done."

Sam nodded. The complex would memorialize the victory over the false Ra, and she couldn't help thinking of Teal'c and the symbiote inexorably growing within him. Three weeks, he had said, was too long to wait, and now that Hor-Aha had refused to let them open the Stargate—

I'll have to do it, Jack had said to her, softly, sitting by her side in the garden behind their house.

We'll figure something out, she had said, but she still hadn't come up with anything.

The problem was that Pharaoh was right, it was a huge risk, even if they went somewhere else first. If they dug up the gate, got it working again, there was nothing to stop Ra or any other Goa'uld lord from dialing in and attacking. And they had only just defeated Ra the first time around, there was no reason to think they'd get that lucky a second time. In Danyel's time, the SGC had built a titanium iris that blocked the gate, kept anything from materializing, but here, where copper tools were an expensive rarity, that was hardly an option.

"Sam?" Sethnakht was looking at her, and she forced a smile "Sorry."

He shook his head. "What's wrong?"

Sam sighed. There was no point in not telling him, and he might see something she had missed. "I'm worried about Teal'c. His symbiote is almost mature, and he will die without it."

"And the symbiote will become a Goa'uld," Sethnakht said.

"We won't allow that to happen," Sam said. "But it will mean Teal'c's death." She looked away, not wanting him to see the tears that prickled at the corners of her eyes. "We asked Pharaoh to let us use the Stargate to find him a new symbiote — we know a place where we can steal one, with only minimal risk — but he refused."

Sethnakht nodded. "I can understand his point."

"So can I," Sam said. She knew what was at stake — there was Ellie to think of, always, and Aset and Tamit and their lovely house by the river, with its garden and the lotus flowers painted on the walls. "But — it's Teal'c."

Sethnakht nodded again, slowly. "So. There's nothing else we can do today. Let us consider the problem, you and I." He smiled. "Because I know you'll think of nothing else anyway."

"I think I'm missing something," Sam said, and shook herself. "Tamit! Take Ellie, will you?"

"You can go, too, Ankhaf," Sethnakht said, and the scribe scrambled to his feet. Sam loosened the ties that held Ellie on her back — the baby squirmed, waking — and Tamit took her into the shade, clucking to her. Sethnakht seated himself on the edge of the granite block, opening his parasol, and Sam settled herself next to him.

"Danyel must have had this problem in his own time,"

Sethnakht said. "What was his solution?"

"A metal iris," Sam answered.

Sehtnakht snorted. "All the copper and gold and silver in the kingdom wouldn't cover that circle. Even if I could work out how to shape it, which I could. And then how would you move it aside to use it?"

"Precisely," Sam said.

"Wood, perhaps?" Sethnakht squinted at the piles of timber waiting for the workmen. "Or must it withstand attack?"

"I don't think so," Sam said. She was starting to see the glimmering of an idea. "That's maybe not necessary. The iris kept anything from materializing fully, but allowed the wormhole to form. But if there's anything inside the gate, the wormhole won't form, just as it won't close if there's something sticking into it."

"So if your object is to keep any of the Goa'uld from opening the door from the other side," Sethnakht began.

"Then all we have to do is place something inside the gate," Sam said. "It doesn't even have to be heavy, just—large enough."

"Heavy linen," Sethnakht said. He stopped. "Or the sail of a boat."

"Yes!"

"Rigged so." Sethnakht handed her the parasol, fumbled for a piece of charcoal. He found it, drew a circle, and then a cross inside it. "If a mast is placed behind the gate, with the sail attached—"

"And then we draw the sail forward, through the ring," Sam said. "That would keep the wormhole from forming."

"And to open it, we withdraw the sail," Sethnakht said, "and let the wormhole form naturally."

"Yes," Sam said again. "OK, we'll need some kind of quick-release on the front side, and some way to be sure that all the rigging comes back with the sail, so that nothing is left in the ring—but that's easy."

Sethnakht nodded. "But how will we know when to open

the ring for you?"

"We'll set specific times," Sam said. "You'll clear the ring for, oh, five minutes, max, and if we don't dial in, put the sail back and wait for the next time."

"Safer for us," Sethnakht said. "But much more dangerous for you."

"That doesn't matter," Sam said. "Not if we can save Teal'c."

"I'll speak to Pharaoh as well," Sethnakht offered, and Sam nodded.

"Thank you. It can only help."

There was little point in waiting, Sam thought, so she and Sethnakht went straight to the palace, their little entourage in tow. It was the fourth hour of the day, and the chamberlain gravely informed them that Pharaoh was on the archery range with his men, but that the Lady of Egypt would be pleased to receive them in his stead. The Lady of Egypt was not the Fighting Hawk's wife, but his mother, the extremely redoubtable Queen Nithotep.

Unlike Danyel, Sam was not a history person, and she'd gotten the impression in school that the abasement of women was a historical constant, at least until the late twentieth century. It had been a considerable surprise to her to discover that women not only wielded substantial amounts of power here, but that average women enjoyed an amount of freedom she hadn't imagined. Women owned land and entered into contracts, could sue for divorce or have children without marriage, and every woman from the poorest farmgirl to Pharaoh's mother worked. True, the work was different, but Sam was absolutely aware how much effort went into the logistics and supply for a palace the size of a small military base. Nithotep wielded more power than the Executive Officer at the SGC and cared for just as many in many of the same ways.

She and Sethnakht waited with Ellie, Tamit and Ankhaf in the courtyard outside while Nithotep finished a meeting with someone or other, who at last filed out preceded by three scribes. And then it was their turn.

Nithotep was perhaps a decade older than Sam, fifty instead of forty, small and fine boned, with darker skin than her son, thin as a reed beneath her wig of black hair combed straight around her face in what Sam could only think of as a short bob. Her eyes were painted with blue minerals, and her sheath dress was of white linen stamped with geometric patterns that looked something like a net of dark blue. It covered her from just above the ankles to just below her breasts, thin spaghetti straps over her shoulders the only covering above the high waist.

"My Lady Queen." Sethnakht sank into a deep bow, and Sam followed.

"Architects," Nithotep said, coming around the little table and looking at them. "Is this a matter that pertains to building? Or to the matter of Teal'c, of which my son has informed me?"

"The latter," Sethnakht said, with a glance at Sam. "I think we have devised a way by which the gate could be unburied, and yet be inoperable most of the time."

Nithotep's eyes flickered from Sethnakht to Sam. "I understand that you very much wish to help your friend. But you must see how my son decides. He is the guardian of this realm, and he cannot put the wellbeing of any one person above that of his people, no matter who that person may be."

"I do understand that, my queen," Sam said. It was never a good idea to look away from Nithotep. It seemed dishonest. "I too do not wish to endanger this realm, or my own family. But Sethnakht and I have an idea that we think will make it much safer to use the Stargate. We can block it in such a way that an incoming wormhole cannot form. It would only need to be open for a few minutes at carefully planned intervals in order for us to come and go."

"And this would mean the Goa'uld could not use it, Sa-Mantha?" Her eyes were very sharp.

"I won't say it's impossible," Sam said. "If they dialed at

exactly the right moment, yes, they could use it. But it would be a tremendous coincidence for them to accidentally hit on precisely the right few minutes rather than any other minutes in the last three years."

"And at any other time the Stargate would not work?"

"That is correct, my queen," Sethnakht said.

She nodded slowly. "Tell me how this is accomplished."

Even with all Sethnakht's work gangs diverted to the project, it took some days to free the Stargate and erect the mast and sail behind it. The youngest of Pharaoh's river captains produced a sail that could be split lengthwise to make a single long strip of reed matting, and offered advice on the rigging that drew it through the gate. Jack spent most of that time drilling the unit Hor-Aha had detached to guard the gate, and allowed that he was satisfied. They were mostly veterans who had fought the Goa'uld before, with a sprinkling of level-headed recruits, all armed with zats and staff weapons. If somehow the Goa'uld managed to dial in during the seconds between the release of the sail and them dialing out, then they'd have to hold to gate for thirty-eight minutes. Maybe less, but as he watched Sergeant Basa put them through their paces, he thought they could do it. He just really hoped it wouldn't come to that.

Hor-Aha and his attendants, including the Queen Nithotep, arrived in the middle of the afternoon, as the workers were stirring from the noon rest. Sam and Sethnakht showed them around the gate, still with a mound of dirt filling the lower curve of the ring. Jack trailed behind the royal party, watched as Sam demonstrated the sail's release and the team ready to draw it forward again as soon as the wormhole vanished. It looked good to him, and he wasn't surprised to see Pharaoh nod several times.

And then it was his turn, Hor-Aha coming toward him across the hot sand, trailed by a servant with his parasol and his sandal-bearer and the rest of the court. Jack bowed—it was easier to do it when you thought of it as a salute — and Hor-Aha nodded in acknowledgement.

"So, O'Neill," he said. "Once again you confound me."

"You were right," Jack said. "But — there had to be another answer. And Sam's good at that."

"She is," Hor-Aha agreed. "And her solution seems to be a good one. Show me what you've done."

"Right." Jack gestured to Basa, who waved his men into position. "The chance we'll need this is pretty small, I know Sam's told you that. But just in case —" He went though the plan, a small group in front of the Stargate to draw fire, the bulk of the men on either side to pick off the Jaffa as they came through.

Hor-Aha nodded again. "That is a post of great danger, before the gate."

Basa cleared his throat, and Jack said, "Go ahead."

"With respect, Lord, those men all volunteered — there were more who were willing, but these were all O'Neill said we needed. All of them have fought at Teal'c's side, and wish to see him safe and well."

"Teal'c is blessed by his friends," Hor-Aha said. "Very well."

"We're doing everything we can to protect them," Jack said. "We've got breastworks ready, and the main attack's going to come from the sides."

"Show me these breastworks," Nithotep said, and Basa bowed. "At once, Lady."

They turned away, followed by most of the court, and Jack realized she'd done it on purpose. He was left almost alone with Hor-Aha, and that usually wasn't a good sign.

Pharaoh smiled as though he'd guessed the thought. "I will give you leave to do this, never fear. You have countered all my worries, and I know the debt I owe Teal'c. This small risk I will gladly take for him. But I wished to ask you — Sa-Mantha accompanies you? And Danyel?"

"I couldn't stop them," Jack said, honestly. "And I'm glad to have them."

"And what of Ellie?" Hor-Aha asked. "Should not her mother remain behind?"

Jack looked away. "Teal'c deserves the best chance we can give him, and that means all of us. Look, I don't think—if something happens, Aset will take care of her. Danyel's given her the deeds to the house and the farm."

"And I will care for her as though she were my own," Hor-Aha said. "Should something happen. But it will not come to that."

Jack looked at him, a young man, rather ordinary-looking in spite of the heavy wig and the gold collar spread across his sweating chest, the kohl smudged at the corners of his eyes. A young man, but also a father, and offering the one thing he had that might make things easier. Jack swallowed hard, wished he had the words to say how grateful he was. Danyel would, and he'd make Danyel send a letter, but for now—

"Thank you," he said.

Hor-Aha extended his hand, and Jack took it, clasping Pharaoh's wrist.

"You are welcome," Hor-Aha said. "But it will not be needed."

"Amen to that," Jack said.

CHAPTER EIGHT

THE SUN was rising as Sam made her way down to the dock, the dew cold between her toes, her shadow stretching behind her almost to the walls of the house. Jack was up before her, as she'd expected, a black silhouette against the molten light, fishing pole in hand as he studied the currents. The sound of her foot on the boards of the dock wasn't loud, but he turned at once, relaxing as he saw who it was. She held up the basket she was carrying and he smiled.

"What've you got there, breakfast?"

"Bread and beer," she said, and settled herself cross-legged beside his stool. "Ellie's still asleep, but I—wasn't."

"Me, neither," Danyel said, behind her, and she looked up to see his rueful smile. "I don't suppose there's enough for three?"

"I think so," Sam answered, and poured the first cup of beer. One of them would have to drink out of the jar, but that was fine. A bird broke from the reeds, wings whirring, and in the courtyard a cock crowed.

"OK, kids," Jack said. "What are you up to?"

"Nothing," Sam said, with honest surprise. She swallowed her mouthful of bread. "Ellie was asleep, for once..." She let her voice trail off, and Jack looked at Danyel.

"Talk."

"I don't have anything to say," Danyel said.

Sam leaned forward to look at him around the wall of Jack's knees. "Are you all right?"

She could feel Jack's silent laugh, and Danyel shook his head. "I'm fine."

"The hell," Jack said. "You're so quiet it's unnatural."

"So you'd rather I was talking so that you could ignore me?"

Danyel asked.

"Maybe."

They could go on like that all day. Sam said, "I want to know what's wrong."

There was a little silence then, Jack frowning at his fishing line, Danyel staring into the sun. The river breeze was still cool, and she hunched her shawl further on her shoulders, glad she'd worn it.

"I'm worried about the timeline," Danyel said at last.

"Oh, is that all?" Jack said. "Everything else is going to be a piece of cake —"

"No, of course not," Danyel said. "But you're not taking Egeria into account."

"You said yourself, the symbiotes can't be trusted," Jack said. "Why should we believe it?"

"Because Egeria appears about now," Danyel said. He sounded unusually subdued. "And if this is Egeria, and we don't let her take a host and go do what she's going to do — the vanishing of the Tok'ra is an even bigger change to the timeline than Ra taking Earth's Stargate."

"But we don't know," Jack said again.

"It almost doesn't matter," Danyel said. "Look, the only thing I can think of is to talk some poor bastard into becoming Egeria's host and sending them off through the Stargate before we bury it again. And I don't — I can't do that, Jack."

"You're not going," Sam said.

Danyel gave her a look. "You might at least let me say it. Besides, who else is there who knows what they're getting into?"

"Other people at the temples," Sam said. "Some of the people who trained to become hosts."

"We shot most of them," Jack said. "The ones who wanted to be chosen were pretty much Goa'uld supporters."

"And the rest of them — why would they do it?" Danyel slid forward so that he could look at both of them. "Look, it's not like I want to do this, but I don't see an alternative."

"These are the Tok'ra," Sam said. "They're the good guys, right?" Danyel looked dubious at that, but she plowed ahead anyway. "I bet somebody at the temple would want to help fight the false gods, and I can't think of a better way to do it."

"But they don't know—"

"And you know too much," Jack said. "Suppose this Egeria isn't the right one, suppose it's lying? If some Goa'uld turns one of those weird hand things on you, what does that do to the timeline?"

"OK," Danyel said. "That's a problem, yes—"

"So we find a volunteer," Jack said. "Worst case, Pharaoh finds us somebody who was going to be executed, and we give him to Egeria."

"I don't think that's a good idea," Sam said.

"Whatever." Jack pulled in his line, glancing over his shoulder at the house. Following his gaze, Sam saw a lamp moving in the courtyard, and heard the wail of a hungry baby.

"Sam's right," Danyel said. "I think—"

"You think too much," Jack said. He pushed himself to his feet, and extended a hand to help Sam. She let herself be hauled up, and Jack looked down at Danyel. "And it's time for breakfast."

"That's not going to solve anything," Danyel said, but he was smiling.

"No," Jack said. "But it might shut you up."

"For a while," Sam said, grinning, and started back up the path to the house.

It was early evening before all the preparations were complete. Jack took a long look at the fading sunset behind the buildings that would someday be a city, and reached for his watch. Danyel already had his in hand, ready to set it to match.

"Seven-oh-six," Jack said, and Danyel nodded, his fingers deft on the tiny bezel.

"OK, got it." He held out the watch to Aset, who took it with careful respect. Danyel had taught her to tell time during the rebellion, Jack knew, along with half a dozen others who were now dead. Now she would be the one to say when the Stargate would be cleared, ready for them to dial in. He checked his own watch again out of reflex. Twelve hours from when they opened the gate, Aset would order the sail removed, leave it clear for exactly ten minutes. If they didn't dial in, she'd do it again six hours after that, then four hours from then, then two hours, and one final time two hours after that. Twenty-six hours. Surely that would be enough time—and it would be, he told himself firmly. Plenty of time. Get in, get a larva, get out: that was the mission.

"Ready?" Sam called from the DHD. They were all dressed in the long sand-colored robes Danyel said people wore on Abydos, hot and confining after a few years of near nakedness. Jack felt for the zat hidden beneath the folds of his robe, and hiked a sleeve irritably out of his way. The mark on his forehead, Ra's insignia drawn in kohl and sealed with something Sam had saved from her pack, was itching, but he managed not to scratch. Teal'c seemed unbothered, and Jack told himself it was just because the mark was on scar tissue, not on normal skin.

"We're good," Danyel said, from just outside the reach of the expanding wormhole, and Teal'c nodded as well. He was dressed in Abydonian robes, too but he still carried his staff weapon.

"Jack?" Sam called again, and he shook himself.

"Yeah, ready. Dial the gate."

He moved to join the others as the sailors dragged the reed sail out of the gate opening. Sethnakht raised his arm the moment it was clear, and Sam began pressing buttons. The first chevrons lit, the ring groaning as it turned. Danyel was watching it with something like hunger, and Jack moved closer to Teal'c.

"How're you doing, Teal'c?"

The Jaffa slanted a glance at him. "I am well enough, O'Neill."

He looked all right, but Jack had seen him look pretty much the same with a two-inch wide hole punched through his biceps. "OK," he said, in a tone that he hoped conveyed, I'm trusting you.

The last chevron lit. The wormhole exploded with a whoosh, then stabilized to a shimmering pool. Sam hurried to join them, slinging a bundle over her shoulder.

"OK, kids," Jack said. He couldn't help being a little wary of the wormhole, no matter how often he'd heard Danyel talk about it, or how often he'd been told his other self had walked through its circle. Before, he'd done it in the jumper, and that was somehow different.

"OK," Danyel said, and stepped into the blue light. Teal'c followed him, the event horizon swallowing him, and then Sam. Jack looked over his shoulder to see Hor-Aha lift his hand in blessing and farewell.

"The true gods protect you," he called.

Jack lifted his own hand and snapped a salute, then turned to face the Stargate. He took a deep breath and stepped into its embrace.

Danyel and Teal'c had chosen good planets for their intermediate stops. The Stargate had been completely unguarded on two of them, and the third was attended only by an elderly woman, who collected a small silver ring that Teal'c had apparently brought for the purpose, and let them go on their way. This final gate was unguarded, too, just the great sweep of the ring gleaming in the cloudy moonlight, trees crowding dark around them. Teal'c concealed his staff weapon in the brush by the DHD, and Danyel entered the address for Abydos. The Stargate lit, driving back the shadows.

"Are we expecting guards?" Jack asked, looking at Teal'c. He'd asked before, but the Jaffa didn't comment.

"There will be guards, O'Neill. But there will also be visitors. The prim'tah ceremony is a time for rejoicing, for families to gather. We should pass unnoticed."

"Let's go, then," Jack said, and stepped into the wormhole.

He emerged in shadow, in a long hall of stone lit by a double row of Goa'uld braziers. There were Jaffa in armor at the base of the steps leading up to the gate platform, but they were fairly relaxed, for Jaffa, aiming staff weapons without actually charging them.

"Kree!" the leader shouted, and Danyel stepped hastily forward.

"We are here for the prim'tah of my sister's son," he said. "May we pass?"

The leader hesitated, but only for a moment. "Go, then. And hurry. The ceremonies have begun."

"Thank you," Danyel said, ducking his head, and Jack followed, resisting the urge to say something stupid, Sam scurrying at his elbow.

They came out of the temple into sunlight bright enough to make him blink, reflecting off pale sand and stone, the cloudless sky dazzling. The only spots of color were the clusters of sun-faded tents that lay beyond the twin obelisks that stood before the temple gate. Smoke rose from cooking fires, and Jack could hear laughter, and children's voices raised in a sing-song chant.

"They are singing of the prim'tah," Teal'c said, his expression unreadable, and Jack couldn't repress a shudder.

"OK, Danyel, now what?" he asked, and Danyel looked over his shoulder.

"We find a quiet spot to put up our tent—"

"Oh, that's what I've been carrying," Sam said, not without irony.

"And then we go looking for the larvae," Danyel finished. "Let's try over there."

Danyel negotiated a spot at the edge of a group of faded blue tents, not so close that they could easily be overheard, but close enough that at first glance they seemed to belong to that group, and they busied themselves setting up the tent and establishing their camp.

"We'll go look for water," Jack said, once the tent was up, and Danyel nodded.

"The public well should be just inside the temple," he said. "They'll probably keep the larvae somewhere nearby."

"That was my thought," Jack said, and reached down to haul Sam to her feet.

There was already a ragged line of men and women heading for the temple, most of them carrying water jars. Jack eased into the line, Sam at his side, both of them smiling blandly. There was a definite holiday feeling to the crowd, everyone relaxed and cheerful, and little groups of kids were playing between the tents. A ball knocked against his ankle, and he stopped it without thinking, A boy, maybe ten or so, stood looking embarrassed, and Jack kicked it back to him.

"Everybody's so happy," Sam said.

"It's a big deal," Jack said. The whole idea gave him the willies, but he kind of understood what it was supposed to mean to a Jaffa. And that was all the more reason to get a larva and get back to Earth so they could bury the Stargate again.

They made their way into the temple, paused for a moment as though they were enjoying the relative cool. Jack let his eyes rove around the shallow entrance hall. That tall doorway led to the Stargate; there were smaller doors as well, two to the left, and three on the right. There weren't any Jaffa warriors in evidence, but that probably just meant that they were inside the chambers. He followed Sam to the well, held their jar while she ladled it full.

"Any ideas which one it is?" he asked, and she shrugged. "We'll have to get a closer look—"

A trumpet sounded, the flat dissonance of a ram's horn, and suddenly everyone was scuttling back against the walls, leaving a wide path through the center of the hall. Jack copied them, pulling back until he and Sam were both flattened against a wall of carvings. The trumpet sounded again, louder this time, and a procession emerged from the middle of the right-hand doors. Two Jaffa warriors in full armor led the way, followed by the trumpeter, and then a quartet of women in tall headdresses. They were followed in turn by a pair of men who carried a golden box slung on a pole between them. It was faceted almost like a diamond, and each face was embossed with Ra's symbol and a cartouche. Another pair of Jaffa warriors brought up the rear.

"I don't have to know how to read Goa'uld to guess what's in there," Jack said, in Sam's ear.

"And now we know where they're kept," she said.

"Yeah." Jack wished he thought that did them more good. There were bound to be guards watching the larvae, and it looked like it was an awkward scramble from that room back through the hall and into the gate room. He wished he still had some demolition charges. Blowing up the DHD behind them was probably the best way to delay pursuit—but he didn't, so they'd have to find something else. "Let's go."

By the time they reached the tent, the sun was nearing the horizon. Danyel had kindled a small fire, and was holding something that looked like a cross between a sponge and an ear of corn over the flames. Teal'c was reclining on one of the blankets, his face unreadable, and Sam dipped water for each of them.

"Please don't tell me that's dinner," Jack said.

"I'll have your share, then," Danyel answered. "No, really, it's very tasty. Sort of like, I don't know, kettle corn, maybe."

"Maybe," Jack said. Danyel's comparisons tended to be optimistic. "Well, we know where they keep the things."

Danyel handed the stick to Sam, who gave it a dubious look, but kept it over the fire. Danyel smoothed a patch of sand, began drawing in it with a smaller stick. "OK, here's the gate, and its hall. And here's the entrance hall, with the well, and these are the side chambers—"

"That one," Jack said, and pointed.

"Yeah." Danyel kept drawing, adding lines that ran through the back of the temple, connecting the side chambers with the gate room through doors beside the gate. "OK, that's what I would have — these rooms all connect, here, past the chamber with all the gate addresses, and we can get into the gate hall this way, maybe take the guard by surprise."

"Assuming we haven't already alerted them by shooting the guards that are watching the prim'tahs," Jack said.

"There may not be any," Danyel said. "There weren't any on Chulak."

"There were guards escorting the one we saw being taken out," Sam said.

"I think that's just an honor guard," Danyel said. "More to emphasize the importance of the whole event than to protect the larva — I mean, what Jaffa is going to harm the symbiotes they need to survive?"

"Not everybody here's a Jaffa," Jack said.

'Yes, but they're not going to risk it, either," Danyel said. "Look, after dark, Teal'c says things will quiet down a little. The families who've already gotten the prim'tah will be celebrating, and everyone else will be getting ready. We should be able to slip into the temple and get into the chamber where they're keeping them — quietly neutralizing any guards that are there, if there are any."

"See, 'quietly neutralize' just never works out that way," Jack said.

Danyel ignored him, retracing one of the lines with his stick. "Then we take this back corridor into the gate hall, and that's where we'll probably have a fight. But if we can knock out the Jaffa quickly enough, we'll have plenty of time to dial the gate. Once we're through, we dial out again immediately, and keep moving until we can dial Earth."

Jack pulled his watch out from under his robes. "OK, we

need to wait until dark, that's, what, another three hours?"

"Full dark, yeah, I'd say so." Danyel nodded.

"That'll be—OK, give it another couple of hours after that, just to let everybody get settled, and we'll be right on schedule for Aset to open up the gate for us."

"I do not think that will happen tonight, O'Neill." Teal'c rolled to a sitting position, pointing out past the flap of the tent. Jack turned, to see a Goa'uld ship settling gently onto the tip of the pyramid behind the temple. An instant later, its noise washed over them, followed by a wave of cheers. People were emerging from their tents, shouting and pointing, and there was another blast of trumpets from the temple.

"Ra will preside over special ceremonies in the temple tonight," Teal'c said, "and in the morning he will show his favor to certain of his warriors by himself being present at their sons' prim'tah. The temple will be nearly empty then—but not tonight."

"Crap," Jack said. He closed his eyes for a second, calculating. "Twelve hours from now, that makes it about twenty-one hours before we can try. That's cutting it really close."

"It won't be so bad," Sam said. "And if Ra's going to be in the temple all night—well, we don't have a choice."

The rams' horns sounded from the temple steps again, and all around them people began to move, filing slowly toward the temple. Sam frowned.

"What's this all about?"

Teal'c gave a thin smile. "We must welcome our god, Samantha Carter."

"Crap," Jack said again, and pushed himself to his feet. "I don't suppose we can bring the kettle corn thing."

"No, O'Neill," Teal'c said.

CHAPTER NINE

THE RAM'S horn trumpet sounded again, closer this time, marking another procession of priests and Jaffa, and Jack glared out the opening of the tent. They had been going strong since sunrise, leaving them no opportunity to get into the temple, and his nerves were definitely beginning to fray.

"You know, if he blows that thing one more time, I'm going to—" He'd been trying to watch his language since Ellie was born, and finished, "stick it where the sun don't shine."

Teal'c tipped his head to one side, clearly about to ask for an explanation, and Danyel said, "Really, don't ask."

"Then I will not." Teal'c settled back on his blanket, propping himself comfortably on one elbow. "This should be the last ceremony of the morning. Ra will speak to his people when the sun is at the zenith, and the temple will be quiet then."

"That doesn't leave us much time," Sam said.

"The temple will begin to empty before Ra speaks," Teal'c said. "If we are there when the trumpet sounds, it will be easy enough to conceal ourselves in the shadows. Few guards will remain."

"That'll work," Jack said.

Danyel unwrapped the last of the rounds of bread and tore it into quarters. Jack took his share without eagerness, but he knew he'd need to eat. There wouldn't be time later, and he'd need the calories. The others were doing the same, washing it down with the last of the water they'd brought from the well. Without turning, Jack flattened his hand against his blanket, feeling the container they'd readied for the larva. It would seal tight, protect the thing from damage, and, not incidentally, protect them from it, though both Danyel and Teal'c swore the symbiotes would be too young to take a host. Still, Jack thought, there was no point in taking chances.

They finished their meal, and Jack checked his watch again. "Time," he said, softly, and the others began slowly getting to their feet. They would leave the tent behind, and Jack glanced quickly over it to be sure there was nothing that would betray its origin. He couldn't see anything — the humans taken by the Goa'uld had brought their livestock with them, and an Egyptian goatskin tent was indistinguishable from an Abydonian one. He reached under his robe to be sure his zat was accessible.

"Everybody ready?" he asked, and the others nodded, Sam with a quick fierce smile. It still impressed him how well she'd taken to guerilla warfare. "Then let's go."

Teal'c was right, there were fewer people moving toward the temple. Jack checked the urge to hurry, trailed along behind a trio of chattering women. Sam tucked her arm into his, the pot for the larva cradled in her other arm; Danyel followed, apparently deep in conversation with Teal'c. The obelisks loomed ahead, and they started up the shallow steps, drawing aside to let a group of armored Jaffa hurry past them.

"Hopefully that's a good sign," Danyel said. He didn't seem to expect an answer, and Jack ignored him, following the three women into the entrance hall. As they approached the well, Sam caught his sleeve. He turned to see her settle onto one of the stone blocks, fiddling with the strap of her shoe. Out of the corner of his eye, he saw Teal'c melt into the shadows between the torches. Danyel leaned one shoulder against the wall, contriving to give the impression that he was part of a group waiting their turn at the well.

Then the trumpet sounded. Jack put a hand down, pulled Sam to her feet, and together they shuffled after the rest of the stragglers. As they passed the first shadowed alcove, they slipped inside, and a moment later Danyel and Teal'c joined them. The rest of Ra's congregation filed past, and the sound of their footsteps died away. Jack waited a few seconds more, then peered cautiously out. The hall was empty as far as he could see, and he motioned for Danyel to take point. Danyel nodded, his zat unfolding, but in that instant there was the whine and the blazing light of transporter rings.

"Oh, crap," Jack said under his breath, and waved frantically for everyone to stay put. The rings disgorged Jaffa, a good dozen of them, and then Ra himself, resplendent in cloth-of-gold. He wasn't wearing the mask, and it looked as though he'd acquired a new host recently. His female attendants no longer supported him, just provided a decorative escort, though one cradled the heavy mask.

"What?" Danyel hissed, and Jack lifted his finger for silence.

"Ra," he mouthed, and Danyel made a face, flattening himself against the stones.

Teal'c had his zat ready, the look on his face suggesting that he really wanted his staff weapon. So did Jack, for that matter, but nothing much short of claymores would even the odds. There had to be at least two dozen Jaffa out there now, plus the handmaidens and four or five guys in robes who were either minions or — worse and more likely — lesser Goa'uld in Ra's service.

"What are they doing?" Sam said, very softly.

"Looks like they're getting dressed for the ceremony," Jack said, equally quietly. The handmaidens were fluttering around Ra, smoothing his robe and polishing his fingernails. The one with the mask stood on tiptoes, her eyes downcast, and Ra took his mask, turning it as though he was inspecting it for damage.

"Come on," Danyel murmured. "You're going to be late —"

Teal'c glared at him, and Danyel relapsed into silence. Jack refrained from looking at his watch. There was still time, plenty of time... He was lying to himself and knew it, his gut tightening. If they couldn't get to the gate in time, Earth's Stargate would be closed forever, or at least until sometime in the 1920s, which wouldn't do them the slightest bit of good, either. Ra would have to leave before noon to preside over the ceremony, he told himself, and that left them about an hour to steal a larva and dial out again.

Then, finally, Ra lifted the mask, settling it onto his head. The handmaidens fussed again with his robe, drawing out the hem in luxurious folds. A trumpet sounded, and the Jaffa who seemed to be in charge of this group shouted something that started with "Jaffa, kree!" and at last the whole procession began to move. More trumpets sounded in the distance, and Jack felt his knees sag just a little. Still, he made himself wait until the last Jaffa was well out of sight before he checked his watch. The number made him wince, and he knew Sam saw.

"How long?" she asked.

"Thirty-three minutes." Jack risked another look, decided the coast was clear. "OK, let's do this."

The entrance hall was empty, no Jaffa left behind. Jack paused in the doorway of the corridor that led to the symbiotes' chamber, but he could see nothing but the flicker of Goa'uld torches. Maybe a shadow moved, beyond the light, but he couldn't be sure. He motioned for Teal'c to cover him, and edged down the corridor, keeping close to the shadowed wall. He could hear water as he came closer, paused just inside the entrance to let the others come up. The noise was good, would help cover their movement, the zat blasts. Even flattened against the corridor wall, he could see its source. A ribbon of water fell glittering from an elaborate ceiling rosette, and splashed into a glass-walled cylinder that seemed half full of writhing pink eels. The top edge of the cylinder was banded in gold, and golden spikes stood out from it like the rays of a sun. He risked a further look, saw only a single woman, a priestess by her headdress, twirling a spindle as she sat beside the tank.

Now or never, he thought, and waved the others forward. He popped into the doorway after them, ready to provide covering fire. There were three Jaffa, caught by surprise with their helmets open and their staff weapons leaning against the wall beside them. Teal'c dropped two with well-placed zat blasts; Danyel got the third, but not before he'd fired once. The priestess screamed, spindle clattering to the stones, and Jack brought her down with a single shot.

"Which corridor leads to the gate room?" Teal'c asked, scooping up one of the staff weapons, and Danyel pointed.

"That one."

"Cover us," Jack said, grabbing a staff weapon himself, and put himself between the larva tank and the doorway by which they'd entered. "Sam, get one of those things."

She was already moving, hiking up the skirts of her robe to free her legs. She unstoppered the jar and climbed up onto the platform that held the cylinder, bent around the spikes to dip the jar into the water. Jack looked back toward the door. No sign that anyone had heard them — but then there was the sound of zat blasts from the direction of the gate room.

"Better hurry, Sam," he called.

"I'm trying," she answered. "These things are slippery."

He risked another glance over his shoulder, saw her leaning over the edge of the tank, her hand brown among the thrashing larvae. She gave an exclamation of triumph, pulled back with a foot-long symbiote wriggling in her grasp. Jack caught a quick glimpse, pink, blind, embryonic, its three-fold jaws opening and closing ineffectually, and then she dropped it into the jar and pressed the lid solidly home.

"Got it!"

More zat fire punctuated her words, and Jack grimaced. "Great. Let's go."

They fell back toward the corridor that led to the gate room, Jack covering their retreat. So far, at least, they hadn't attracted any other attention, but he knew that wouldn't last. A staff blast scorched past them as they reached the end of the corridor, and Danyel looked over his shoulder.

"We, um, we may have a little problem."

"There are still four Jaffa left in the gate room, O'Neill," Teal'c said. "We cannot reach the DHD."

"Crap." Jack leaned past Danyel's shoulder, snapped a shot

at a Jaffa as he dove for a better position.

"They're going to be calling for reinforcements," Sam said. She wound the jar more tightly into the cloth sling, settled it on her hip.

"We may have a break there," Danyel said. "Teal'c says they won't want to interrupt Ra."

"That's helpful," Jack said. OK, the Jaffa were in cover, tucked in behind the columns that lined the hall; the DHD was in the open, and even if they could get to it, there wouldn't be time to dial. No, they'd have to take out the Jaffa first. "Is there any other way across there?"

Danyel looked around. "Maybe?"

"Could you be a little more definite?"

One of the Jaffa was moving, trying to work his way up the hall, and Jack snapped off a shot that knocked him back.

"If we go back the way we came, there's another corridor that comes out over there," Danyel said. He nodded to a shadowed alcove almost directly across the gate room. "But it's a long way around."

"Too long," Jack said.

"O'Neill," Teal'c said. "I believe they are calling for assistance."

Sure enough, one of the Jaffa was talking into a golden armband. Jack grabbed his watch: eighteen minutes before Aset would unblock Earth's gate. "We're going to have to rush them," he said, and Teal'c nodded.

"I will try for the gate itself," he said.

Jack saw it instantly, the converging angles, the shots it would give him and Danyel and Sam, and braced himself.

Teal'c leaped forward, startlingly fast for such a big man, and Jack swung into the open to cover him, Danyel and Sam at his heels. Sure enough, the first Jaffa broke cover, and Jack picked him off. Danyel caught the next one with a pair of zat blasts, and Teal'c and Sam caught the last two in unexpected crossfire. Jack grinned, and only then saw the curl of smoke rising from the DHD.

"Oh, crap!"

Sam was already on it, stripping off the sling to pry up the panel. "It's OK," she said. "I can fix this."

"You got twelve minutes," Jack said. "Danyel, cover the side entrance. Teal'c, with me."

They took up positions on either side of the hall, sheltering behind the pillars, where they could more or less cover the main entrance. Jack looked at his watch again, seeing the minutes tick away. "Sam."

"Almost there," she answered, never looking away from the crystals.

"They are coming, O'Neill," Teal'c said, and Jack heard the sound of armored feet on the stones of the entrances hall. He braced the staff weapon fired as soon as he saw movement at the end of the hall.

"Sam!"

"Almost —"

Jack fired again, and a Jaffa tumbled down the steps. They could hold them off for a little while, but if the Jaffa commander sent his men around to the side corridors, they'd be trapped.

"Got it!" Sam yelled.

Jack risked a look at his watch. It was time, past time, and that meant —

"Dial direct!" he shouted. "Danyel, cover us."

He heard the gate begin to turn, the heavy chunk of the chevrons locking, and fell back as Danyel fired past him at the approaching Jaffa. And then he and Teal'c were at the DHD and the wormhole lit behind them in a whoosh of light.

"Go!" he yelled. "Teal'c, Sam, go!"

The Jaffa were entering the gate room, and he ducked instinctively as a staff blast screamed past him.

"This is a bad idea," Danyel said, and Jack shoved him toward the gate. He backed after him, firing his own staff weapon. A Jaffa fell, then two more, falling in a tangle of limbs, and staff blasts shot past him, vanishing into the event horizon. And then at last he was close enough, and he made a jump for the gate, tumbling out of the wormhole and down the familiar steps outside Pharaoh's palace in a tangle of robes. More staff blasts passed overhead, and then the gate winked out. There was sudden, blessed silence. Jack picked himself up, pleased to find that he was only bruised, and Sam cried out.

"Aset! Oh, my God!"

CHAPTER TEN

ASET LAY sprawled on the ground just beyond the DHD, her head and shoulders in the lap of a young soldier who held a fairly clean-looking kilt against her side. The cloth was bloody and her eyes were closed, her hands lax in the dirt. Teal'c dropped to his knees at her side.

"O'Neill!"

Jack went to one knee beside them, wincing as the big man gently uncovered the wound. A staff blast through the Stargate had caught her in the side between ribs and hip, the flesh torn and blackened. At least the blast had cauterized most of the major vessels, or she'd be dead already, but as it was—He grimaced and looked away. She wasn't going to survive this.

"Teal'c, my brother," Hor-Aha said, his voice reflecting the same shocked knowledge. He beckoned to the nearest of his men. "Quickly, bear her to the temple. Perhaps—" He stopped, shaking his head.

"Yes." Teal'c interlaced his fingers with her unresponsive ones. "We must try."

They brought her into the temple, into a cool antechamber, and laid her on a bed hastily spread with linen and a pillow. Temple servants brought lamps until the narrow room glowed, and the scent of the oil warred with the smell of her burned flesh. A small boy was set to fan her, keeping the flies away, and the senior priest came hurrying with soft linen heavily smeared with honey. He laid it gently over the wound, not daring to move her to bind it tight. Danyel made a strangled noise and turned away. Sam went after him, laying a hand on his shoulder, spoke softly in his ear. It was the best they could do, Jack knew, and to use so much of the precious stuff on what they had to know was a hopeless case… Tears prickled in his eyes, and he cleared his throat. Teal'c looked up, his own eyes suspiciously bright.

"I cannot lose her, O'Neill."

Aset's eyes opened then, vague and unfocused at first, but then her gaze sharpened. "Teal'c," she whispered, and the ghost of a smile crossed her lips. "You are well."

"But you are not," he began, and she freed her hand from his, reaching clumsily to cover his lips.

"Shh. It is well." She closed her eyes again, a flicker of pain racing across her face.

Jack stepped back, looking for the priest, but the man had seen the same thing, and beckoned to an acolyte. The youth poured a thick liquid into a shallow dish, and the priest held it to her lips, dribbling it into her mouth with the ease of long practice. Poppy syrup, Jack knew. He knew, too, that it was all they could do for her. Make her comfortable, and wait for her to die. Ellie would miss her, and there could be no explanation; Hor-Aha would give her a tomb fit for a queen, and none of it was fair. Even if they'd been back in his own time, with all the resources of Landstuhl available, this one would be touch and go. Here in Egypt, five thousand years before antibiotics and artificial skin — He shook his head, focused on what he could do.

"Teal'c," he said softly. It had been more than twenty-four hours since the Jaffa had entered kelnorim, and Jack could tell that this was going to be a long and painful vigil.

"O'Neill." Teal'c did not look up, his hands closed again around Aset's limp fingers.

"You need to take a break, buddy," Jack said.

"I cannot."

"Teal'c." Jack groped for the words. "She'll need you later."

Teal'c closed his eyes. "Yes," he said, and pushed himself to his feet. He disappeared into a side chamber, and Jack stood for a moment, looking down at Aset. At least the poppy syrup had soothed her.

"Damn it," Danyel said. "There's got to be something."

"Like what?" Jack asked, and turned away before he could answer. He made his way back out to the temple's grand entrance, stood for a long moment looking out at the deepening night. Twenty-six hours since they'd left—twenty-eight, now—and so much for thinking they'd won. The reed matting swung in the breeze behind the gate.

"Jack?" Sam came to take his arm. "I've sent one of the soldiers for Tamit and Ellie."

Life goes on, Jack thought. The baby needs to be fed, even when her favorite aunt lies dying. He nodded. "Good idea."

He wrapped his arm around her waist, glad to have her there, guiltily glad it wasn't her on the bed inside. She rested her head against his shoulder.

He didn't know how long they stood there. The moon cleared the horizon, a misshapen coin, and a night bird called from the river. A pair of torches moved by the palace, vanished again, and he could smell the fading smoke of a hundred hearths. Not fair, not by a long shot, and there was nothing he could do.

"Jack." That was Danyel, his voice sharp and worried. "Jack, Teal'c's—he's got an idea."

"What?" Jack blinked, pieces fitting together. "Oh, no, that's not a good idea at all."

"Tell me about it," Danyel said. "But—have we got a better one?"

"Egeria?" Sam looked from one to the other. "Come on."

Teal'c was sitting cross-legged beside Aset's bed, his face calm. "O'Neill. Egeria has spoken to me. If Aset agrees, she will take her as a host and heal her, and promise to share her body as you tell me the Tok'ra do."

"That's if we believe her," Danyel said. "If she can be trusted."

"You yourself told me she was mother of the Tok'ra," Teal'c said.

"In my timeline," Danyel said.

"Yeah," Jack said. "The Goa'uld don't exactly have a great track record here, Teal'c."

"And if we do not," Teal'c said, "Aset will die."

"What's worse?" Jack asked. "Being dead, or being a Goa'uld?"

Teal'c looked down at the woman on the bed. Her breathing was shallow, her eyelids fluttering a little as the poppies' effect wore off. "If Egeria betrays her—" He stopped. "I will not permit it."

"But—" Danyel began, and Jack grabbed his shoulder.

"OK," he said. "But if it doesn't work—"

"We will have done all that we could do," Teal'c said. "And I will do what I must."

Jack nodded. "Sam?"

"It's right here." Sam unwound the jar that held the symbiote from its sling.

"Do it," Jack said, and hoped none of the priests would return before it was finished. How he was going to explain this to Hor-Aha—but he'd cross that bridge when he got there.

Teal'c reached out to take Aset's hand. "Aset," he said. "Aset, hear me."

She's not going to answer, Jack thought, but to his surprise, Aset opened her eyes.

"Egeria can save you," Teal'c said. The lips of his symbiote pouch gaped open, the winged head of the Goa'uld emerging. "If you are willing, she will join with you, and save you."

Aset blinked hard, tilting her head as though to see. Her eyes widened, but then she nodded. "Yes," she whispered, and closed her eyes again.

Teal'c closed his eyes in turn, and the Goa'uld—Egeria, Jack reminded himself, it was a Tok'ra, the first Tok'ra—wormed its way out of the pouch. There was a moment when it hovered, wings spread, and then it leaped for Aset's throat. She choked, and the thing had vanished, burrowing into her flesh.

"Damn it," Danyel said. He was looking sick, and Sam grabbed his hand.

"It's OK," she said, but didn't sound very sure.

"Give Teal'c the new symbiote," Danyel said, his voice tight.

Sam nodded, and brought the jar to Teal'c, crouching at his side. She opened it, and Teal'c shook himself, reached in to take the larva. It squirmed for a moment, as though trying to escape, then seemed to sense a Jaffa, and dove into the pouch. Teal'c's head snapped back, and then he steadied.

"Aset? Is she—?"

"I am well." The words were barely a thread of sound, but it was Aset's voice, not a Goa'uld's. "Or I will be. Egeria says it will take time, and I must sleep..." Her eyes closed again.

"Her breathing is better," Sam said.

Jack scratched his head. "OK," he said. "That's—weird, but hopeful."

"If she is Egeria," Danyel began, and shook his head. "Actually, I have no idea how this will all work out."

"We'll figure it out tomorrow," Jack said. "For tonight, I'm sure Pharaoh will put us up."

"I will remain here, O'Neill," Teal'c said.

Jack nodded. "Do you want company?"

Teal'c smiled. "It is not necessary. But thank you."

CHAPTER ELEVEN

Cheyenne Mountain
2008 AD

GENERAL Jack O'Neill looked down the briefing table waiting for somebody to say something. Mitchell had just laid out the situation with the Tok'ra, with considerable interjections from Daniel about everything. Landry was pacing while Vala was being uncharacteristically silent, Teal'c characteristically so. And Carter... Well, it was about time for her to come up with a brilliant plan, wasn't it? "So?" he prompted.

"We could attempt to use Ba'al's facility," Carter said reluctantly. "I'm fairly sure I can figure out how it works. That would allow us to use the Stargate to get to the right time, or at least to the right era. But we still have a problem."

"Both of Earth's Stargates are buried at that time," Daniel said. "The Antarctic gate is under the ice, and after the rebellion against Ra the Giza gate was buried."

Jack's brows twitched. "The Antarctic gate... It's in a crevasse. It's not inoperable." And he ought to know, having found out the hard way.

"And then we're in Antarctica. In 3000 BC." Carter pursed her lips. "How do we get from Antarctica to Egypt? How do we even get out of the crevasse? Remember, we found the body of a Jaffa down there. He couldn't get out."

"Climbing gear," Jack mused. "Proper equipment..." They hadn't had cold weather gear or anything but emergency supplies, and he'd been wounded. A well supplied team might be able to get out onto the glacier. But then. Antarctica was a long way from Egypt.

"The Giza gate can't be buried," Vala said, and everybody

turned to look at her. "It can't," she said, folding her hands on the conference table. "Because somehow Egeria left Earth, right? She didn't stay. So she must have used the gate. Therefore it can't have been buried the entire time."

Mitchell raised a finger. "I think she's onto something there."

Daniel shook his head. "OK, they unburied the gate and Egeria dialed out. What, it was open for a few hours in several hundred years? There's no way we can know exactly when."

"Actually, maybe there is," Carter said, looking down the table, and that was his regularly scheduled Carter, always coming up with a technical solution. "At any given moment most of the Stargates in the galaxy are inoperable. We found that out back in the first year of the program. If you just randomly dial gate addresses out of a database, less than fifty percent will connect. Now, some of those are gates that are permanently offline, destroyed or inoperable for one reason or another, and some of them are busy. The gate is already being used, and that's especially true of worlds that have a lot of traffic. It may take sixty or seventy repeats to get through because somebody is always dialing in or dialing out."

"Like trying to call the cable company," Jack huffed.

"Exactly like, sir," Carter said.

"Daniel Jackson has used the telephone analogy before," Teal'c said.

"It's exactly like a phone." Carter turned to Daniel. "So what do you do if you need to call someone, but their line is always busy? You know they have to get off the phone sometime, but you don't know when. Especially if you have a lot of numbers you have to call."

"Leave a voice mail?" Mitchell suggested.

Daniel sat up straighter. "You use a predictive dialer."

"OK, kids," Jack said. "What's a predictive dialer?"

"It's a program you use for phone banking or telemarketing, sir," Carter said. "It dials dozens or even hundreds of numbers at once, and then only puts through to the live operators the ones that get a connection. That way you don't waste time having your employees dial numbers that are inoperable."

"It's that little click click click on the line you get when a creditor is calling you," Daniel said helpfully. "That way you can hang up before they put a live person on and they'll think it was a bad connection."

Jack blinked. He wasn't generally pursued by creditors. After all, he'd had a steady salary since 1973, give or take the year he was retired, and he was the kind of guy who paid all his bills on the fifteenth of the month, every month.

Carter looked like she was trying not to smile. "Because if you don't say anything their computer can't recognize that the call wasn't dropped."

"Oh, hey, my car loan does that all the time," Mitchell said. "I didn't realize what that was."

"Same with Bloomingdales," Vala said, patting his knee.

"My college loans can't tell," Daniel said. "They've got that dialer turned up so high they can't tell if they've got a live person or not."

Mitchell blinked. "I didn't know your college loans were chasing you."

"Yeah well, your rich Uncle Sam may have paid for your school, but I still owe nearly $30,000 on my doctorate." Daniel shrugged. "I figure I'll have it paid off by the time I'm sixty."

"Can we focus here?" Jack said.

"Sorry, sir," Carter said, though of course it hadn't been her being the peanut gallery. "My point is that Ba'al's device must have a predictive dialer program. Otherwise it would spend a huge amount of time and memory displaying inoperable functions." Jack opened his mouth, but she was right ahead of him. "It would waste resources displaying inoperable gates. It seems to display the options available at any given moment, calculating the gate that would need to be dialed and the temporal deviation caused by any one of a dozen possibilities. For example, the wormhole passing through a single solar flare could have a dozen different outcomes depending on which gate beyond it the wormhole was connecting with. These are immensely complex and memory intensive calculations. There is no reason to do hundreds of extraneous ones every few minutes when you can eliminate the unworkable ones with something as simple and low tech as a predictive dialing program."

Jack nodded slowly. "So you're saying you should be able to use Ba'al's device to tell when Earth's Stargate was operable?"

Carter nodded. "It should work, sir. Essentially, it's like having a predictive dialing program call your phone every thirty seconds until you pick up."

"My car loan does that too," Mitchell said to Daniel under his breath.

"I thought that was illegal," Daniel said.

Jack gave them a quelling look.

"It is," Carter said.

Landry turned around. "So what you're saying is that you can use Ba'al's device to find a window when the Stargate was operable and use that to follow the Tok'ra."

Mitchell and Carter looked at each other. "Carter thinks we can," Mitchell said. "So let's do it."

Landry hesitated, and Jack thought he knew what was going through his mind — sending them all into danger for his daughter. But it wasn't for Carolyn. It was for the timestream. It was just that Landry needed someone else to make that call.

"You have a go," Jack said. "Go knock yourselves out, SG-1."

"Why are we just sitting here?" Daniel nudged Cam's shoulder. They were sitting on the floor of Ba'al's installation with their backs against the only thing around to lean on, the base of the instrument console. On the other side of Daniel, Teal'c had closed his eyes and opened his hands, meditating or something. On the other side of Cam, Vala was snoring softly, her head drooping over onto Cam's shoulder. Their packs and weapons were arranged around their feet.

Cam looked at his watch for the seven hundredth time. Nine hours and forty eight minutes. "We're waiting for the right solar flare," he said.

"And waiting," said Daniel. "And waiting."

Carter stuck her head over the top of the console looking surprisingly perky. "Sorry, guys," she said. "We've got to wait for the right moment on our end, one that connects with a clear gate. This could take quite a while. But as soon as it does connect we've got to move fast."

Daniel blinked. "What's put you in such a good mood?"

"Chocolate." Carter held out a bag of fancy foil wrapped squares. "Want some?"

Cam looked at it thoughtfully. "Yeah, actually, I do." He picked through the bag looking for one of the milk chocolate ones.

"You got into some bad habits in Atlantis," Daniel said.

"No kidding." Sam pulled out a square labeled 'dark chocolate truffle cream' and started unwrapping it. "When you're on a long deployment where you can't get much of anything, it really makes you appreciate stuff when you've got it. I never realized how lucky we were to be able to come home at night, and you never know how long that's going to last."

Daniel opened his mouth and shut it again, clearly thinking the same thing as Cam. "You mean the *George Hammond*," he said quietly.

Carter looked a little uncomfortable. "I don't know for sure that I'm going to get it." She studiously didn't look at Cam. And that was about all this stepping on each others' feet. If Carter were going to stay at the SGC with her level of experience and rank, she needed to be either the exec or get SG-1. Either of which would be all over Mitchell's feet. And Cam was pretty sure he wasn't seriously in the running for the *Hammond*.

"Hey, you know it won't be me," he said. "Not that I wouldn't love it. But." Cam shrugged. "There are way too many people ahead of me."

"You've got the 302 experience," Carter said.

"And you've done a tour on *Odyssey*," Cam said. He bit into his chocolate. "And you're a grade ahead of me. And you've got administrative experience."

"For what that's worth."

"It's worth a lot at staff grade," Cam said. He'd been breathing down Carter's neck since his first year at the Academy, when he'd been in her flight as a freshman. She was a junior, and she'd always have that two years up on him, but he'd gotten the best tactical aircraft right away while she'd gone through a series of research positions. Her work on wormhole physics might have been more important, but it didn't look as good on the record as four years in an F-16. And then there was that little bit about the Congressional Medal of Honor. Not to mention that he looked like a poster boy for the Air Force and always had. There had never been a female starship commander, and he only knew of three women in 302s. It was still a boys' club, just the boys and Carter.

That was changing, of course. About a quarter of the lieutenants in the program were women. It looked a lot different for the kids who were nineteen, not thirty nine. But he was thirty nine, and Carter was forty one. They were on the front edge.

"You'll get the *Hammond*," he said.

Daniel nodded slowly. "Cam's right. We'll miss you. But it's your time."

"I don't know," she began, but a flashing light on the console distracted her, and she bent over the datascreen. "I think this is it!"

Cam gave Vala a quick nudge. "Hey!"

Carter's hands flew over the board. "We've got a window open in 2492 BC. Not a big one, so let's get going! I'm going to go ahead and tell the gate to dial." She punched keys, and the vast ring began to turn, the first chevron flaring to life.

"What?" Vala said, startling awake.

"Time to go, sleepyhead," Cam said, getting to his feet.

"Come on."

Teal'c, of course, had merely opened his eyes and was getting up.

Cam looked at Daniel as he reached down and gave Vala a hand. "2492. What have we got?"

"Early First Dynasty," Daniel said. He looked rueful. "We don't have a very complete chronology in that period. But this is what I was telling you about the other day. It's roughly the period of the creation of the Narmer palette, the one showing the defeat of King Scorpion."

"So there may be Goa'uld," Teal'c said, lifting his weapon to port arms.

"It's a good bet," Daniel said.

"I knew it was going to bite me in the ass," Cam said.

Carter stuffed her bag of chocolate into her pack as the sixth chevron lit. "OK. We're set."

"Everybody be ready for trouble," Cam counseled. "Daniel says there may be hostiles."

"We are ready," Teal'c said. He dropped back to be the last through the gate as the wormhole exploded in a blue kawoosh.

"Right." Cam took point and plunged through the event horizon, hoping for one fleeting second that Carter absolutely, positively knew what she was doing and they weren't going to emerge under a ton of sand or in a crevasse in Antarctica.

There was a moment's disorientation, the swooping sensation of wormhole travel, only it seemed to go on longer than it ought to, longer and longer. He was just on the point of deciding that something had gone badly wrong when suddenly he was out, stumbling through under a star studded night sky, the gate in a plaza lit around by torches.

He stopped, and there was a soft ooof as Vala plowed into his back. "Would you mind clearing the place where other people have to step?" she said.

He took a step forward, raising his hands slowly. "Sorry," he said. "I think we've got a problem."

Daniel, then Carter, then Teal'c emerged, looking around with the same wonderment that Cam felt, wonderment and dread. Ahead of them the great pyramids at Giza loomed against the bright night sky, tips capped with shining stone or metal, while about them a bunch of low buildings clustered alive with lights. The Stargate stood in a wide courtyard well lit with a hundred torches, and there were about a hundred guys covering them, some of them with zats, some of them behind barricades.

A young man in a white kilt that came to his knees stood up behind one of the barricades, gold bracelets on his upper arms like emblems of rank, and called out to them in what was clearly an official tone of voice.

"What did he say?" Cam asked Daniel quietly.

"He said drop your weapons or die."

Cam eased his P90 to the ground. "Daniel?"

Daniel rattled off a long bit in a language of course he didn't understand.

"What are you saying?" Cam muttered as Teal'c, Vala and Carter followed his lead and carefully put their weapons down.

"I'm saying we aren't Goa'uld," Daniel said.

"Are you sure they aren't?"

Daniel shook his head almost imperceptibly. "I don't think so. I don't see any Jaffa." He took a step forward his hands raised, speaking to the officer again. That was the thing about Daniel, Cam thought. He was brave as all get out and he'd play a hunch as far as it went. He was probably saying something about how they were friends and how they hated Ra, which if these guys weren't working for Ra was a fair bet would be a winner.

The officer replied, and several men stood up and came around the barricades, zats at the ready.

"He says they're going to take our weapons," Daniel said quietly, translating as they went. "And we will come quietly to prove our good intentions." Even Cam caught one word in the last sentence just as Carter made a strangled noise behind him. "We may plead our case before his officer, the distinguished O'Neill."

CHAPTER TWELVE

Egypt
2492 BC

ASET WAS still sleeping, Teal'c sitting at her bedside. Her color was improving, and Jack knew that if he lifted the bandage, he would see signs of impossible healing. Already the chief priest had his suspicions about this miracle, and Jack wasn't looking forward to explaining this to Hor-Aha. Well, you see, this one is actually a good Goa'uld, and her descendants are going to bring down Ra and the rest of the System Lords in about five thousand years. If he were Pharaoh, he wouldn't buy it, either.

"O'Neill!" One of the young officers came dashing in, his eyes wide. "You must come at once! Travelers have come through the gate!"

"What?" Jack shook his head. "How?" Out of the corner of his eye, he saw Sam hand Ellie to Tamit, and hurry to join him.

The young officer looked at his sandals. "Apparently we did not secure the gate, O'Neill."

"Damn it," Jack began, and stopped himself. "Is it secure now?"

"Yes, O'Neill."

"What kind of travelers?" That was Danyel, rubbing his eyes, zat unfolded in his other hand.

"Not Goa'uld," the young man said. "But—strange. Sergeant Basa has them under guard."

"On my way," Jack said, and the young officer dashed out. Jack paused long enough to collect a staff weapon, and stalked toward the temple steps. He checked at the top, his eyes sweeping across the group waiting for him. His men were drawn up in careful order, zats and staff weapons pointed at a group in what were unmistakably Air Force uniforms. Five of them, and three were hardly strangers: Teal'c — Teal'c with hair, which was unexpectedly weird, and the gold First Prime's tattoo still in place, looking indefinably older; and Danyel, looking younger; and Sam. Sam with long hair in a pony tail and what looked like a colonel's eagles on her collar and the same incredulous recognition on her face.

"Holy crap," he said, and looked at Basa.

"O'Neill." The sergeant raised his hand in salute. "These came through the gate — very like what happened before, when you, the other you, arrived. They swear they are no friends of Ra —"

"Well, they would, wouldn't they?" Jack said.

"Perhaps so," Basa agreed. "But you were not his friend, and these — are they not more of you?"

"Not me," Jack said. That seemed important, somehow. "But, yeah, a couple of them do look vaguely familiar."

This Daniel grinned at that, almost in spite of himself, and the tall good-looking one took a half step forward.

"General O'Neill?"

"Boy, have you got that wrong," Jack said, in English. "It's Colonel O'Neill. And I'm retired. Very, very retired."

"Not so much," Daniel said, with a pointed look at the soldiers.

The pretty, dark-haired woman was looking at him curiously, and then her eyes widened. "Oh," she said.

The woman who looked like Sam — who probably was Sam Carter, in some weird twist of time and physics that was going to make his head hurt just to think about it — made an odd strangled noise, and valiantly looked away. Jack glanced over his shoulder to see Sam and Danyel descending the steps. The other Sam, the colonel said, "Uh, sir?"

"Not sir," Jack said. "I'm retired."

"They — I'm guessing they must be us from the original timeline." That was his Sam, her eyes bright. "Or something very like it."

"I knew this would give me a headache," Jack muttered. He

said, more loudly, "OK, kids, this is — weird. What are you doing here?"

"We're here because the timeline is in danger," the good-looking one said. He really did look like a recruiting poster, Jack thought. "Again."

"You people seem pretty careless about it," he said.

"I'm guessing this has something to do with a videotape we found in a First Dynasty canopic jar," the younger-looking Daniel said.

"That damn videotape," Danyel said. He shook his head. "It seemed like such a good idea at the time."

"General O'Neill," the good-looking one said. He'd gotten a grip on himself, looked as though he was determined to get a word in before things got any stranger. "I'm Lieutenant Colonel Cameron Mitchell, this is Vala Mal Doran, and I'm thinking you know Colonel Carter, Dr. Jackson, and Teal'c."

"Colonel," Jack said, and shook his head. "And I'm a colonel. Was a colonel. Not a general." He looked at Basa. "They're friends. Or at the very least, they're enemies of our enemies."

"Unless they are evil ka," Basa said. "Sent to deceive us."

"I suppose that's possible," Jack said. "But I don't think so. Those two —" He pointed to Mitchell and Carter. "They serve the same government I used to, and I'm sure they wouldn't ally with Ra or any other Goa'uld."

Basa gave a reluctant nod. "As you say, O'Neill."

"Come on in," Jack said, in English, and motioned for them to follow up him up the long stairs. "We probably need to talk."

The temple servants found them stools and cushions and brought jars of beer and a plate of dates and almonds into the room outside the area where Aset slept. Teal'c, his Teal'c, came reluctantly to join them, his eyebrows rising as he saw the other Jaffa. Jack busied himself getting the beer handed round, got everyone served in time to hear Danyel — his Danyel — say, "OK, this is the part that you don't know about because it didn't actually happen."

Jack took a long drink of his beer, and saw Mitchell do the same. Their eyes met, and Jack thought he recognized the look. Probably anyone who dealt with Daniel Jackson — either one of them — developed it after a while. Sam and the other Sam — Carter, he was going to call her Carter, just like he would any other Air Force officer — were both listening with rapt attention, even though Sam, his Sam, had heard the story before.

"We really needed a ZPM," Danyel said. "So I had this — well, not-so-bright idea, as it turned out. We knew from tomb paintings that Ra had one, but didn't know what it was, so I thought we could use the time-traveling puddle jumper we found on Maybourne's planet to go back and get it." He paused. "You still have the jumper, right?"

Both Daniel and Carter had odd looks on their faces, and the dark woman, Vala, looked even more innocent. Mitchell said, firmly, "Yes."

"Good," Danyel said. "Though, of course, we still have ours —"

"Danyel," Jack said. "Focus?"

"Yes, sorry." Danyel frowned. "So, anyway, we got into trouble, and couldn't get back to our own time, so we made that videotape to try to insure against changing the timeline."

"And it worked," Sam interjected.

"Which was good," Danyel said, "because we did change the timeline. Jack —"

"Not me," Jack put in.

"Right, our Jack, the Jack from my original team — he decided that we might as well lead a rebellion because it was going to happen anyway, only he and Sam and Teal'c were all killed." The ghost of something bleak and bitter crossed Danyel's face. "And Ra took the Stargate. But, like Sam said, we'd left that videotape, and sure enough it was found, and the Air Force dredged up Sam and, well, me, the me from that new timeline, and dragged Jack out of retirement, and sent them off in the puddle jumper to fix things. After first collecting Teal'c, who was still Apophis's First Prime."

"Indeed," the two Teal'cs said, in almost the same moment.

"Does your head hurt?" Jack said, to Mitchell. "Because mine does."

"I'm wondering what you put in this beer," Mitchell said.

"The other me got killed on Chulak," Danyel went on. "But I was still here, trying to run a rebellion, and we ended up saving the Stargate and driving Ra out. And presumably fixed the timeline, though I am wondering how much stayed the same, given that she's apparently on the team." He nodded to Vala.

"You're not still holding that against me," Vala said, with what Jack thought was a distinctly sharp smile.

"Yes," Danyel said, and Daniel said, "Maybe."

They looked at each other, and then Daniel shrugged. "She grows on you."

Vala pouted, and Sam and Carter stifled identical grins. His Teal'c tipped his head to one side, and the other Teal'c said, "Indeed."

"Be that as it may," Jack said, perhaps more loudly than was strictly required. "What are you doing here?"

"Yeah," Mitchell said. "About that puddle jumper. It was stolen by a trio of rogue Tok'ra — who kidnapped Carolyn Lam to fly it, before you ask, you still need an ATA gene to fly it —"

"Who's Carolyn Lam?" Sam asked.

"General Landry's daughter," Danyel said. "Our — their — commanding officer. I assume?"

Carter nodded.

Mitchell raised his voice just a little. "These Tok'ra are trying to go back in time to find Egeria so that she can restore the Tok'ra as a species."

"What?" Jack sat up straight, almost spilling his beer.

"I thought the Tok'ra were on our side," Sam said.

"That's infinitely debatable," Daniel said.

"But Egeria is here." Teal'c's voice cut through the confusion. He looked at his other self as though willing him to understand. "My symbiote was nearly mature. I could not risk it taking a host, though O'Neill and Danyel and Sam were willing to open the Stargate to find me a new prim'tah. I descended deep into kelnorim to persuade it to delay, and learned its name and its — different — nature. It has taken a host, a willing host, to save her life. Egeria lies within, in the body of Aset."

"What?" Mitchell began.

His Teal'c gave a slow smile. "This does allow us greater freedom of action, Colonel Mitchell."

"We can't just shoot them," Mitchell said, though he sounded like he didn't want to say it. "The Tok'ra are our allies."

"That might be precisely what we need to do, to save the timeline," Vala said. "But we need to find them first."

"But if you lost the puddle jumper," Sam said, "how did you get here?"

"We found this device of Ba'al's," Carter said. "It linked up Stargates and solar flares in such a way that the wormhole could be diverted into the past. In a controlled fashion."

"That would require an awful lot of power," Sam said. "And computing capacity. And how do you know that the receiving gate is available?"

Jack realized abruptly that having two Sams was going to be a lot more — geeky — than he'd expected. "Kids," he said. "Can we stay on-topic?"

"So we've found Egeria," Mitchell said. He shrugged. "I suppose we could just wait for the Tok'ra to show up. Unless they already have?"

"Not as far as I know," Jack answered.

"Or we have the puddle jumper," Daniel said. "Their puddle jumper. The records here may well tell us where we should look."

"OK," Jack began, and stopped as Basa appeared in the doorway.

"Your pardon, O'Neill," the sergeant said. "But Pharaoh wishes to speak with you. At once."

Carter watched Jack get up to answer Pharaoh's summons

exactly the same way he always did when someone important called. Well, not exactly the same. This Jack was thinner than her Jack, but he moved more stiffly. No ibuprofen, no supplements for joint health, no knee replacement… Well, and he was wearing his underwear. Her Jack didn't usually run around town wearing a pair of boxer shorts and nothing else except a couple of gold chains around his neck like an aging hippie.

She had to admit that this Daniel and Teal'c looked good in their little white kilts, but she couldn't even look at the other her. Of course it wasn't the first alternate her she'd encountered. There'd been one particularly weird time where she'd wound up with fourteen of her. Of other her. And then there was Quantum Her, which had been the first strange time she'd run into herself from an alternate reality. But this her… Her hair was more or less pixie cut like Carter's used to be, though Carter's had grown out into a long ponytail while she was in Atlantis, and she looked distinctly… buxom. Carter could feel a furious blush rising in her face. The other her didn't look like she blushed much. She was tan and confident.

A teenaged girl had come to the door and now came in holding a fretting baby, saying something to other her as she crossed the room. Other her took the baby with expert hands and popped her on. Just…popped her on to nurse, all the while talking about temporal physics with the Daniels. Carter blinked.

Daniel looked at Carter, an ironic smile tugging at the corner of his mouth. "The road less traveled," he said.

Vala blinked, and then her smirk grew into a wide grin. "I never knew you'd look so good with a shaved chest," she said. "And shaved legs. You have such pretty legs when they're nice and clean." She beamed at other Daniel appreciatively. "You know, I think he's better looking than you."

Jack figured he knew what this was about, and he wasn't wrong. The Fighting Hawk, Hor-Aha, was pacing his outer receiving room and turned with a snap when Jack entered. "You may go," he said to the guards, and Jack stood up straighter. Hor-Aha looked at him directly. "O'Neill, you said that the Stargate was secure and that there was no danger in this adventure of yours. Now I hear that other travelers have come through the ring."

"Yes," Jack said, "I take full responsibility for that. It was one of my men who did not secure the gate."

"It is secure now?"

"It is," Jack said. You've got to face the music when one of your guys screws up. That's how it goes. "It won't happen again."

"These other travelers," Hor-Aha said, pacing around the back of the room, around the brazier that stood there to give warmth against the chill of the desert night that came in through the skylight, "They are not Goa'uld?"

"No." Jack swallowed. This was going to be fun to explain. "They seem to be from the same future that we came from, or at least that Danyel came from. Several of them are people I've never met before, but some of them are, well, us."

Hor-Aha's eyebrows rose. "You?"

"Not me, me. But another Danyel, Sam and Teal'c. And two other people," he added.

"Another Danyel, Sam and Teal'c." Hor-Aha shook his head. "This is deep water for me, my friend."

The 'my friend' was a good sign. "It's pretty deep for me too," Jack said.

Pharaoh looked at him keenly. "So what have they come seeking? Or is it that they come to our aid in the face of some new crisis that we have not yet seen?"

Jack took a deep breath. This was going to involve some heavy explaining. "I don't know about another crisis," he said, "but Danyel says that in his time the defeat of the Goa'uld was accomplished with the aid of the Tok'ra, a band of Goa'uld who had rebelled against Ra and who had pledged themselves to be friends of humanity. We did not believe them at first, but they were as good as their word, and many of them died beside us in the fight against the System Lords. One of them even joined with Jacob Carter, Sam's father, who was a willing bridge between our peoples. The new Daniel says that the first Tok'ra, Egeria, began her life on Earth in this period..."

Hor-Aha interrupted. "Is this true? Do you know this?"

Jack winced inwardly. "We know she's here. She was Teal'c's symbiote."

"Was?" Of course he caught that word.

"She's joined with Aset to save her life."

Hor-Aha slammed his hand down on his desk hard enough to make a roll of papyrus jump off onto the floor. "O'Neill! You let a Goa'uld join with Aset?"

"If she is the mother of the Tok'ra, she must not be allowed to die," Jack said. "Or the defeat of the Goa'uld in the future may not happen."

"And if she is not?" Hor-Aha snapped. "If she lies?"

"Teal'c will kill her with his own hand," Jack said.

Hor-Aha looked at him keenly. "Will he? When she is one with Aset, whom he loves?"

Jack didn't look away. "If Teal'c can't do it, I will. I give you my word."

"At the slightest hint of treachery," Hor-Aha said. "You will slay her. Or I must do so now. Do you not understand that the safety of my people must come first? We have already taken an incredible risk for Teal'c, and you say no harm has come of it. But this must end. The next time you make a decision such as this joining without my order you will be dismissed from my service and stripped of your rank. Do you understand?"

"I do," Jack said. It was about what he'd expected.

Hor-Aha held his gaze for a moment, then turned away. He might be young, but he'd learned how to command. Once a reprimand was taken, it was time to let it drop. "What do these strangers want from Egeria?"

"I don't..." Jack began, but he stopped as Hor-Aha's head turned sharply. There was shouting in the antechamber, panicked voices raised in supplication and alarm.

An unearthly glow was growing at the skylight, a white blue light that should not, could not, have been there, could not have any good reason on this planet to exist.

"Oh crap," Jack said as Hor-Aha dashed out the door to see what was going on. He shaded his eyes, looking up through the skylight instead as the lights grew brighter, the blinding landing lights of a Goa'uld mothership.

CHAPTER THIRTEEN

SAM AND the other her, the one who was a full colonel in the Air Force, heard it at the same time, both their heads turning at the same moment to the sound of engines. "That's not right," Sam said, coming to her feet with Ellie still at her breast.

"That's a Goa'uld mothership," Carter said, her gun rising as she turned toward the door.

"How could we have led them here?" the dark haired woman named Vala exclaimed.

"You didn't," Teal'c said, Sam's own Teal'c for whom they'd risked so much. His eyes sought hers unerringly, filled with awful knowledge. "We did."

"We dialed direct," Danyel said. "We were out of time. Teal'c, wait!" he shouted, but Teal'c had already run back into the room where Egeria slept.

The other her turned around and looked at her. "You've got to get out of here," she said, her mouth tightening as she looked at the baby.

"You mean we've got to get out of here," Sam said. "This palace used to be Ra's. It's the first place he'll come."

"I thought Ra left Earth for good?" Danyel demanded from Daniel.

"He did until you screwed it up," Daniel snapped back.

"Boys and girls, let's all calm down," Mitchell said. "We don't know this is Ra, and we don't know it's not supposed to happen. Teal'c, you and I will go check it out. Everybody else chill a second. We've got a badly wounded woman and a baby here." He looked at Sam. "Do you know a way out of here that doesn't go past the stargate?"

She nodded.

"OK. Daniel, help their Teal'c get the wounded ready to travel." He looked at his Teal'c. "You're with me." Sam couldn't help but notice that he stopped short of any sort of directive to the other her, like he couldn't actually order her to do anything. Or maybe he just assumed she'd go with him and Teal'c, because she did, following them into the hall taking up the rear position with her big gun like she did this every day of the week.

Sam looked at Danyel and Vala, shifting Ellie onto her shoulder. "Let's get a pallet for Aset. There's a back way out of here but I don't know how long it will stay open."

Mitchell dodged through the doors of the palace, ducking from one carved pillar to the next, Teal'c and Carter behind him. If he'd been the type, he would have been swearing a blue streak. Ra probably had a couple of thousand Jaffa on that mothership, and he doubted there were fifty staff weapons on the whole planet, leaving aside the idea of taking on armored Jaffa with a bunch of guys armed with spears and bows. How these guys had done it in the first place escaped him, but they probably weren't going to get lucky twice. In the land of par for the course this was about the usual level of SG-1 disaster. Only with about twice as many of SG-1.

Daniel and Vala had to roll up the rug behind them while he and Teal'c and Carter held them off. It was going that way.

Mitchell motioned Teal'c to wait a second, then dodged through the next doorway and into the recess behind a pillar that looked out across the courtyard. Unfortunately the pillar was already occupied by both O'Neill and a young guy with a bald head and a white kilt. A soldier scurried behind it from the other side, reporting something to the young guy, his back straight with military precision. Mitchell realized belatedly that the young guy must be the Pharaoh.

"Too many," O'Neill said.

"Too many what?" Mitchell said.

O'Neill shook his head while Pharaoh and the soldier were

talking. "At least thirty Jaffa have already ringed down inside the pyramid. They're securing the pyramid first."

"Not good," Mitchell said.

"Tell me about it." He looked at Pharaoh as he spoke, and O'Neill replied something incomprehensible, his face serious. Then he turned back to Mitchell, grabbing his arm with wiry strength. "He's just given the evacuation order for the palace. You should get your people out of here."

"And you, sir?" Mitchell couldn't help but think of O'Neill as a general, even if he was wearing boxers. And really pretty much he was acting like a general, even if the pharaoh didn't look a lot like Hank Landry.

"I'm sticking with Hor-Aha," O'Neill said. He glanced back toward the pyramid of light towering over Giza. "He's going to surrender to Ra." Mitchell made some movement of demurral, and he looked back, his voice dropping. "What else is he going to do? Ra can level his kingdom in a couple of hours and kill everybody in it. We're not going to win, Mitchell. Now get the hell out of here!"

Daniel slammed a fresh magazine into his P90, wishing they'd come better armed—a couple of missile-carrying drones, say, or a MANPAD system. Or maybe a whole squad of Marines. Or all of the above. He'd be the first to say that they were good, but he didn't really like the idea of taking on Ra with a handful of stolen staff weapons, about as many zats, four machine guns and a couple of pistols. Plus bows, spears, and slings. He wondered how the hell they'd managed it the first time. He'd have to ask, as soon as they were in cover, because it looked like they were going to have to do it all over again. But they had done it, he reminded himself, and we did it on Abydos, though that hadn't started off with a ticked-off Goa'uld at the height of his power.

His other self—Danyel, everyone called him, with the accent on the second syllable, just the way they'd pronounced it on

Abydos — Danyel was talking urgently to what looked like the senior temple priest, gesturing with the hand that wasn't holding a zat. Daniel started toward him, wanting to know what the other him was planning, but Danyel was already turning away.

"OK," he said. "Sam's got Aset ready to travel, and we've got the use of a litter and two bearers from the temple —"

He broke off, and Daniel swung around, lifting the barrel of the P90 as he recognized Mitchell.

"We've got to get out of here," Mitchell said. "The Pharaoh's ordered everyone to evacuate."

"Torches," Sam said, deftly winding the baby into a sling against her chest. She was fussing, frightened by the noise and confusion, and Sam soothed her with one hand.

"We've got flashlights," Mitchell said.

Sam nodded, and turned to direct the litter bearers. Danyel said, "Where's Jack?"

"Staying with the Pharaoh," Mitchell said. Sam gave him a single stricken look, and Danyel's mouth tightened, but neither said anything. Their Teal'c lifted his head.

"That is ill-advised."

"No choice," Carter said tightly. It might not be her Jack, but she couldn't help but be affected.

A pair of shaven-headed men emerged from the alcove carrying a gaudily painted litter. A part of Daniel's mind tagged it as ceremonial, never intended for serious use, and he hoped it would stand up to it. The woman on it was wrapped securely in plain linen, her eyes closed, heavy black hair spilling over the pallet. She was beautiful, Daniel saw, beautiful in the same way Sha're had been, and as he looked away he met his other self's ironic smile.

"Robes?" he said. "Something to cover the uniforms?"

Sam nodded, the baby clutching at her breast. Another echo of Abydos, or rather, Daniel thought, Abydos had been an echo of this. She spoke to the girl, who nodded, and returned a moment later with an armful of heavy wool. Daniel took one, saw without surprise that it was a heavy cloak, and slung it around his shoulders. The rest of the team did the same, Vala wrinkling her nose at the smell of sheep that rose from the coarse fabric. The girl had brought a scarf for their Teal'c as well, and he wound it carefully around his head, hiding Apophis's mark.

"This way," the other Sam said.

She led them toward the door that led to the sanctuary, but before they entered it, she ducked behind a pillar. Her Teal'c shoved hard on a door whose outlines were almost hidden by the wall paintings, pushing it in to reveal a set of shallow steps descending into darkness. Daniel rummaged for his flashlight, flicked it on, and offered it to her. She took it with a nod of thanks, and started down the stairs, the light playing ahead of her. Daniel followed, Mitchell at his back, and the men with the litter made their way carefully after them. Carter stopped to light the door as the two Teal'cs pushed it closed again, and Daniel lengthened his stride to catch up with Vala, wishing he'd kept his flashlight. The baby was fussing again, and the circle of light at the head of the group bounced as Sam soothed her.

"She's very good at that," Vala said, and let her light play over the painted walls. "Do you think our Sam has unsuspected qualities?"

Daniel refrained from pointing out that Carter had helped raise Cassie from the day they'd found her, had been more or less her guardian since Janet's death. Instead, he reached for the flashlight. "Can I see that?"

She handed it over, mercifully without comment, and he swung the light over the half-finished paintings. Half-defaced paintings, he amended. It looked as though the priests had already begun removing Ra's name and titles, and Danyel looked over his shoulder with a shrug.

"We thought we'd won," he said.

"Apparently not," Daniel answered, and Mitchell said, "Hey."

There was light showing ahead, and the ground underfoot

sloped gently upward. Sam gestured for the litter-bearers to halt, and edged forward. The tunnel took a sharp bend, Daniel saw, presumably to disguise the exit. Then Sam ducked back, raising her hand in warning.

"Jaffa. Three of them."

Danyel muttered something, and squeezed past the litter. Sam shook her head, already unwinding the sling that held the baby. She handed her to Tamit, and Danyel shook his head.

"I'll go. Keep Ellie quiet."

Sam hesitated, then nodded. Mitchell said, "The plan?"

"I'll distract them," Danyel said. "You take them out—quietly, if you can."

Easier said than done, Daniel thought, and edged past the litter. The woman, Aset, lay unmoving, eyes still closed, only the slight movement of her chest betraying that she still breathed. He drew his zat, let it unfold with a whine and click, and both Teal'cs moved forward, readying their staff weapons. Danyel took a breath, and stepped out into the open.

"Our lord Ra has returned! All praise to him!"

"What are you doing here?" The Jaffa sounded more annoyed than alarmed, and Daniel heard heavy footsteps as the rest of the Jaffa came closer.

"Now!" Mitchell said, and he and the Teal'cs stepped out into the open, firing as they moved. Daniel moved to cover them, but the Jaffa were already down, smoke rising from their bodies.

"Nice shooting," Danyel said, looking at his Teal'c, and the other Teal'c dipped his head.

"Indeed."

"Let's go," Sam said. "We don't have much time."

Daniel looked over his shoulder to see the litter-bearers already lifting their burden. They made their way through what looked like an upper-level official's house, past the reception room, and into the deserted kitchen courtyard. Sam fiddled with the latch on the back gate, then waved them through. "Follow the road down toward the river," she said. "Hurry, but—"

"Don't look like we're hurrying," Mitchell finished. "Aren't they going to be suspicious if they see her?" He waved to Aset.

"Ra shouldn't be interested in refugees just yet," Danyel said. "At least, we hope not."

Sam nodded. "And if we're lucky—"

"They won't notice us at all," Danyel finished.

Daniel followed them out of the courtyard, tugging up the hood of his cloak to cover his unfamiliar haircut. He couldn't resist one last backward glance, though things were suspiciously quiet behind them. Ra's mothership balanced on top of the pyramid, lights glowing, impossibly large and dangerous. Even as he looked, a light flashed, and there was the faint sound of transport rings. They couldn't stay and fight, he knew that, but he still wanted to try, to do whatever they could to protect the people who'd been left in the palace. The only thing they could do was get away, and hope to fight another day.

Cam breathed carefully through his mouth, trying not to take in any more dust or the sheep-stink of the heavy cloak he was still wearing. He and Carter were taking six, hoods up, P90s ready beneath their robes. So far, there was no pursuit, and he'd like to keep it that way. Lights glowed and flashed on the horizon behind them from the mothership topping the pyramid, and it took willpower to keep from looking back to check it every few seconds. Ahead, the litter-bearers kept a steady pace, the woman they carried still deeply unconscious. Tok'ra, he amended. If that really was Egeria—and he didn't seriously think it wasn't, there was no way a Goa'uld could have known to tell that particular lie—then part of their job was done. Of course, they still had to rescue Carolyn Lam, and capture the renegade Tok'ra—oh, and defeat Ra for the second time—but he supposed he should try to think of it as some kind of progress.

"They are good, these guys," he said quietly, and Carter gave him a quick smile.

"Well, they're us."

"Yeah." Cam wished he felt more reassured by that. Yes, they were SG-1, in some form or other, but that still made only eight of them, plus an Egyptian army of maybe a couple of thousand men at the absolute maximum, against Ra. He'd never really wanted to be Han Solo.

They were coming up on a small compound, a handful of buildings surrounded by a low wall. The river was close at hand, a dock stretching out to the muddy water, and the walls looked more like they'd been built to keep out stray animals than to withstand a siege. The top of a tree peeped over the mud bricks in one corner of the compound, and the air smelled not unpleasantly of smoke and cattle.

Sam organized them with brisk efficiency, dispatching her Teal'c and the litter into the back of the main house, and sending the girl — Tamit — off in another direction. She led the rest of them into what had to be the main room of the house, a large, bare room furnished with a single brightly painted armchair and a scattering of stools and small, low tables. A low brazier stood in the center, fuel piled ready for a spark. The floor was beaten dirt, but the walls were a riot of color, a frieze of flowers and hunters, spears poised over fish that swam beneath the blue line that marked the water.

The other Teal'c reappeared, looking impassive, but on second glance, Cam thought he saw a faint worried crease below the paler mark where the tattoo had been.

"Aset sleeps, Samantha," he said. "She is healing well, but it will take time still for the blending to be complete."

"How long?" Danyel asked, and the Jaffa shook his head.

"I cannot say. But she — they — are both aware of the situation."

"But what exactly are we waiting for?" Sam asked. "I thought Egeria would be able to heal her right away, like the Goa'uld usually do."

"It takes time for a blending," Carter answered. "For a Tok'ra to join with a host properly. It's easy to just take over, harder to leave the host autonomy."

That was a good sign, Cam thought, meant that Egeria was keeping her promise. He shrugged himself out of the cape. "OK, first things first. Carter—I mean, Dr. Carter—"

"Sam," she said, firmly.

"Sam," he agreed. "Is there a back way out of here? If Ra comes looking, we'll need to move fast."

"Yes." Sam's smile reminded him of Carter at her most reckless. "There's a cellar—we used it as an arms store in the rebellion—and tunnels that lead to the river and behind the stable wall. The river would probably be best, especially after dark. It comes out just under the dock, and there's a boat ready."

Never underestimate any version of Sam Carter or her ability to provide a technical solution, Cam thought. "OK, that's good. Next step—"

"Drive out Ra," Danyel said. His voice was bitter. "Again."

Sam rested her hand lightly on his bare shoulder. "And there is this Tok'ra problem to deal with. And your friend to rescue."

"Ra's the immediate threat," Cam said. "If the Tok'ra are coming here looking for Egeria, they'll be walking into a trap."

"We'll need to make sure that doesn't happen," Carter said.

"Yes, but how?" Daniel glared at his other self, who glared back at him.

"And we cannot destroy Ra," Teal'c said—their Teal'c, Cam thought. "If he is destroyed now, that will change the time line. We must drive him away from Earth and prevent him from taking the Stargate, as you tell me he did before when the timeline was disrupted."

"Last time we harassed him so badly that he couldn't get a lock on the gate," Danyel said.

"He's not going to fall for that again," Daniel said, and his other self nodded.

"Much as I hate to say it, no."

"Sa-Mantha!" That was the girl, Tamit, darting through the

door from the courtyard. She followed with an outpouring of words that made both Daniels and the other Teal'c start to their feet, reaching for their weapons.

"Someone's coming," Sam said, and broke off to give a string of orders. Danyel added something, and the girl dashed off again. "Not Jaffa, she says, but—"

"Be prepared," Vala said, with her brightest smile, and unfolded her zat.

"Teal'c," Cam said. "Daniel. Cover the door. Carter, Vala, if you'll take the window—"

They were already moving, fanning out to take up position. Danyel opened his mouth as though he wanted to protest, then closed it again.

"Aset is below," their Teal'c said.

"Get her ready to move," Danyel said. "Sam, help him. We can't use the bearers."

"No," Sam agreed.

"I'll close the trap," Danyel began.

"If it comes to that." Sam's voice was firm. "Let's see who it is first."

She touched his arm again, and she and Teal'c disappeared into the inner rooms.

"Somebody has to hide the trap door after it's closed," Danyel said. "We never got around to fixing that."

There wouldn't be many options with a dirt floor, Cam thought. He didn't much like the idea of leaving anybody behind, but Danyel at least spoke the language, could blend in. He could hear voices in the courtyard, and risked a look past Carter's shoulder. A heavy-set guy with a shaved head had thrown back the gate, and half a dozen men with spears were standing in the courtyard, surrounding a dark-skinned woman in a dusty shift.

Danyel said something in Egyptian, sounding dismayed

"The Lady of Egypt," Daniel translated. "Hor-Aha's mother, the Queen Nithotep."

"Wonderful," Cam said, but Danyel had already pushed past Teal'c and his other self, hurrying out to meet her. He called something, and Daniel translated softly.

"He says, greetings to the Lady of Egypt, a bright moment in a terrible day."

The queen cut him off with a gesture, her voice sharp and strained.

"She's a bearer of ill tidings," Daniel said. "She's setting her men on guard. And he's inviting her inside to share her news and take refreshment."

Sure enough, the soldiers were taking up positions beside the gates. Danyel walked respectfully ahead of the queen, taller than she by more than a head. Behind him, the queen's remaining escort had his spear ready to hand, and Cam wondered if Danyel knew it.

"It's OK," Danyel called. "Let us in."

Cam lifted his P90 to port-arms, stepped back so that he could cover the door. Danyel entered, the queen and her escort following, and her dark eyes swept the room. She said something that made Daniel grin, and Danyel bowed, offering her the painted armchair. She seated herself, and the young soldier came to attention at her side. Nithotep was a small woman, not young, with the dust of the road clinging to her skin and her heavy wig. The kohl around her eyes was smudged, her dress dirtied, but there was no question that she intended to take charge. Tamit came hurrying with a basin and a cloth, and the Lady of Egypt allowed her feet to be bathed. Danyel seated himself cross-legged at her feet, saying something deferential. Cam recognized their names, and did his best to look stalwart and useful as her eyes met his. She spoke then, voice sharp, and Danyel translated.

"The Lady of Egypt says that the palace has fallen—has been surrendered to Ra to save the lives of the people. The soldiers are disarmed, and command is given to the Jaffa. Pharaoh himself is Ra's guest, which is to say his prisoner. O'Neill—"

Danyel paused, just for an instant, and when he spoke again, his voice was unnaturally controlled. "Jack's been taken prisoner, too. Ra picked him out from among the others, she doesn't know why." He listened again. "Pharaoh is held in the palace, but Jack's on board the mothership. She wants us to rescue Pharaoh — to help him as we helped his father."

"To do that," Carter said, "we should probably start by rescuing General — Colonel O'Neill."

"He's on the mothership," Daniel said. "We might have an easier time getting Hor-Aha out."

Either one was going to be close to impossible, Cam thought. Brute force was definitely out of the question, with all the Jaffa around. What they really needed was —

"I have a clever plan," Vala said. "I can pass myself off as a minor Goa'uld, get us into the palace that way."

She had been a host, Cam thought. There was still naquadah in her blood, it might work, at least long enough to get them in. But she wouldn't pass if they came face to face with Ra, or any other Goa'uld.

"You just want to get your hands on some of the jewelry," Daniel said.

"It's very pretty," Vala agreed, and bestowed her best smile on the queen, who looked distinctly unimpressed.

"She isn't Goa'uld," Danyel translated. "Even the Lady can see it."

"We can do better than that," Sam said, from the doorway to the inner rooms. Aset stood beside her, Teal'c at their backs.

"I believe we can." The voice was a woman's, but with the peculiar resonance of a Goa'uld. Or a Tok'ra, Cam reminded himself, and kept his hands quiet on the P90. The young soldier said something sharp, and readied his spear, but the queen lifted one hand to stop him. She said something, the words like the crack of a whip, and Daniel sucked in his breath.

"I hadn't thought you'd betray me," he translated.

"But I have not!" The Goa'uld timbre was gone from her voice, and Aset dropped to the floor at the queen's feet. "I have not, Great Lady, truly. It is still I, still Aset. Egeria has saved me, made me whole, and she wishes to help us against Ra. To be Tok'ra, against Ra, in truth."

She tipped her head, and now it was Egeria who spoke. "What that one suggested has merit. But I can face Ra directly, and use any tool or weapon of the Goa'uld. I am in your debt, all of you, and I wish to repay."

"Let me get this straight," Danyel said. "You're going to pretend to be a Goa'uld—"

"A survivor of the rebellion, come to offer allegiance to Ra," Egeria said. "Perhaps with useful intelligence I have gained while I was in hiding? And of course I must bring my attendants."

"That—I almost hate to say it," Daniel said, "but that might work."

Cam turned the idea over in his mind. Yes, it would work, and it was the best thing anybody had come up with so far. "All right, then," he said. "So what does a well-dressed Goa'uld entourage wear, anyway?"

Carter grinned. "No pants."

Danyel had been translating softly, and the queen nodded once.

"The Lady of Egypt agrees," Danyel said.

CHAPTER FOURTEEN

JACK O'NEILL was pretty sure that something unpleasant was about to happen. That was how this went. There's the 'take him to the mothership' part and then the 'take him to see the System Lord' part and then the really bad part. Not that he'd done that part before personally. Well, not him, him. But he'd gleaned enough from Danyel to know that the other him had. Way too often. So. Here it went with that part, hauled in to face Ra with his hands cuffed behind him, two big Jaffa to keep him in line, while Ra lounged around in a seriously overdone cloth of gold outfit that looked like it was off the back lot of a B movie.

Only not. Ra paced toward him, his white shenti no different than that of Hor-Aha, his eyes darkened with kohl, his arms banded with bracelets. "You are the one," he said.

"One what? One great guy?" Jack thought he ought to get some points for that. Not that you did from humans, and he bet the Goa'uld didn't do any better.

"Don't toy with me, O'Neill," Ra snapped. "Do you think I cannot tell that you are not from this world?"

Oh boy.

"You may be dressed like these humans and may even pretend to be one, but I know what you are." Ra snapped his fingers and one of the Jaffa along the wall produced a small white box, holding it out carefully and deferentially. Ra took it from him with his finger tips, holding it delicately. His other hand was encased in a hand device, each finger chased with gold. "You see?" He held it out toward Jack and Jack tensed, prepared for intolerable pain.

Instead, nothing happened.

Or rather, the only thing that happened was that the little

white box lit up, lines of incomprehensible letters scrolling across a tiny screen. Ra smirked with satisfaction. "You cannot deny it."

"Deny what?" Jack said.

"That you are one of them. You are not the only one who has meddled on this planet, nor the only one I have killed. But the others were useless, uncertain, children of bastard birth who did not know, who could not tell me where their hidden places were, where their elders kept watch. But you are one of them yourself, are you not, O'Neill?"

"I don't know what you're talking about," Jack said.

Ra waved the white box at him. "This!" he said. "It does not lie. The others spoke of a time travel device, but only the woman could operate it. I have torn her mind to shreds and she knows little—one spaceship, one device—she does not even know the dialing address for the treasure she knows lies hidden! But you do, do you not, O'Neill? You know the way to the Lost City. You know how to operate this time travel device. You know all your people's secrets. Perhaps you are even the one of which the rumors speak, that gadfly Myrddin who would champion humans against the Goa'uld?"

"Never heard of the guy," Jack said. This was starting to sound…not good at all.

Ra shook his head. "Your race is dead. You are nothing. And your pitiful descendants will be nothing except hosts for us."

"I wouldn't bet on that," Jack said, twisting his arms against the Jaffas' grips.

"I would," Ra said and raised the hand device. "Your mind will be open to me and you will tell me what you know when you can bear the pain no longer."

Ra was right about one thing, Jack thought as he sank to his knees, screams ripping from his throat. That thing was excruciatingly painful.

Daniel thought they looked quite a bit like a Goa'uld entourage, all things considered. A little weedy, but then since Egeria had supposedly been in hiding, that was more or less to be expected. Aset/Egeria didn't entirely look the part of Supreme Overlady in Sam's best dress—truth to tell, by ancient Egyptian standards, Sam's best dress wasn't all that nice, but there wasn't a lot they could do about that. It was a plain white linen sheath, good material but a conservative cut, falling from a band just below the breasts to just above the ankles with straps made of contrasting cloth. Aset's own jewelry would have to do, as Sam didn't have anything nice but a pair of gold stud earrings and a watch that was decidedly not period. Aset at least had appropriate earrings.

Teal'c, of course, looked the part already. Their Teal'c, Daniel amended. In his immaculate white shenti and gold bracelets he looked like Egeria's First Prime, even if they'd had to draw Ra's tattoo on his scarred forehead with kohl. Fitting out himself and Cam was a little more difficult. Danyel's clothes fit him, but...

"Are you sure it's supposed to look like this?" Cam said for the fourth time. Danyel's shenti was a little short on him, a couple of inches above the knee. On Cam it looked like he was wearing a towel around his waist and nothing else.

"You look fine," Danyel said absently, hunting in a chest for sandals. Daniel supposed this must be his bedroom, though the low carved bed with its tufted wool mattress looked big enough for a small army.

"I'm kind of..." Cam gestured to his chest. "...bare."

"Vala will like it," Daniel said. His own shenti at least fit. And he was a little more used to the idea of wearing one. No, they hadn't worn them on Abydos, but at least the concept was familiar.

Danyel handed over a pair of worn leather flip flops. "These are going to have to do. They're too big for me, but they'll probably fit you."

"Thanks," Cam said dubiously. "How the hell are we supposed to fight our way in and out of stuff in flip flops?"

"You get used to them," Danyel assured him.

Daniel shrugged. "I see teenagers at home skateboarding in them."

"I'm not a teenager," Cam said. He tugged the shenti down a little further. "Let's go."

Out in the main room the other team was gearing up. While Aset/Egeria and her entourage went straight to Ra, the other group would try to get aboard the mothership. That was Carter's team, Carter and their own Teal'c and Vala, with Danyel along to translate. Also presumably Danyel knew how the pyramid was laid out, which he really didn't. Going through it five thousand years later was not at all the same thing. Sam would presumably be staying here with Nithotep and the baby.

"Ready?" Cam said, trying to look as professional as a guy can while wearing a towel and flip flops.

"Ready," Carter said. Her mouth twitched. She struggled.

"You know you want to," Daniel said.

Carter burst out laughing. "It's just that he keeps losing his pants!"

Vala cast an appreciative eye over Cam's chest. "I think he looks perfectly splendid."

"I never said he didn't," Carter said.

Nithotep gave them all a stern look, despite not having understood a word of it. Some things didn't require translation.

"She asks if we are through clowning and ready to save lives," Danyel translated quickly.

"We are ready," their Teal'c said, coming to stand a pace behind Aset, a staff weapon in his hand. "Let us begin."

"Right," Cam said. It was time to get this mission back on track. He looked at Aset/Egeria. "We'll follow your lead."

Egeria looked him up and down, then looked at Danyel. "One of you to each side, I think, preceding me while my First Prime follows. I think that is the proper disposition of human servants. You do not need to keep your eyes down, as that way you could not guard me, but try to look humble."

"Of course," Danyel said with a deep half bow that managed to look both proud and graceful at once. Cam didn't think he could do that on a bet.

Vala leaned in close, her hair brushing against his shoulder as she whispered in his ear. "Just look submissive, darling."

Cam shook his head. Vala was utterly irrepressible. "Carter? You ready?"

Carter nodded. "We'll be thirty minutes behind you. No radio contact."

"Got it," Cam said. "Let's go, people." And he led a Tok'ra lady in procession out into the cool Egyptian night.

Carter watched the first team head up the road, the amusement of seeing Cam pantsless yet again fading quickly. "OK," she said, and turned back to the others. "We give them thirty minutes, and then we go."

"And in the meantime, we eat," her other self said briskly. Tamit brought around a shallow basket piled with flat loaves of bread, and Carter took one without enthusiasm. She wasn't really hungry, but she knew her other self was right. They might not get another chance for quite a while, and she nibbled half-heartedly at the bread and the sour cheese that came with it. The queen mother was regarding her dubiously, and Carter reached into her pack for the bag of chocolates and offered them around. Vala and Teal'c took them gratefully enough, but Sam's eyes went almost comically wide.

"Oh, my God, chocolate! I've missed that even more than coffee."

Danyel said something to the queen mother, and offered her a square. She unwrapped it, sniffed it, and then took a cautious bite. From her expression, she wasn't entirely certain, but she finished the square.

"What about your weapons?" Carter said to Sam, and her other self looked almost wistful.

"I wish," she said. "I'm staying with the queen mother. We'll be your backup if anything goes wrong."

But. Carter closed her mouth over the word. If it was her Jack—

Sam said, "I'm a physicist. An engineer now, and an architect. You're leading an assault team, and I know my limits. Much as I'd like to go with you, I'd be a liability. Here, I'm an asset."

She was right, Carter realized. She would be—not a liability, Carter refused quite to believe that, but she wasn't a soldier. And someone had to mind the store, just in case things went south. Sam must have seen her face change, for all that Carter tried to hide her thoughts, because she gave a wry smile.

"Besides, I'd have a really hard time not killing Ra if I had the chance, and that would defeat the whole purpose of this." She shook herself. "In the meantime, let's go over the plan of the pyramid one last time."

Dirt floors were useful for this kind of briefing. Sam sketched the outlines of the pyramid, laying out the main corridors and the tunnel entrance that they would use. Sam had built that, Carter realized, Sam at the head of a team of rebels, digging in secret to link up with spies in Ra's temple.

"You are certain that the exit will be unguarded," Teal'c said, staring at the drawing as though he was memorizing the map.

"As certain as we can be," Sam answered. "Pharaoh had it watched of course, but those guards will have been withdrawn, and no one in Ra's service knows about it."

"What about ring platforms?" Vala asked.

Sam pointed. "Here and here. But they are guarded, or at least they always have been." She looked around the little circle. "Anything else?"

There was nothing. Carter forced herself to take another mouthful of the bread, and Danyel handed her a cup of the thin, weak beer. Safer than the water, she told herself, and drained it. "What was that tunnel for?" she asked. "Originally, I mean."

"Well, first we wanted access to the pyramid," Sam said, with another quick grin. "Then I had this idea. If we filled the end of it with flammables, burned out the supports—I made them wood at that end—I thought we could probably collapse a corner of the pyramid so that Ra's ship couldn't get a lock on the Stargate."

"You remind me of my dad," Carter said, without thinking.

"Really?" Sam looked faintly embarrassed. "I never knew mine. He was killed in Vietnam when I was a baby. My mom raised me."

"My mom died when I was in my teens," Carter said slowly. "Dad took care of us as best he could. That's part of why I went into the Air Force."

"Mom would have had a heart attack if I'd even suggested it," Sam said. "I had the hardest time talking her into letting me get a car, never mind flying a plane. I can't imagine..." She shook her head. "She was determined to keep me safe. She wasn't going to lose me like she lost Dad."

"Did you ever know George Hammond?" Carter asked, and Sam nodded.

"He was my father's wingman, the one who brought back his body. Danyel said that in your time he commanded the SGC?"

"Yes."

"I remember when I was little he used to send me Christmas presents," Sam said. "But Mom didn't like having him around—too many bad memories, I think. She lost touch. That—I'm sorry about that, from what Danyel's said. He must have been an amazing man."

And that was more of what the Stargate had done, Carter thought. The time loop that had thrown the team back to 1969, when they'd given Lieutenant Hammond a note from his future self in order to get back to their own time—she'd wondered how that had changed him, and if it had, indirectly, changed her father. And now she knew. In her time, Hammond had saved Jacob Carter's life that day in Vietnam, and maybe he had taken a crazy risk because he knew that somehow he was going to survive.

Somewhere in the back of the house, the baby began to cry. Sam looked up, listening, and a few minutes later Tamit appeared with Ellie in her arms. Sam started to get to her feet, but the queen mother said something and held out her arms. Tamit handed her the baby, who quieted abruptly. She said something more, and Danyel translated.

"The Lady says she left men still loyal to her in the palace, who will aid us if they can."

"More important, let us know if anything goes wrong," Sam said. She stood up. "Well."

Carter looked at her own watch. "Time."

Her other self nodded. "Good luck," she said, and held out her hand. Carter took it, her own hand but with unfamiliar, unexpected calluses. Sam turned to embrace Danyel then, and Carter thought she heard her say, "Bring him back."

Danyel's arms tightened briefly, then he released her, and opened the door. It was dark still, only the first hint of dawn showing in the eastern sky. As the queen mother's guard unbarred the gate, Carter looked back to see the three women standing in the door, the queen mother, Sam now with the baby at her breast, and Tamit holding a lamp, shielding the flame from the night air. Soldiers flanked them, spears at rest but ready, and Nithotep lifted her hand in blessing and farewell.

"The wings of the true Horus shelter you from the false gods, and the Lady of Light bring you safely home," Danyel translated.

"Thank you," Carter said, and they moved out into the night.

CHAPTER FIFTEEN

THE PALACE and the area around the pyramid was busy as an anthill. Ra's Jaffa had already corralled enough of Pharaoh's workers to create a seemingly endless stream of bodies carrying things in and out of the pyramid. Others scurried around the edges of the working groups: courtiers and servants, Carter guessed, trying to salvage what they could of their lives without drawing Ra's notice. At least it gave them some cover, and kept the Jaffa occupied.

They found the entrance to the tunnel easily enough, hidden in one of the outbuildings — a stable, by the smell — and she and Teal'c stood guard while Danyel wrestled the trapdoor open. There would be no one to spread straw back over it, but it opened on an ordinary-looking cellar The entrance to the tunnel itself was hidden behind a stack of coarsely made storage jars: double bluff, Carter thought, with approval, and flicked on her flashlight.

The tunnel was low, but wide enough for a man carrying weapons to walk comfortably. Even Teal'c didn't have to bow his head, though he did glance warily at the bricks shoring up the walls. Only the ceiling was timbered, no surprise in this wood-poor land, and the tunnel ran straight and true. Torches and lamps would foul the air, Carter thought, as would a horde of soldiers, but with flashlights and only four of them, it was surprisingly clean and efficient.

Danyel took point, leading them briskly along the corridor. They'd sealed the walls with what looked like some kind of mud plaster, and it was flaking away in spots, but the basic structure seemed sound enough. They'd covered maybe a hundred yards when the brick gave way to timber, and Danyel's pace slowed.

"Almost there," he said quickly. "It's just wood and plaster between us and the corridor, so—let's keep it quiet."

"Of course, darling," Vala said, and drew her zat, letting it unfold. Danyel looked annoyed, then realized her intent and swallowed his complaint.

"Let's go."

The tunnel ended a few yards further on. It was sealed by a wooden panel set into a frame of heavy timber and crossed by more timber bars. Danyel drew a thin knife and scratched at the panel's edge, opening a thin crack that glowed with artificial light. He applied his eye to the gap for a long moment, then straightened.

"Clear," he said, and began methodically to cut around the other edges—through plaster or paint, Carter guessed, that hid the panel from the other side. Once all four sides were clear, he and Teal'c lifted away the heavy bars and set them carefully out of the way. Teal'c stepped back to cover him, and Carter lifted her P90 as well. Danyel braced himself, and hauled the panel back and in. Plaster split and rattled on the stone floor of the pyramid. It wasn't really all that loud, but Carter winced, bracing herself for discovery. Light spilled in over them, but nothing happened, and she let out her breath in a sigh of relief. Danyel heaved the panel out into the corridor, and scrambled out after it.

"Clear," he said again.

Carter gestured for Teal'c and Vala to go, followed them a moment later. She'd been in pyramids before, on enough planets that she'd lost count, but it felt weird to know that this was Earth. She shook that thought away, and turned to help Danyel set the panel back into place. It would pass a cursory glance but not a close inspection, and she hoped Ra's Jaffa were still busy securing the palace complex.

"Which way?" she asked, and Danyel pointed.

"Up. To the mothership."

Cam gave his shenti another downward tug surreptitiously, keeping his eyes on Teal'c ahead of him. The other Teal'c, the one without hair. It was more than a little odd having multiples of his team running around, but not nearly as weird as the time he'd stolen a battlecruiser from himself. All in a day's work at the SGC, he said to himself.

They were waiting in the antechamber of the palace, or at least he supposed that's what it was, with giant carved columns and lots of Egyptian hieroglyphics, lit here and there by torches and a little more weirdly by Goa'uld portable lights. Dawn was coming outside, but as yet the skylights illuminated nothing. Beside him, Daniel shifted from foot to foot, probably trying to adjust his towel too. One thing you had to say about security in these outfits — there wasn't any way to conceal a weapon. He and Daniel wore their zats perfectly openly on their belts, and Teal'c had his staff weapon in hand.

It had caused raised eyebrows, but nobody had tried to take it yet, not after Egeria forbade them to in her unmistakably Goa'uld voice. Ra's Jaffa were pretty confident themselves.

At last the doors opened. "The Lady Egeria," Teal'c intoned solemnly, preceding her into the hall.

Aset/Egeria stepped forward, her eyes golden. "My Lord Ra," she said, her voice dropping into its lowest register.

He came forward, a ribbon device on his hand, and Cam saw Daniel tense, though Ra did not so much as glance at them. His eyes were for the lady. Cam had to admit that Aset was beautiful, and with that air of command she captured attention. "Egeria," he said. "How is it that I do not know you?"

"I was carried in the body of one of your Jaffa," she said, and held out her hands to rest them lightly on his own. "One who escaped the slaughter of your men. But I was near maturity, and when that time came I took a host who pleased me. Since then I have lived in quiet, hoping that you would return."

"I am pleased that you have survived," Ra said. His eyes roved over her face.

"And now I have come to pledge myself to you," Egeria said, and the beads in her hair rang as she moved her head. "It would be an honor to serve so distinguished a master."

"And my pleasure to have so beautiful a servant," Ra said.

Cam saw Teal'c's fingers tighten on his staff weapon, but otherwise the Jaffa did not move.

"It is good to return to civilization," Egeria said. "I have spent too long in hovels." She looked about the palace appreciatively. "I hope that I may come with you when you leave this world?"

"Most assuredly," Ra said with a smile. "It is only the least part of my domain. My servants will find rooms for you and your entourage aboard my ship. In the meantime, I hope that you will make yourself comfortable in this palace. It is mean, but for a short while..."

"I am sure your hospitality will lack nothing," Egeria replied. "Come. Let us speak further."

Danyel had been on the prison levels of a ha'tak before, both as a prisoner and as a rescuer, and he didn't think it was actually getting any easier with practice. The corridors here were dark, there weren't too many Jaffa, but they came and went unpredictably, and there was still no sign of Jack. Something was nagging at the back of his mind, the weird conviction that he'd done this before — rescued Jack from a System Lord with the help of Sam and Teal'c, but the third, the alien, wasn't Vala, but — the ghost of memory was gone, leaving only frustration. It was an Ascended memory, it had that peculiar, unmistakable flavor, the certainty that there were tremendous secrets just beyond his reach. And this was not the time, he didn't need the distraction, except maybe he did, if it was something about rescue. Whatever it was, though, it dangled just out of reach.

He controlled his thoughts with an effort, took another quick look around the edge of the door: the main corridor was still clear. Behind him, Carter was bent over the console, searching the ship's database to find where Jack was held. Teal'c dragged the last Jaffa body out of sight behind it, straightening with a grunt, and Vala came to join him, smiling at him over her unfolded zat.

"Isn't this fun? Just like old times."

"The old times we shared involved me getting kidnapped and tied up," Danyel reminded her. "And you nearly getting me killed. Oh, and I still haven't been to Atlantis."

"You are still annoyed about that," Vala said, with an air of discovery, and Danyel nodded.

"Yes. As a matter of fact—yes, I am."

Vala pouted, and he looked away, peering down the corridor again. Jack a prisoner, Jack tortured, Ba'al with that smug lying smile—he was almost there, and then it slipped away.

"Got it!" That was Carter, turning away from the console. "Three levels down, along the lateral corridor."

Danyel let her take point, Teal'c at six, kept his own zat cocked and ready. Luckily, the corridors were nearly empty—not only were Ra's Jaffa busy with the palace, but he was beginning to suspect that Ra hadn't waited to collect a full complement before he headed to Earth. If so, it was the first stroke of luck they'd had so far.

There was more light ahead, a hum of machinery and the sound of scuffling feet, and then the cry of a man in agony. Jack. Danyel started forward, but Carter caught his arm.

"Wait."

Danyel froze, all too aware of what he'd almost done, aware, too, that his instinct had as much to do with whatever it was that he couldn't remember than with the present situation. "Sorry."

"General O'Neill?" Vala asked softly, and Danyel didn't bother to correct her. Carter nodded, her expression grim.

Danyel flattened himself against the corridor wall, eased sideways until he could take a quick look into the cell. Jack hung suspended from the back wall, his head down, body slack. There were two Jaffa on guard, eyes front, faces impassive, and a third held a pain stick, his head tipped to one side as he considered his next move. Danyel bit back a curse, and held up three fingers. Carter nodded again, and turned her attention to the locked door. After a quick examination, she pried open a panel, and reached in.

"Teal'c," she said. "Ready?"

"Yes," the Jaffa answered, and she did something to the machinery. Sparks flew, and the door slid open. Teal'c fired twice, three times, and there was silence.

"Pretty," Vala said, and folded her zat.

Danyel ignored her, pushed past the others and the Jaffa bodies to get to Jack. The cuffs that held him were locked, and he turned to look, but Vala tossed him the keys. Teal'c came to help, and together they got Jack down onto the cell floor. He looked terrible, his face pale and drawn, but his eyes opened slowly.

"Ow."

Danyel closed his eyes in relief, and Carter grinned. Jack dragged himself to a sitting position, wincing.

"About time," he said. "And you might have left one alive for questioning."

"We could put you back and try again," Danyel said, and kept a steadying arm on Jack's shoulders.

"No, no, just—" Jack accepted Teal'c's hand, and hauled himself to his feet. "File it for next time."

"Right." Danyel stood, carefully just in reach in case Jack stumbled.

"Glad to see you're all right, sir," Carter said. "Look, they're probably monitoring the cell, so we need to get going. And the sooner we're out of the pyramid, the better."

Jack was shaking his head. "Sorry, Colonel, we've got one more stop. Ra's got your friend Carolyn Lam."

The quarters given to Egeria were those of the Queen Mother, Teal'c saw, and he repressed a frown. Of course they were. They were the nicest ones besides Pharaoh's own, which were no doubt reserved for Ra himself. Egeria would not know that, but Aset did, and for a moment dismay chased across her face before Egeria spoke. "These will do," she said regally and favored Ra with a smile. "I will send my servants to prepare my bath. I am fatigued from my journey. Also," she plucked at the fabric of Sam's best dress disdainfully, "better clothing."

"It will be as you wish," Ra said smoothly. After all, what was it to him? A bit of plunder from humans who had defied him. "I will return to my ship, as I have business to attend to."

"So soon?" Egeria favored him with an intimate glance, and Teal'c tried not to grind his teeth together. "I had hoped you would talk with me a little while."

"Perhaps I could do so," Ra said, and sank into the finest chair in the room. "While your servants are about their business."

Daniel Jackson bowed gracefully from the waist. "We will do our best, Lady," he said, and trotted out of the room followed by Cameron Mitchell. Which was the plan, of course. They were now loose in the palace to do what they could.

Teal'c went and stood behind Egeria's chair, protective as a First Prime should be. Aset would know he was there and would let no harm come to her.

"Tell me of your realm and of your person," Egeria said. "I am eager to know you better."

Cam drew Daniel aside as soon as they were around the corner and out of sight of the two Jaffa who guarded the door to the Queen Mother's rooms while Ra was in them. "OK," he said. "Let's stop and think. Where would Ra keep the Pharaoh?"

Daniel reached up as though he were going to adjust his glasses, but of course he wasn't wearing them. "He's probably claimed Pharaoh's rooms for himself. So he's being kept somewhere secure. Sam said there wasn't a prison attached to the palace, so if he hasn't been taken to the mothership he's likely in a storeroom somewhere. They're the only rooms in a palace of this era that aren't connected to anything and don't have a skylight."

"OK," Cam said. "We're servants. We can go visit the storerooms, right?"

Daniel nodded. "They'll be around the back, past the smaller courtyards that have living quarters around them. I don't see Jaffa widely through the palace. Mostly they're guarding the entrances. We can probably take out the guards with zats."

"Good." Cam unfolded his zat. "Let's do this thing."

The third storeroom was the charm. Cam looked around the corner and gestured Daniel back. Two big Jaffa guarded the door, but there didn't seem to be anything other than a bar across it. After all, it was a pantry, not a high security prison. Cam tucked his zat inside the waistband of his shenti and ambled out, ignoring Daniel's weird gestures. Daniel knew what the score was and he'd have the surprise.

"Hey guys," Cam said in a language that was utterly incomprehensible to the Jaffa, his hands empty and visible. "Can you give me a hand with a problem here?"

One of the Jaffa stepped forward shaking his head, saying something that probably universally translated as, "Dude in a towel, go away."

Cam pointed to the storeroom. "I need to get some stuff out of there. Clean towels. For my master, Ra's guest."

Ra's name seemed to go over at least, as the other Jaffa leaned his staff weapon against the wall, saying something that probably meant, "Dude, this area is restricted."

"I've got a problem," Cam said with a disarming grin, and drew his zat. Which unfortunately caught on the folds of his skirt, but one swift jerk took care of that just as Daniel fired and the first guy crumpled. "Like that," Cam said, shooting the other one without raising his hand from his hip. It didn't matter where you hit someone with a zat. Hitting the guy in the legs dropped him all the same.

Daniel hopped around the corner with an exasperated look. "What was that about?"

"It worked, didn't it?" Cam picked his skirt up off the floor and tried to rewind it around his waist.

Daniel shook his head. "Is that a zat in your shenti, or are you just glad to see me? Honestly."

He unbarred the door while Cam fixed his little wardrobe malfunction and opened it, saying something in Egyptian. Presumably it was something along the lines of 'we're here to rescue you.'

"Danyel!" The speaker was the young man with a shaved head Mitchell had seen O'Neill talking to earlier, shorter than they were but seriously ripped, and he clutched Daniel's forearm in a handshake before he stopped, looking at him more carefully.

More Egyptian, presumably explaining that he wasn't Danyel but the other Daniel.

"OK," Cam said. "Let's get out of here. We haven't got a lot of time." He handed Hor-Aha the zat. A staff weapon was easier to manage in a shenti anyhow.

CHAPTER SIXTEEN

"CAROLYN!" Carter's voice was sharp with relief. "Where is she?"

"In a sarcophagus," Jack answered. He stretched cautiously, testing his muscles. Everything still hurt, but nothing was actually injured. The pain sticks worked directly on the nerves, and the sensation was out of all proportion to the damage.

"I don't suppose you know where they are," Danyel said.

"I knew I forgot to ask Ra something," Jack exclaimed. "I had it written down somewhere — no, I don't know where the sarcophagi are. I kind of thought you might have some idea."

"Yes, sir, we do," Carter said.

For a second, Jack thought about telling her to stop calling him sir, but it occurred to him that it was a good way to remind him that this wasn't really Sam. Sam didn't call him sir except on very special occasions — and that was something else he really didn't want to think about right now.

"We do?" The dark-haired woman — Vala — gave Carter a quick look. "I mean, yes, we do." She favored him with a toothy and completely insincere smile.

"Colonel Carter is right," the other Teal'c said. He looked really odd with hair, Jack thought. "We must hurry. Ra's men will soon realize you have escaped."

"This way," Carter said.

"How far?" That was Danyel, and Jack thought he knew what prompted the question. He would resent it, except that his knees were feeling as though this might be a relevant bit of information.

"Two levels up," Carter answered. "In the port quadrant."

Well, it could be worse, Jack thought. It could be all the way on the other side of the ha'tak, and there might be an entire regiment of Jaffa between them and it. Of course, there still might be, so it was probably better not to borrow trouble. Teal'c took point, staff weapon ready—good move, Jack thought; he was the one most likely to confuse the Jaffa—and Carter settled in six. Vala moved slightly ahead and Jack wasn't surprised to find Danyel at his elbow.

"I'm fine," he said, and Danyel nodded.

"Uh-huh."

"Not my first rodeo."

"I know."

"Fine." They had reached a set of narrow stairs, probably for maintenance, and Jack hauled himself up, trying not to flinch as his knees cracked sharply. "You do know the way out, right?"

"Carter does," Danyel said, far too cheerfully, Jack thought. And that wasn't fair, because this was Carter—she was Sam with Air Force training, after all, and nobody made colonel on good looks and astrophysics—but he hated having to trust himself to anyone else. And, OK, maybe that tendency was just a little bit worse after the last few hours with Ra and his men, but—He shut that thought away in the box with everything else he couldn't afford to think about right now, and concentrated on keeping pace with the others.

There were more Jaffa on this level, a lot more. Teal'c cast around for an alternate route, one that didn't take them through the main corridors, but even the smaller passages were busy. They finally stopped to regroup in a small storeroom on the level below the sarcophagus room.

"What the hell is he thinking?" Jack said. Frustrated as he was, he kept his voice well down. "Why aren't these guys out subduing the planet?"

"Because he's spent a little too long in a sarcophagus?" Carter said. If she was as irritated by the situation as he was, she didn't show it.

"Unless maybe he's got something he really wants to protect," Danyel said. "If so—"

Teal'c was shaking his head. "I do not think so, Danyel. This is not a security deployment." He smiled, and Jack blinked, trying to remember the last time he'd seen their own Teal'c smile like that. "I think Colonel Carter may be correct. He has spent too much time in his sarcophagus."

"Well, I never thought much of him," Vala said. "But how are were going to get past his stupidity?"

Carter and Teal'c exchanged glances. "I think we're going to need a diversion," Carter said. "Teal'c, Danyel, and I will draw them off, and Vala, you and General O'Neill will go after Dr. Lam."

"Split up?" Jack frowned. "I don't think that's a good idea, Colonel."

"It's not what I'd choose," Carter agreed. "But I don't see a better alternative. We're not going to find a way around all these Jaffa." She grinned then, a sudden, wholly mischievous expression. "Besides, as you've repeatedly reminded me, sir—you're retired."

Jack felt a momentary flash of anger, but it dissolved immediately into a chuckle. He'd deserved that, and, anyway, she was right. He didn't see a better option either. "OK, Colonel. We'll do it your way."

The Jaffa didn't know Hor-Aha by sight. In a plain white shenti like theirs the three of them looked the same, three servants bound on an errand. Nobody stopped them in the back corridors of the palace. After all, the attention was on Ra and on the massive mothership hovering. Hor-Aha's men seemed to have melted away, or at least Daniel hoped that was what had happened to them.

Hor-Aha hesitated, and Daniel stopped beside him. "We have to go."

"My wife," Hor-Aha said, looking toward the mothership with an expression Daniel expected he himself knew far too well. "My sons. I don't know where they've been taken."

Daniel made his voice as confident as he could. "We'll find them," he said. "But not this way. You have to lead Egypt, and you can't do that if you're taken prisoner again."

Hor-Aha paused, then nodded gravely. "And you and your friend have risked your life to come for me. I cannot repay your risk with foolishness." His dark eyes were sharp. "Ra has O'Neill too."

"We know," Daniel said. "Colonel Carter has gone after him."

The pharaoh shook his head. "I am confused by this multiplicity."

"So are we."

Cam, who of course hadn't understood a word of all that, looked back testily. "Are we going or not?"

"We're going," Daniel said with what he hoped was the same tone of voice Jack had used to pry him off Abydos.

"All right," Carter said. They had stopped again at the base of a stairwell, and it seemed as good a time as any to check supplies. "C4?"

Teal'c shook his head. "I have only two blocks, Colonel Carter."

"I have seven," Carter said, with satisfaction. "And detonators. We ought to be able to do something useful with that."

"Hey, whoa," Danyel said. For a second, he sounded so much like her Daniel that it was disorienting. He was older, browner—and a lot less clothed—but it was still hard not to treat him the way she would their Daniel. And, of course, they'd been the same person only five years ago, which was maybe even more confusing. "We've got to be careful what we blow up," he said. "Ra's got to be able to take off. We need him gone, not dead. Unfortunately."

It was a very Daniel objection, and Carter nodded. "I was thinking weapons systems. Target them, and Ra can't defend himself either, so that's another reason for him to leave."

"I'd expect them to be pretty well guarded," Danyel said.

Teal'c cocked his head to one side. "I believe that if we were to target the power crystals that govern the power flow to the main weapons array, we would not only divert attention from the sarcophagi, but Ra will find it difficult to repair the damage quickly."

"Pretty much what I was thinking," Carter said. She rearranged the blocks of C4 in her pockets, putting them ready to hand, and slid a fresh magazine into her P90. "And explosives are the last thing Ra's going to be expecting given how primitive the planet is."

"Except that he is thinking about the Ancients," Danyel pointed out.

"Who aren't supposed to interfere," Carter answered.

"And isn't — aren't those power crystals in the main engine compartment?" Danyel asked. "How are we going to get at them?"

"There weren't as many Jaffa toward the stern," Carter reminded him. "It looked as though Ra had most of them guarding his quarters. We'll call this Plan A."

"I'm almost afraid to ask about Plan B," Danyel said.

"We blow up whatever looks interesting that's a long way from the sarcophagi," Carter said.

"It's better than 'retreat to the Stargate under fire,'" Danyel said.

"I believe that is generally Plan C," Teal'c said.

The lowest decks of the ha'tak were quiet, only a handful of Jaffa guarding the obvious entry points. Carter worked her way around them — there were times when she felt as though she'd spent a good quarter of her professional life sneaking around Goa'uld motherships — and they came out at last onto the level just below the main engineering controls.

"There should be a ring platform on this level," she said, and Teal'c nodded.

"I believe so — this way."

The platform was unguarded. Not too surprising, Carter thought, considering that the receiving platform was in Ra's palace, and line-of-sight beaming would just drop them outside the pyramid. Or maybe inside it, on the lowest level? That would be more useful. She studied the controls, not wanting to touch anything in case the system was being monitored. Yes, it should be possible to ring down into the pyramid itself, though there was no way to tell exactly what would be waiting for them. Plan D, she thought, and pointed to the nearest stairs.

"Let's go."

The upper corridors were still uncrowded, though there were more Jaffa in evidence, and once a couple of technicians hurried past, talking in low tones about hull integrity testing. The door to the engine compartment was open, light spilling out from the central towers, and Carter gestured for the others to take shelter in the cross corridor behind her. She leaned out carefully, made sure the main corridor was empty, then darted across to flatten herself against the wall beside the door. The hum of the machinery covered the noise as she armed her zat, and she waved for the others to take their places. Teal'c peered quickly into the compartment, then held up two fingers. Carter nodded, and checked her own side: three technicians in sight. She held up three fingers, waited for Teal'c's nod, then pointed for Danyel to cover them. He nodded, and Carter turned her attention to the compartment.

"Go," she said, softly, and together she and Teal'c stepped through the open doorway. She dropped the first of her targets before he knew what hit him; the second barely had time to turn before she shot him as well. The third was reaching for something, his own zat or a communicator, there was no telling which, but she brought him down before the device was in his hand. She heard staff blasts behind her, turned to see Teal'c stepping over the first body.

"We are secure, Colonel Carter," he said.

She nodded, shoving her zat into her belt and reaching for the first block of C4 and its detonator. "Cover the door."

She didn't wait for his answer, made her way along the racks of crystals. Every ha'tak was just a little different, but finally she found the drawer she wanted, slid it out. She set the first block of C4 in place, set the timer for fifteen minutes, moved on to the fire control panel. Another block there, and another in the backup trays, and she turned back for the door.

"OK—"

"Colonel Carter!" Teal'c's shout was punctuated by staff weapons fire. "We have Jaffa."

Carter drew her zat. "We must have missed somebody."

"Or they're monitoring remotely," Danyel said. He flattened himself against the wall inside the door as another zat blast ripped past him. "I hate to ask, but how long—?"

"Fifteen minutes," Carter said. "Um, more like eight, now."

"We cannot fight our way past them," Teal'c said. His voice was unchanged, but Carter had long ago learned to read the tilt of his eyebrow, and recognized concern when she saw it. She slapped the door controls, sealing them in the compartment, then zatted the box. It exploded on the second shot: the Jaffa weren't getting past that any time soon.

"This way," she said, and saw Danyel's face change from alarm to understanding.

"Access hatch," he said, and Teal'c nodded.

"Indeed."

Sure enough, there was a narrow tube-and-ladder leading down to the next level. Carter let herself slide down fast, landing in a crouch ready to cover them, but this corridor was empty, at least for the moment. Above them, alarms began to sound, the noise spreading. Danyel hit the floor beside her, and then Teal'c, and then there was the sharp crack of explosions as the timers went off.

"Well, as diversions go, that's fairly impressive," Danyel said, and Carter grinned.

"Thanks. I think it's time for Plan D."

"The rings?" Teal'c asked, and she nodded.

"Let's go."

CHAPTER SEVENTEEN

IT WAS nothing at all like Abydos, Daniel mused as they hurried along the road beside the Nile in the growing dawn. Not really. Abydos had revolved around the naquadah mines, the original reason that Ra had transported people from Earth against their will—people from this time and place, taken as slaves to endure backbreaking labor. Even after Ra's death the mines had remained. There was no Nile on Abydos, no life giving water, and the only thing the Abydonians had to trade was naquadah. Better to trade their own work than to be slaves, but the mines were still the center of life.

Here it was the river. It was omnipresent, a whisper at the edge of consciousness. Even now, even in what Daniel could blithely term Early Dynastic Egypt, these people were much richer than the Abydonians had ever been. It was entirely different in ways that bothered Daniel like an itch he couldn't scratch, almost Abydos sometimes and then not. He wondered if the other him felt the same way. Probably he'd had time to get used to it in eight years.

Daniel looked at Cam, still hurrying along the road. "You think we can bring them back with us?'

"Bring who back?" Cam's thoughts were clearly still on the mission.

"The other us," Daniel said. "I mean, he...I...got stuck here eight years ago for him...me. And the other us are from an alternate future, but they still don't belong here. We could take them back with us."

Cam looked at him sideways. "You think they want to come?"

"I probably do," Daniel said. "The other me. I think he probably does."

"And then what?" Cam asked. "Two of you around the SGC?"

"Why not? Stranger things have happened."

"That's true." Cam lapsed into silence to consider what some of them had been. "If they want to," he said at last.

"You don't sound convinced."

"I'm not," Cam said.

They had managed to reach the sarcophagus level, but there were too many Jaffa on guard for them to venture any closer to the sarcophagi themselves. Or, rather, Vala thought, there were too many random Jaffa wandering the corridors. She didn't doubt that General O'Neill, or this version of him, anyway, could take out the trio that seemed to be on permanent guard.

"We'll have to wait for Colonel Carter's diversion," she said, and settled back into the ventilation duct where they had taken up their position. O'Neill had pulled the covering grate back into place, and through it they could see the entrance to the sarcophagus room as well as a long sweep of corridor.

"Let's hope it's a loud one," O'Neill said.

Vala grinned. She'd been a little worried about him — he wasn't a young man, and Ra's interrogation had been harsh, but he seemed to have himself well in hand. And she'd known plenty of men like him, tough, wiry, indomitable. It was almost a pity he was so obviously taken.

She rummaged in her pockets, came up with a candy bar and held it out to him. "Want to split it?"

He started to wave it away, and then his eyes focused. "Is that —?"

Vala glanced at the wrapper. "Baby Ruth." She would never understand the Tau'ri. "Do you want half?"

"Yeah, thanks." He settled himself more comfortably against the conduit that ran the length of the vent, and stretched his leg, wincing slightly. Vala broke the bar in half and, after only a tiny struggle, gave him the larger piece. O'Neill took it, his eyes closing for a second in what looked like pure bliss. He saw her watching, and gave an almost sheepish smile.

"It's sweets," he said. "There just aren't any. What there is, is flavored with honey, and—it's just not the same."

"Daniel says he missed coffee that way," Vala said.

"Sam misses chocolate," O'Neill said. He looked down at his empty hand. "I suppose I should have saved it for her."

"I'll never tell," Vala said.

O'Neill grinned, and shifted his weight to peer out into the corridor. "How much longer do you think—?"

An alarm sounded in the distance, a two-toned wail, and then the same alarm sounded closer, and again closer still.

"Not much longer at all," Vala said, and edged forward herself. The corridor was filled with running Jaffa, the air echoing with shouts of "kree!" but the movement was purposeful, and heading away from them. She hoped Carter knew just how much trouble she was getting, and watched the corridor empty.

"OK," O'Neill said, after a long moment in which they could hear nothing but the alarm. "I'm opening the grate. You go first."

Vala started to protest, then realized that she was younger, fresher, and wearing body armor. "All right," she said, and O'Neill pulled the grating back and in. Vala dropped lightly into the corridor, turning quickly through a full circle, and was relieved to find it still empty. She signaled to O'Neill, who landed grimacing beside her.

The door of the sarcophagus room was open, and a single Jaffa stood in the gap, staring away from them toward the source of the alarm. O'Neill took four quick steps, closing the gap, and brought him down with one quick shots. He was through the door an instant later, quicker than Vala would have thought possible, dropped a second Jaffa in his tracks. She followed, slipping through as the door was closing, and brought down the last Jaffa herself.

"OK," O'Neill said. He was breathing a little heavily, but seemed to be all right otherwise. "Four sarcophagi. Which one's got the prize?"

Vala folded her zat and turned to the console, adjusting the display. Four people had gone into the sarcophagi, three Goa'uld—Tok'ra, really—and a human, and only two were left alive. Her breath caught, and then she saw that the human was one of them, and she was well on her way to being healed. The Tok'ra, though... So many of them carried genetic programming or even implanted devices intended to keep the System Lords from torturing information out of them. She looked over her shoulder to see O'Neill studying the controls of the furthest sarcophagus, and even as she opened her mouth to warn him, he put his hands on the controls. The lid split, the two halves spreading like wings, releasing light and a nasty smell. O'Neill drew back.

"Whoa, that's—unpleasant." He slapped at the controls, closing the lid again. "I thought these things were supposed to be infallible."

Between the smell and O'Neill's expression, Vala was glad she hadn't seen what was in the sarcophagus. "They were Tok'ra," she said, and somehow managed to keep her voice light. "They've developed ways to defeat the sarcophagi. And cheat the System Lords." She looked at the screen again. "We want the two in the middle."

O'Neill worked the controls of the one on the left, and the wings of the lid folded smoothly back. There was light, but no smell. The light faded, and a slight, dark-haired woman sat up, blinking hard.

"General O'Neill?"

She sounded doubtful, and Vala couldn't blame her. Even by SGC standards, O'Neill was out of uniform. Carolyn turned her head, and her face relaxed a little.

"Vala! So SG-1's here."

"Of course," Vala said, trying to sound like Cam. "We've come to rescue you."

O'Neill offered his hand, and helped her out of the sarcophagus. "What about the other one?"

Vala was very tempted to say, *oh, just leave him*, but common sense prevailed. The Tok'ra knew too much to be left behind. "I suppose we'd better bring him."

"Give me a zat first," Carolyn said.

O'Neill grinned and produced one from somewhere—probably from one of the Jaffa, Vala thought. There was no place to hide a weapon in those skimpy shorts he was wearing. Carolyn took it, and touched the sarcophagus controls. For a moment, there was only the fading light, and then a slight, dark haired man sat up, one hand to his forehead.

"Marik," Carolyn said. "I hope you have the mother of all headaches."

"We both do," the Tok'ra answered, with a grimace. "And I'm Leymac. Marik is still recovering."

"Sounds like you earned it," O'Neill said.

"Definitely," Carolyn said.

"My friends here really aren't very happy with you," Vala said. "I suggest you come—meekly."

"However you like, as long as we get out of here," Leymac answered. "I don't suppose I could have a weapon?"

"Absolutely not," Vala said cheerfully. "Let's go."

They reached the ring platform before Ra's Jaffa had fully worked out where they had gone, with time enough for Carter to study the controls and make fine adjustments. Teal'c was glad: their situation was precarious enough without beaming completely blind, and he felt almost relieved as the rings rose to surround them.

The rings drew away, and he realized that they were standing utterly exposed, the open platform not fifty meters from a team of Jaffa. They had their back to the platform, and seemingly hadn't heard anything, but that luck wouldn't last long.

"Crap," Carter said, and lifted her P90.

The odds were terrible, Teal'c thought, even with surprise on their side, but he readied his staff weapon, prepared to fight.

"Wait!" Danyel grabbed his arm, pointing, and Teal'c turned to see one of the Egyptians waving to them from the shelter of a pillar.

"Quickly," Teal'c agreed, his staff weapon still lowered and ready, and they backed cautiously away until they reached the shadows between the pillars. Danyel said something quickly to the young — priest, perhaps, Teal'c thought, looking at the neat hands, the spotless linen. Or a scribe. But not a soldier.

"The Queen Mother has reactivated her old networks," Danyel said. "They were told to watch for us. He has a way out."

"Great," Carter said, and moved out after them.

Teal'c followed more slowly, his eyes scanning the shadows. When he had been Apophis's First Prime, he had arranged such deceptions himself, rebels and troublemakers lured into traps by apparent friends. But Danyel knew the man, and they had successfully driven Ra from Earth before. It was important to remember that, and not be deceived by the lack of technology.

It was unpleasant to be thinking like a First Prime again, to be racking his brains for memories of tricks and tactics. He had enjoyed that freedom as much as any, after the System Lords were defeated. There wasn't much to be said for the Ori, but at least they weren't Goa'uld.

The priest led them through the shadowed halls, talking quietly to Danyel the whole way. At the end of the maze, he let them out into the pre-dawn light. He had robes for them as well, and Teal'c and Carter swung them on, Carter wrinkling her nose at the smell of goats. Teal'c accepted his philosophically, and they made their way out of the palace compound.

"This way," Danyel said, and pointed down the line of an irrigation ditch.

"I thought the road was back that way," Carter said, but followed.

"It is," Danyel said. "Irer said Ra posted Jaffa at a roadblock. We're going to loop around and get behind it."

They would have to hurry, Teal'c thought, glancing at the

sky. Light would come quickly as the day rose. Luckily, though, Danyel knew the ground, and brought them safely around the roadblock. Looking back, Teal'c could see them, blind to everything outside their circle of artificial light, searching each group of travelers. They came back up onto the road just behind one such group, and Carter let out a long sigh.

"OK. Now where?"

"Back to the house," Danyel said. "With any luck, the others are there ahead of us."

"Indeed," Teal'c said, and hoped it would be true.

Troops had been filtering in throughout the night and into the false dawn, veterans of the first rebellion as well as more than a few of Jack's new recruits. Priests and scribes arrived as well, and a handful of the palace women. The Queen Mother sent the women with children and the older men south to estates still held by loyalists, refugees who would also serve as messengers and seeds of this new revolt. The palace cook had arrived, too, and took up residence in the kitchen wing, commandeering women and servants and the household stores. That was a load off Sam's mind, though her supplies wouldn't last long even with everyone reduced to soldiers' commons. Either they would have to rescue Pharaoh and find a way to drive Ra out, or they would need to be resupplied, and she was betting on the latter. That had been the hardest part of the first rebellion, too, keeping everyone fed and armed while Ra had control of the harvest. It wouldn't be as bad this time, she told herself, and crossed the courtyard to the house.

The Queen Mother was still holding court in the main room, a cup of beer at her side and a scribe at her feet. One of the palace women stood ready to do her bidding while two more slept on a pallet in the corner, their backs turned to the flaring lamps. Sam had sent Tamit to bed with Ellie a while ago, intending to snatch a few hours' sleep herself before the baby woke to nurse, but so far she hadn't found the time.

Nithotep gave her last orders to a middle-aged priest, who bowed and backed away, then beckoned for Sam to take the cushion at her feet.

"There is no news as yet from the palace, Sa-Mantha."

"No news is good news," Sam said, and Nithotep cocked her head. "A saying. Of my people." She wondered if she'd actually managed to say what she meant, or if the meaning had drifted off the way it sometimes did. Especially when she was so tired.

"A just one," Nithotep said, gravely. She looked at Sam, and her face softened. "And you should rest, Sa-Mantha."

"And so should you, Lady," the waiting woman said. "I beg you, let us put you to bed, just for a little."

Nithotep shook her head. "I will wait a little longer. There is still much to be done."

And still a chance that they would hear something from the palace, Sam knew. Nithotep was waiting not just for news of Pharaoh, but for news of her son, of her surviving family. "I'll wait a little longer too," she said, and the Queen Mother smiled again.

"Then we will wait together."

"Lady." The voice from the doorway was soft but distinct. "The Royal Architect is here."

Nithotep turned her head slowly, and Sethnakht came to kneel at her feet. For the first time, Sam could see how tired the Queen Mother was, and how afraid.

"What news?" Her voice was utterly controlled, however, and Sethnakht lowered his head even further.

"Great Lady, as I left the palace, I saw the Jaffa in an uproar, recalled to the palace and then to the pyramid."

An hour ago, Sam thought. In another hour, maybe two, they would know if the plans had succeeded. She met the Queen Mother's eyes, and Nithotep smiled.

"May the word be good," she said.

CHAPTER EIGHTEEN

THE JAFFA were swarming on the lower levels of the mothership. Jack froze again, halfway down yet another narrow flight of stairs, and flattened himself against the wall. The others did the same, and below them a troop of half a dozen Jaffa stomped past. Even after they were out of sight, Jack waited, and, sure enough, heard still more heavy footsteps approaching. He waved the others back, followed them as quietly as he could manage, and stopped at the top of the stairs to meet Vala's eye.

"I don't think we're getting out this way, either."

"All right," she said, though he thought her good humor was starting to wear a bit thin. "Let's see, this would be—"

"Plan Z," Jack said. "How about a way off the ship that doesn't involve going through a small army of Jaffa?"

"We might be able to use the rings," Vala said, but she sounded doubtful.

"So far, the platforms have all been guarded," Jack said. "We could probably take them out, but—"

Carolyn cleared her throat. "What about the puddle jumper? The one we came in?"

"You know where it is?" Jack asked. That was sounding a bit more promising.

"If she doesn't, I do," Leymac said.

"I do," Carolyn said, and glared at the Tok'ra.

"Can I fly the jumper out of wherever it is?" Jack squinted, considering the options. Get into the jumper, and he could set the cloak, put up the shields, and they'd be pretty much invulnerable. He liked that idea quite a bit.

Carolyn considered the question. "Yes," she said at last. "It's some kind of docking bay, not a regular glider bay, though."

"It looked like a maintenance bay," Leymac said. "The hanger door was large enough to take the jumper and the two gliders that had it in tow."

"How'd you manage to let him catch you?" Jack demanded. "A puddle jumper can outfly anything Ra has in his arsenal."

"That may be," Carolyn retorted. "But I'm a doctor, remember? Not a pilot."

"If you'd done what Marik told you," Leymac began, and Carolyn turned on him.

"I repeat. I'm not a pilot. And why the hell should I do what a kidnapper tells me?"

"Because it's better than being captured by Ra," Leymac snapped.

"OK, kids, that's enough," Jack said, and they subsided, Carolyn flushing to the roots of her hair.

"This has promise," Vala said. "Lead the way."

Carolyn threaded her way through the ha'tak's corridors with only a couple of wrong turns. The corridors were mostly clear of Jaffa now, presumably ordered away to deal with Carter's diversion, but Jack kept his staff weapon ready just in case.

The hanger was nearly deserted, only a couple of technicians bent over a device attached to the puddle jumper. Beyond them, Jack could easily make out the edges of the hanger door—plenty of clearance—and then the panel that controlled it. "All right," he said softly. "Dr. Lam, Leymac, fan out—take cover behind those consoles there. Once you're in position, Vala and I will take out the technicians. Then Dr. Lam and I will get the puddle jumper operational, and Vala and Leymac will get the hanger door open." He looked at Vala. "You do know how to do that, right?"

She nodded, with a bright smile that he didn't find very reassuring.

"OK, move out."

Carolyn and the Tok'ra moved off, keeping low, and Jack

frowned at the technicians.

"I just hope to hell they haven't started dismantling things," he said, and Vala shook her head.

"They don't know how."

"I hope you're right," Jack muttered.

"I am." Vala looked around. "Does this remind you of a movie?"

"What?"

"The one that Colonel Mitchell likes so much. And Colonel Sheppard—Star Wars."

"Star Wars?" Jack said. He was not going to go there, not on a bet.

"Mm." Vala nodded. "Daniel doesn't like them."

"Try him with Indiana Jones," Jack said, before he could stop himself, and she smiled brightly.

"Oh, an excellent idea! I'll do that."

First Carolyn and then Leymac had made it to cover. Jack looked at Vala. "Ready?"

"Ready," she answered, and they fired almost simultaneously. The technicians dropped without a sound, and Jack started for the jumper at a dead run. Carolyn caught up to him a moment later, and the jumper's systems came on around them as they stepped through the open rear hatch.

Jack slid into the pilot's chair, running his hands over the controls. "Get those cables unhooked," he said over his shoulder. "Don't worry about finesse, just get us loose."

"OK," Carolyn said, and he heard the snap and slither of cable as she obeyed.

Through the windscreen, he could see Vala and the Tok'ra at the door controls, but he made himself focus on the jumper's systems. Think at it, they'd told him, and he frowned at the board, telling it to show him its status. The controls lit, and then a heads-up display, tracing lines across the windscreen. Power, damage, screens, cloak, weapons, all at least functional, all ready to go, and he set his hands on the controls.

"How're you doing back there, Doc?"

"Almost — there, that's the last one."

Jack risked a glance over his shoulder, saw Carolyn kick a last thick cable off the end of the ramp. "Take second seat," he said.

There was a rumble from outside, and the hanger door began to move, three triangular pieces drawing away from each other. An alarm began to sound, and he could see Vala doing something to the controls. Carolyn tumbled into place beside him, and he told the jumper to rise. It lifted, sluggish at first, the ramp not quite dragging on the hanger floor, and he brought it down again at the end of the hanger to let Vala and Leymac scramble aboard.

"Hurry," Vala called. "They're going to override from the pel'tac."

Sure enough, the triple doors were starting to slide back the other way. Carolyn did something that brought the ramp up into place, and Jack aimed the jumper at the rapidly narrowing gap. He could see exactly what it needed to do, but couldn't find the right controls. "Crap —"

The jumper shimmied, tilted sideways, so that it would have been standing on its wing tips if it had had them, and slid through the gap just before it closed too far. Invisible, Jack thought, go invisible, and a light flared on the board. The cloak was on, the shields were up, and they'd be back at the house in minutes.

"What did I tell you?" Vala exclaimed. "Just like those movies."

Cam settled himself on the cushion that was currently serving as a chair, very glad that he'd managed to snatch a couple hours' sleep and reclaim his pants. How the Egyptian men managed to sit like this without showing off everything they had was still a mystery to him. Daniel managed it, of course, though from Jackson's expression, he was glad to be back in uniform, too. A servant appeared with a cup of beer, and Cam took it with a smile of thanks. So far, so good. Hor-Aha was safe, even if Ra still had the royal family prisoner somewhere, and Carter and Teal'c and Danyel had made it safely back from the pyramid. They'd managed to rescue O'Neill, too, and he and Vala were presumably rescuing Dr. Lam, which was better luck than Cam had been expecting. They should be on their way back by now, assuming that they'd managed to get out of the pyramid about the same time as Carter and Teal'c, and he glanced toward the door again. Daniel gave him a look as though he wanted to kick him under the table if there had only been a table, and Carter stifled a yawn. The Queen Mother had gone to bed — taking over the best bedroom, Cam noticed — but Hor-Aha was awake, still listening to his men's reports, his expression unreadable. Daniel translated in an undertone, but it was hot in the house, and Cam fought to stay awake.

After a while, one of the men brought around bowls of stew — lentils, Cam thought, poking curiously with his spoon. But it was hot and savory, and he was almost surprised to find his bowl empty. He mopped up the last traces with his share of the round of bread, and hoped the calories would give him a little extra energy. They all needed sleep, more sleep than the few hours snatched on their return, but nobody was willing to go to bed until everyone was back.

Daniel caught his eye, came quietly to sit beside him. "The latest word from the palace," he said. "Ra's man are swarming like a kicked anthill, and there's no sign that Vala or O'Neill have been captured."

"That's good news," Cam said. He eased his back, wishing he could have a real chair, but the only chair belonged to Hor-Aha. Cam understood the principle perfectly well — no one stands taller than the king — but his back was definitely a democrat. Much longer in this position, and it would be an anarchist.

"Look, if you want to take a break —" Daniel paused. "I mean, it wouldn't be a problem, wouldn't offend anybody, or anything like that."

Cam's instinct was to refuse — never admit to weakness —

but he had learned better, and besides, this was Daniel. Daniel could be pretty tactful about dealing with other people's weaknesses. He nodded. "I'll just be in the courtyard," he said, and hauled himself to his feet.

It was later than he'd realized, well into the afternoon, and already smoke was starting to rise again from the kitchen. Somehow Sam was providing for all of them, though he guessed she was burning through supplies meant to last for months. He made a slow circuit of the courtyard, working the kinks out of back and legs, and at last the pain settled to a dull ache. His right hip, the one with two pins in it, was stiff as hell, but at least it wasn't going to give out on him. He supposed he should go back in, but couldn't muster much enthusiasm for the idea. As he finished another round, he saw that Carter had come out as well, and stood squinting in the lowering sun.

She shaded her eyes at his approach, and shook her head. "I wouldn't go back in. Daniel's arguing with himself, and it's getting a little personal."

"The Pharaoh's handling this pretty well," Cam said. "All the weird, I mean."

"He's had time to get used to the idea," Carter said. "Multiples of us, anyway."

"Guess so," Cam said. He glanced toward the gate and the empty road that led toward the palace complex.

"Vala will manage," Carter said. Cam thought she might be trying to convince herself.

"Yeah, she's good. Sneaky."

"Sneaky's definitely an advantage here," Carter said, and Cam nodded.

Something moved in the air above the gate, a pinpoint shape that was nothing like a bird. An airplane, except there weren't, couldn't be, any here, and his heart kicked in his chest as he squinted into the sun, searching for the distinctive downswept wings of a Goa'uld glider. But, no, there weren't any wings at all, just an odd, boxy, distinctly unaerodynamic shape.

"The puddle jumper?" Carter said.

"It looks like it." Cam could see it clearly now, the squared-off shape with both drive pods extended. Carter was grinning like an idiot, and Cam doubted he looked any more restrained.

"Nice job, Vala," he said, and ducked back into the house. "Daniel!" He hadn't kept his voice down, and Hor-Aha gave him a sharp look. "The puddle jumper's in sight. Looks like our guys made it out."

Hor-Aha said something, and Danyel shook his head, answering. The Pharaoh's face relaxed a little, and he tapped Danyel on the shoulder. Telling him to go ahead, Cam thought, the gesture the same in any language. Sam was already on the move, brushed past him without a word, and the two Daniels followed. Cam went after them, Teal'c at his shoulder.

The puddle jumper slowed, circling, while the Egyptians in the courtyard pointed and stared. Cam would have expected more fear, but of course they'd seen the puddle jumper before. A couple of the older men were slapping each other on the back, and Cam picked out O'Neill's name among the unfamiliar words. Another man with the gold armbands of an officer had the smug expression of a man who'd just won a hefty wager. Never bet against O'Neill, Cam thought. Any of them.

The puddle jumper swung around again, dropping lower, and there was a rush to clear the courtyard as it settled slowly between the walls. It landed gently, to a storm of cheers, and the rear hatch lowered. Figures emerged, Vala first, then a nervous-looking Tok'ra and Carolyn Lam holding a zat on him, and finally O'Neill, looking tough and tired and unbeatable. O'Neill's men raised another cheer and he lifted his hand in answer. Hor-Aha came to meet him, the crowd parting before him, and he and O'Neill clasped hands, O'Neill saying something that made Hor-Aha smile slightly.

And then it was back to the main room for another briefing, the air hot and smelling of too many bodies. Hor-Aha made a speech, running down the score, and Daniel translated softly:

the prisoners had been rescued, thanks to the strangers from the chappa'ai, and there was a core of resistance both here and at the palace. But the royal family was still held, and that would need to be dealt with before they could attack Ra directly. If they could attack Ra directly, or if they needed some other plan.

O'Neill nodded. "I think we need to get the queen out of there first, and the kids. But I know I'm going to need some sleep before I can think straight." He'd spoken in English, Danyel translating, and Hor-Aha gave a wry smile.

"He says he knows Ra won't harm his family while he thinks they can be used as hostages," Daniel translated. "And he, too, needs to eat and sleep. But in the morning, we'd better have a clever plan."

CHAPTER NINETEEN

RA HAD given them the Queen Mother's rooms, the second best, as befitted the only other Goa'uld in the palace. Teal'c searched carefully once their escort had left, and was sure there were no surveillance devices hidden in the room. Even so, they stood close, and kept their voices down.

"Do you think they have had enough time to get away?" Egeria asked softly.

Teal'c considered. The Jaffa were definitely on alert, teams forming to sweep the area, others called to the pyramid, and he nodded. "I believe so."

"Then we must report that our servants are missing," she said.

Teal'c nodded again. This was the tricky part of the plan, but it was the only way they could hope to stay in Ra's favor. Egeria took a deep breath, and moved to the door.

"Jaffa!"

The men on duty came to instant attention, but their eyes were wary. They were, Teal'c knew, in an awkward position, expected both to keep the "goddess" confined and to do her bidding.

"My servants have not returned," Egeria said. "And I have neither bath nor my evening meal. Must I speak to Ra himself?"

"Great Lady," the senior Jaffa said. He licked his lips, visibly trying to decide upon he right response. "Great Lady, there has been some disturbance. Perhaps your servants have been delayed?"

"Delayed for no little time," Egeria snapped. "And I am still without service. Find them for me. And send someone with at least the meal."

The Jaffa bowed his head, relieved to have an order he could obey. "At once, Great Lady."

"See to it," Egeria said, and slammed the door. She turned back to Teal'c with a wry smile—Aset's smile—and held up her hand to show it trembling.

"You did well," Teal'c said, and it was Aset who answered.

"So far, so good. Do you think—Egeria thinks we will still have to speak with Ra."

"I believe she is right," Teal'c said, reluctantly. "He will have questions, particularly when your servants are not found. But you are his match."

"I must be," Egeria said.

It was some time before the Jaffa returned, but at least they escorted a handful of servants carrying trays, and one carrying a covered basket. Egeria lifted her eyebrows at that, and the man carrying it bowed even more deeply.

"A gift from our lord Ra," he said, and opened the basket. "That you may be clothed more as befits your station."

Egeria plucked at the fabric disdainfully, even though Teal'c knew she must recognize the dress as belonging to the young queen. And the jewels, too, collar and bracelets and gilded sandals: all the queen's, and Egeria waved for the man to put the basket aside. "It will do for now," she said. "Where are my servants?"

"Forgive me, Lady," the nearest Jaffa said. "We have been unable to find them."

"What?" Egeria mimed shock and anger. Teal'c drew himself to attention, a First Prime responding to his mistress. "Why not?"

"Perhaps because they have joined the rebels."

It took all Teal'c's willpower to keep from reaching for his staff weapon at the sound of Ra's voice. The System Lord stood scowling in the open door, the fingers of his left hand tipped in gold. From the movement of her eyes, Egeria saw that, too, but she matched anger with anger.

"Why would they do that? They know what it is to serve their goddess. More likely they've been taken prisoner."

"And what do you know of prisoners?" Ra asked. He waved for the human servants to leave, but the Jaffa remained, two on each side of the door. Too many if it came to a fight, Teal'c thought, especially with Ra in possession of a hand weapon.

"I would have to be deaf to have missed what your Jaffa were up to," Egeria answered. "And I worked hard to train my people."

Ra seemed to relax slightly. "The Jaffa say they are not within the palace. We may receive an offer to trade them, as I have one or two prisoners of value. If so — well, if I must use them, I will repay you, never fear."

"I would expect no less from one as great as you," Egeria said, and gestured toward the waiting platters. "Would you do me the honor of joining me?"

Ra lifted one perfect eyebrow. "You find this adequate for the gods?"

Egeria blinked once, lifted her chin. "I do not, though I would not have said so had you not asked. But this body must be fed, and I — would be glad of your company."

"Ah." Ra smiled. "Would I had the time. Another day, I think, and we will have the chance to know each other better. But for now, alas, I have other matters to attend to."

"I eagerly await that other day," Egeria said.

Ra chuckled, and for a moment Teal'c thought he would kiss her, but he settled for chucking her under the chin. "As shall I," he said, and turned away.

The Jaffa followed, closing the door behind them, and Egeria shuddered.

"It was well done," Teal'c said, softly. "And now we know Dr. Jackson and Colonel Mitchell are still free."

She nodded, visibly collecting herself. "I'd better change," she said, and dragged the basket of clothes into the inner room.

Teal'c watched her go, uncertain of the best response. He wanted to embrace her, to embrace Aset and tell her how brave she was, how strong, and how much he admired her, but it was Egeria who had spoken, who had been brave and strong. No, he told himself firmly, it was also Aset. They were Tok'ra, one could not act without the other. He looked at the meal — a roasted duck, bread, dates — and could not muster an appetite. Instead, he went slowly to the bedroom door.

"Aset?" He had spoken without thought, winced as he realized who he had called, but the word could not be taken back.

She looked up from where she knelt by the basket, still sorting through the young queen's clothes, and her face was transformed by an entirely familiar smile. Surely this was different, Teal'c thought. Shau'nac had never smiled so, as though her thoughts were her own.

"I am here."

"And so is she," Teal'c said. He hadn't meant to have this conversation now, but he couldn't seem to stop himself.

"She is." Aset sat back on her heels, regarded him steadily. "We did well, did we not?"

"You did."

"So."

There were no stools, just the queen's bed, and she stood, gestured to it. Teal'c seated himself beside her, his legs crossed, their backs against the painted wall. All around them, the gods marched in procession for the birth of the child Horus, and at their feet, the peoples of Egypt went about their lives, fishermen, hunters, weavers, scribes and priests, a fluteplayer and a dancing girl and a maker of sandals.

"If this has changed things," Aset said, at last, and Teal'c closed his eyes.

"I do not know."

"I would rather have died than lose you," Aset said. "But to live and have you still... seemed best of all."

"And so it is," Teal'c said, but knew he didn't sound convinced. He shook his head. "I am sorry, Aset. I do not know what I think."

"I am I," she said.

"And yet Egeria lives within you," Teal'c said. "She is here, she listens, she is part of you."

"It is I who speaks," Aset said. She touched his cheek, and when he did not resist, turned his head to kiss his lips. "It is I who kiss you, not her."

"And what does she conclude?" Teal'c asked. He took her free hand, laced his fingers with her, feeling their bones solid beneath the flesh. He expected her to bow her head, to let Egeria speak, but instead she gave a wicked grin.

"She is embarrassed. Interested and embarrassed. Remember, she is young, and I have had my share of lovers. I have assured her she will have no complaints."

Teal'c laughed in spite of himself, as she had meant him to, but he sobered quickly. "I had hoped our children would be born free."

It was the first time he had spoken so openly of his feelings, and Aset's smile softened. "They will be more than free. As will you and I."

"We will not live to see the end," Teal'c said. "Nor will anyone who remembers us."

"She will," Aset said. "And when Ra is destroyed, when the Goa'uld are finally beaten, they will know all too well where this began."

Teal'c rested his arm on her shoulders, her skin warm beneath his touch, leaned his head against her fragrant hair. "May it be so," he said.

Jack rested his back against the wall and took a sip of the beer Danyel had brought them along with the morning porridge. He felt better than he had expected. His knees hurt, yes, but only a little worse than usual, and the pain stick had left no lasting damage. OK, his back was a little sore, but that was as much because they'd had to give up their rooms to Hor-Aha and the Queen Mother. Pallets on the floor were a lot less comfortable than his nice big bed. He felt a little bad about SG-1, who'd been bumped right down the ladder to one of the back storerooms, but not bad enough to offer to swap.

Ellie gave a screech of intense disapproval, and Sam put down the spoon with which she was trying to feed the baby a last bite of porridge, reaching for a rag to wipe her face.

"I'll take her," Jack offered, and Sam gave him a grateful look.

"She's all yours," she said, and set the baby in his arms.

"Aren't you my sweetheart?" Jack exclaimed, and lifted Ellie into the air. She giggled, but the movement made his shoulders ache. He set her on the pallet between his legs, and she promptly lunged over his knee, grabbing for the battered wooden duck that was currently her favorite toy. She crammed the tail into her mouth and stared at him over it.

"Wouldn't you rather have some more porridge?" Jack asked, feeling as though some attempt at adult guidance was required. "How about some bread?" He tore a piece from the center of the loaf, but Ellie turned her head away, pursing her lips in definite refusal.

"I think she's probably had enough," Sam said. She was eating her own porridge hastily, before it cooled completely. "Tamit can give her more later if she's hungry."

"How are we doing for supplies?" Danyel asked. He held out a piece of crust, and Ellie took it, the duck still in her other hand. She considered for a moment, and stuffed both of them into her mouth, gumming them happily.

"Your turn to wash the ducky," Jack said.

"Three more days at this rate," Sam said. "The Queen Mother has sent for grain from one of her manors to the south, but getting it here without drawing Ra's attention is going to be a trick."

"Yeah," Danyel said. "Ra's bound to be keeping an eye on the river traffic."

"Hey, Danyel," Jack said. Now was as good a time as any to ask, safe at home with the baby pounding his thigh with a wooden duck. He took the duck away, and Ellie shrieked, flailing for it. He gave it back to her, wincing in anticipation, and she resumed her pounding. "Why would Ra think I was an Ancient?"

"What?" Danyel held out another crust, and this time Ellie dropped the duck to grab it. Jack moved the duck out of reach.

"Me," he said. "An Ancient. Why would Ra think that?"

"I — well, I suppose because you have the Ancient gene," Danyel said. "I mean, you know that's how you fly the jumper, right? But how Ra knew that —"

"He brought out this little box," Jack said, miming the shape. "It went all sparkly when it saw me."

"OK, so Ra had some Ancient device that he's using to test for Ancients," Danyel said, dubiously.

"But why?" Sam asked, and Danyel nodded in agreement.

"Why bother looking for Ancients? They're mostly dead, or too busy Ascending to bother with the Goa'uld. As far as we know, they weren't particularly active here on Earth."

"As far as you know," Sam said. "From everything you'd said, it wouldn't take many of them to cause the Goa'uld some serious headaches."

"No, that's true," Danyel said.

"So maybe there were Ancients here who helped humans," Sam said.

Ellie was reaching for the duck again, making increasingly urgent noises, and Jack handed it back to her, bracing himself. She seemed content to chew on it now, however, and he relaxed a little. "Maybe it's time we gave Ra a serious headache," he said. "Ra thinks I'm an Ancient. We've got two puddle jumpers, the one I just stole, and the one we left parked at Saqqara. Two identical puddle jumpers, both capable of going invisible — if we handle things right, Ra will think we've got a whole fleet of them."

"And I really don't think he's going to hang around to find out how well a mothership stands up to Ancient drones," Danyel said slowly. "We know how badly that can go for him. You — the other you — took out a fleet of motherships with the drones from the Antarctic chair installation. Granted, that was a lot more drones, but he's only got one ship."

"And he won't know how many of us there are," Jack said. "Two invisible puddle jumpers — Mitchell and I can make them seem like a whole squadron."

"Mitchell doesn't have the gene," Sam said. "She — Carter told me. The doctor is the only one who can fly it."

"OK, that makes it a little harder," Jack said. It meant he'd have to do all the fancy flying, but still, he thought, he could manage that. "Kids, I think we've got a plan."

"Part of a plan," Sam said. "There's still the Queen and the boys to think about."

"Yeah." Jack's hands closed a little tighter on Ellie, who squirmed in protest. "We'll figure that out, too."

CHAPTER TWENTY

THE SUN was rising over the palace compound but there were no sounds from the temple, none of the familiar ritual of the morning. Instead, there were Jaffa on guard at the entrance to the pyramid, and more Jaffa marching purposefully toward the courtyard gate. Teal'c craned his head, but couldn't see which way they turned. Not toward the house, he thought, and hoped it was true.

"Teal'c?"

It was Egeria who spoke from the doorway of the bedroom, and he turned, dipping his head.

"Look at this," she said. She held out a palm device, the finger-stalls dangling. "It seems Ra trusts us this far."

Teal'c stared for a moment, embarrassingly glad she had not put it on before she told him. If he had been faced with the device, the gold disk nestled in her palm, the glittering fingers — his reaction would have shamed them all. "Indeed."

"It was in the basket with the queen's dress," Egeria said. "We didn't see it last night."

"You must put it on," Teal'c said, though his throat tightened at the wrongness of the idea. "Ra will expect to see you wearing it."

She nodded, and worked her fingers into the pieces. She had a little trouble with the fastenings, and after a moment Teal'c moved to help her, tugging the last closure into place.

"Your fingers are cold," Aset said.

"It's early still," he answered, but he guessed she knew that was not the entire cause.

Aset looked away, moving her fingers carefully in the device's embrace. "We — this is new to both of us," she said. "Egeria knows how it should work, but she's never used one."

Teal'c took a deep breath. This was Aset, Aset and Egeria together, and unless he ceased to believe in them, he would have to trust that they would use even Goa'uld tools for good. "I hope it will not come to that," he said. "We cannot fight Ra directly."

"No." This time it was Egeria who spoke. "But I can't say I'm sorry to have a weapon of my own."

That was a sentiment Teal'c could share, and he nodded, his hand tightening on his staff weapon. "Yes—"

The door was abruptly flung open, and he swung to face it, bringing his weapon to bear. Half a dozen of Ra's Jaffa stood there, their captain to the fore.

"What is the meaning of this?" Egeria drew herself up, the beads in her hair clashing. "How dare you interrupt me?"

"Your pardon, Lady," the captain said. "Ra requires your presence. Immediately."

Egeria lifted her chin. "We will come. And I am sure Ra will be less than pleased by your discourtesy."

Teal'c took a tighter grip on his staff weapon and placed himself at Egeria's shoulder. To his relief, the other Jaffa said nothing about their weapons, but hurried them toward the throne room.

Egeria checked in the doorway, and Teal'c's breath caught in his throat. A body lay sprawled before the throne, a palace servant in fine linen now scorched and bloodied, and beyond it stood the young queen, her children clutched against her skirts. Ra glared at her from the throne, then waved to the nearest Jaffa. The Jaffa shoved the queen to her knees, settling the baby wailing. She clutched him more tightly, but said nothing.

"How dare you defy me?" Ra demanded. "How dare you stand against your god?"

The queen said nothing, holding the wailing baby tight against her breasts. The older boy buried his face against her shoulder, too afraid to cry.

"You see what this has earned him," Ra went on, pointing to the body. "A deserved death, and the end of all chance of rebirth. His body will be given to the jackals, and scattered into so many pieces that even the gods themselves could not find and restore him. Tell me why the same should not be done to you!"

"Gracious Lord," Egeria said. Teal'c could see the tension in her shoulders, prayed Ra was too distracted to notice. "What has happened for you to summon us in such haste?"

"This woman conspires against me," Ra answered. "She and this slave would have sent word to my enemies." He turned back to the queen. "And I would have honored you for your beauty, raised you up among my servants, had you but proven worthy." He gestured to the Jaffa. "Still, perhaps she will serve someone as a host. Take her to the ship."

Teal'c stiffened, and made himself relax again, hoping none of the other Jaffa had noticed. It would be almost impossible to rescue the queen from the cells on the mothership — Ra wouldn't be taken by surprise a second time.

"Gracious Lord," Egeria said again. "If I might offer a suggestion?"

Ra lifted an eyebrow.

"Perhaps she could be of more use to you here," Egeria said. "If she remains in the palace, the rebels will try to rescue her because she is their queen. It will be an excellent opportunity to crush them utterly."

There was a moment of silence, and then Ra smiled slowly. "I was correct, Egeria, I shall certainly enjoy getting to know you better. Jaffa! Return the woman to her cell, and the children with her. Then double the guard — but discreetly."

The leader of the Jaffa bowed his head. "At once, Lord." At his gesture, two more Jaffa hauled the queen to her feet and turned her toward the door.

"And you, Egeria," Ra continued. "You will join me."

Egeria dipped her head. "I am honored —"

"Your pardon, Lord." That was Ra's First Prime, standing impassive in the doorway. "There is a message from our scouts."

Ra waved his hand. "Later."

"Forgive me, Lord," the First Prime said. "I fear the matter is urgent."

For a moment, Teal'c thought the System Lord was going to lose his temper, but then Ra sighed. "We must postpone our discussion, then, Egeria. Nean'tac, I trust this will merit my attention—"

He swept out, still talking, the Jaffa coming to attention around him, and Egeria drew herself up. "Jaffa! I wish escort to my quarters, a decent meal—and has anyone found my servants?"

"At once, Lady," a Jaffa said, bowing, and the senior officer remaining shook his head.

"No, Lady, there has been no sign of them."

"Then I will require staff from among the humans here," she said firmly. "See to it. Come, Teal'c."

He bowed, impassive, and followed her from the throne room. At the door of the queen's quarters, she dismissed the escort, and stalked into the bedroom without a backward glance. Teal'c remained in the outer room long enough to be sure no one lingered, then came to join her. Egeria was huddled on the bed, her head in her hands, and when she looked up there were tears on her cheeks, leaving tracks of kohl on her skin.

"I don't know if I've made things better or worse," Aset said. "What if I've only made it harder for Jack and the others?"

Teal'c wrapped his arms around her. She was trembling with reaction, and he tightened his hold, kissed her hair. "It would have been worse to let Ra take them to the mothership," he said. "And we will find a way to warn O'Neill."

"We must," Egeria said. "Or they will be walking into a trap I have set for them."

Sam woke at mid afternoon with the muzzy feeling of someone who had been up all night and then slept during the day, her breasts aching with the need to nurse. The whole house was sleeping, visitors sprawled on mats and curled up in corners wherever they could, the best bedroom given over to Pharaoh and his mother, who had presumably taken the opportunity to nap while they could. But Ellie…Ellie wouldn't be asleep at this time of day.

She wasn't. The other Teal'c, the Teal'c from the future that wasn't hers, was playing with her in the courtyard, one eye always on the road. A shadow moved in the entrance to the gatehouse, Colonel Carter keeping watch in the shade, her camo uniform blending with the colors of the mud brick.

"Here is your mother," Teal'c said to the baby quietly. He looked up at Sam and she could swear she saw his mouth quirk in a smile. "I believe she is growing hungry."

"Well," Sam said scooping her up. "Some bread and some me. Thank you for watching her."

"I do not mind," Teal'c said. He put his large hand on the baby's head for a moment as he released her. "I like children."

"Do you have children…" Sam began and stopped, worried that she was stepping on a sore subject.

"I have a son named Ry'ac," Teal'c said, and this time he actually did smile. "He has grown into a fine young man and has recently married."

"Oh." Sam hauled Ellie up on her shoulder as Ellie flailed around with pudgy bare feet. "That's wonderful."

Teal'c nodded. "Perhaps he has grown well despite my choices rather than because of them, but I am very proud of him."

"Isn't that the way it works?" Sam sat down. Ellie wanted to nurse now, and she was going to flail until she did. The next thing would be a piercing scream, and it seemed cruel to wake everybody up, as tired as they all were.

"Perhaps," Teal'c said. He glanced down at Ellie with a smile, not looking away from her as most of the rest of his team did, like they'd never heard of breastfeeding before. Maybe the Jaffa were a little more sensible about these things than people from her own culture had been.

Sam settled Ellie on the left, brushing an errant strand of brown hair back from her face, soft and fine against her baby cheek. A thought occurred to her. "Daniel said that the other me knew my father."

"That is correct." Teal'c nodded slowly. "As did I. General Jacob Carter was a fine man. It was an honor to know him. I owed him my life."

"Oh." Sam looked over at him, then away. "I didn't. He died in December 1969, before I was two years old." Teal'c didn't say anything, so she went on. "He was killed in action over Vietnam. His plane was shot down and he tried to bail out, but his parachute didn't open." Sam had told this story so many times that her voice was even, and after all she didn't remember any of it. "His wingman, George Hammond, tracked where he fell and his body was recovered. I think he blamed himself somehow."

Teal'c nodded again, his eyes rising to the endless azure sky. "George Hammond. Lieutenant George Hammond."

"Yes."

"We met him," Teal'c said. "A few months before that time. It must have been shortly before he was sent to battle."

"How..."

"It is a very long story involving temporal physics." The corner of Teal'c's mouth twitched. "If you would like a technical explanation you had better ask Colonel Carter. But the result was that we were transported into the past, to the summer of 1969, and there you gave Lieutenant George Hammond a note from his future self, asking him to help us return to our own time. Which he did."

"Oh." Sam felt a frisson down her spine, the touch of the fascinating and marvelous. "Time travel."

"Indeed. I did not consider greatly at the time that you were, of course, already there."

Sam nodded. "In the summer of 1969 I was learning to walk. We were at Pope Air Force base in North Carolina. My dad got sent to Vietnam in the fall. It was his second tour."

"General Jacob Carter said that his life was saved by George Hammond, and in that battle he won the Distinguished Flying Cross and then returned home to his wife and daughter. Your brother, Mark, was born two years later."

Sam blinked. The pieces fit together, beautifully and perfectly as they always did once you understood. "You changed it," she said. "That's why I'm so different from your me. She changed it when she gave George Hammond the note from himself. He knew he couldn't be killed in Vietnam because he was going to live to be an old man and send the note! He couldn't be killed! So he took risks that he otherwise wouldn't have, and one of them saved my father's life." She met Teal'c's eyes. "George Hammond was always guilty. He always said to my mother that he felt responsible for my father's death because he should have done something heroic and insanely brave to prevent it. And in your world he did."

"In my world he did," Teal'c said gravely. "George Hammond and Jacob Carter were lifelong friends. He died nearly four years ago after his symbiote, Selmak, died."

"Symbiote?"

"Your father chose to become a Tok'ra host like Aset," Teal'c said. "He had contracted a fatal disease. I believe you called it lymphoma. Selmak's host was dying of old age, and Selmak offered to become one with your father and save his life if your father would share that life with him."

"Cancer," Sam said. "An incurable cancer?"

"He chose to become the host of the Tok'ra Selmak who healed him of the disease. Together they were a powerful force in the war against the Goa'uld." Teal'c leaned back against the wall. "He himself rescued me and General O'Neill in a ha'tak when our glider malfunctioned and left us adrift in space."

"My father flew a space ship." Sam shook her head. She could still see the color picture that had been beside her mother's bed, that young man a decade younger than she was now, stiff and formal in his uniform, posed in front of the flag like everybody else. She'd looked at it a million times, wondered what he would say if he could talk, wondered what he would have wanted. Wondered what it would have been like to know him. Well, now she knew that.

"He flew it exceedingly well," Teal'c said.

She shook her head. "And so that's the right future? That's the good future and I'm some kind of mistake?"

"I do not believe so," Teal'c said. His eyes rested on Ellie. "I do not believe that either of you are a mistake. You are different, products of different lives and different experiences, and hence you have made different choices. But I do not believe that either of you are wrong or have failed." He leaned back against the wall, stretching his long legs out before him. "Perhaps you wonder if you should be her. And yet she wonders if she should be you."

Sam blinked. "Why?"

"You have what she does not, just as she has what you do not. And you are as valued here — king's architect, builder of a new world — as she is in her place. It is no little thing, what you do, and you do not seem unhappy."

"I'm not," Sam said. "Actually, I'm really happy. I like my work and I like my family and..."

"And you would not return to the future if you could?"

Sam shifted Ellie, switching her to the other side. That was the operative question, and they hadn't had time to talk about it. "No," she said quietly. "I don't think so."

Teal'c nodded again. "Then it is as it is. Perhaps given all the worlds there may be, each of us plays all parts somewhere. I do not know."

"Neither do I," she said. "But you have to start somewhere."

Jack stuck his head out the door. "Sam? We need you for a minute for a logistics thing. Hor-Aha wants you."

"Coming," Sam said, getting to her feet, and Teal'c smiled.
"As I said," he said.

CHAPTER TWENTY-ONE

SAM HANDED Ellie off to Tamit, and she and Teal'c made their way through the crowded halls to the main room. Hor-Aha was already holding court, and Jack hoped he'd managed to get a decent night's sleep somewhere along the way. The Queen Mother was missing, but SG-1 was huddled in a corner, finishing the last of their breakfast. Jack lifted a hand in greeting, intending to talk to Mitchell, but Hor-Aha looked up at their entrance.

"O'Neill! A word with you."

"Of course, sir." Jack moved to join him, nodding to the chamberlain Irer and an officer with heavy gold bracelets, a commander of a hundred spears whose name Jack couldn't remember.

"We are discussing the best way to get the grain ration to our people," Hor-Aha said, "and it has occurred to me that you might be able to circumvent the river journey with your invisible machine."

"Bring supplies in the jumper?" Jack blinked. "Yeah, that could work. It depends on how much it will lift—hey, Mitchell!"

"Sir?" Mitchell set his bowl aside and came to join them.

"Do you have any idea what the carrying capacity of a puddle jumper actually is?"

"I don't know that we've ever found its limits," Mitchell answered. "Several hundred tons, with the inertial dampeners adjusted right, and probably more than that."

"Thanks." Jack looked back at Pharaoh. "Colonel Mitchell says it's possible. But now that we're talking about the jumper, I had another idea about them."

Hor-Aha waved his hand. "Say on."

"We actually have two jumpers now," Jack said. "The one we just took from Ra, and the one that we — Sam and Danyel and I — left at Saqqara. I believe that we can use them to attack Ra's mothership, and in the process make him believe that we have not two, but a whole fleet of jumpers, and that they are manned by the Ancients who long opposed the Goa'uld." Quickly, he outlined his plan, then repeated it in English for Mitchell's benefit.

"That could work," Mitchell said. "But Dr. Lam's going to have to be the one who flies it."

"Sam told me," Jack said. "I figured I could do any fancy flying that was required."

"This is very promising," Hor-Aha said.

"And if Pharaoh pleases," Irer said, "while O'Neill brings the jumper from Saqqara, perhaps the other one could fetch the grain."

Jack nodded. "That would work —"

"My lord!" One of his men was striding toward them.

Hor-Aha turned sharply, a flash of fear in his eyes before he had himself under control.

"My lord, there is word from the palace."

"Say on." Hor-Aha's voice was steady, but Jack could guess the effort it took to seem unmoved.

A stocky man in a common shenti shouldered his way past his escort, dust still clinging to his feet and his sweating chest. He bowed his shaved head, and only then did Jack recognize him by the gesture: Ankhmerwer, another of the senior chamberlains. Jack didn't think he'd ever seen him without the collar of his office and a massively fashionable wig.

"Pharaoh. I bring news of the queen — good news, for now," he added hastily, and Jack saw Hor-Aha's shoulders relax just a fraction.

"I listen gladly," Hor-Aha said.

"I have spoken with Aset and Teal'c," Ankhmerwer said, "and they are safe and well. The queen and the princes are likewise unharmed."

Hor-Aha's eyes flickered closed for an instant. "Thank all the gods."

"They are being held in the overseer's house beside the granary," Ankhmerwer said. "I have seen with my own eyes that they are there and treated fairly. And, my lord, they are not well guarded."

"We must act, then," the commander said, and Hor-Aha cocked his head.

"And yet?"

"Aset claims it is a trap." Ankhmerwer paused. "I saw no sign of it, lord. There are guards enough, but they are distracted—Ra calls for them at all hours, and his household is in constant upheaval. And they do not yet know the palace, or their servants. That will not last forever."

"But Aset says it's a trap," Jack said.

"Yes, O'Neill." Ankhmerwer took a breath. "Forgive me that I raise a painful matter. But Aset is a Goa'uld now. She lives as one of the gods, and Ra has given over to her the queen's quarters and the queen's jewels. Perhaps she has cause to dissuade us from a rescue."

"Not Aset," Sam said firmly.

"No. What does Teal'c say?"

"Very little," Ankhmerwer answered. "And again I beg your pardon, O'Neill, but it must be said. He loves Aset. And he is Jaffa."

"Oh, for—" Jack glowered at the chamberlain, who met his gaze squarely.

"It must be considered, O'Neill."

"What's going on?" Mitchell asked quietly.

Jack ignored him, saw out of the corner of his eye that their Daniel had arrived to translate, and focused on Hor-Aha instead. "This is Teal'c we're talking about," he said. "He gave up everything to fight the Goa'uld."

"He loves Aset," the commander said. "We cannot pretend

it isn't so."

"And Aset fought the Goa'uld with us," Sam said. "She was with us at Saqqara, and when Ra fled — she was as brave as anyone when it looked like Ra was going to take our last outpost."

"That is so, Sa-Mantha," Hor-Aha said. "And yet. She hosts a Goa'uld."

"A Tok'ra." Danyel had joined them. "The mother of the Tok'ra."

"And you tell me they will change the course of history," Hor-Aha said. "Though not yet."

"Yes," Danyel said, a little too firmly.

Jack said hastily, "One way or another, we have to get the queen out of there. OK, this may be a trap — me, I think that if Aset says it's a trap, it's definitely a trap. But Ankhmerwer is right that this may be our best chance, to get in there while Ra's people are still disorganized."

"What are you proposing, O'Neill?" Hor-Aha asked.

"Let me take a scout party in," Jack said. "Me and Danyel, maybe, just to take a look around. We can check out this trap, maybe even make contact with Teal'c and Aset, but, either way, we'll have a better idea of what we're up against. And in the meantime, Colonel Mitchell and his team can go get the other jumper so we won't be losing any time."

Hor-Aha was silent, considering, but finally gave a slow nod. "We must — if they can be reached, we must save them, O'Neill, for I do not know if I can bear to see them used against me." He stopped abruptly, and Jack winced in sympathy. If it was Ellie — but that didn't bear thinking of.

"Go, then," Hor-Aha said. He had control of his voice again, and his face was like a statue's, stiff and unflinching. "See if this trap can be drawn."

Cam listened to O'Neill outline his plan, and nodded reluctantly. Whatever else they did, they could definitely use the second jumper, and he could see that it was important to find out for certain what was going on at the palace. It was just... He lengthened his stride as they left the main room of the house, caught up with Teal'c.

"I've got a question for you," he said, and glanced quickly over his shoulder to be sure that none of the alternate thems were anywhere in earshot.

Teal'c gave him a look that might have been wary. "I will answer if I can."

"Egeria," Cam said.

"Ah." Teal'c looked over his shoulder, too, then stepped deliberately into the shadow of one of the outbuildings.

"It's not that I have anything against Aset," Cam said, following him. The mud brick walls were thick enough that they couldn't be overheard from inside, and they'd be able to see anyone approaching. "And it's not that I don't trust your other self. It's just that whenever there are Tok'ra involved, everything seems to go south really quickly."

"Indeed," Teal'c said. "We have seen that too often. But if this is Egeria, she must be allowed to create the Tok'ra, or the time line will be damaged far more than it was before."

"If," Cam said. "What about Anise's idea that one of the others, one of Marik's people, was carrying the Tok'ra that becomes Egeria?"

"That cannot be," Teal'c said. "They have no queens left, so logically none of them could become Egeria."

"Unless they were lying," Cam said. "Which, you've got to admit, is not all that unlikely."

"Indeed no," Teal'c said. "Certainly either Anise or the Tok'ra Council lied to us."

"Right now, I'm going to bet it was Anise," Cam said.

"She had more cause," Teal'c agreed.

"And that brings me back to my question," Cam said. "O'Neill and the others, they're sure this is Egeria. But that's what they want to believe, because Aset was going to die if she didn't get a symbiote to heal her. And the symbiote was going to die if it didn't take a host, because O'Neill was planning to kill it. But I can't help wondering if the little snake could have somehow figured out that claiming to be Egeria was the one thing that would get it a host."

"You are asking if my counterpart's prim'tah would have sufficient awareness to have deduced Egeria's role, and to claim it when it was threatened," Teal'c said.

"Yeah. Pretty much." Cam leaned against the bricks, grateful for the shade. "Would it?"

"I do not know," Teal'c said slowly. "I never carried a prim'tah for so long, to a point past maturity. However..."

There was a long silence, Teal'c staring across the sun-baked courtyard, his face even more neutral than usual. Cam had learned to wait out those silences, and at last the Jaffa blinked, focusing again.

"When Shaul'nac tried to save Tanith," he said. "You were not there, Colonel Mitchell, but—"

"I've read the mission report," Cam said. An ugly business, another time the Tok'ra had betrayed them, and it had cost the life of a woman Teal'c had loved.

"Yes." Teal'c might have looked relieved. "Shaul'nac always said that she spoke to the symbiote who was Tanith only in the depths of kelnorim, but it seems to me that Tanith might have learned some things without her realizing it, either by somehow tapping into her consciousness, or by somehow observing—overhearing, perhaps—while he was still in her pouch. He had an excellent understanding of Tok'ra politics, as well as of the tensions between the Tok'ra and the Tau'ri, that I suspect may have come from such observation."

Cam carefully didn't look at Teal'c's stomach, even though he knew perfectly well there was no symbiote there. "Is that possible? For a larva to hear? Or to pick somebody's brain like that?"

"For an immature prim'tah, I do not believe it is," Teal'c answered. "But one at maturity, ready to take a host, and perhaps even a little younger? I could not discount the possibility."

"I was really hoping you'd say I was just looking for trouble," Cam said.

"I, too, would prefer to believe that," Teal'c said. "But—I believed Shaul'nac, against all my training and everything I had been taught. Against the evidence of the prim'tah I carried then, even. And my other self loves Aset."

"Yeah." O'Neill wasn't going to want to hear any doubts—he'd made that perfectly clear when he was talking to the Pharaoh. And Cam couldn't blame him. Aset was clearly family, and it had been O'Neill that made the call to let the symbiote take her as a host. But that didn't mean that "Egeria" was telling the truth. He straightened slowly. "Let's just keep the possibilities in mind, right?"

Teal'c nodded. "Indeed."

Mitchell sidled up to Carter in the storeroom where she was switching clips for her pistol out of her backpack and into her pockets. She stopped, stretching a hair band out one handed and redoing her long pony tail. "Have we got a plan here?" Mitchell asked quietly.

Carter nodded. "I'm going with Jack and Daniel—their Jack and Daniel, not ours—into the palace. You and Vala and Carolyn need to go to Saqqara to get the other jumper. If that's cool with you?" Her eyes searched his face belatedly, conscious once more that she might be stepping on his toes. SG-1 was his, and this wasn't Atlantis.

"That's cool," Cam said. It was always a good thing to have Vala for backup.

"And the other me," Carter said. "She knows where the jumper is." She gave him a flat little stressed smile that he'd first seen on the drill field when he was eighteen years old, the first time cadet Carter had drilled the flight and marched him straight into a rhododendron bush. Right turn and column right are not at all the same thing.

Cam dropped his voice. "That's got to be weird."

"It's not the first time I've seen an alternate me." Carter bent over her pack again, shuffling things around inside.

"Yeah, but." The other hims he'd met were all pretty much him. Same Air Force, same haircut. Of course some of the alternate teams they'd encountered that time didn't have a Cameron Mitchell with them. The ones of him who'd made choices that led him in a different direction didn't come walking through the Stargate. Nor did the ones of him who were dead. There must be a bunch of him who'd never made it out of Antarctica, who'd had a full military funeral instead of SG-1. "It's gotta be weird, you know?"

Carter shrugged and didn't look up. "Yeah."

She was two years older than he was. It had been twenty years since they'd stood on that field together, assigned to the same flight in 1988, when he was a freshman and she was a junior. Carter was forty. The clock was running for her in a way it wasn't for him. Cam figured he'd get married someday. There wasn't any hurry. Sooner or later it would happen, and the right woman was worth waiting for. There would be kids on down the line, but that wouldn't screw him over any more than it had screwed over his dad or Carter's dad. Lots of guys had kids. It wouldn't end his career, like it would for Carter. If she stepped back to have a baby she was never going to get back to the front of the line.

"She's named for my mother," Carter said. "Eleanor. She was killed in a wreck when I was twelve." Carter didn't look up from the interior of her backpack. "Except that she wasn't. In that other reality she died of cancer five years ago, when she was sixty one. She smoked all the time, the other me said. She never quit. It caught up to her eventually." Carter shuffled more things around. "My mom quit when she was pregnant with Mark, because they knew then that you shouldn't smoke when you're pregnant. She smoked with me of course, but I don't see it did any damage. I just remember her smoking, the way she'd sit on that avocado gabardine couch in base housing with her legs crossed and her hair in a big beehive with a cocktail glass in one hand." She looked at Cam sideways. "Your parents do the gabardine couch too?"

"Oh yeah." Cam grinned. "We had shag carpets, man! And some wild parties, let me tell you. They went to some crazy ones. My mom bought my dad a keychain with a lucky rabbit's foot on it so she could tell which one was his."

"What?"

Cam grinned bigger. "Key parties. Don't you remember that whole big scandal about Air Force wife swapping? The key parties where all the guys would put their car keys in a punch bowl and then the women would draw one to go home with? My mom didn't want to swap but she liked the parties, so she made sure she could always figure out which one was dad."

"I cannot see my dad doing key parties," Carter said, but she was smiling back. And that was a good thing, the whole point of this little segue into obscure Air Force history. "I really can't."

"Mine didn't swap. At least I don't think so. But there was some pretty heavy drinking going on. It wasn't all canasta in the good old days." Cam picked up his pack.

"It's not all canasta now," she said.

"Don't I know it?" Cam grinned back. "You know, six of one and half dozen of the other. But what we've got's not bad, right?"

"Not a bit," she said. She zipped up her pack looking a lot more cheerful. "Not at all. Have a good trip to Saqqara."

"Will do," Cam said.

CHAPTER TWENTY-TWO

CAM SETTLED himself in the stern of the little reed boat, thankful that for this mission at least he got to wear his own clothes. The sun was halfway up the sky, and it was hot and humid on the river, in the eighties and rising he'd guess. Clouds of gnats circled over the water, the surface broken occasionally by the tell tale bubble of a fish nabbing the unwary one. It looked like the lazy rivers of Cam's childhood, hot summer days spent with his grandfather out on the water. "Good fishing here," he commented.

Sam — the other one — stepped into the boat just ahead of him, surprisingly nimble in her print sundress. "That's what Jack says." She looked at him sideways. "He does bring home some big ones sometimes."

Cam stood up as Carolyn and Vala came down the path, stepping out of the boat and offering a hand for them to step past him. "Keep low," he said. "Just crouch down and stay in the middle of the boat and go on forward. Sam's going to take the front oar." She was already settling in at the bow, the oar across her lap. "Just like a canoe," he said. "You guys are in the middle, and Sam and I get to row."

"I'll be the queen of the Nile," Vala said, lifting her chin as she let Carolyn go ahead of her. "You do the work, Cameron."

"Do you know how to row?" Cam asked. "Because if you do, it's all yours."

"Actually I don't," Vala said cheerfully.

"I thought not." He looked with approval at the way Carolyn wasn't tipping the small boat at all, moving into position in a crouch. "Good job there."

"Summer camp," Carolyn said, with the first smile he'd seen

since they rescued her. She looked worn, as she ought to after what she'd no doubt been through, but like she was holding it all together. Carolyn was probably tougher than she looked. Lots of doctors were.

"Try not to tip the boat over," Cam said, handing Vala in. "Please."

"I have no desire to be muddy and wet," she said.

"There are enormous crocodiles," Sam said. "Really big ones. That eat people."

Vala looked nonplussed. "I said I'd be careful."

Cam pushed off and jumped in as he did, not getting more than one foot wet in the process. The little boat wallowed about six inches above the water, but it seemed stable enough. Enormous crocodiles. Fun times.

"How far is it to Saqqara?" he called up the boat.

"About eight miles." Sam put the paddle to the water, and he dipped his neatly on the other side. "It's not far. But it's upstream. The current's not bad this time of year, not like it is during the flood. And the prevailing winds are upstream, which is nice."

Cam could already see that. Out toward the middle of the river larger boats with single lanteen sails were heading upriver, transports probably. One was about forty feet long and seemed to have four or five cows on deck, chewing placidly on a pile of straw. Wouldn't want them to start moving around, he thought. There was a lot of river traffic. They were pretty unremarkable.

The sun rose higher and the temperature climbed. The sun was warm on his forearms.

"Crocodile," Sam said, pointing. One about four feet long was lying on the muddy riverbank, looking sleepily at the passing traffic. "That's one of the little guys."

"How big do they get?" Carolyn asked.

"Eight, nine feet." Sam shrugged. "Supposedly bigger, but that's the biggest I've seen."

"Cool," Cam said. "No swimming."

"Pretty much," Sam said. "Actually, we pipe the water off and filter the sediment out. And the sewage, of course."

"Right."

"We've got a basic charcoal filtration system for drinking water. Don't worry. It doesn't change the timeline. We know that the Egyptians knew how to filter water through several layers of sand, coarser and then finer and then finest, to get safe drinking water. Otherwise everybody would be dead of cholera. We just add a little activated charcoal."

"The Egyptians knew that?" Carolyn sounded dubious. Cam was too.

Sam didn't stop rowing. "This is actually a very sophisticated society. Remember, these guys built the pyramids."

"I thought the Goa'uld built the pyramids," Cam said.

"Actually, Danyel has a theory that they learned from us," Sam said. "The Goa'uld don't really create technology. They just borrow it from anybody they encounter. In this case, they learned a lot from humans. That's why they've been kidnapping people off this planet for a couple of thousand years."

"A couple of thousand years?" Vala sat up straighter.

Sam glanced over her shoulder, then back to the river. "Danyel says that we realized after we started using the gate in your timeline that all of the humans we encountered in the Milky Way were descendants of people seeded from Earth. Well, here we are while they're doing the seeding. It amounts to Ra kidnapping people and selling them as slaves to the other system lords. And it sucks."

"Yeah," Cam said. "Oh yeah."

"Of course sometimes it doesn't go their way. We found a bunch of documents the first time we beat Ra that were basically one of the other system lords giving him hell because they'd paid Ra for permission to round up a bunch of people in what we're guessing is Hokkaido, the northernmost island of Japan. Only it didn't work out and the locals kicked the system lord's butt. So the system lord complained to Ra. Ra blamed it all on the interference of mysterious Ancients."

"Do you think that's possible?" Carolyn asked interestedly.

Sam shrugged, her back to them. "I don't know. Danyel says that there is a cluster of the ATA gene there five thousand years on. Whether that means that there are Ancients there now — your guess is as good as mine. We've been trying NOT to alter the timeline, which means not using the puddle jumper to jet all over the world and visit Japan!"

"Right." Carolyn sounded vaguely disappointed.

"But the big deal here is that Ra thinks that there are Ancients on Earth who are interfering," Cam said. "That's our in. We convince him that the Ancients have a bunch of puddle jumpers and weapons, and he gives up and goes home."

"Exactly," Sam said. "His ships are no match for Ancient technology. Only we don't actually have anything except the puddle jumper."

"Two puddle jumpers," Carolyn said. She squared her shoulders. "OK."

"You're not going to have to do any tactical flying," Cam said reassuringly. "O'Neill's going to do that. We'll just back him up and make it look like we've got a fleet."

"An invisible fleet," Vala said. "Which is a nice thing."

"Yeah." Cam couldn't help but wish for a 302. Now that would be a nice thing.

"I can't wear that," Carter said, scowling at the plain boatneck dress Daniel held up to her. "Where am I supposed to put my pistol?"

"A towel and flip-flops," Daniel quoted. Carter supposed this was fair payback for her remark about Mitchell's pantslessness.

"Actually, the pattern of her tan is going to be a problem," the other Daniel said. "Try this one."

He held up a tunic with short sleeves that fell low enough to hide the line where her T-shirt sleeves had been. "Sorry about the pistol, but pockets aren't an option."

Carter sighed and took the dress.

"She'll look like a servant," Daniel said.

"Which isn't exactly a problem," Danyel said. "We're supposed to blend in with the palace servants, remember?"

"That's not my point." Daniel glared at his other self.

Carter had spent enough time among the Goa'uld to know exactly what Daniel meant. "Any human is vulnerable," she said. "Not just servants."

"We're all servants as far as Ra's concerned," Jack said. He had given up his boxers for the sort of kilt the other men were wearing, and a pair of beaded sandals. "Which is why I intend to stay well out of sight."

"Yes, about that," Danyel said. "Ra's just been reminded of your existence. Don't you think it might be better to let me go alone —"

"Nope," Jack said, with enough good-humored force that both the Daniels stopped short. Carter cleared her throat.

"He has a point, sir."

"We are not going to spend any time where Ra can see us," Jack said. "We're going to get in, check out where the queen's being held, and get out. Discreet reconnaissance, with an emphasis on discretion."

Carter had never believed that when her Jack said it, either, but she'd never found a good way to argue with him. "Yes, sir," she said, and went to change.

It was a long hot walk back to the palace compound, sand sliding uncomfortably in her sandals. Neither the heat nor the sand seemed to bother Jack and Danyel, though after a bit Danyel did deploy a painted parasol. Sunshade, she corrected herself. At least that sounded a little more dignified. There wasn't a lot of traffic on the road, not heading toward the palace, and she touched the ripped seam of her dress that gave her access to her pistol.

"Do we actually have a plan for getting in?" she asked.

Danyel grinned. "Well, I could be a palace official, and you could be my servants."

Jack rolled his eyes. "You should have shaved your head if you wanted to play it that way."

"There's a wig in Carter's basket," Danyel said. The thought of Danyel, any version of him, in one of the heavy horse-hair pageboys she'd seen on Hor-Aha's officials — it was calculated to make her giggle almost as much as Mitchell losing his pants again.

"If you tell them you're an official, you'll probably have to talk to Ra's First Prime," Jack said. "And that would be a bad idea."

"OK," Danyel said. "So what's your plan?"

"Let's see if we can't find someone who's on their way to sell goods to the palace," Jack said, "and take their place."

"Assuming there is someone," Danyel said. "If that's what you wanted, why didn't we just bring supplies from home?"

"Because we don't have anything to waste," Jack began, and then broke off. "See? We won't have to worry about it."

Carter squinted into the sun. An older woman was coming toward them, a basket topped with leaves tucked under her arm. She was scowling, and Jack's cheerful greeting didn't seem to improve her mood. Danyel interjected something that sounded polite, and got an elbow in the ribs for his pains. After a minute, though, the woman nodded, and handed over the basket. Danyel fumbled in his own basket, and handed Jack a pouch. Jack produced a couple of baked-clay tablets and the woman took them with a nod and a genuine-looking smile. She moved away, calling something over her shoulder that Danyel translated as, "The true gods bring you luck."

"So what was that about?" Carter asked.

Jack peeked under the leaves, then tucked them back into place. "We're going to go sell Ra some fish, Colonel."

"Apparently not very many of the palace's usual suppliers want to go there," Danyel said. "There are all kinds of rumors about the Jaffa locking people up for no good reason."

"And do we know that won't happen to us?" Carter asked.

She didn't think she liked this plan very much at all.

"It's just a rumor," Danyel said. "She didn't know anyone it had actually happened to, and she said her sister earned a beaded necklace doing laundry just yesterday."

"We hope," Carter said. "Can't we just sneak in the way we did before?"

"That doesn't take us to the right places," Jack said. "Besides, these are very good fish."

There were half a dozen Jaffa on duty at the palace's main gate, and she saw Jack give them a measuring glance before he approached, holding out his basket. Carter kept her head down and did her best to look like a servant while they haggled, and then the team leader waved them through the gate.

"We're to go straight to the kitchen buildings," Danyel said under his breath. "And not hang around."

"OK." It look an effort not to look over her shoulder, but Carter managed it, though her shoulder blades tingled in anticipation of a staff blast. To her surprise, the palace compound was relatively free of Jaffa. There were guards at the entrance to the palace itself, of course, and more moving in and out of the pyramid, but most of the people she saw were human, scurrying back and forth without meeting each other's eyes. The Queen Mother had agents here, she remembered, and hoped no one else would recognize them.

At the kitchen door, Jack lifted his voice in a nasal cry that made Danyel roll his eyes.

"It's a traditional fisherman's call," he said. "Jack gets a kick out of it."

"Hey, it works," Jack said, and turned to smile at the buxom woman who appeared in the doorway. "Hey, Merymaat, want to buy some fine fresh fish?"

The woman's painted eyebrows rose. "O'Neill —" She broke off, shaking her head, and beckoned them inside. Even in the kitchen's antechamber, it was sweltering, and the air was heavy with baking bread and what smelled a lot like roast chicken. Jack said something, still grinning, and Danyel translated.

"He's asking Merymaat what she knows about the young queen. And Aset and Teal'c."

The woman took the basket, automatically checking over the fish as she spoke.

"She says she doesn't know anything about a new god, nor has she seen Teal'c, but if we want to know about the queen —" Danyel stopped, gave Jack a sharp and disapproving look. "Apparently Jack and I can take her dinner as soon as it's ready."

"Sir," Carter said.

"Have you got a better idea?" Jack asked, and she shook her head.

"Not at the moment. But I'm working on it."

CHAPTER TWENTY-THREE

THERE wasn't much to do but wait. Danyel settled himself cross-legged on the floor in the antechamber, thanking Merymaat for the bread and oil and lentils that she dished up from the palace stores. Ra was banqueting tonight, Merymaat said, with food brought from the mothership rather than from her kitchen. She claimed to be just as glad, though Danyel suspected she took it as an insult, too. But tonight there were just the duty Jaffa and the human servants to be fed. And the prisoners. Jack flirted idly as he ate, earning a rap on the shoulder with the heavy wooden spoon that was Merymaat's unofficial badge of office, and then at last the queen's meal was ready, covered bowls and rounds of bread packed neatly into a basket.

"I'll go," Danyel said firmly.

"We'll both go," Jack said, with equal force.

"Carter doesn't speak the language," Danyel pointed out. "One of us ought to stay with her."

"Merymaat speaks a little English," Jack answered.

That was true, they'd taught all their operatives some English in the first days of the rebellion, protection against being overheard or betrayed. Merymaat had been with them then, an assistant cook who'd lost a child to the Goa'uld, a boy of fifteen taken as a host. Her son was lost, of course, but there had been others who were saved...

"I remember still," she said, in English, and included Carter in her smile. She held out the basket. "You go now."

Carter looked as though she still wanted to protest, but Jack stared her down. Danyel took the basket, and Jack hoisted the jar of beer onto his shoulder.

"Back in a few," he said, and stepped out into the gathering dusk.

Danyel followed him across the dusty courtyard, head down, the basket heavy in his hands. There were a pair of Jaffa at the door of the overseer's house, and one of them frowned at Jack's approach.

"You're new."

"Yeah," Jack said. "I just got back—I'd been hiding, after the gods were driven out, and it's really good to be back again. Good to see you all back."

Don't overdo it, Jack. Danyel kept his head down, the basket under his arm. But at least the queen might hear, and recognize their voices, not be surprised by their sudden appearance, which was probably why Jack was doing it.

"Nice to see that someone appreciates us," the other Jaffa said, in his own language, and pointed to Danyel. "You. Open the basket."

Danyel whisked off the lid, let the Jaffa poke through the various dishes. The first Jaffa shook the beer jug, and stepped back, waving them inside.

"We'll wait and take the dishes back," Jack said, and the first Jaffa nodded.

"Yes, I know. Go on."

It was dark in the overseer's house, and the air was stale, smelling of lamp oil and sweat. Shadows moved on the far side of the room, resolved as Danyel's eyes adjusted into the queen and the two little boys. She had the younger at her breast, nursing, but the elder glared at them from the shelter of her skirts. Her eyes widened, and Jack put his finger to his lips.

"Keep it down, and I think we'll be all right," he said, softly.

"I should have known," she said, with a laugh that almost broke into a sob. "And Pharaoh?"

"Safe and well," Danyel said. He busied himself setting out the dishes, clattered the pottery so that the guards would hear something familiar. "He sent us to rescue you."

"Thank the true gods," she breathed. "Tell me what to do."

"Well, that's what I'm not sure of," Jack said. He moved from window to window, peering through the cracks in the shutters. "How many guards are there?"

"Just those two," the queen answered, and filled a plate for the older boy. "At least that I have seen. The back door is barred, I can see that through the cracks, but I don't hear anyone posted there. I believe it could be opened without anyone seeing you."

"And that doesn't strike you as a little odd?" Jack came back to join them, accepted the cup the queen held out to him.

"It does," she said. "But there are not as many Jaffa as before, and I do not think they intend to keep us here much longer. I'm willing to take the chance."

"Aset and Teal'c sent word that this is a trap," Danyel said. He looked at Jack. "Well?"

Jack shrugged. "The armory overlooks this house, it would be easy to put an observer there. I don't see one, but I wouldn't expect to."

"So — we try it?" Danyel went to the rear door. "The hinges are on this side, we wouldn't have to get the bars off."

Jack shook his head. "Teal'c says it's a trap, and I believe him. Let's make sure we know what we're up against before we risk the kids." He looked back at the queen. "How often do the guards come in here, search the place?"

"Never," she answered. "As I said, I don't believe they intend to keep us here much longer."

"And we're not going to leave you here, either," Jack said. "Trust me."

"She has a point," Danyel said. "If Ra moves them to the mothership — even if this is a trap, it's going to be easier to deal with that than getting them out of the pyramid."

Jack was rummaging under one of the couches, came up with a sturdy-looking staff. It was no ornamental badge of office, Danyel thought, but as thick as his wrist and banded in bronze.

"See, finding stuff like this doesn't make me feel good about the situation," Jack said. "No way the Jaffa would leave that here unless it was a trap."

"They have staff weapons," Danyel pointed out. "I'm not thinking a big stick is going to worry them much."

"You're just arguing," Jack said, and the other man sighed.

"Yeah. I know. You're probably right, but—"

"Let's get the hinges off if we can," Jack said. "That'll give us an extra option. And then I think we need to talk to Teal'c."

Danyel nodded. "How much more time do we have?" he said, to the queen, and she shrugged.

"You had better hurry."

Between the staff and the commando knife Jack had carried beneath his shenti, they managed to carve out the mud brick around the pins that held the strap hinge in place. It wouldn't pass a close inspection, Danyel thought, kicking and smoothing the fragments of broken brick out of sight against the base of the wall, but if the queen was right and the Jaffa didn't look too closely, they might just get away with it. And it wouldn't take much of an effort to pull the hinges free—the queen herself could probably do it, if she had to.

"You in there!"

Jack swore under his breath, and Danyel dropped to his knees beside the table just as the main door flew open.

"Are you finished, lady?" the Jaffa demanded.

The queen gave him a wounded look. "Nearly. May I be permitted to feed my children?"

The Jaffa gave them a searching glance, and Danyel slid his hand under the low table, his fingers closing over the heavy staff.

"A little longer," the Jaffa said then, and pulled the door closed behind him.

"OK," Danyel said, after a moment. "That wasn't right."

"Nope," Jack said. He looked back at the queen. "That doesn't mean we're not going to get you out of here. We'll figure out how to break this trap, and then we'll be back."

"I believe you," the queen said, but her voice wobbled just a fraction on the words.

As far as Cam could see the puddle jumper was in good shape. It was parked in a tight ravine on the edge of the desert on what would eventually be known as the Saqqara Plateau. Daniel had said that in a few hundred years this site would hold the tombs of Hor-Aha's descendants, incredibly rich archaeological sites where the movie camera that the alternate team had buried had finally come to light, the message from the past that had begun all this, at least as far as Cam's stream of history knew.

Now it was nothing. There was bare rock with a few lonely thorn bushes clinging to it, a vista that looked out over desert on one side and the unbelievably green river valley on the other side, marshes clinging to the edges of the Nile like a fringe.

The jumper was cloaked but right where Sam said it would be. She walked confidently up to it, holding her hands out in front of her like a mime, touching the edges of something invisible.

Carolyn looked doubtful. "It's there?"

"It's here," Sam said, taking her hand and putting it against a surface they couldn't see. "Right there."

Carolyn nodded. "OK."

"Just think about it being visible," Sam said. "That's what Jack does."

Carolyn frowned, closing her eyes, her mouth moving as though she whispered only to herself. For a long moment nothing happened, and then there was a shimmer like a heat mirage above the surface of a road on a long, hot day. Under her hands the puddle jumper decloaked, smooth metal resting against her fingertips. Carolyn squeezed her eyes shut, an unbelievable look of peace suddenly crossing her face.

"What is it?" Vala said.

She smiled, opening her eyes. "It just feels really good."

"Maybe it likes you," Vala said.

"Maybe so," Sam said seriously. "Jack says that Ancient things have personalities. That it's weird how they respond to people." She shrugged. "He said the jumper never really liked him. It acted like an old horse with a flaky rider."

"I think it likes me," Carolyn said, running her hand along its side as the tailgate came down slowly. The lines of stress that had bracketed her mouth since they rescued her were gone. Cam and the others followed her into the jumper, the tailgate rising quietly behind them. There was a soft sound as the ventilation systems came on, the hot desert air being replaced by the cool breeze of air conditioning. Lights came on, the control board coming to life as Carolyn slid into the pilot's chair.

Cam sat down beside her in the copilot's position. "OK," he said. "You've flown a jumper before, right?"

"Only once," she said. "And that was with a Tok'ra holding a gun to my head." Carolyn ran her hands over the control surfaces. "It was kind of dicey."

"Well, this will be a lot nicer," Cam said. He was a good trainer. He'd had a lot of people who were nervous in the chair the first time. "So take some time, familiarize yourself with the controls, relax, don't hurry." Once they got in the air it would be about two minutes back, so there was no need to have his pants on fire right now. "Just take some time to figure out how everything works and how the systems work for you."

Sam and Vala sat down behind him, Sam looking over his shoulder interestedly. "What's that light?" she asked.

Vala squinted, no doubt trying to read the Ancient.

"I think it's something in communications," Carolyn said. She frowned as though thinking at it, asking the jumper to show her something. A cascade of blue lights appeared, letters displayed against the inside of the windscreen, Ancient letters dancing like falling water. "I think it's saying that the jumper has seventeen incoming messages waiting." Carolyn looked sideways at Cam. "How could that be possible? We just got here with the other jumper a couple of days ago, and if General O'Neill just sent us a message surely he'd send one, not seventeen?"

Cam glanced back at Vala and saw the same thought in

her eyes, though of course she voiced it first. "Maybe there are Ancients on Earth," she said. "And they've been calling."

There was a pair of Jaffa waiting at the kitchen door. "Oh, crap," Jack said, but it was too late, the path too exposed, for them to turn back without attracting unwanted attention. He pasted on his most guileless smile, and kept walking toward the door, Danyel at his heels.

"Was there a problem with dinner?" he asked, and he could almost feel Danyel wince.

The nearest Jaffa frowned, but before he could say anything, a familiar figure loomed behind him.

"You," Teal'c said. "The lady will speak with you. Now."

Danyel made a graceful bow. "Yes. At once. Absolutely."

"Both of you," Teal'c said. His face was set in his usual impassive stare, but Jack through he detected a glimmer of humor in the big man's eyes. "You will keep a civil tongue in your head, too."

You've just been waiting to say that, haven't you? Jack swallowed the words, and managed a polite bow. "Right away. Yes."

"The woman, too," Teal'c said. "Perhaps these will please the lady."

Jack set his jar down inside the door. Carter came to join them, her face carefully controlled, and they followed Teal'c back across the courtyard, the other Jaffa at their heels. They were heading toward the palace, Jack realized, and hoped none of the other guards remembered him. He kept his head down, and they passed into the maze of corridors without anyone raising the alarm. They were heading for the Queen Mother's rooms, but of course that was where Ra would house his fellow deity. The doors swung open at their approach, and Teal'c dipped his head.

"I bring more servants for your consideration, Lady."

"Excellent." It was Egeria who spoke, out of the mask of Aset's face. She waved a beringed hand, dismissing the escort.

"Leave them here. I will decide later."

"Yes, Lady," the senior Jaffa said, and bowed himself out, closing the door behind him.

"I'm glad we caught you." That was Aset, relaxing into herself again. "Did you not get my warning? Ra has set a trap—"

"We heard," Jack said. He kept his voice down, and scanned the walls for Goa'uld technology.

"We are safe," Teal'c said. "I have searched and found no listening devices."

"Well, that's good news," Danyel said.

"About the queen," Jack said.

"She is bait in Ra's trap," Egeria said. "To recapture Pharaoh."

"Why am I not surprised?" Jack said, and was pleased to draw an answering smile from Aset.

"There is a watcher in the armory, and a dozen Jaffa within easy call," she said. "They have left the back door apparently unguarded to tempt a rescue, but the watcher has a perfect view. I'm glad you didn't try anything, O'Neill."

"So am I," Jack said. "All right, kids, it's time for a change of plans." The floor underfoot was stone, and he looked at Teal'c. "You wouldn't happen to have some charcoal, would you?"

Teal'c reached into the gilded brazier, produced a charred stick. Jack took it, began to draw lines on the floor. "OK, here's the overseer's house, and the granary, and that's the armory. Show me where Ra's men are placed."

"Here," Egeria said, and drew a cross halfway down the armory. "That is where his watcher sits. And the dozen men are here, on the far side, where you would not see the guard change, or anyone bringing food and drink."

Crap. Jack frowned at the crude map. The obvious approach was covered by the watcher in the armory; the other side was too exposed, visible to anyone crossing the courtyard, or looking from the entrance to the pyramid.

"We're not going to get in without being seen," Carter said.

"Yeah." Jack sighed. "We're going to need a diversion."

"I really don't like that idea," Danyel said.

"What? You haven't even heard my plan."

"That's because you don't have one yet," Danyel answered, and Jack saw Carter grin.

"Of course I have a plan," he said. "We need a diversion. That's a plan."

Daniel waited, cocking his head to one side, and Carter said slowly, "You said that's an armory? What kind of weapons are in there?"

"Egyptian ones," Danyel said. "Spears and bows, mostly, plus shields and some bronze ingots for making more."

Carter made a face. "Do the Goa'uld know that?"

"I don't know." Danyel looked at Teal'c, who shrugged.

"I do not think Ra has ordered any kind of inventory yet, Colonel Carter. Why do you wish to know?"

"I was thinking," Carter said. "We need to drive them out of the armory, right? If they thought something was going to explode — they'd withdraw, right?"

"Very likely," Teal'c said. Jack thought that was approval in his face.

"I have some C4 with me," Carter said. "A chain of little explosions, running from the back door forward to where the watcher is placed —"

"You'd need something to make them think there was more coming," Jack said. "Otherwise, they're just going to go after you. A fake device, maybe."

"Sorry, sir," Carter said. She looked down at her dress. "That I didn't bring."

"I have this," Egeria said. She held out a Goa'uld tablet. "Would that help?"

Carter took it, nodding. "It just might."

It was full dark by the time Carter finished modifying the tablet. She had pried it apart and repurposed the various components, so that the original casing was now webbed in wires that held a dozen blinking crystals. It was very impressive, Teal'c thought, though he should not have been surprised. Sam could have done the same thing.

She saw him looking, and flashed him a quick smile. "So what do you think?"

"If I were confronted with that, I would hesitate," he answered, and her smile widened.

"Couple it with a few explosions, and they ought to retreat."

"That's the plan," Jack said. "What is it with you and explosives, Carter?"

Carter shrugged, but her smile didn't entirely vanish. "Bombs are fun?"

"If you say so." Danyel added a fuse to the last of the half-dozen packets Carter had improvised from her packages of C4. "OK, these are all ready. Two with timers, the rest with—"

"Snap and toss fuses," Carter prompted. "Just like a grenade, really. Break the seal, and you've got thirty seconds to get rid of it."

"Yeah." Danyel regarded them warily.

They were little bombs, Teal'c thought, not likely to cause any real damage. Confusion, yes, and with zat fire, and surprise on their side, it should be enough to make the guards fall back. "Are you sure I should not go with them, O'Neill?"

Aset laid a hand on his arm. "You cannot."

"She's right," Jack said. "If anything goes wrong—you're our back-up, Teal'c."

"As you say." Teal'c couldn't pretend to like the idea, but he had to admit that O'Neill was right. It was just—he hated being trapped here, playing at being First Prime, unable to do anything to drive the Goa'uld away. "Very well."

"OK," Jack said. He gave a last glance at the plan sketched on the stone floor, then deliberately rubbed his sandal across it, scuffing it out. "Danyel, Carter, you'll get into the armory and set off the charges. Use your discretion about the interval, but no more than a minute apart. When the second one goes off, I'm heading for the back door of the overseer's house. I'll get the queen and the boys, and head for the tunnel entrance. We rendezvous at the other end of the tunnel, outside the palace. Got it?"

Danyel nodded.

Carter said, "Yes, sir."

"Then let's go." Jack turned for the door.

"Good luck, O'Neill," Teal'c said. Jack lifted a hand in answer, and the door closed again behind them.

"Now," Egeria said. Her eyes seemed to flicker gold, but then Teal'c realized it was a trick of the lamplight. "We will wait a little, and then we will inform Ra."

"What?" Teal'c hand tightened on his staff weapon.

"We must time it just right," she said. "We must warn Ra before the first explosion, but not in time for him to send reinforcements. And we must tell him there will be more attacks, from all quarters, sow as much confusion as we can. Attacks through the Stargate, so that he takes men from the walls."

"Why tell him at all?" Teal'c demanded. Only a Goa'uld would think of such a thing—but, no, this was Egeria, Egeria and Aset, and he would not believe that possible.

"We must make him trust us," Egeria said. "Teal'c, if I am to do what Danyel says I will, Ra has to take us with him when he leaves. Even if Pharaoh would leave the Stargate unburied long enough for us to leave, you and I cannot just walk through the gate and proclaim ourselves goddess and First Prime, we must have a sponsor among the gods, and who better than Ra? But to do that, he must believe we are loyal to him."

Teal'c nodded slowly, suppressing the niggling doubts. "Very well."

CHAPTER TWENTY-FOUR

THE FIRST message played in the quiet coolness of the puddle jumper, picture projected in two dimensions on the inside of the windscreen. A woman with long black hair pinned up at the back of her neck spoke to them earnestly, her recorded voice swift over unfamiliar syllables. She wore a wrap top the color of polished wood, lusterless, like raw silk. Her eyes were dark over broad cheekbones, epicanthal folds accented by the dark eyeliner she wore, beautiful and very, very human. And yet this woman was an Ancient, an Ancient or one of their children or grandchildren. She or those before her had walked through the Stargate from Atlantis, left their city to sleep and sought refuge and peace on Earth.

A refuge now destroyed by the Goa'uld.

Cam shook his head. If he were her, he'd be pissed. He'd also want to know where another puddle jumper had come from. The wall behind her didn't betray where she was, but he'd bet good money on Hokkaido. He'd bet he knew her distant descendant, Dr. Miko Kusanagi of the Atlantis Expedition. Even driven underground they must have some of their communications equipment still, some way of monitoring air traffic and radio signals, otherwise they wouldn't have been able to fight off the system lord's slave raid. They'd probably picked up the jumper and wanted to know who it was. After all, if only someone with the ATA gene could fly it, it had to be one of them. Maybe they hoped it was more of their people. Maybe they hoped it was desperately needed reinforcements.

Only it wasn't.

The second message began to play, the same woman again but her shirt was different. A different day. They were calling again. Daniel would be able to understand spoken Ancient, but none of them could.

Carolyn's hand moved toward a key.

Sam shook her head. "Don't do it." Carolyn looked back at her. "Don't reply," Sam said. "We can't. Remember? We're trying not to change history. We can't interact with the Ancients or their descendants in 2492 BC. If the Ancients know about the future or have access to the Stargate, that will change everything! Right now they're cut off from the gate. If they don't have any jumpers left or won't have them in the next few years, then even if they knew the Goa'uld no longer controlled the gate, they couldn't get to it. But if they still have a jumper and we make Ra leave the gate, there's nothing to prevent the Ancients from using it. And that will change the entire history of the Milky Way! The Ancients on Earth have to stay underground or everything's different."

Reluctantly, Carolyn moved her hand away. "Maybe they could help us."

"Maybe they could," Cam said. "But they'd want access to the Stargate in return, I bet. And we can't do that."

"So we just let them call and call with no answer?"

Cam nodded. "Sooner or later they'll decide it's just a glitch and there is no jumper here. We just leave it be."

Carolyn took a deep breath and a long look at the woman in the picture, speaking earnestly into the camera. "OK." She turned it off. "Then I guess we should recloak the jumper and get busy." She gave Cam a wobbly smile. "The only Ancient armada is us."

"Yeah," Cam said. He put his hand on her arm. "Don't worry. You'll do them proud."

The back of the armory was in deep shadow, but there was no way to miss the Jaffa who stood leaning on his staff weapon beside the narrow doorway. It gave access to a narrow workroom, Danyel remembered, used mostly for repairing leather goods. The bronze work was done in the smith, far enough from the other buildings to reduce the risk of fire. It was a small room, and Danyel guessed — hoped — most of the Jaffa would be inside the armory itself. But first they had to get past this guy.

"That one looks pretty alert," Carter said in his ear. "And I can't make the shot from here. What now?"

"Good question." Danyel glanced around the courtyard again. At least the back door wasn't meant to be observed — it was defended from within, the inner door fitted with a bar, so that a single soldier could watch over both the stockpiled weapons and the workroom door.

"I guess we need a diversion," he said, and Carter gave him a look. "Give me the basket."

She handed it over, and Danyel tucked it under one arm. "When you get your shot, take it," he said, and stepped out of the shadows.

He made no attempt at concealment, but even so he was within twenty feet of the door before the guard stiffened to attention.

"Who's there?"

"It is I," Danyel answered. He kept his voice calm and easy, an ordinary person on an ordinary, insignificant errand.

"Stop where you are." The Jaffa lifted his staff weapon, fire coiling in its opened tip.

Come on, Carter. "I'm sent with bread," he called, and lifted the basket slightly.

"Our meal came hours ago," the guard said. "What folly is this —?"

A single bolt of zat fire split the night, and the Jaffa sprawled forward into the dirt. Danyel grabbed the staff weapon, blinking to clear his sight, but there was no reaction from inside the armory, or anywhere around the walls. Carter darted to join him, and he handed her the staff weapon so that he could drag the Jaffa into the deeper shadow at the base of the wall. The door loomed open, a single lamp casting a faint light within.

If there had been another guard, he would already have given the alarm, and Carter nodded as though she'd read his thought. "Go."'

Danyel ducked inside, zat unfolded and ready, swiveled to cover every corner, but as he'd expected, the room was empty. "Clear."

"It's a start," Carter said, as she joined him. She set the basket on the table and began unloading the improvised bombs. "Let's hope the door isn't barred on the other side."

Danyel checked it, eased it open on its leather hinges. It was weird, she was his original Carter, the one he'd worked with for eight years before he'd gotten himself lost in the past, but she felt like a stranger now. "No, we're good."

"Right." Carter stuffed several of the bombs into her pockets, handed him the two with the timers. "You know how to set those, right?"

"My timeline only diverged a few years ago," Danyel answered. "I know how to use the timers."

"Right," Carter said again. The apologetic grimace was disconcertingly like Sam's. "Sorry. I forgot."

"No problem." Danyel eased the door open a little further, and together they peered out into the dimly-lit armory. The space was more crowded than he had remembered. There were racks of spears and shields toward the main door, as well as spears and unstrung bows, but the near end of the workshop was filled with the detritus of the peace, bronze ingot, stacks of hides, bundles of wood and huge unidentifiable baskets. The Jaffa had set up a powered light near the observer's narrow window, but they had shielded it and kept it turned low to keep from betraying their position. There were maybe half a dozen of them, more than he'd hoped, but the darkness and the clutter ought to provide enough cover.

"Up the right side," Carter said softly. "Behind that pile of metal?"

Danyel nodded — they didn't really want to burn the armory

down — and said, "And if I can get to it, closer to the main door?"

"Yeah." Carter squinted into the dark. "Four minutes, and four minutes forty-five?"

"Right." That should give him enough time to plant them and get back to Carter. He twisted the dials, hiding the flashing lights, and slipped forward between the piles of baskets. He could hear the Jaffa talking, though he couldn't make out the words. They sounded bored, though, and maybe a little fed up with the whole plan, and Danyel hoped they'd stay distracted.

He made it to the spot Carter had indicated without being seen, and crouched in the shadow of the piled bronze to wedge the first explosive into the space between two ingots. He slid the second device into a pile of arrow shafts, sweeping the floor around it in the probably vain hope of keeping any fire from spreading. No matter how careful they tried to be, they were probably going to set the place on fire — but it would be worth it, if they could rescue the queen.

He rejoined Carter, saw her check her watch, and nodded. She cracked the first of the fuses, and lobbed the bomb gently over the nearest pile of baskets. It landed with a definite thud, but before the Jaffa could react, the explosion came. Danyel ducked in spite of himself, saw Carter toss the next bomb, and then another. The Jaffa captain shouted, trying to get his men into order, and Carter aimed the next bomb directly at the observer. There were more shouts, mixed with screams from a wounded man, and someone fired blindly into the dark, the staff bolt crackling overhead. The captain shouted again, ordering his men after the attackers. Carter hefted the fake device, judging the distance, threw it so that it bounced and rolled almost to the captain's feet, and in the same moment the first of the timed devices went off, toppling the pile of ingots and knocking over a long rack of spears and shields. The Jaffa hesitated, but their captain shouted again, urging them forward. A second voice called for backup.

"Time to go," Danyel said, and Carter nodded.

They backed toward the workroom door, weapons ready. The Jaffa fired again, and then the second device exploded, drawing their fire. Danyel kicked open the workroom door, zat ready, and Carter ducked past him, darting into the shelter of the wall. He saw her beckon, and hurried across to join her in the shadows.

"Well, that certainly got their attention," he said, and Carter grinned.

"Let's just hope it gave Jack enough time—" She broke off, her face changing, and Danyel spun to look himself. More Jaffa were pouring out of the palace, armor snapping into place. Light flashed from the pyramid and the mothership perched at its tip, and an amplified voice shouted in Goa'uld, warning of intruders in the compound.

"That's not good," Danyel said. They weren't going to be able to meet up with Jack, he could tell that immediately. The best thing, the only thing they could do was to try and get out themselves, if they could manage it without getting killed or captured themselves—"Damn, we should have saved some of those bombs."

"I did," Carter said. "Only two, though."

"Nice."

"They come in handy," she said, and looked over her shoulder again. "OK, you said there was a side gate?"

"It'll be guarded," Danyel warned, but pointed along the wall. "This way."

Jack flattened himself against the mud-brick wall of the granary, staff weapon pressed against his side, waiting for the first explosion. There was a patrol, but it didn't come by here more than twice a night—more proof, if he'd needed it, that this was a trap—but if Danyel and Carter didn't get a move on, he was going to risk running into them. Something moved by the granary door, a slithering shadow, and he started to charge the staff weapon before he realized what it was. The cat hesitated, dead mouse dangling from her jaws, then darted away across the courtyard.

Jack let out his breath with a sigh. Danyel would have quoted a prayer, or some appropriate invocation; he was having a hard time not swearing aloud. Come on, he thought. It was times like these he really missed radio. Come on.

And then it happened, a flat crack that couldn't be mistaken for anything but what it was. A second explosion, louder, sounded almost on its heels, and he scurried across the gap, flattening himself against the back wall of the overseer's house. He waited for a moment, hoping the queen would hear and be ready to leave, but there was no sound of movement from inside. OK, he thought, plan B. Again. He lifted the bar carefully from its brackets, trying to make as little noise as possible, and eased the door open.

It was even darker inside, in what had to serve as the queen's bedroom, and he made himself wait until he could make out the pale lump of the pallet, the shapes of baskets and a tall jar, before he risked moving. The room was empty, and a dim light flickered in the main room; the queen said something, soft and soothing, and one of the boys made a smothered, unhappy sound.

"You will remain here until the alarm is past," a Jaffa said, and Jack swore under his breath. Fine. Plan C. There were more explosions from the armory, and shouted orders, and then the sound of a voice on a loudspeaker. That also wasn't in the plan, and Jack knew he didn't dare delay any further. He took a step, and kicked open the inner door, bringing his staff weapon up in the same moment.

"Get down!" he shouted, and the queen threw herself flat, sheltering both little boys beneath her body. Jack fired, dropping the Jaffa, swung around to find there were no other guards.

"He was alone," the queen said. "All the others went to join the fighting." Both boys were crying, and she sat up swiftly, pulling them against her. "Hush, hush now, we're all right. Your father's general has come for us, and all will be well."

The older boy checked his sobs, nodding, but the younger one buried his face in his mother's shoulder. She rose, lifting him with her, but the hiccupping sobs continued. "I'm sorry, O'Neill—"

"It's OK," Jack said. "Don't worry about it. We just need to move fast now."

The queen nodded.

"Prince," Jack said, the plan forming as he spoke. "I'm going to carry you. We're going to pretend to be a family, servants running away from the fight."

The queen nodded again, and slid her heavy wig from her head. She hadn't shaved her scalp in several days, and the new stubble was shorter than a Marine's. "Yes. We are running to the temple for shelter—who would think I would go there?"

"Exactly." Jack hoisted the older boy to his hip, a warm disconcerting weight. "Hold on tight, now," he said, and set the staff weapon reluctantly against the wall. He hated to leave it behind, but no servant would be allowed to carry one. Instead, he tucked his zat out of sight in his waistband, and held out his spare to the queen. "You know how to use this?"

She nodded. "I do," she said, and slipped the folded weapon between her breast and the still sobbing child.

"Let's go," Jack said, and herded them out the back door.

Danyel flattened himself in the narrow space between the scribes' workroom and their barracks next door. Carter pressed in tight beside him, stolen staff weapon ready.

"This doesn't look good," she said.

"No." No, it didn't, not with the Jaffa pouring out of the pyramid and spreading out across the courtyard, effectively blocking them from reaching the tunnel. The palace was in an uproar, light blazing up as servants lit torches and human attendants joined the Jaffa. Right now, there was confusion, but it wouldn't be long before someone got things under control.

"What about this gate?" Carter asked.

Danyel risked a glance out of their hiding place. The side gate, intended for servants coming and going from the river, would be barred for the night, and should be guarded, but— He squinted, wishing there were a way he could get new glasses. It looked as though most of the guards had been pulled away from the gate. "It's clear," he said, "but there's no cover."

"Time for another diversion," Carter said, and her teeth gleamed white as she grinned.

"Let's not blow up anything vital," Danyel said, but she was already sliding through the gap between the buildings, an improvised bomb ready in her hand.

"So pick something non-essential," she said over her shoulder, and Danyel paused.

"OK. OK, there, that little building, the chief scribe's house." The chief scribe and his family had joined Hor-Aha; there was a decent chance the building was empty. Certainly there were no lamps inside, no sound of movement.

"Right." Carter was busy with the C4, shaping it to stick against the wooden door. "OK, there's no timer, so when I break this—"

Danyel nodded. "Run."

"Yeah." She looked around. "Back where we came from ought to be far enough—"

"Just—hurry," Danyel said. He heard her take a breath, and then her shoulders moved.

"Go!"

They raced for the shelter of the scribes' barracks, had barely pressed themselves into the narrow space when the bomb went off, a blast of heat on Danyel's back. He didn't look, kept pushing forward, hearing the new shouts, screams of fear and confusion. He hoped no one had been in the house, and put that thought aside. Ahead, the gate was unguarded, the Jaffa on duty drawn by the explosion, and he nodded.

"We're clear."

"Go," Carter said again, and moved to cover him.

Danyel sprinted across the open courtyard, flattened himself against the gate. The Jaffa were gone, but the heavy bar was still firmly in place. It would take both of them to lift it. He unfolded his zat, and waved Carter across. "Help me get the bar down."

Carter set her staff weapon against the wall, and grabbed one end of the bar. Together they levered it free, and Danyel hauled on the massive door. It groaned, but moved, and he put his full weight against it, dragging it further open. Carter snatched up the staff weapon again, covering them both.

"Trouble," she said.

Danyel glanced over his shoulder, saw a troop of Jaffa running toward them, their officer shouting orders. "One last bomb?"

"Yeah." Carter had it in hand, snapped the fuse and threw it toward the oncoming Jaffa. "Go!"

Danyel slipped through the open gate. There was no cover there, nothing but open ground between the road and the gate, that and the track the led to the reeds bordering the river. He turned toward the road, but he could see Jaffa there, coming in from the checkpoint further up the road.

"That way," Carter said, and pointed to the river.

"Um, that's not a good idea," Danyel said, but he couldn't see another choice.

"Why not?"

"Crocodiles."

Carter looked over her shoulder, gave a little shrug. "Better than Jaffa," she said, and plunged toward the reeds.

CHAPTER TWENTY-FIVE

THE PRINCE clung like a limpet, burying his head against Jack's shoulder. In the queen's arms the baby was wailing, but that was all right, made them look just like all the other civilians fleeing for the temple. Jack kept his head down, putting his body between the queen and the onrushing Jaffa, steering them both to the shadows as much as possible without it looking suspicious. If they could just make it to the temple — and then they were there, scrambling up the steps, the baby's shrieks seeming even louder in the lamp-lit antechamber.

"Silence, there!" someone shouted, and the queen ducked her head, curling her body around the baby as she tried to quiet him. There were a lot of people in the outer precinct, Jack realized, servants and priests awakened by the fighting, most of them half-dressed and confused as well as afraid.

"Back," he said quietly, and the queen edged toward the wall, still cooing to the baby. His cries had eased, and now he snuffled unhappily against his mother's breast. The queen rocked him, bouncing back and forth, and looked at Jack.

"Where now?"

Jack looked quickly around, trying not to be too obvious. They were on the right side, at least, but they needed to get into the inner corridor, where the tunnel opened, and right now the priests were blocking those doorways, keeping the servants herded together in the outer rooms.

"O'Neill."

Jack turned slowly, stitching a look of confusion onto his face. "Sorry?" He stopped abruptly, recognizing the chief priest of Horus, who gave him a conspiratorial smile.

"We were told to watch for you. This way."

Jack touched the queen's shoulder, and they slipped into the shadows, following the young priest. He was a nephew of the queen mother's, Jack remembered, or at least some sort of cousin, and he had her delight in politics.

"Has Danyel been here?" he asked.

The priest shook his head. "No, O'Neill, though we will watch for him."

Crap. Danyel and Carter should have been at the temple ahead of them. Jack killed that thought, made himself concentrate on the business at hand. "Can you close the tunnel behind us?"

"That was my intention, O'Neill. But we must hurry. Right now, everything is in disarray—"

But not for much longer, Jack thought. It wouldn't take long for the Jaffa to figure out Carter's bombs were ineffectual, and then they'd go looking for the queen. And then the place would be locked down tight, and once the Jaffa knew what they were looking for, it would be impossible to hide.

"Here," the priest said. They had reached the end of the side corridor, where the lamplight barely reached and the wall painting looked chipped and tattered. Chipped because it was the hidden entrance, Jack realized, and set the prince down to help work the panel loose. More paint fell, and he winced. The priest met his eyes.

"It will hold a little longer, I think. If there is no search."

"So we'd better hurry," Jack said.

The queen ducked under the low lintel without hesitation, but the prince hesitated.

"I—there might be scorpions."

The queen's breath caught in something between a laugh and a sob. "There are none, my son. Take my hand."

"I'll light the lamp as soon as we get the door closed," Jack said. "Hang on just a little longer."

He ducked into the tunnel after the boy, stooped to help the priest work the panel back into place. He found the lamp where it should be, and flint and tinder with it, and coaxed the flame to life. In its wavering light, the queen's face looked drawn and thin.

"Can we rest, O'Neill? Just for a little while?"

"We need to keep moving," he said. "But soon. When we get to the end of the tunnel."

She nodded, and shifted the baby to her other shoulder.

"I can take him for a bit," Jack said. "If you'll carry the lamp."

"No," the queen said, with a sideways smile. "Though I thank you. But you must have your hands free."

In case of trouble. Jack nodded. "Let's go."

Carter's penlight swept quickly over the reeds, picking out a narrow path, and then she'd hooded it again. Something coughed away to their right, and Danyel grimaced.

"Was that—?" Carter began, and he nodded.

"Yeah."

Carter flicked the light in that direction, and two gold disks shone briefly out of the dark. Danyel caught a glimpse of a narrow, lumpy head and one thrashing foreleg, and then the crocodile turned away, vanishing among the reeds. A few moments later, there was a splash as it entered the water.

"Well," Carter said, and sounded distinctly shaken. This was probably not the time to tell her that was one of the small ones, Danyel thought. He looked back the way they'd come, wondering if maybe it wouldn't be better to try for the road after all, but he could see lights and movement, the Jaffa fanning out to search.

"There should be a boat," he said, and hoped he was right.

"And if there isn't?" Carter gave him a look.

"Well, I don't think swimming is a good plan," Danyel said. "There will be a boat. The fishermen always leave them here."

"I hope so." Carter shone the light ahead of them, picking out the trail. "How many shots does it take to bring one of those things down?"

"From a zat?" Danyel paused. "I've never really tried."

"I'll file that as 'a lot,'" Carter said.

They were getting close to the river's bank, the ground soft and muddy underfoot. In the distance, they could hear shouted orders, but Danyel couldn't make out the words, hoped they were going in another direction. The fishermen who served the palace usually left their boats drawn up along here, convenient to the kitchen gate; surely there would be one.

"There," Carter said, and Danyel gave a sigh of relief. There were three of them, drawn up together in a narrow cleared space. They were all small, but they'd definitely hold two people. Carter's light flicked over the nearest one, picking out paddles and rope and a roll of linen. There was a box of hooks, and baskets for the fish as well.

"OK," Danyel said. "You go first."

They got the boat down to the river's edge, and Carter scrambled into the bow, keeping her body low. Danyel pushed it the rest of the way in and clambered after her, groping fro the paddle. The boat rocked alarmingly, and then steadied.

"OK," Carter said. She had found her paddle, held it with reassuring competence. But of course she'd been through all the Air Force survival training, not to mention eight or nine or ten years with SG-1, so of course she'd know. Not like Sam, though Sam had learned. "Now what?"

"We're heading downstream, which is a mercy," Danyel began, and a beam of light stabbed out from the bank.

"Crap," Carter said. "Get down."

Danyel stretched out on the boat's damp bottom, reaching for the roll of linen to pull it over them. His head was pressed into Carter's thigh, the toe of her boot digging uncomfortably into his belly. He could see the light sweeping overhead, bright through the coarse cloth, but so far it hadn't focused, hadn't found them. He lay still, counting his heartbeats, a hundred, two hundred, five hundred. He could feel Carter tensed against him, ready to explode into action if they were spotted, but the light swept over them at irregular intervals, and never settled. The boat drifted, bobbing gently on the current. Danyel thought they might be traveling sideways, but there was no way to be sure. All they could do was wait.

The stable area was quiet for now, but Jack knew it wouldn't last. He busied himself hiding the trapdoor again, brushing the dirt over it until all the cracks were hidden, while the queen nursed the baby, and the older boy sprawled beside her, sound asleep. He moved to the window again, seeing lights moving along the palace walls, looked back at the hidden trapdoor. Danyel and Carter weren't coming: if they were, they'd have been here by now. And he didn't dare wait much longer, or he and the queen and the children would be caught by the sunrise before they could get into the safety of the countryside.

"We need to go," he said, and the queen made a face.

"So soon?"

"The night's half over," Jack said. Half over, and I don't know where half my people are. He looked around, found a stick, and carved words in the dirt floor: *gone fishin'*. Only the team would know what that meant, that he'd been there, and was safe, at least for now. "We need to go," he said, gently, and the queen rose with a groan.

"Come on, son," he said, and picked up the older boy, who stirred, complaining, but didn't wake.

The queen shifted the baby to an easier position and squared her shoulders. "I'm ready," she said, and followed him into the night.

They took the long road, the track that wound away from the palace into the desert, and then back again to join the main road. Once they had to hide from a Jaffa patrol, crouching among scrub and stones until the men were past, but otherwise the night was quiet. At dawn they found themselves near a small village, and traded Jack's necklace for food and a full waterskin, gossiping while they ate. The Jaffa had been through during the night, searched all the houses, and found nothing. Still, it was better not to linger, just in case they were to return. Jack took the hint, and moved them on.

And then it was just walking, a man and a woman and their children, ordinary people on the road from one village to another, unremarkable. The older boy demanded to walk for a while, and Jack carried the baby so that the queen could watch him; when the prince grew tired and cranky, Jack carried him again.

Finally, the house loomed on the horizon, a thread of smoke rising above the compound's walls, and the queen drew a shaken breath.

"O'Neill. I did not entirely believe —"

"Nor did I," Jack said, quietly. "But here we are."

Their approach had been seen, and soldiers came to meet them, Hor-Aha at their head. He embraced his wife, who promptly burst into tears. The baby set up a wail as well, and she laughed through the tears, bouncing him to silence. Hor-Aha rested his head on her shoulder, tears bright in his own eyes, then stooped to embrace his son.

"I'm in your debt, O'Neill," he said. "Again."

"Don't worry about it," Jack said. "Did Danyel and Carter make it back yet?"

Hor-Aha paused, and shook his head. "We have not seen them."

Damn. Jack turned to look over his shoulder, squinting into the sun as though he could will them into existence, conjure them up out of the dust of the road. "They'll be here," he said. Whatever he had to do to make it happen.

The boat ground to a stop, its flat keel digging gently into the mud. Danyel tensed beneath the concealing linen, waiting for a searching light to find them, for someone to shout from the shore. There was no way of telling how far they'd come, how long they'd been drifting with the current. A while, certainly, long enough for the damp to settle into his skin, so that he was very grateful for the warmth of Carter's leg against his chest. Maybe it was long enough, maybe they'd come far enough — and in any case, it wasn't safe to stay grounded like this. There were the crocodiles to worry about, and a beached boat was bound to draw intelligent interest as well. He propped himself up carefully on one elbow. The boat wobbled under him, but didn't break free.

"Careful," Carter said.

"Yeah." Danyel folded the linen down from his face, peered cautiously over the edge of the boat. It was still dark, the moon down and the first hint of the dawn lightening the eastern sky. There was a mist on the river, obscuring the far bank; they lay across the current, the boat's bow resting gently on a finger of mud that extended from the near shore. Nothing was moving, not even a night bird, and he sat up slowly, shivering as the night air hit him. Carter did the same, and shoved the crumpled linen toward him.

"You'll want that."

"Thanks." Danyel wound it around his shoulders, trying to keep the driest parts next to his skin. He'd warm up soon enough once they got moving, but for now — it wasn't very pleasant.

Carter fumbled for her paddle. "Where are we?"

"I'm not entirely sure." Danyel found his own paddle at last, wedged into the stern. They were surrounded by mist and black water, the bank a darker shadow, the stars fading overhead. It was about an hour before true dawn, from the position of the stars. "Downstream from the palace."

"I had kind of figured that out," Carter said. "So what do we do now?"

"We get off this sandbank," Danyel said. "And then — keep going downstream, I think. We'll find a village soon enough, there are enough of them along the river. We'll get our bearings there."

"OK." Carter dug her paddle into the mud, pushing them away, and Danyel backed water at the same time. The boat rocked, but didn't move.

"Again," Carter said, and pushed harder. The paddle slipped, flipping a clot of mud away with a splash, but this time the boat rocked free. Carter fell forward, caught herself, and Danyel backed water as hard as he could.

"Quick, before we're stuck again—"

Carter dug deep with her own paddle, and together they got the boat turned and steadied, steering around the tip of the sandbank. Danyel relaxed a little, setting himself to paddle, and after a moment Carter matched his stroke. Down the river, then, he thought, and when the sun comes up, we'll know where we are. We'll find a village and make our way home—his home, not Carter's. And Carter—Carter wasn't dead. They'd really done it, fixed the time line so that SG-1 had never taken the puddle jumper back in time to find Ra's ZPM. Jack, the original Jack, and Teal'c, and Carter had never been killed in the rebellion. It was as though a weight lifted from his shoulders, a guilt he thought he'd put behind him long ago. It had been his bad idea that had started it, his bad idea that had gotten them all killed, but they'd managed to fix it, Jack and Sam and Teal'c and the other self he hadn't met. No one had died, and he—had Abydos again. Or something better.

He was grinning like an idiot, and Carter glanced over her shoulder. "What?"

He thought for a moment about parrying the question, pretending it was nothing, but in that moment he couldn't bear anything less than honesty. "You're alive," he said, and Carter looked back at him again.

"What—oh."

"It worked," Danyel said. "We managed to stop my stupid plan from ever happening, and everything's all right. Well, more or less, and assuming that we manage to drive off Ra, but—"

He stopped, not sure he was making sense, but Carter nodded. "Doesn't it bother you?" she asked, after a moment. "Being stuck here, I mean. We could probably bring you back, I don't think it would disrupt the timeline too much."

"It doesn't," Danyel said. "Bother me. And I don't want to go back. I'm happy here." He paused, trying for a lighter touch. "Besides, two of Jack in one place..."

"Might be awkward," Carter agreed, but he thought she'd heard what he hadn't said.

They paddled on in silence, the light slowly spreading along the horizon, paddling just hard enough to keep the boat steady in the current. The air was warmer now, with day approaching, but Danyel was still glad of the linen around his shoulders.

By the time the sky had lightened enough for them to see the opposite bank, Danyel was fairly sure he knew where they were. They were still upstream of the house, but only by a few hours' walk. If they were lucky, they were still above the potters' village, and they could get food and water there. He was definitely hungry, and once the sun came up, they'd need water.

The sky to the east glowed, red, then gold, Horus ascending, and the first white-hot sliver of the sun-disk rose above the horizon. It was no wonder people worshiped the sun, he thought, not for the first time. Sunrise over the black land came like a blast of trumpets, the god leaping up with a shout, pouring light and life onto the plains. Carter shipped her paddle and they drifted as the sun rose, the enormous disk pulling free of the horizon, the haze puddling at its base as though it was formed from a bed of molten iron.

"It's spectacular," she said at last, when the sun had risen far enough that they could no longer look at it. "No wonder you want to stay."

That wasn't why, or not the only reason. But he couldn't deny that it was part of it, either, these moments of pure, heart-stopping beauty. An ibis lifted from the reeds, black against the glowing sky, and his breath caught in his chest. "It doesn't hurt," he said, and lifted his paddle again.

The current was flowing faster here, and there was more debris in the river, coming probably from one of the villages they had passed in the dark. Danyel did his best to steer around the largest of the floating objects, but first one and then another thumped against the low sides. Something else scraped unpleasantly against the underside of the hull, and a few minutes later Carter said, "I hate to mention it, but my feet are getting wet."

"Yeah. Mine, too." Danyel couldn't see a hole, but he could definitely feel that there was more water than there had been. It was coming in more quickly, too. He could see the smoke of cooking fires rising from the potters' village, a mile or so ahead, maybe a little less. They'd probably make it, if the leak didn't get any worse.

They covered maybe a third of the distance before Carter had to stop paddling to bail, and it wasn't long after that that Danyel began angling toward the bank. The reeds grew thickly here, breaks had the trodden, polished look of crocodile wallows: not at all where he would have chosen to land, but choice didn't have anything to do with it.

Carter emptied another pot-full of water over the side. "It's gaining on me," she said, and Danyel nodded.

"I'd noticed." He dug his paddle deeper into the current, the boat wallowing, awkward. "I'm going to put us ashore there—"

Carter dropped the pot she'd been using to bail, picked up her paddle, and together they drove hard for the bank. At last the bow touched the slick mud, and Carter drove her paddle hard into the ground. Danyel sloshed his way forward, and together they dragged the boat the rest of the way onto the shore. Water spilled out over the stern, and finally Danyel saw where a seam had split. There would be no repairing that, not with anything they had in hand. That meant they'd have to walk the rest of the way, first to the village and then home: not impossible, not even that difficult, but first they had to get out of the reeds.

Carter drew her zat, letting it unfold to check the mechanism. Danyel did the same, scanning the ground for what he hoped would be a safe path. And then they both heard it, a grunt and a roar and a rushing through the reeds. Danyel flung himself aside, saw Carter dodge the other way, and then they both brought zats to bear. They fired together, and then again. The crocodile staggered as it turned, but gathered itself for another rush. Danyel backed away, firing, heard and saw Carter's zat blasts hit home along the animal's back. And still it kept coming, slower now, but still digging its claws deep into the mud, hauling itself forward. The narrow jaws opened, showing crooked teeth and puffy flesh. Danyel aimed for the head, the tiny brain, and fired twice more. Carter fired, too, and the crocodile roared. It lifted its head, and then, abruptly, collapsed.

"Come on," Danyel said. He wasn't entirely sure the thing was dead, and he didn't want to wait to find out. "Let's go, we've got to get to the high ground, to the road..."

Carter gave the crocodile a wide berth—he guessed she wasn't all that sure it was dead, either—and together they scrambled up onto the road. They stood for a moment, breathing hard, and then Carter folded her zat.

"How big do you think it was?"

"About the biggest I've seen," Danyel said. It had to have been over nine feet long, even allowing for the exaggerating effects of pure terror, and it had taken far too many shots to finally put it down. Two shots to kill a human, but a crocodile?

"I hit it at least six times," Carter said. "And I'm guessing you did the same." She shook her head. "That was one tough crocodile."

"They grow that way here," Danyel said, and couldn't avoid a quick glance into the reeds. "We should probably get moving."

"Good idea," Carter agreed, and they set off down the road.

CHAPTER TWENTY-SIX

"COLONEL Carter will no doubt return in good time," Teal'c said.

Cam shaded his eyes, looking out over the river in the early morning light. "Yeah." He didn't like it. He didn't like it one bit. Carter and Danyel had been gone way too long with no explanation that could be good. If they'd been captured...

Carolyn came and stood with them, a steaming mug of tea in her hands. She looked better, had some color in her face again, and Cam gave her a smile. "How's it going?"

"Not bad. I've had a look at some minor injuries, but there's nothing that stitches and time and rest won't fix." She took a quick sip and then stopped to blow on the surface of the tea to cool it. "Where's Colonel Carter?"

"Not back yet," Cam said. He understood why this job had given General O'Neill gray hair. He thought he could see some hairs turning himself.

Teal'c frowned, turning abruptly, and Cam cut off whatever Carolyn had been going to say to follow his gaze in the sky with the long practice of someone used to spotting aircraft.

"What's that?" Carolyn said, looking up at the glint of silver that approached far too rapidly.

"I believe it is another puddle jumper," Teal'c said evenly.

"Crap." Cam swung around. "Teal'c, get O'Neill and Hor-Aha. We've got a problem here. And get Daniel too."

Carolyn grabbed his arm. "Wait. Does that mean...?"

"It means the Ancients got tired of us not answering the phone," he said.

The other puddle jumper vanished suddenly, cloaking no doubt when it registered the mothership parked at Giza. But that didn't mean it was gone. There was a wind that came from nowhere, a cloud of dust blowing up from the courtyard, whipping around Teal'c as he hurried back into the house. Sam came out, shading her eyes and looking up, O'Neill just behind her, and Cam jogged over to him.

"What's up?" O'Neill shouted above the whipping wind.

"Another puddle jumper," Cam said, his P90 at port arms. Best to be prepared, though he didn't think it was likely the Ancients would shoot first and ask questions later.

"Landing," O'Neill said, straightening himself up as the wind began to die. In a moment a familiar stubby shape materialized, a puddle jumper just like theirs.

Only not. This jumper had been through the wringer. Cam could see that in a heartbeat. The surface was pitted and scorched, the windscreen cracked along one side, and the surface was not smooth because here and there bits had been welded on, panels removed and cable tacked across the smooth hull. This puddle jumper was an old wreck, barely flying, held together with spit and duct tape. The back gate opened.

It was the woman from the messages, her hands held well away from her body as she carefully came down the ramp. She wore loose trousers of heavy brown cloth and a white wrap shirt, her black hair pulled back in a long pony tail. Her eyes went to the weapon in Cam's hands, flickered over the others and back to him, saying something that of course he didn't understand.

"Hi," Cam said, the muzzle pointed away from her. She clearly knew what firearms were. "I'm Colonel Cameron Mitchell." Of course that would mean as much to her as whatever she was saying did to him.

Daniel came hurrying out of the house and stopped, sizing up the situation in a moment. "OK." He burst into another long series of words Cam didn't understand.

O'Neill nudged him. "Here we go again."

"Welcome to the Black Land," Daniel said in Ancient. "This is the realm of Hor-Aha, who is the Lord of the Two Lands. I am Daniel Jackson."

The woman nodded back gravely. "I am Ai, First Engineer of the Mishihase."

"You're an Ancient?"

Ai put her head to the side. "I do not know what you mean."

"Are you one of the people who came to this planet from the city of Atlantis?" Daniel asked.

Her expression cleared and she came to the end of the ramp, her hands still held plainly in view. "No. My mother's father was one who came as a man, and my father's mother came as a baby in arms, carried through the Ring with the other transport orphans from Tinun. My other grandparents were Mishihase." Her eyes flickered over the assembled group, Hor-Aha appearing in the doorway behind with Teal'c. "But you must also be a child of Atlantis, or at least far-kindred."

Daniel nodded, conscious of everyone waiting for him to translate, but feeling like he ought to go on a bit first.

"Some of us are, though I am not. O'Neill is, and also Dr. Lam." He gestured to them respectively.

"Which settlement are you from?" Ai asked, her brow creasing. "I didn't think that any of the other gateships survived, and yet we picked one up on our sensors."

"From none of them," Daniel said, taking a deep breath. "It's a long story." He switched back to English. "This is Ai," he said. "She's the engineer of a group of descendants of the Ancients that I think, though eastern history is not my specialty, are probably in the Kuril Islands or Hokkaido, a place called Mishihase." That was his best guess, anyway. "I think this is going to be a long conversation, folks. It's probably best if I sit down and talk to her and we don't all stand in the courtyard to do it." Hor-Aha looked confused, and Daniel repeated the whole thing again in Egyptian.

"OK," Mitchell said, herding people back toward the house.

"You do that, Daniel. Figure out what her story is. But you know..."

"I know I can't tell her too much," Daniel said. "I get that." Though how he was supposed to make any of this make sense to someone who could perfectly well look at their stuff and tell it had never come from this time and place, or from the Goa'uld either...

He invited her to come inside and have refreshment, sitting quietly in a corner of the main living room while everyone else tried not to stare. O'Neill brought them something to drink, bending over with a raised eyebrow in his white boxer shorts and gold necklace to deposit two stoneware cups of beer like the most surreal cocktail waitress Daniel had ever seen. He was never going to let Jack live this down once they got back. Provided their timeline stayed intact and they could get back.

Ai took a polite sip. "You said you were not from one of the settlements?"

"No," Daniel said. And that was a line of questioning he ought to avoid, at least until he got a better read on her. "How many are there?"

"There were seven originally," Ai said. "When we came to this world as a refuge we knew that our numbers were too small for us to be viable as a population. We had dropped below genetic viability, and we could not replicate our great cities with the very limited supplies we had and the small group of people who could build the things we used. We were refugees, Daniel Jackson, not a colony. Many of those who came were people of the City, not soldiers or engineers or builders. Many of them were people who had been evacuated to the City from other places, from other stands against the enemy—children, non-combatants, the old. Even we get old, Daniel Jackson."

"I know," he said. "And so you split up?"

"We divided into seven settlements, as we knew our footprint on this world must be lighter. Our scouts and ambassadors had come here for some years, and we knew a number of friendly peoples who would welcome the things we brought. We brought doctors and better ways of fishing and farming, things that were useful. There were seven places where it seemed we could live among friends and benefit one another. I am from the settlement in Mishihase."

"The clusters of the ATA gene," Daniel said. It all made sense. Seven clusters around the globe, the ATA gene spreading from places where the Ancients had once lived, southern Britain and the horn of Africa south of the Gulf of Aden, the Yucatan Peninsula and the Bulgarian Black Sea coast...

"The ATA gene?"

"That's what we call the genetic marker that allows one to use your technology," Daniel said.

Ai nodded. "Yes, we know what that is. It's recessive, and therefore becomes rarer the further removed one is from the people of Atlantis." She crossed her legs, taking another sip of the beer without looking away from his face. "I am the only one of my three siblings who express it."

"Which is why you can fly a puddle jumper. Er, gateship."

"Yes." Ai nodded again. "I carry it from two grandparents, a double recessive expressed from each parent." Her eyes slid away to Carolyn, who was talking with Sam on the far side of the room. "But your friends are also children of Atlantis?"

"Through many, many generations." Daniel shook his head. He was going to have to come out with it sooner or later. "How did you know about the Goa'uld?"

"As you no doubt know, those who came from Atlantis have lifespans many times longer than the people of this world. When they had dwelled here many years these other travelers came, the parasites you call the Goa'uld. We thought they might become friends, but we were wrong. They came first on a slave raid, surprising the people of the Circle Sea settlement and killing many and taking many more. After that we fought. We did not have many gateships left by then, as time and age took their toll, but we did what we could. We used an installation beneath the ice armed with the last weapons of Atlantis, and for a time we drove them off. Years passed. And then they returned. Once more we drove them away. Once more they returned." Ai shook her head sadly. "But we are not what we were. Those who came from Atlantis are gone, for the most part, for age catches even us. This is the last gateship we have, the last on the planet. I risked all on this flight, bringing no one with me for I could ask no one to share the danger, in hopes that the other gateship we sensed was that of friends who could help us, some scattered remnant of our people. Without the gateships, contact between the settlements has been lost, and when last the Goa'uld raided Mishihase we barely managed to protect ourselves." Her eyes searched his face. "So who are you, Daniel Jackson? If you are also children of Atlantis and their allies, where do you come from? Who are your friends descended from through many generations? I do not believe your doctor is from the Circle Sea or the Coast of Birds. Her face is more like to Mishihase, but I have never seen her before."

Daniel took a deep breath. "We're from the future," he said.

It took a while to get through the explanations, and Cam was beginning to wonder just how much Daniel was telling her as they sat in the corner and sipped the thin beer. He was about to go over and remind Daniel that he was supposed to be getting information, not giving it, when there was a shout from the compound. He turned to the door, felt his shoulders sag with relief as he saw the other Daniel and Carter crossing the dusty compound. They looked as though they'd been dragged through a mud puddle, but it was obvious they were unhurt, and he couldn't help grinning.

Neither could O'Neill. He slapped Danyel on the back and offered Carter an approving nod to go with the grin. "We were starting to think the crocs got you."

Danyel rubbed a streak of dirt on his jaw. "Yeah, well."

"You know better than to go swimming," O'Neill said.

"We didn't have much choice," Danyel answered. "Look, I'm filthy and dead tired and I want a bath and bed, and I'm sure Colonel Carter feels the same."

O'Neill waved his hand. "Go, go."

Danyel paused, gave him a sudden grin. "And yes, thank you, it's good to be back."

"Crocodiles?" Cam said, to Carter, who nodded.

"Yeah. One really big one that didn't like where we decided to land."

Which begged the question of what they were doing on the river in the first place, Cam thought, but he knew the simple answer — escaping — and Carter looked just as tired as Danyel.

"Tamit will draw you a bath, too," O'Neill offered.

"Thanks," Carter said, and she trudged after Danyel toward the back of the compound.

Cam glanced back at the main house — he really should go find out what Daniel was saying — but before he could move on, one of the Egyptian soldiers came trotting over to O'Neill. Cam thought he heard his own name, and sure enough O'Neill lifted a hand.

"Hang on a minute, will you? Seems this Marik wants to talk to us."

"I don't really want to talk to him," Cam said. He sighed. "Do we know what he wants?"

"Nope." O'Neill squared his shoulders. "I guess we should find out, Colonel."

Hor-Aha had ordered the Tok'ra confined in a small room at one end of the stable building, with a high window too narrow for a man to fit through, and a single door. It was open, Cam saw, letting in what breeze there was, and Marik was sitting against the back wall, the guard watching him impassively. Marik scrambled to his feet at their approach, and the soldier laid his spear across the opening, barring his way.

"Colonel Mitchell," Marik said. "And General O'Neill. Thank you for coming."

O'Neill looked at Cam. "He's all yours."

"Thanks very much," Cam said, under his breath. He said, more loudly, "What do you want, Marik?"

"To make amends," Marik answered.

"Boy, that's a tall order," O'Neill said.

Cam pretended he hadn't heard, though he pretty much agreed. "Did you have something particular in mind?"

"You're going to fight Ra," Marik said. "No, no one's told me, but there isn't any alternative. Let me fight with you. I'm Tok'ra, it's what I was born to do."

"Sorry." There was no way in hell he was going to let Marik out of that cell, not after the trouble he'd already caused. Cam shook his head for emphasis. "You're staying right here."

"I can be of use to you," Marik protested. "I'm from your own time—"

"And were willing to screw up the timeline to get what you wanted," Cam said. "Sorry. You're staying right here."

He turned on his heel, and O'Neill moved with him, nodding. "Good call, Colonel."

"The Tok'ra are just pure trouble," Cam said, with more bitterness than he'd meant, and headed for his own quarters.

"So."

Jack looked up to see Danyel looming over him, and made a gesture that encompassed both the empty stool beside him and the beer jar. Danyel gave a little smile and seated himself, reaching for the ladle.

"Do we actually have a clever plan?" he asked, after a moment, and Jack sighed. He'd been hoping to avoid that question just a little longer, but, no, no one—least of all Danyel—was going to let him off the hook.

"I told you my clever plan," he said. "And now we've got three puddle jumpers."

"One of which barely flies," Danyel said. He paused. "But, on the plus side, we've got someone else with the ATA gene and a working knowledge of Ancient policy."

"What exactly did you — I mean him, the other Dr. Jackson." Jack shook his head in frustration. "What did he tell her?"

Danyel gave him a sideways look. "You know I wasn't here."

"Uh-huh."

Danyel sighed. "Well, if it was me — I'd have told her the truth. It just makes sense."

"Not to mention you're a terrible liar," Jack said. "And she's an Ancient."

"Not exactly," Danyel said, in the tone of voice he reserved for lost causes. "She has the ATA gene, just like you."

"But she's actually met some Ancients," Jack said. "She's a lot closer to one than I am."

A shadow crossed Danyel's face, was gone so quickly Jack couldn't be sure of what he'd seen. "That has good and bad points."

Jack rested his back against the wall. "If you — the other you — told her what's going on, what's that going to do to the timeline?"

"Potentially bad things," Danyel said. "But — I assume I, he, got some kind of promise, and she must know what it would mean to her descendants. The Ancients are gone, Jack, even now. She's got nothing to gain by changing the future."

"That you know of," Jack said, but he felt obscurely reassured. "OK, we go with that for now. Which leaves us with 3 invisible spaceships and somebody who was around the last time one of Ra's buddies got his butt kicked. That has to improve the odds."

"What does?" That was Sam, dropping to sit cross-legged beside them. She had a shallow basket under her arm, held it out to reveal rounds of bread still warm from the oven.

"Ai," Danyel said, and Sam blinked before the name registered.

"Oh, right. She seems very sensible. And she has a lot of courage, flying here in that wreck." She paused. "I think we ought to give her as many parts as we can spare."

"You're assuming she's going back," Jack said.

"We can't just keep her," Danyel said.

"Can't we?" Jack reached for his beer, not meeting their eyes. "That's one way of making sure she doesn't tell anybody anything that's going to change the timeline."

"That's — not a good idea," Danyel said.

"It would be wrong," Sam said briskly. "And, from a practical standpoint, extremely difficult. Unless we're planning to destroy the puddle jumpers, which I think is a bad idea, we'd have to keep her locked up forever. We're not going to do that."

"We're not?" Jack smiled in spite of himself.

"No," Sam said. "We're not."

Vala eyed the stranger — Ai, she called herself, a child of the Ancients. Vala wasn't at all sure how she felt about the Ancients in general. No matter how much Daniel argued that the Ancients couldn't act, that there were good reasons to think that intervention would only make things worse, and the Ori were certainly some evidence of that, she found it hard to come up with a description more positive than "unhelpful." But Ai wasn't an Ancient, she reminded herself, and even if she had been, she wasn't one of the Ascended ones who had all the power, but never intervened. She was more like Myrddin, or really one of Myrddin's grandchildren, and from the look of the puddle jumper, her colony was well on its way to losing itself in the local population.

She looked lost, Vala thought, standing there with her arms folded just a little too tightly across her chest. There was a line between her eyebrows, the faintest hint of a frown, not displeasure but concentration — and had she been wearing that egg-shaped pendant before? It was remarkably undecorative, a pale gray ovoid much smaller than the hen's eggs she bought at the grocery store when she was trying to live like one of the Tau'ri, and Vala frowned in turn. If I was an Ancient, I'd have a way to translate unfamiliar languages discreetly, she thought, and put on her brightest smile.

"Darling!" she said, and made sure her voice was loud enough to reach Mitchell and the rest of SG-1, huddling beside the other puddle jumper. "That's a very pretty necklace. You don't mind letting me take a look?"

She reached for it as she spoke, and saw the moment that Ai surrendered.

"No, it's not just jewelry," Mishihase's First Engineer said. "It's a translator."

"A translator!" Vala repeated, for Mitchell's benefit. "How very clever of you!"

She had Mitchell's attention now, and Teal'c's, and they both turned and came to join her, Teal'c's eyebrows rising in unspoken question. Ai's mouth tightened, and then she relaxed with a rueful smile.

"You can't blame me for trying. It's always wise to find out as much as possible about strangers."

"Indeed," Teal'c said. "Then we may presume that this is an Ancient device?"

"It only works for those with the blood marker," Ai said.

"So it wouldn't do me or Teal'c any good," Mitchell said. "OK, I got that, not that I wanted it anyway. What I am concerned about—how much did Jackson tell you, anyway?"

"Enough to understand that you are worried about changing your people's past," Ai answered. "And, yes, that is a grave thing. But I submit that it is more important to drive Ra from this planet, and for that I believe you will find me useful."

"That doesn't necessarily mean we can afford to let you go," Mitchell said, and there was what sounded like genuine regret in his voice.

"Let us ford that stream when we reach it, and not before," Ai said. "In the meantime, do you want my help or not?"

Mitchell smiled slowly. "Yeah. We do."

CHAPTER TWENTY-SEVEN

HIS OTHER self was sitting cross-legged in the shade of the courtyard wall, squinting at a scroll unrolled in his lap. A younger scribe sat with him, busy with ink and reed pen, making notes as Danyel dictated to him. Daniel hesitated, not wanting to interrupt, but his other self looked up before he could back away.

"Nothing important," Daniel said quickly. "I can come back."

"No, we're done." Danyel looked at the scribe, who dipped his head.

"I will make the copies, Danyel, and bring them to Pharaoh."

"And one for Sa-Mantha, too, please."

"Of course." The scribe finished gathering up his equipment, and disappeared into the house.

Danyel looked up at him, squinting again. "I'd suggest going inside, but it's a lot less crowded here."

Daniel nodded. He was abruptly overtaken by a memory of everyone on Abydos crowding into Kasuf's tent. He and Sha're had ended up jammed into a corner, and she had ended up in his lap, which hadn't exactly helped him pay attention to the matter at hand... He shook the thought away. This was Egypt, not Abydos, and he had something equally important to deal with. "I wanted to talk to you about coming back with us," he said.

"I don't — I'm not sure that's possible," Danyel answered.

Daniel settled himself in the dirt at his other self's side, rested his back against the brick wall. This early in the morning they were still cool, and the shade was pleasant. "I think it is. In fact, I think you can all come back. If you want."

"It's taking a hell of a risk with the timeline," Danyel said.

"Not to mention that having two versions of us in the same place—I'm surprised we haven't had problems already. I've been worried about Sam. And Teal'c."

And not about us, Daniel thought, unsurprised. Or at least not that either of us would admit. He said, "That's right, you—our timelines diverged before that."

"Before what?"

"Before—" Daniel stopped, trying to think of a good way to sum up a situation that had been bizarre even by the relaxed standards of the SGC. "Due to an unfortunate incident involving massive energy weapons and a black hole, we ended up with I think it was sixteen versions of SG-1, all from different alternate universes, but no entropic cascade failure. The Carters and Dr. Lee theorized that the universes were all similar enough that there wasn't a problem. And our universes—well, they're different timelines within the same universe."

"I think that still makes them different universes," Danyel said. "Though certainly it would explain why you and I aren't having problems."

"And Sam and Teal'c—and Jack, though that's not entirely relevant in this case—may have been from a more different universe, but they're now firmly established in this one."

Danyel pushed his glasses into a more secure position. "I think I want to talk this over with Sam."

Daniel nodded. "Yeah."

"So." Danyel gave him a sidelong glance. "What did you really want?"

"I think you should come back," Daniel said. "All of you."

"I'm already there," Danyel pointed out. "Or—you know what I mean."

Daniel nodded. "And I say this without false modesty, two of us would be useful. As would two of Sam, and Teal'c—"

"Teal'c can't come," Danyel said. "Egeria needs him." He smiled then, not entirely pleasantly. "And what about Jack? One retired colonel, one active-service general—that's a bit awkward, don't you think?"

"We've done weirder," Daniel said, thinking of Jack's teen-aged clone, and Danyel nodded.

"OK, point. But—"

"You don't want to come back," Daniel said. He blinked, started. How had Mitchell noticed that, and he hadn't? This was himself he was talking about, he ought to know what he'd want. "That's what this is about. Never mind all the arguments, you don't want to leave."

Danyel tipped his head back so that it was resting against the wall. "No, I—I suppose I don't."

Why the hell not? Daniel swallowed the words, knowing how he'd react to a direct question, and narrowed his eyes at his other self. "And so you're going to talk everyone else into staying?"

"They can make their own choices," Danyel said. "Ask them."

"We will," Daniel said. "But—they're your friends. And it's a dangerous place to raise a child. Snakes, scorpions, diseases that could be cured in a heartbeat at home..."

"You think I don't know that? That Sam doesn't know that?" Danyel glared at him, then shoved himself to his feet. "Do you really think the SGC would just, I don't know, give us our old jobs back? Jobs Sam and Jack never actually had?"

"It would be a waste not to," Daniel answered, standing with him. He wasn't entirely sure it was true, but it was better to get them back first, and then worry about the details. "Are you being fair about this? This may be what you want, but what about them?"

Danyel's fists tightened. "That's a low blow."

"Is it?" Daniel paused, ready to duck when the other man took a swing at him. "Remember what happened the last time we stayed behind."

For a second, he thought Danyel was going to hit him, but then Danyel shook his head.

"No," he said. "This isn't Abydos." He turned on his heel

and walked away.

"Isn't it?" Daniel called after him, but there was no response.

"So this is the plan?" Carter asked. She hoped she didn't sound quite as dubious as she felt, but from the expression on Mitchell's face, he was thinking the same thing. "We're going to use the two — sorry, three — puddle jumpers to bluff Ra into leaving Earth for fear that the Ancients will retaliate."

"After you and her, the other you, figure out a way to keep Ra from taking the Stargate with him," Mitchell said. "Yep. That's it."

"I am in agreement with Colonel Carter," Teal'c said. "There are many unanswered questions about this plan."

"You think I hadn't noticed?" Mitchell asked. They were sitting in the doorway of the storeroom that they had been allotted as quarters, making the most of a mild breeze. Vala had acquired a parasol somewhere, Carter noted without surprise, as well as a jewel-handled fan. She could probably have a handsome young soldier to wave it for her if she made an effort.

"It's a typical Jack plan," Daniel said. He was looking tired, Carter thought, probably from the strain of translating so much. "OK, kids, let's try this incredibly unlikely idea, and see if we can't make it work."

He had O'Neill's intonation down perfectly, and Carter grinned in spite of herself. "The basic idea makes sense," she said. "We know that Ra doesn't want to risk being attacked by the Ancients — his mothership won't withstand a direct attack — and we also know he doesn't want the other Goa'uld to know he's screwed up. So if he leaves, and they bury the Stargate — he won't be back."

"It's the 'and now Ra leaves' part that I have doubts about," Daniel said.

"The main thing is to figure out how to make sure Ra doesn't take the Stargate," Carter said.

"Well, how'd they do it the last time?" Mitchell asked, after a moment.

"I don't think it was a problem," Carter said, and looked at Daniel. "Was it?"

"I've been talking to Daniel," Vala said. "The other Daniel, the mostly naked Daniel. He told me that they had the advantage of surprise. Ra panicked and fled, and they buried the Stargate behind him. He thought it simply wasn't worth Ra's time to come back, not now that he has other sources of human slaves seeded throughout the galaxy."

"I didn't think 'mostly naked Daniel' was speaking to you," Daniel said.

Vala smiled. "He changed his mind."

"You are not going to make me jealous of myself," Daniel said.

Mitchell cleared his throat. "So is there any reason to think that Ra won't react the same way this time?"

"I believe he has more at stake," Teal'c said. "From his perspective, he has been attacked. The Tau'ri invaded Abydos and stole a prim'tah. If he is to maintain his standing, and the loyalty of his Jaffa, he must punish them."

"So he's not going without a fight," Mitchell said.

"I do not believe so." Teal'c's expression was impassive.

"Great." Mitchell let his head fall back against the mud brick wall.

Carter reached for her water bottle and took a careful swallow. The biggest technical problem was to make sure that Ra couldn't take the Stargate with him, and that meant finding enough power somewhere to counteract the mothership's lifting beams. Maybe the time travel device — it had to use enormous power — though she didn't really like the idea of messing with one of Janus's devices. Maybe the gate itself? If she could figure out a way to tap the wormhole… Yes, if the wormhole could be tapped, she could increase the power in the jumper's inertial dampeners exponentially, use the jumper itself as an anchor. "I need to talk to Sam," she said, and the rest of the team gave her a startled look. "I have an idea."

"Save it for later." The voice was so like their own Jack's that she automatically pulled herself to something closer to attention. O'Neill stood at the corner of the building, incongruous in his linen shorts and heavy gold necklace. "We've got another problem."

The main room was even more crowded than the last time Pharaoh had held court, and it smelled strongly of sweat and garlic. Jack left them wedged into a corner by the door, and elbowed his way toward Hor-Aha, who sat in the center of the room, listening to a young man with a shaved head.

"A scribe or a priest," Daniel said, almost to himself. "A message from the palace?" He broke off, said something in Egyptian to the nearest gold-braceleted officer, and grimaced at the answer.

Mitchell prodded him. "What?"

"I'm not—"

"Share with the rest of the class, Jackson."

Daniel gave him a look. "Ra is preparing an assault. He knows where we are."

"That's not good," Carter said, and saw the same knowledge on the others' faces. Hor-Aha had maybe two hundred men, crack troops by his standards, but the Jaffa would cut them to pieces in a pitched battle. A guerilla campaign would stand more chance of success, but still—the odds were daunting.

Hor-Aha rose to his feet, and the room quieted, all eyes turning to him. He looked ordinary, Carter thought, just another skinny sun-browned guy with eyeliner and a heavy wig. She could see the sweat on his chest, and the worry lines bracketing his mouth. It was his father who defeated Ra the first time, not him. She hoped Jack was right, and he was up to the job.

The Pharaoh said something, and Daniel tipped his head to one side, began translating in a weary whisper.

"My people, there is word from the palace that Ra intends to attack within days. We're sending away the women and children, under the queen's command — his wife, not the queen mother — and keeping only those men of fighting age. They will defend our person and my house — this house — while our commander O'Neill once again faces Ra directly, with the weapons of the Ancients at his command. And together we will drive the false gods from the face of this world."

There was a cheer in answer, but Sam caught the same worried speculation in the Egyptians' eyes. This plan of Jack's was a huge gamble, there was no denying that. And if they couldn't pull it off, Hor-Aha's men had almost no chance of defeating the Goa'uld.

Hor-Aha lifted his hands again, and the room quieted as he began to speak.

"He's giving his orders," Daniel said. "Dividing up duties. Sending away some of his people —"

An older man burst out in complaint, but Hor-Aha shook his head firmly, took the man by the arm until he bowed in agreement.

"And some of them don't want to go," Daniel said. "Hor-Aha's telling him he's needed to take care of the young queen, and the princes. Ah. The plan is to be out of this house by sundown tomorrow, with the women and children sent south by water, and the rest of the men dispersed to other places. And we're going to stay here with the puddle jumpers and get ready to make Ra think we have an armada."

Hor-Aha finished with raised hands and something that might have been either exhortation or blessing, but Daniel didn't bother to translate. Instead, he looked at Mitchell. "So we're really going to do this?"

"Have you got a better plan?" Mitchell asked, and lifted a hand. "Gen — Colonel O'Neill! If I might have a word?"

Jack grinned, came slouching over to join them, but Carter recognized the worry in his eyes. "Absolutely, Colonel."

"Where exactly did this information come from?" Mitchell's voice was very even.

"From Aset and Teal'c." Jack met his eyes squarely. "You got a problem with that, Colonel?"

"I might." Mitchell took a careful breath. "You have to admit, it's very convenient for Ra. He makes us move well before we're ready, and to put the noncombatants on the move, which makes them vulnerable."

"Teal'c," Jack said. "And Aset." Danyel had come to join him, his eyes narrowing as he picked up the thread of the conversation.

"And Egeria," Mitchell said. "If it really is Egeria. Teal'c— our Teal'c—and I have been talking, and he thinks it's possible that a mature larva could effectively overhear what its Jaffa host was thinking, and could have figured out that claiming to be Egeria would save its life."

"That's pushing it," Jack said.

"I believe it is possible, O'Neill," Teal'c said.

"But you've got no proof," Danyel said.

"And neither have you," Daniel pointed out.

"What we have," Danyel said, "is, first, our Teal'c's word that this is Egeria. Second, she saved Aset's life, and third, we've spoken to Aset since Egeria took her as a host. It's clear that Egeria is acting like a Tok'ra, not a Goa'uld."

"We thought we were talking to Tanith's host, too," Daniel said, and Jack lifted his hand.

"OK, putting all that aside—what exactly do you expect us to do differently, Colonel Mitchell?"

Mitchell pulled up short, frowning. "I don't think there is anything, not at this point. But I think we do need to be aware that this 'Egeria' may not be on our side."

"We're going to need Aset's help," Danyel said, "Aset's and Egeria's. With her help, we've got a chance to reinforce Ra's fear of the Ancients, maybe manipulate him into making mistakes. She's incredibly useful."

"If you can trust her," Mitchell said, doggedly.

"I'd trust her with my life," Jack said. "And, yeah, I know

that's exactly what I'm doing. End of discussion."

Carter saw Mitchell's mouth tighten, but they both recognized that tone of voice. This wasn't an argument they could win, anyway, not when Jack was the Pharaoh's right-hand man.

"OK," Mitchell said. "What about Marik? Do you want to use him?"

"To do what?" O'Neill asked. "He can't fly a jumper, and he's a hell of a loose cannon. And if you think I'm going to trust him — you're out of your mind."

"You're trusting one Tok'ra," Cam said.

"It's not the same," O'Neill said.

He was right, Carter knew, and she cleared her throat. "How are you planning to let Teal'c and Aset know what to do?" she asked.

"I'm going to tell her," Danyel said. "I'll be heading to the palace once we're done. Nobody got a good look at me —"

"You hope," Mitchell interjected.

Danyel ignored him. "And anyway, all us humans look alike."

Carter opened her mouth to protest, and closed it again. If they were going to tell Egeria — and if they trusted her, they had to tell her; they needed all the advantages they could get — then sending a messenger was the smart way to do it. There was no risk of anything being garbled as it was repeated, or of a written message falling into the wrong hands. Plus there was a good chance that Aset didn't read Egyptian, and sending a note in Goa'uld was just stupid. No, the best thing was to let O'Neill and his people handle this part of the plan, and hope they knew what they were doing. She looked at Mitchell. "In that case, Colonel, I'd like to talk to Sam. I've got an idea of how we can keep Ra from taking the Stargate."

Mitchell nodded. "Go ahead."

"You said within days," Vala said, looking at O'Neill, and Carter stopped to listen. "How long do you think we have?"

"They won't come tonight," Jack said. "But tomorrow — it's possible. So we get as many people away tonight ourselves, and we have the jumpers ready to take off at first light."

"Why first light?" Daniel began, and then answered his own question. "For the Egyptians, of course. The true gods supporting us against the false."

"Well, there is that," Jack said, with a sudden grin. "But mostly I need my sleep."

CHAPTER TWENTY-EIGHT

AI HAD helped them rig working lights in the back of the jumper — Sam's own jumper, or so Sam thought of it, for all that Jack was the only one of them who could fly it — and was now curled in one of the front seats, drowsing if not entirely asleep. Carter slanted a glance toward her, and gave a little smile.

"Well, you can't blame her," Sam said, softly. "She's had a busy day."

Carter nodded. "Maybe we ought to send her back to the house and let her get some proper sleep?"

Sam considered — the idea sounded lovely, in fact, and just because she couldn't take time to sleep was no reason to punish anyone else — but finally shook her head. "No, once we get these crystal paths mapped out, she knows where the jumper systems link in."

"Yeah." Carter sat back on her heels, wiping the sweat from her forehead. Inside the jumper, it was still warm, though the night chill was beginning to seep in through the hull. "I'm worried about burning out the crystals when the wormhole opens."

"I think we're better off trying to make the connection — tap the wormhole itself — after it stabilizes," Sam answered. "I still think it might be better to use the time travel device as a power source. It's self-contained, and we don't have to worry about tapping the wormhole itself."

"Do we really know how it works?" Carter asked. "Well enough to make that big a modification, I mean. And —"

Sam nodded. "It's Janus. No, you're right, I don't want to fiddle with his work too much."

"It never ends well," Carter agreed.

They worked in silence for a little longer, tracing the jumper's modified power paths, and finally Sam straightened, one hand going to the small of her back. "That's the last of them."

"Yeah. They should hold." Carter worked her shoulders. "I wish I had a cup of coffee."

"You sound like Danyel." Sam settled herself against the wall where she had replaced the padding, and reached for the jug of water. "Sorry, I don't even have beer."

"That's probably just as well," Carter said. "I'm beat."

"Me, too." Sam passed the jug across, and Carter took it, drank carefully.

"What about the baby?" she asked, after a moment, and Sam sighed.

"I sent her and Tamit with the Queen," she said. "They should be all right regardless — regardless of how long it takes," she corrected, and knew Carter guessed what she had been going to say. "Not very comfortable for me," she said. "I'll have to pump and dump."

"What?"

"Manually express breast milk. Otherwise I'll hurt like hell." She shrugged. "Fortunately Ellie's getting big and eating real food some, so my volume is dropping. It's not as bad as it could be." She glanced at the other her, who was watching her with an expression of weird fascination. "Do you have children?"

"I'm not — not exactly," Carter answered, and leaned against the padded hull. "Cassandra — I guess you'd say she's my foster daughter. We found her on another planet, the last survivor, and a good friend of mine adopted her. After Janet, my friend, was killed in action, I kind of took over from her." She paused. "Not that I'm needed all that much. Cassie's grown now. She's just finished college."

Sam took another drink of water. She was hungry, too, but she'd finished her share of the day's rations long before. That was something Ellie wouldn't have, college, an entire world to travel. She'd spend her life here, the boundaries drawn by how far she could walk in a day, by the length of the Nile and the rhythm of the flood.

"You could come back with us," Carter said. "All of you. We could use you, that's for sure."

Go back. Sam took a long breath, and let it out slowly. Go back — no, go forward, because this was not her time, not the life where she'd been adrift and miserable, but the world that was supposed to have happened. The world where her father had lived and her mother had died and she'd become this other person, a colonel in the Air Force, this tough, competent other self who sat next to her in an Ancient spaceship in the middle of the night drinking water that tasted of the pottery that held it. A world where she would be nothing, an inferior copy — the same mousy self she'd been before. "I don't think that would work very well," she said.

"It would be a little weird," Carter said. Sam looked at her, and Carter shrugged. "OK, maybe it would be a lot weird. But we always need physicists, especially ones who can work with very strange things, which —" She waved at the jumper and the softly glowing crystals. "Clearly that's not a problem for you."

"That's not, but there are other problems," Sam said. "I haven't been a physicist for five years. I've been an engineer, a mathematician, an architect — I've been helping build what's going to be one of the greatest cities of the ancient world, and I'm happy doing it. I'm useful, and I'm happy. I don't actually want to leave."

Carter nodded as though she understood — and if anyone would, Sam thought, it was her other self. In this, at least, they weren't so different after all.

"I'm going to be offered the *George Hammond*," Carter said abruptly, looking down at her lap and then up as Sam must have looked blank. "The new battlecruiser. The only woman ever to command a starship."

"That's good, isn't it?" Sam asked.

"Yes. Of course it is," Carter said firmly. "But."

"But?"

"It will be two years, maybe three or four. If I do this, it's ending the old SG-1 forever. And it's closing a lot of doors in my personal life that won't ever open again. And I guess I'm a little…ambivalent."

Sam settled against the bulkhead more comfortably. "Isn't everyone? Always? Or maybe it's just us." Carter smiled at that, as she'd meant her to. "You've got to do the thing you really want to do, whatever that is. Do you want the *Hammond*?"

"Yes," Carter said.

"Then do it. Pay up the price willingly and be glad you had the choice."

Carter nodded, glancing around the puddle jumper and out into the night beyond the tailgate. "Like you're doing."

"I'm glad you gave me the choice to come back. But my answer is no."

"I think my answer is yes," Carter said slowly. "Yes. I want the *Hammond*." Her eyes focused somewhere beyond the wall, as though she were already seeing the distant reaches of space she'd travel, galaxies millions of light years from home, worlds replete with mysteries waiting to be solved. "I should tell Ai I've been to Atlantis," she said. "I should tell her that what her grandparents did was worth it."

"I expect she'd like that," Sam said. She looked at the other face so like her own—alike and not. Less sun damaged, but with lines of stress beginning at the corners of her eyes, beginning to bracket her mouth. "Besides," she said quietly, "don't you think he'll wait for you?"

Carter closed her eyes a second, a different smile transforming her for a moment. "I expect he will," she said. Then she rummaged briskly in one of her pockets, pulled out an energy bar and held it up with a wordless question. Sam nodded, and Carter broke it in half, held out one of the pieces. The smell of chocolate and sugar was suddenly strong in the night air, and Sam took it eagerly. It had been five years since she'd had chocolate, even chocolate chips in an oatmeal-granola sort of base, and she took careful, tiny bites, savoring every crumb. The last time she'd had chocolate was with the other Daniel, her reality's Daniel, sitting in the near-empty mess hall trying to figure out how to stay part of this — thing — they'd stumbled into. She could still see him clearly, floppy hair and heavy glasses and the absolute certainty that they were made for better things. We did it, you know, she thought, though she didn't believe in ghosts. And you were right, we were, we are, better than we realized.

In the front of the jumper, Ai stirred, waking, and Sam looked at Carter. "Why don't you take a break? Ai and I can run the first set of diagnostics."

For a moment, she thought Carter would refuse, but then the other woman nodded. "Wake me when you're done," she said, and took the seat Ai had vacated.

Sam watched her go, amazed again at the trust she'd earned, then shook herself and smiled at Ai. "Back to work."

The moon was setting, a bright thin curve against the stars. The gods' sickle, they had called it when he was a boy on Chulak, and told the tale of how the gods harvested the very stars, scything them from the sky in glittering clusters like grapes from the vine. Even before he become First Prime, he had known that the story was not literally true; once he had risen in Apophis's service, he had understood it as a metaphor for the wars between the System Lords, whole planetary systems wiped out in a fit of pique. Now, leaning against the edge of the window in a Tau'ri palace, he wondered if there were not some deeper truth behind it, some metaphor for knowledge that preceded the Goa'uld. Danyel would know, or if he did not know, he would guess, and for a moment he missed those evenings spent in speculation. He closed his eyes, conjuring up the narrow house, the comfortable main room, the baby asleep and the adults relaxed around the remains of the meal, Danyel holding forth while Jack teased and Sam considered and he and Aset held hands, fingers clasped tight enough that he could feel the delicate bones.

That time was past. He turned away from the window, back into a room filled with lamplight, dozens of them placed in the niches and on the low tables. That was Aset, he felt sure. She loved light, loved lamps, and now she could demand all the oil she needed. There was no harm in it, and it made her seem Goa'uld, to indulge in such careless pleasure.

The door opened then, one of the palace servants bowing her into the room. They had found more suitable robes for her aboard Ra's ship, vivid scarlet spangled with gold, and there was more gold woven into her heavy hair. Goddess indeed, he thought, in spite of himself, in spite of knowing better, and bowed deeply. She smiled in answer, but spoke to the hovering attendants.

"Leave us."

They backed away, bowing, the last one closing the door behind him, and Aset came to take his hands. She shimmered in the lamplight, and she smelled of her favorite musky scent. She had been bathing in perfumed waters, Teal'c guessed, perfumed and strewn with flowers, and he wrenched his mind away from that thought.

"Is there any word?" That was Egeria, and Teal'c took a breath, her perfume almost overwhelming.

"Not yet. Though I would not expect an answer so soon."

"I would." Egeria gave him Aset's smile, a wry twist of painted lips. "If they're to survive—they have to act."

Teal'c nodded. "Indeed. But it is too great a risk to send a messenger."

"But they must," Egeria said. "How else—we cannot aid them if we don't know their plan."

"We know what their plan must be," Teal'c pointed out. "We have warned them that Ra plans to take the Stargate, and therefore they must prevent it. That is enough."

"It's not," she said. "If we don't know how they plan to stop him, we may inadvertently interfere. They have to tell us."

A serpent of unease coiled at the pit of Teal'c's stomach. What she said was true enough, but it was equally true that what they did not know could not be betrayed. "This is how we have always managed," he said, and could not help the hint of disapproval in his tone.

She shook herself then, and it was Aset who answered. "You're right, I know — though so am I! It's just that I'm worried."

"As am I." Teal'c regarded her gravely. "We must not let our concerns drive us to make mistakes."

"Yes." Aset took a deep breath. "That's so. And in the meantime —" She took his hand, smiling, and tugged him toward the gilded bed.

CHAPTER TWENTY-NINE

THE AIR was still and smelled of the river and the muddy reeds. Overhead, the stars had faded, and the first light of dawn grayed the sky. Jack looked to the east, where the sky was lighter still, a hint of pink showing on the low-lying clouds. Time he got things started, he thought, and turned away from his jumper. The other Teal'c was waiting with Basa, along with the other Daniel and Vala. The team from the future — and there was a phrase he'd never expected to use — were already sweating in their armored vests, though it was the hair and the tattoo that made Teal'c look so odd.

"Ready to move out?" he said, to Basa, and Mitchell peeled himself off the jumper where he'd been leaning.

"Time?"

"Time," Jack said.

Teal'c looked at Mitchell. "Sergeant Basa believes he has a man on duty who will let us in the side gate undetected."

"The guard is a man of mine, one I trained from a boy," Basa said to Jack, who nodded.

"Is that going to work?" Mitchell asked.

"We relied on inside men last time," Jack said. "It tended to work. Besides, if the gate doesn't open, I imagine Colonel Carter's already provided you with something that will bring down a wall."

Vala smiled broadly. "As a matter of fact..." She held up several packets of C4.

"And for the armory door, too," Jack said.

Teal'c nodded, massively competent as always. "If all goes as planned, I believe we will have little difficulty securing weapons for Sergeant Basa's men."

"And if it doesn't go according to plan?" Mitchell asked. "No offense, but how often does that happen?"

"I do not believe that it will materially affect the outcome," Teal'c answered, with a sudden smile.

Mitchell nodded. "Good enough for me."

"The main thing," Jack said, to Basa, "is to protect Pharaoh in case we fail. Make sure Sergeant Irer knows his job is to keep him safe. And yours is to keep the Jaffa too busy to attack the house."

"Yes, O'Neill," Basa said. "Be sure of it."

They clasped hands, and Jack nodded again. "OK."

He watched them form up, not the neat formation of his cadet days, but a differently disciplined line. One of Hor-Aha's servants hauled back the gate, and Teal'c and Basa and Basa's men vanished into the fading dark. Teal'c's staff weapon, Jack thought. A couple of P90s, every zat he'd kept around the house, which was exactly three of them since Ellie was born, plus spears and bows and slings. And that was his fault, for not keeping a proper armory here, just like the whole attack was his fault. If he hadn't talked Hor-Aha into letting them go look for a new symbiote for Teal'c, everything would have been fine. Except that Teal'c, his Teal'c, would be dead.

It was not a useful line of thought. He closed it down and walked back to the puddle jumpers, lined up as though on a flight line. Carolyn Lam turned at his approach, and held out a thermos and a stack of pottery cups.

"Coffee?"

It was instant and awful, tasting of the fire, and he closed his eyes in momentary bliss. "Too bad Danyel isn't here."

Mitchell took a sip from his own cup, and made a face. "I don't know, he'd never stop complaining."

"Not until he finished the thermos," Jack said. "OK, kids, have we got any last questions?"

There was a resounding silence, even the Ancient woman shaking her head. She was the real unknown quantity, Jack thought. Not that he really believed she was going to betray them, or at least he didn't think she was going to do anything that would help Ra, but her jumper was a flying wreck. Carter and Sam had gone over it, swapping out as many damaged crystals as they could manage, but it was still going to be a beast to fly. At least they all had a decent number of drones to work with, and Ai had to be a better than average pilot, or she never would have gotten the thing here in the first place.

"One more time," he said aloud. "Sam, you're with me, Carter with Ai, Mitchell with Dr. Lam. We're going to wait until just past sunrise, and then we're going to head for the pyramid. We're going to take turns uncloaking — uncloak, recloak, change position as quick as you can — and then I'm going to get on the loudspeaker and tell Ra he's parked in no-parking zone and has two minutes to move his car." Ai was looking blank, and Jack stopped. "I'm going to tell him he has two minutes to begin preparing for lift-off, or we Ancients will express our disapproval. I don't think he's going to leave, but it's worth a try. If it doesn't work, then we redeploy. Ai, Dr. Lam, you'll attack the mothership, I'll handle any death gliders, and see if we can't change his mind."

"A mothership carries a lot of gliders," Mitchell said.

"We're invisible, remember?" Jack looked around, projecting a confidence he didn't entirely feel. One puddle jumper against a flight of gliders — even with the drones able to follow a target on their own, it would be a hell of a fight. "They're more likely to run into one of us by accident than to actually shoot us."

Dr. Lam looked a little relieved, but he didn't think either Mitchell or Carter was buying it. "And the Stargate?" Carter asked. "If Ra tries to take it, who stops him?"

"We do," Sam said, firmly. "I'm more confident in the crystals on our jumper. And Ai's is definitely out."

Carter looked as though she wanted to protest, but finally nodded. "OK."

"Copilots will handle communications," Jack said. He'd

rather do it himself, and probably would, but the other pilots would have enough to worry about. "Anything else?"

Mitchell shook his head. Ai said, "Thank you, Colonel O'Neill, for letting me fight with you. We have owed the Goa'uld this for a long time."

"You're welcome." He could see the light gathering on the horizon, the limb of the sun pushing up out of the east, far beyond the river. "All right," he said. "Time to go."

Danyel attached himself to the crowd of servants entering the palace gates, head down, the basket he'd offered to carry for an older woman tucked under one arm. None of the Jaffa looked twice at him, and he breathed a sigh of relief as the door closed behind them.

"Where can I take this for you?" he asked, and the old woman smiled and pointed.

"The kitchens, my son, if you'd be so kind."

He carried it the rest of the way, accepted a small loaf of bread for his kindness, and extricated himself as quickly as he could. Dawn was breaking: he needed to find Teal'c and Aset before the attack began. At least the kitchen staff had been able to tell him where they were quartered, and he knew the palace. He threaded his way through the halls, trying to look as though he belonged, fetched up at last at the door of what had been the Queen Mother's rooms. There were Jaffa on guard, of course, and he bowed deeply even before they could bar his way.

"Your pardon, but I have a message for the Lady Egeria."

The senior of the two gave him a wary look. "Wait here," he said, and disappeared into the room. A moment later, the door opened, and the other Jaffa gestured for him to enter.

Aset was looking splendid. Danyel blinked in spite of himself, seeing the scarlet robe, the gold in her hair and on her arms. And on her hand, too, the golden finger-stalls and disk of a Goa'uld palm device. At least Ra trusted her that far, he thought, and made another bow.

"Lady—"

She lifted her hand. "Leave us," she said, to the Jaffa, who bowed and backed away, closing the door again behind him.

At her side, Teal'c relaxed fractionally, his hands easy on the staff weapon. "It is good to see you again, Danyel," he said softly.

"Is everything all right?" Danyel asked. "Are you all right?"

"We are," Teal'c said, but he shot a quick glance at Aset as he spoke.

"Has O'Neill's attack begun?" That was Egeria who spoke, her voice resonant.

Danyel nodded. "At sunrise. He's coming with the jumpers—"

Egeria lifted her weaponed hand. "Kneel." A beam of light shot from the palm device, slamming him against the wall. Danyel rolled, shaking his head, but a second beam pinned him in place, driving him to his knees.

"Aset!" Teal'c stepped sideways, swinging his staff weapon to cover her.

"Be silent," Egeria said, and in that instant the door slammed open. Out of the corner of his eye, Danyel saw the sweep of Ra's formal robes, and then he was forced to the floor.

"What's this?" Ra demanded. "You are meeting with traitors—"

"Meeting, my lord?" Egeria's voice was richly amused. "Indeed not. I offer this one as a gift for you. This is Danyel Jackson, O'Neill's minion."

The pressure eased at last, and Danyel shoved himself back to his knees, shaking his head to drive away the pain behind his eyes. Teal'c's staff weapon was trained on him, but the Jaffa looked a fraction less impassive than usual. We got it wrong, Danyel thought. Somehow we got it wrong, and this isn't Egeria, not the real one. And now—we are so screwed. He glanced around the room, wondering if there was a way to make Teal'c shoot him—not fatally, he hoped, but enough to keep Ra from questioning him—

"Do not attempt it, Danyel Jackson," Teal'c said, light snapping at the tip of the staff weapon, and Egeria lifted her hand again, holding him frozen.

"Shall I share what I have learned?"

Ra smiled slowly. "By all means. You intrigue me, Egeria."

She bowed her head in regal acknowledgement. "Thank you, my lord. It is as you expected, O'Neill is planning a preemptive attack, and it will begin today—"

There was an explosion outside, from the direction of the pyramid. Jaffa shouted in answer, and Ra's head snapped around. "What is this?"

"Lord!" A Jaffa captain came skidding up. "The ha'tak is taking fire from invisible ships."

"Ancients," Ra snarled. He looked at Egeria. "So O'Neill was one of them all along."

She dipped her head. "Yes, my lord."

And that was wrong, Danyel thought. Maybe there was still hope, if she was still lying—or maybe she was just humoring Ra, hoping to earn his favor.

"Bring him to the peltac," Ra said. "We will meet this attack directly. And you, Egeria, will stand with me and watch my triumph."

"It will be my pleasure, my lord," she answered. She was still smiling as she released her hold, and a pair of Jaffa wrestled Danyel to his feet.

"You know, you really don't want to upset the Ancients," he began, and Egeria turned on him.

"Be silent! If you know what's good for you, you will say nothing."

She swept out in Ra's wake, and Danyel cast a look of appeal toward Teal'c. Come on, he thought. Come on, give me a sign, give me a hint, here, let me know what game we're playing—

Teal'c shouldered his staff weapon, and motioned for the soldiers to drag him away.

Jack eased the jumper into the air, trying to relax into the Ancient interface. The displays lit obligingly, speed, attitude, course, weapons array, everything right where he wanted it on the heads-up, and he tried not to glare at it. In the tactical screen, he could see the other two jumpers rising to join him, forming up in echelon off his left — well, left pod, not wing, but it would do. They were all visible for the moment, high enough already to catch the first of the light, and he nodded to Sam. "Time to cover up."

She reached for the communications board. "Colonel Mitchell, Colonel Carter. Jack says it's time to engage the cloak."

It really wasn't what he was used to from his copilot, but it would have to do. Disappear, he thought, frowning at the controls, and a light blinked on. "Does that mean —?" he began, and realized that the other jumpers no longer appeared in the standard displays. They were there on the tactical, though, right where they were supposed to be, and he looked at Sam.

"Are we invisible? It's hard to tell from in here." He thought the light brightened, but he pretended he didn't see it.

"I'll ask," Sam said, calmly. "Colonel Mitchell, can you confirm that our cloak is working?"

"Sure is," Mitchell answered. "And so's Ai's. How about ours?"

"Looking good," Jack said. "Or, rather, not looking like anything, which is good..."

"We can't see you either," Sam said.

"Next stop, the pyramid," Jack said, and tipped the jumper into a wide turn, heading north and east, following the river. The rising light glinted off its calm surface: they were too high to disturb the water even with a breeze. He glanced at the tac screen again, checking the formation. If he had more experienced pilots, he'd have them in close and tight, ready to give chase or offer support, but Dr. Lam was no real pilot, and Ai was an unknown quantity in combat. At least they had Mitchell and Carter to suggest tactics, but he was under no illusion about how useful that was likely to be. Like trying to defuse a bomb while wearing hockey gloves…

Ahead he could see the pyramid, capped by Ra's ha'tak, lights flashing slowly along its massive sides. The glider bays were sealed, and there were no signs of charged weapons: good news, he thought, and nodded to Sam.

"OK, Sam. It's show time."

She touched the controls again. "Colonel Mitchell, Colonel Carter, are you ready?"

"Ready and waiting," Mitchell answered, and Carter echoed him a second later.

"On my mark," Jack said. "Two… one… now!"

As he spoke, he pitched the jumper up, sent it soaring over the tip of the ha'tak, looped down to drop the cloak and fire a single drone. He swung away immediately, but not before he saw the drone explode short of the ha'tak's hull: the mothership was shielded, Cloak, dammit, he thought, and the light reappeared. The tac screen showed two more hits, but no damage, and then another jumper—Ai's, he thought—flashed into view. Another drone exploded against the shield, and he swung the jumper up and out of range, telling it to uncloak as he went.

"Turn on the loudspeaker," he said, and Sam nodded.

"You're good."

"Ra!" The jumper damped his voice, but he could feel the echo, knew he was reaching everyone in the palace compound. "You've made a mistake coming back here, but we're willing to be generous. Go now, and we'll let you leave in peace. Otherwise—" He stopped, hoping silence would be more suggestive than an outright threat.

"That didn't sound very Ancient," Sam said.

"Everyone's a critic." Jack frowned at the tac display, seeing power building inside the ha'tak. "Crap. Heads up, people, looks like they're arming the guns."

Yes, a port was opening, there on the ha'tak's side. Cloak, he thought again, and felt a shudder as the jumper obeyed. He swung the jumper through a series of quick turns, banked around and to the left, and realized nothing was pursuing him. Instead, light flared from the tip of the ha'tak, a glowing cloud that shimmered and formed itself into a giant head: Ra's head, surveying his palace and his invisible attackers.

Sam gave a nervous laugh. "Pay no attention to the little man behind the curtain..."

"I have been patient," Ra said, "a kindly god, willing to forgive, to restore my people to favor. But no more. You will feel only my anger."

The image winked out, and in the same instant the glider bays opened.

"Ah, crap," Jack said, and dragged the jumper out of the way of the first stream. "OK, kids, it's time for Plan B."

CHAPTER THIRTY

"DOWN," Cam said, and kept his voice calm and conversational. Mercifully, Carolyn didn't ask questions, just angled the jumper toward the deck, swooping low under the skirts of the mothership where it perched on the pyramid. The first flight of death gliders screamed overhead, missing their previous position by less than a meter. The view in the windscreen rocked, but the inertial dampeners kept everything steady.

"Drone," she said, and the jumper released one, sent it shooting up into the ha'tak's underbelly. Shields flared, but there was a shower of broken stone from the pyramid itself. That's an option, Cam thought. Destroy the pyramid and chase Ra off that way. Except it would leave a hell of a lot of collateral damage.

His eyes were still on the tactical display, following the gliders as they fanned out into a search pattern. Whoever was in charge was good, wasn't fazed by the problem of invisible attackers; he was willing to spend gliders to draw them out, spot any pattern that formed—

A drone struck, taking out a glider above them, and Carolyn heeled the jumper over the top to avoid the debris. The gliders were dropping lower now, weaving a defensive pattern around the ha'tak, and he glanced at Carolyn, checking to see if she needed advice. Her face was calm, almost relaxed, her hands easy on the controls, but she was going to be trapped if she didn't—

"Break left," he said, and she tipped the jumper sideways, sliding out between two gliders.

"Thanks."

Another drone hit, and another, taking out gliders at the top of the pattern, and Carolyn frowned in concentration. "Drone," she said again, and Cam said, "Wait—"

It was too late, the drone had already launched, and sure enough a glider made a beeline for their position.

"Oops," Carolyn said, and dragged the jumper almost straight up. One of the glider's shots hit home, but the rest passed harmlessly behind them. Lights flared on her controls, vanished again. "Sorry—"

"They're going to shoot where the drones originate," Cam said. "Fire and turn, that's the plan."

"Right." Carolyn launched a salvo of drones, five of them in a tight bunch that instantly spread to seek new targets. Another glider pounced, but she was already diving, the jumper rolling onto its side. The ground spun in the windscreen as more gliders turned toward the source of the drones, firing blind, and Cam grabbed the edge of the control panel. Carolyn spun the jumper the other way, scraping between two gliders, pulled up and out of the fight.

"OK, that was too close," she said.

"It's only too close if you hit them," Cam answered, and was rewarded by a shaky smile.

Below them, Ai's jumper popped into sight, and the gliders turned to pursue.

"We've lost the cloak!" Carter called, her voice crackling as though they were losing communications, too, and Carolyn flung the jumper into a tight turn, swooping down behind the attacking gliders. She fired drones, taking out two of them; three more exploded—O'Neill's work—and Ai clawed for maneuvering room. She dived between two gliders, who pitched over to avoid her, and one clipped wings with his fellow, went tumbling out of control. The heads-up display placed the crash on the far side of the river, and a thick column of smoke rose from the reeds.

"Come on, Carter," Cam muttered. The jumper was a sitting duck, visible like that, and there was only so much they could do to help.

Carolyn fired again, the drones homing hungrily on the chosen gliders, but the rest of the flight ignored the attack, concentrating on the one enemy they could see. Ai spun through a tight turn, trying to put the mothership between her ship and the attackers, but the gliders stayed glued to her tail. She fired back, but the drones seemed weaker, as though there was other damage, and the jumper rocked as a beam clipped the edge of a pod.

"Carter —" Cam leaned forward as though that would help, urging them on.

A second jumper popped into view, O'Neill hauling the stubby ship into a scorching, impossible turn. He fired a salvo of drones, and another pair of gliders fell. Part of the flight turned to follow him, and he vanished, to reappear a moment later on the far side of the fight. This time, though, a glider was waiting, and the beams stitched a pattern along the jumper's side.

"Cover him, Carolyn," Cam said, and she launched a drone, taking out the glider, then spun her ship toward Ai's jumper, firing as she went.

Ai's jumper disappeared at last — the heads-up showed it pulling out and away, presumably to check the damage — and O'Neill blasted another glider from the sky. And then, abruptly, the gliders pulled away, running for the shelter of the mothership. The bay doors opened, and Cam pointed.

"See if you can —"

"Got it," Carolyn said, and launched a drone. It flew true, but the armored door slid closed again, and it impacted on the surface, leaving only a smear of scorched metal. "Damn, it didn't go in."

"Missed that one," O'Neill said. "Any luck on your side?"

"Nope," Cam answered. "They got the doors closed too fast."

"Yeah." O'Neill paused. "Carter. What's your status?"

"The cloak's back on line," Carter answered, after a moment, "but we're on reduced power. It's affecting the drones —"

"Crap," Cam said. Lights flared across the boards and in the heads-up: the ha'tak was powering up at last.

"Maybe they're leaving," Carolyn said, but she didn't sound like she believed it either.

"Get ready," O'Neill said, and for the first time, he sounded grim. "If he goes for the Stargate — this could get ugly fast."

There was no resistance at the city gate. And only a handful of men at the armory. Basa summoned them to surrender, Daniel translating in a whisper, and they did so with relief, promising that their loyalty had been to the Pharaoh all along. Basa neither believed nor disbelieved, Teal'c saw with approval, but locked them into the small back room and left a couple of men on guard before he began handing out weapons.

"Basa says that Ra pulled most of the Jaffa back to the pyramid," Daniel reported. "They don't know about Aset or Danyel."

Egeria, at least, was probably on the mothership, Teal'c thought. Or she should be, if everything had proceeded according to plan. He looked up sharply as the first explosions sounded from the pyramid, and motioned Basa and his men toward the door. "We must secure the gates," he said. "And make certain Ra's Jaffa cannot leave the compound."

Basa nodded, already dividing his men — slightly less than half to guard the gates, the rest forming up, ready to approach the palace. O'Neill's amplified voice boomed outside, warning the Goa'uld to abandon the planet. Teal'c waved his men forward, ducked out through the armory's narrow door.

Ra's head loomed above them, a hundred times life-size, frowning down on the compound, his voice as loud as thunder, loud enough to shake the ground. "— You will feel only my anger."

Basa's men checked, slowed by the sight and sound, a godlike illusion, and even Basa looked pale.

"It's a trick," Daniel said, and repeated himself in Egyptian. "Teal'c, tell them it's a trick."

"It is an illusion," Teal'c said strongly, heard Daniel translate.

"It is unreal, a phantom — it cannot harm or even see you. I am Jaffa, I have seen this before. It is a picture —" He couldn't find an analogy that would make sense — Chulak's technology had been more advanced than this — and from the look on Daniel's face, neither could he. "It is not real," Teal'c said again, but he could see that they were wavering. "Look!"

He lifted his staff weapon, took aim at the looming face. One of the Egyptians cried out, covering his eyes, and Teal'c fired, the blast rising into the bright sky. It passed through the image as though it wasn't there — as though it was what it was, a trick of projected light — and was gone. The image didn't waver, but didn't respond, either, and he saw Basa's eyes narrow.

"See?" Daniel said. "It doesn't even know we're here."

Basa shouted something, waved his men forward, and, when they were slow to respond, grabbed the nearest one by the arm and shoved him forward.

"To the palace," Teal'c said, and Daniel translated.

The main doors stood wide, and the great hall was empty, a stool overturned and the leopard skin askew on the great throne. Teal'c turned in a careful circle, staff weapon ready, but nothing moved among the painted pillars.

"Well, this is interesting," Vala said. "Do you think he's actually leaving?"

"Not without a fight," Teal'c said.

Something did move then in the mouth of the corridor that led behind the throne. Teal'c turned, his weapon snapping up to cover the opening, but Daniel caught his arm.

"Wait!"

"Do not fire, I am a friend!" The English words were accented, but understandable, and Teal'c relaxed just a little. An older woman emerged from the shadows, her wig disordered, her hands held well clear of her body.

Basa visibly relaxed, saying something, and Daniel said, "Basa says this is the priestess Mutnod, who has served Pharaoh and his father."

"The Jaffa have gone," she said. "They have left the building. There are none here but servants, and they will obey you. But — they have taken Danyel."

"What?" Vala's yelp was sheer surprise, but Mutnod took it for disbelief.

"I regret, Lady, but it is so. They have taken him to the pyramid, before the fighting began."

"Crap," Daniel said. He looked at Teal'c, the question obvious, and Teal'c nodded.

"Take Vala, Daniel Jackson, and see if you can find him. We will keep the Jaffa pinned down."

Daniel nodded. "As long as he's in the pyramid —" He broke off, shaking his head.

Teal'c tilted his head gravely. If Danyel had been taken aboard the mothership — there was very little they could do to save him. "Indeed," he said, and hoped the priestess was right.

Danyel worked his wrists cautiously, testing the bonds that secured his hands behind his back. They were just as solid as they'd been five minutes ago, and five minutes before that, and he looked back at the pel'tac's viewscreen, where death gliders swirled, searching for an invisible enemy. So far, so good, Jack, he thought. You've got them literally chasing their tails...

If he looked sideways, he could see Egeria watching from beside Ra's throne, Teal'c impassive one step behind and to her right. His back hurt from being thrown against the wall, and his forehead stung as if he'd been burned, though he didn't feel quite as bad as he usually did after being questioned with a hand device. Of course Egeria hadn't questioned him, exactly, but so far neither had Ra, and he was hoping maybe Ra would be too busy to think of it.

"Nean'tac." Ra pushed himself to his feet. The Jaffa at the main controls turned, bowing, but not before Danyel saw the gold mark of a First Prime on his forehead.

"My lord?"

"The commander of the gliders is to be punished. Their showing is deplorable." In the viewscreen, another glider exploded, and Ra's frown deepened. "See to it now."

"Now, my lord?" The First Prime held his ground, even as he kept his eyes carefully downcast.

"Yes, now. See if his second can do any better." Ra moved to the controls, his fingers tapping impatiently on the gilded surface. "Go!"

"Yes, my lord." Nean'tac bowed again, even more deeply, and disappeared from the control room.

"And you." Ra turned again, and Danyel braced himself, unable to keep from flinching at the sight of the raised hand device. "You're no Ancient."

"No," Danyel said. "No, I'm not, but—"

Ra ignored him. "You must learn to be more careful, Egeria. He cannot be effectively questioned for some days yet. Their minds require a knife's blade, not a hammer."

"My apologies, my lord," Egeria answered. "I am new to this, and perhaps I was carried away."

"Your zeal is forgivable, but inconvenient," Ra said. "As for you, Daniel Jackson... I knew all along you had the Ancients on your side. You could not have defeated me otherwise."

"Yes, well," Danyel said. "We certainly have their help now, and you probably ought to be thinking about doing what Jack said, because frankly you're getting slaughtered out there—"

Ra lifted his hand, and the nearest Jaffa swung his staff weapon, catching him in the back of his knees. Danyel fell forward, unable to catch himself with his hands bound behind him. He worked his way back to his knees to find Ra smiling down at him.

"So you admit that the Ancients are aiding you."

"You see their fleet in action," Danyel said. "They've taken us under their protection—"

Ra backhanded him, hard enough to send him sprawling. Danyel winced, tasting blood where the hand device had cut his mouth, and the impassive Jaffa hauled him upright again.

"The Ancients are a dying race," Ra said. "Their protection is worthless."

"It's working out all right so far," Danyel said, in spite of knowing better. This time, he was able to ride the blow, and the Jaffa caught him before he fell.

"You are a fool to defy me," Ra said. "As you shall soon learn. In the meantime—" He turned back to the controls, waving the Jaffa pilot out of the way. "We shall do what we should have done when first we abandoned this wretched planet. We will take the gate of the gods, and leave you bereft."

Danyel swallowed his instinctive protest. Jack had a plan, he and Sam knew how to stop this, they would make sure it didn't happen—and if that meant he couldn't get back, well, it was worth the sacrifice… He jerked at his bonds again, the thin shackles biting his wrists. There had to be a way off, somehow, if Egeria or Teal'c could only help him—

Ra rested his hands on the controls, fingers spread, and the ha'tak shuddered gently. The view in the screens changed as it rose serenely from the tip of the pyramid and hovered above the Stargate.

CHAPTER THIRTY-ONE

JACK SWORE under his breath as the ha'tak rose ponderously from its perch on the tip of the pyramid. At least the gliders were out of the way, but there were lights flashing on his controls that he didn't like. He glared at them, trying to think a question, and the indicators resolved themselves.

"Crap," he said. "Sam, we've lost drones."

"Oh, boy." She leaned forward, scanning the indicators. "No, OK, we've lost launch controls, if I can just get them back on line —" She was unhooking her safety webbing as she spoke, scrambled back into the rear of the jumper.

"Sam —" Jack couldn't spare her another glance as he brought the jumper around again, but he could hear a sudden hiss and pop, and a yelp.

"You all right?"

"Fine, I'm fine."

"I'm losing something else — looks like the cloak."

"Hang on."

There was another snap and the smell of ozone, and one set of indicators flashed from red to green.

"The cloak's back," he called, and swooped under the ha'tak as it moved toward the Stargate. If only he had drones, this would be the time, but those indicators glowed even brighter red, flashing angrily. On the tac screen, he could see Ai following, saw her jumper flash into view for the instant that she launched a drone, and then disappeared again. The explosion was impressive, but didn't seem to do any real damage.

"Drones, Sam?"

"Working on it."

He swung the jumper up and around, watching the ha'tak's

guns track wildly. In a minute, they'd start firing blind, and that was only going to make things more fun. Drop the cloak, he thought, and made a quick visible pass at the pel'tac, skimming the surface before pulling away. Cloak, damn it—The console beeped at him in complaint, but the systems obeyed.

"How are we doing?"

"Almost—Got it!" Sam yelled, and the weapons indicators flashed brilliant green.

"Nice work," Jack said, and fired a salvo toward the pel'tac. The explosions blossomed, but the mothership's shields held. A warning flashed from the tac screen, and the ha'tak's upper guns fired, beams slicing the air far too close for comfort. They'd just been waiting for him to take the shot, to get an approximate aiming point... He rolled the jumper down and away, but the edge of one beam clipped a pod, sent him momentarily out of control. There was another yelp from the back, and the acrid smell of smoke, but he ignored it and the warning lights flickering across the console, and brought the jumper down toward the Stargate.

"Ready, Sam?"

"No!" For the first time, she sounded harried. "I've lost—that last shot took out the DHD, and I can't reroute. We can't dial the gate."

Really? Jack glared at the jumper controls, and they glowed brighter in answer. "Crap," he said, and keyed communications. "Carter, Mitchell. We've lost the DHD. One of you is going to have to dial the gate."

"And fast." Sam scrambled back to the copilot's seat. "We have to lock in before Ra can set his beams."

Jack tapped the console. "Carter! Mitchell! Come on, answer me." There was only silence.

In the copilot's seat at Ai's right, Carter punched buttons, trying to get the com system to respond. Ai brought the ship up and around again, the craft wobbling as though they were losing power.

"Can we dial the gate from here?"

Ai shook her head. "We cannibalized the dialing mechanism years ago."

"Damn it." Carter punched buttons, got no result. "Why doesn't Mitchell answer?"

"I think they've lost com," Ai said. Her face was showing the strain, but she nursed the jumper into a careful turn, lining up for another shot at the pel'tac. She released the drones, and for a moment the ha'tak's progress seemed to slow.

"We have to have the gate open if we're going to hold it," Carter said. Ai didn't answer, probably because she was stating the obvious, and Carter scanned the tac screen again. "Mitchell!"

"Mitchell!" Jack's voice crackled from the speakers. "Carter! Dial the DHD!"

"Put me down there," Carter said.

"What?" Ai looped the jumper, bringing them down toward the courtyard where the Stargate stood. The ha'tak loomed overhead, lights flickering on its underbelly. "You're out of your mind."

"Somebody has to dial the gate," Carter said. She grabbed up her helmet and P90, glad of the extra clips stashed in her pockets. "If you have a better idea—"

"Sadly, no." Ai brought the jumper down almost to the ground, and there was a whine and a rush of sand and air as the rear hatch began to lower. She was slowing, too, not quite to a hover, but to a safe speed, and Carter made her way to the back, head down against the blowing dirt.

"Now!" Ai called, and the jumper slowed even further.

Carter took a breath, and ran down the wobbling ramp. She jumped and rolled, came up with the P90 ready, air swirling around her from the passage of at least one invisible ship. The ha'tak loomed overhead, impossibly enormous, blotting out the sky, but she made herself focus on the DHD. Ai had made a perfect drop, only a couple of meters from the device, and she slung the P90 as she ran toward it. Still no Jaffa, still no sign of the other jumpers, just the ha'tak's shadow creeping toward her, and she pressed the first symbol. It didn't really matter what address they dialed, just that the wormhole was open, ready to feed the jumper's modified systems; she pressed the symbols for what would someday be the alpha site, watching the chevrons light and lock as the gate began to turn.

A blast from a staff weapon shot past her, and she grabbed for her P90, swung and fired in the same movement. She was horribly exposed here, just the console to protect her, and she made herself small, trying to see where the shots had come from. She heard the last chevron lock, and there was the familiar burst of light and energy as the wormhole opened.

Another blast struck the ground a few feet away, and she risked a second shot. The Jaffa were in the pyramid, she thought. If she could just get to the nearest outbuilding—but it was ten yards away, and might as well have been a hundred, for all the good it did her. She hunkered down behind the DHD, poked the muzzle of the P90 around its base, looking for a decent shot. Something moved in the dark behind the pyramid's entrance, and she fired a burst, as much to keep them down as in any real hope of hitting anyone. Staff weapons fired in return, and she ducked back toward the DHD. One blast clipped her sleeve, fabric and skin smoking, and the next went through her calf, a wave of pain washing over her that for a moment blotted out the rest of the world. She managed to stay upright long enough to loose a long stream of bullets into the open door, then collapsed against the console, groping for a field dressing. At least the blast had cauterized the big blood vessels, she thought, her face screwed up in pain as she tied the dressing into place. She wasn't likely to bleed to death, at least not yet, but—She looked over her shoulder at the outbuilding, now impossibly far, and settled herself behind the DHD. She wasn't going anywhere either.

Jack brought the jumper down level with the wormhole's shimmering center, trying to pretend he didn't see the ha'tak hovering above him. Something like a proximity alarm was flashing on the control board, was joined by the two-toned warble of an audible alarm. Would you stop it? he thought. I see the damn thing. The audible alarm shut off, but the light kept flashing, brighter than ever.

"Sam!"

"I've got it," she said, her voice steady. "Just one more—there, it's done."

The jumper rocked, the air suddenly alive with turbulence, and a whole string of lights popped into existence, a cascade of flashing orange and yellow. "I don't think the ship likes it."

"Just a minute more."

Jack looked up, seeing ports opening on the underside of the ha'tak, weird stubby knobs protruding from their housings. "It's now or never, Sam."

"Got it," Sam said again, and the cascade of lights flashed to solid orange. Jack scanned his boards, trying to interpret the displays. OK, that was the inertial dampeners, feeding through into the tractor, and linking them with the Stargate even as it drew power from the wormhole in an endless loop...

The knobs on the ha'tak's belly glowed, and then shot thin beams of light that converged and merged into a single stream about ten meters above the top of the Stargate. The stream shot downward, enveloping the gate, and the jumper shuddered again. A thread of pale blue light uncoiled from within the wormhole, snaked slowly out toward the jumper.

"Sam?" Jack risked a glance over his shoulder, to see her still fiddling with crystals and dangling wires. The air smelled electric. "Is it supposed to do this?"

"What?" She looked up and he saw her mouth drop open for an instant before she scrambled forward. "I didn't expect that."

"Is it dangerous?" Jack held his hands ready over the controls. The thread of light was moving slowly toward them, weaving slightly as though it was following a scent, and it looked as though it was getting brighter.

"I don't know," Sam said. "I don't think so, I think it's just energy from the gate radiating into the visible spectrum —"

"Should I move back?" Jack interrupted. The tip of the thread was maybe five meters away, homing in.

"No." Sam shook her head. "If you do, we'll lose the gate. We're locked in."

"If it blows up, I'm never going to forgive you," Jack muttered. The ha'tak's tractor glowed white, brilliant as the filament of a light bulb; streaks of green danced in front of his eyes, obscuring the questing thread.

"It shouldn't," Sam said. She was bending over the console, reading numbers and what looked like some kind of graph. "We're already connected to the wormhole, this is just a radiant effect."

The tip of the thread was less than a meter away, and closing fast. Jack flinched as it touched the jumper's skin, but there was no explosion, just a weird tingling that left all the hairs on his arms upright. The air itself seemed to vibrate, a low hum just below the threshold of his hearing. "How are we doing?" he asked, and had to raise his voice to carry in the weirdly thickened air.

"So far, so good," Sam answered. "We can't cut Ra's beam, but he can't take the gate, either."

"Stalemate," Jack said, and hoped the others could figure out the next move.

They slipped through the back corridors behind the temple's public spaces, the torches flickering with each explosion. Vala clutched her zat more tightly, glad she'd remembered to put a penlight in her pocket, and peered cautiously around the next corner. The painted corridor was empty, and she looked at Daniel.

"They are aware, your other selves, that those drones could

bring the whole pyramid down on top of us?"

"I sincerely hope so," he answered, which was not quite the response she had wanted to hear. "Clear?"

"Clear." They scooted across the corridor, took up positions on the opposite side, flattened against the wall. "Where is everyone?"

"The priestess, Mutnod, said they'd gone to the pyramid," Daniel said, "but maybe they've withdrawn to the mothership?"'

"Not all of them," Vala said. She could hear the distinctive scrape of armored feet, and Daniel caught her arm, dragging her into a darkened side corridor. They melted into the shadows, and a handful of Jaffa trotted by, their leader shouting something Vala couldn't quite make out. There were only five of them, though, and she frowned.

"There should be more," Daniel said. "And — that way, back the way they came from, that's where the cells are. So either Danyel's been left behind —"

"Which really doesn't seem all that likely," Vala said.

"Or they've already taken him to the mothership."

"That would not be good."

"That's something of an understatement," Daniel said. He checked the corridor again, looked back at her. "OK, let's take a look in the cells."

"If he's not there," Vala began, and the entire pyramid shuddered. There was a deep, grating groan, stone on stone on metal, and a few fragments of paint drifted to the floor. She caught her breath. It was a sound she'd never really expected to hear again, the sound of a mothership leaving its dock, and Daniel slanted her a wary look.

"What was that?"

"Ra leaving." She hadn't meant to be so blunt, but she was suddenly afraid. They couldn't lose this other Daniel, this man who'd done his best to fix his mistakes, and in the process made a life here in the past. They just couldn't... "Come on."

They hurried down the corridor, past scenes of gods and men, figures that she would probably know if Daniel had time to name them to her, or at least the Goa'uld who had stolen their identities. The pyramid shuddered again, not as hard, and for a moment the stones throbbed underfoot. And then they had reached the cells, hastily abandoned, a few pieces of Jaffa gear still stacked in the corner of the guardroom.

"Danyel?" She risked calling, despite Daniel's irritated glance. "Danyel, are you here?"

There was no answer, and Daniel turned back from the cell doors, shaking his head. "They're empty. All of them."

"We're too late." Vala lowered her zat to her side, the adrenaline washing out of her. "He must be on the ship."

"We still don't know that," Daniel began, but she could tell he didn't believe it either.

"We have to go after him," she said, but Daniel shook his head.

"We can't," he said, almost gently. "At least, not now, not without knowing—" He shook his head. "He's on his own for now."

CHAPTER THIRTY-TWO

THE REMAINDER of the Jaffa were guarding the pyramid's main entrance, a suicide squad left behind to cover Ra's retreat. Teal'c was content to leave them there for now, keep them busy and bottled up so that they couldn't do any more harm, but weren't desperate enough to try anything stupid. Above them, the ha'tak pulled away from the pyramid, rising into the bright morning sky. Drones struck seemingly at random, and the ha'tak's guns answered, firing at an enemy they could not see. And still the ha'tak came on, heading inexorably for the Stargate. The wormhole opened then, the wave of blue steadying to a pool, and Teal'c realized there was someone at the DHD: Colonel Carter.

"Basa!"

The sergeant looked over his shoulder, and Teal'c pointed. The Egyptian took in the situation at a glance, and shoved a man toward him, and then another. "Go!"

Teal'c nodded, hoping that Danyel had been right when he said these men understood basic commands, and motioned for them to follow. More Jaffa fired from the pyramid, and he saw Carter stumble, drag herself into the dubious shelter of the DHD. Above and between her and the pyramid the air was hazy blue, a nebulous shape more or less the size of the jumper slowly taking shape. Something was overriding the cloak — or, no, the energy it was drawing from the wormhole was somehow making it visible.

But that could not be his concern. There was an outbuilding, a guard post, to one side of the square. If he could get Carter into that shelter… He grabbed the nearest Egyptian, pointed at the opening at the base of the pyramid. "Ra's Jaffa are there," he said. "I must help Colonel Carter. Cover me."

He saw understanding dawn, and the man nodded vigorously. "Yes," he said, and spoke quickly to the other men. They dropped into supporting positions — O'Neill and his other self had trained them well — and Teal'c handed the first man his staff weapon.

"Cover me," he said again, and the Egyptian nodded, sent a blast toward the entrance. The others did the same, and the Jaffa's fire tracked toward them. Teal'c took a deep breath, and raced for the DHD. He had covered maybe half the ground before he was spotted, and staff blasts slammed into the dirt to either side. Carter had seen him coming, was offering covering fire of her own. He lowered his head, kept dodging, and skidded at last to his knees beside her.

"You are hurt," he said, taking in the bloody field dressing, the burn that scored her upper arm. Something, a chip of stone, perhaps, had carved a cut across one cheek, and she was squinting with pain.

"I can move if you help me," she said. "Because we can't stay here."

"Indeed not." Teal'c looked around, gauging the distance to the outbuilding, the safest line, the best shelter. Behind and to the right, the Egyptians continued to lay down covering fire, and he looked back at Carter. "Give me your arm."

She cried out as he lifted her, got her arm slung over his shoulder and his other arm around her waist. He didn't give her a chance to think about it, rushed her forward, half dragging, half carrying her toward the abandoned guard post. Staff fire crackled past them, the last shot close enough to singe his ribs, and then they were rolling into the safety of the walls, Carter swearing and holding her injured leg. There was no new bleeding, though, and after a moment, she leaned her head against the wall, eyes fluttering closed for just a moment.

"Thanks," she said, and unfastened the P90 from around her neck. "Here, you'd better take this."

She was right, of course. He was in better shape, should have the better weapon. He took it, checked the clip, took the extra clips she handed him as well. He gave her his zat, and settled against the corner of the building, scanning the courtyard. They were safe for the moment, at least, but Carter needed medical attention. He killed that thought, knowing it was pointless, and took aim at the pyramid.

Danyel sat back on his heels, hoping his guard was sufficiently distracted by the fight outside to miss him tugging at the bonds around his wrists. Unfortunately, they weren't rope, weren't knotted, but there had to be some way to slip free. Or some way to cut them, if he could only get his hands on something sharp. He realized abruptly that Teal'c was looking at him, could see perfectly well what he was trying to do.

Danyel froze, bracing himself to be hit again, but the Jaffa merely looked away. And maybe that was hopeful, maybe it was a sign that there was some other plan going on here, even if Danyel couldn't see what it was.

Ra was poised at the main controls, his hands drawing tiny shapes on the control surfaces. The main viewscreen showed the ha'tak hovering above the Stargate. The tractor beams were engaged, Danyel knew, but so far Jack and Sam's plan was working out.

He cleared his throat. "You know, it's not too late to take Jack up on his offer. If you leave now, nobody's going to stop you."

"Only because they cannot," Ra answered, without looking back. "You will see, you will all see, the cost of my anger." He nodded to the waiting technician. "More power."

Well, that went well, Danyel thought. Nice going, Danny. "They are Ancients," he said. "With Ancient technology—"

"And even Ancients can make mistakes," Ra said. "Look there."

The image in the viewscreen changed, shifted to encompass the Stargate, enveloped in the lifting field. The wormhole was open, because a thin stream of something — energy? matter? — was pouring out of it, to form a shimmering bubble around what had to be the cloaked jumper.

"They have revealed themselves as a perfect target," Ra said.

"Don't forget the rest of the fleet's there to protect them," Danyel said, but knew it sounded weak.

Ra looked at his console. "I do not think there is as large a fleet as you would have me believe. My analysis shows that all I see being done can be achieved with only six ships, and perhaps as few as three. Your protectors are failing, and have been for centuries. They shall not defeat me."

Damn. That was too good a guess, and he wasn't Jack, to bluff his way through. "Your computers don't know everything —"

"Be silent," Ra said, and touched another control. "Launch the gliders again. They are to concentrate on the ship at the gate. Destroy it, no matter what our losses."

The jumper shuddered as another wave of power rolled out of the wormhole, and Jack risked a glance over his shoulder. "Is it supposed to do that?"

"It's not supposed to do any of this," Sam said. Her hands were busy on the crystals, trying to match the fluctuating energies. "But, yes, some instability is to be expected."

Jack could feel the jumper's engines straining to keep up, all the systems laboring to hold the ship in position, to balance the tractor beam that was trying to drag the gate away. Warning lights were flashing all across the boards, though from the feel of things, the jumper would hold together a while longer. *You're just whining,* he thought, and it seemed as though the lights faded a little.

"O'Neill!" It was Ai's voice, high and nervous. "You are visible — the energy bleeding from the gate is showing your position."

"Crap," Jack said. "Sam! Any ideas?"

"I don't think there's anything we can do about it," she called back. "That's how we're holding the Stargate. And I'm kind of afraid to try to damp the visual spectrum—"

More lights flared, and this time there was an audible alarm as well, a blare of sound that made Jack flinch in his seat. "Now what?" he demanded, but he could already see new lights in the tac screen. Ra had launched his gliders. "Damn it. Sam! Forget the cloak, put all the power we've got into the shield."

"On it."

He glanced back again, saw her swapping wires, sparks showering around her.

"O'Neill," Ai said again. "You have lost the cloak. And the mothership has launched gliders."

"Yeah, I see them," Jack answered. "See if you and Mitchell can hold them off—" He stopped, staring at the tac screen as the lead glider rolled and arrowed toward them, spitting fire. "Brace yourself, Sam."

The first shots struck home, rocking the jumper. The shields held, that was the good news, but there was a snap and more sparks and smoke from the back. In the tac screen, Ai's jumper made a quick turn, launching drones, and an instant later Mitchell's did the same. A glider exploded, and then another; a third rolled away, smoking, its pilot fighting for control, but the next came on, firing steadily.

"Damn it," Jack said softly, braced himself as the jumper rocked again. "Sam?"

"How's the shield?" she called back.

"Holding."

"That's good."

The air smelled of smoke again, and the heavy, electric feeling was stronger than ever. Jack tightened his hands on the controls, willing the ship to hold firm. "How about the beam?"

"Holding for how," Sam answered. "But—if we get knocked around much more, I'm going to lose it."

And there wasn't a damn thing he could do about it. Jack grimaced as another shot struck home, steadying the jumper in the roiling air. He couldn't run, he couldn't hide, he couldn't fight back — wait a minute. "Sam! Can I fire the drones?"

"I don't know. It could overload everything."

Overhead, the air was filled with drones and gliders, explosions and the bright flare of beam weapons. And still the gliders came on, diving through the hail of drones to make hit after hit. The shield was holding, but weakening visibly, and the warning lights were flashing again, more steadily and seriously this time. "I'm going to try it," Jack said, and launched three drones.

The jumper bucked and shimmied, and there was a sudden flash of heat in the cabin, as though a hot wind had passed over them. In the tac screen, two gliders exploded, debris raining down around them, and the third swung away, damaged and trailing flame. The Stargate seemed to shiver, and then steadied.

"Don't do that again!" Sam yelled. "It takes too much power. Ra almost got a grip on the gate."

"Damn it," Jack said again. "I don't know how much longer we can just sit here and take it."

"We have to," Sam answered.

Hold on, Jack told the ship. Just — hold on.

CHAPTER THIRTY-THREE

"MY GOD," Carolyn said. "How many gliders has he got in that thing?"

Her hands were still steady on the controls, nursing the jumper up and away from a knot of gliders so that she could send a drone after them without betraying her position entirely. Cam scanned the tac displays, trying to spot a pattern that wasn't there.

"Pick off that ones that are going after O'Neill," he said, and the jumper heeled and shuddered as she released more drones. There had to be eight or ten of them; for a moment they seemed to fill the display, and then broke apart like blossoming fireworks. The gliders jinked frantically, spinning away, but the drones homed in relentlessly. Off to the left, Ai did the same, her jumper flashing into view for an instant before she got it cloaked again,.

"Oh, come on," Carolyn said, and gave Cam a wild glance. "It says it's running low on drones."

"How low?" Cam looked at the screen again, trying to prioritize targets.

"I can't tell," Carolyn said. She brought the jumper around for another pass. "It won't be specific. I think it doesn't want to upset me."

"Think soothing thoughts," Cam said. "Keep it calm." And her, too, but he didn't need to say that. He saw her shoulders move as she took a deep breath. "Can you get a better answer?"

"Twenty-five? Thirty?" Carolyn deliberately uncloaked for an instant as she rose across the nose of a stooping glider. The Jaffa pilot flinched, and the glider clipped wings with the next ship in the flight, sent them both spinning out of control.

"Nice," Cam said, and Carolyn grimaced.

"I don't think it'll work a second time."

"No," Cam agreed. If they were low on drones, there wasn't much they could do to help O'Neill—they weren't making that much difference anyway, there were just too many gliders, and O'Neill's jumper was a sitting duck. "Go for the pel'tac," he said. "Fire one big salvo, see if you can't damage the command center."

"It's shielded," Carolyn said, but she brought the jumper up and around again. For the first time, Cam could feel something ragged in its flight, as though they'd taken more damage than he'd realized.

"See if we can break through," he said, and Carolyn nodded. "OK. I'm giving it everything we've got."

"Go," Cam said, and hoped it would work.

Teal'c stood at attention, one pace behind Egeria and to her right, hoping she knew what she was doing. He did not look at Danyel, still on his knees on the far side of the pel'tac, still worrying at the bonds that held his wrists. Instead, he focused on Ra, still at the controls, his hands spread wide against the planes of light. The jumpers were fighting well, but sheer numbers were overwhelming them; soon O'Neill would have to release the Stargate or be destroyed, and O'Neill would die before he gave in. There had to be something, some way he could help, but he could see nothing yet.

"My lord!" The Jaffa at the weapons station lifted his head. "My lord, they are attacking the pel'tac."

"The shield will hold," Ra answered.

There was no sign of the jumper in the viewscreen, but drones seemed to materialize from nothing, a dozen of them, perhaps more, homing in on the command center. He could see them coming quite clearly, glowing gold and white against the sky's brilliant blue, and Egeria reached back to grab his arm.

"Now," she said, and lifted her weaponed hand. Light shot

from it, caught Ra in the small of the back, folding him over the controls. Teal'c charged his staff weapon, shot the second pilot and the Jaffa at the weapon station, and the drones exploded against the shield. The mothership moaned, the floorplates shifting as the shield absorbed the energies, and Teal'c turned, cut down the Jaffa left to guard Danyel. The ship staggered underfoot, and Egeria swept forward, seized a zat from one of the bodies. Alarms sounded, the deep hooting that warned of weakened shields, potential hull breach, and Egeria turned to him.

"Quickly! You must free Danyel."

Teal'c shook himself, found a knife on the dead guard, and sliced the ties that held Danyel's wrists.

"That was —" Danyel grabbed for the guard's zat and unfolded it, not quite pointing it at Egeria. "This is really interesting, but —"

"You must go now," Egeria said. "To the rings. Somehow, I don't know how, you overpowered your guard, and shot Ra —"

"You hit him with a hand device," Danyel said.

"That can be remedied," Teal'c said. He was beginning to see the shape of it at last, nodded in approval.

"Exactly." Egeria was already working the door controls, surveyed the corridor. "More alarms, Teal'c, tell them there are fires, anything. And destroy the controls for the tractor beams."

"Yes," Teal'c said, and aimed his staff weapon at the panel. It exploded in a satisfying shower of spark and flame. He hauled Ra's unconscious body off the platform, and touched the secondary controls. More alarms sounded, different tones, and he looked at Danyel.

"Aset is right, you must go now. We will handle things from here."

Danyel hesitated for an instant longer, then nodded. "You had me worried," he said. There was an expression on his face that suggested he wanted to say much more, but there was no time. "Good luck," he said, and ducked into the corridor.

"We must give him a little time," Egeria said. "And then—you must shoot Ra, and damage the door, while I call Nean'tac."

"Indeed." Teal'c allowed himself a smile, in spite of everything. "You could have told me the plan, Aset."

She gave him a rueful glance. "But I had no plan. Ra came before I expected him, I saw no other choice."

"Then you are even cleverer than I thought," Teal'c said, and took aim at the door mechanism.

Danyel raced down the empty corridor. There was a ring platform not far from the pel'tac, for Ra's convenience, probably, but at this point, he was hardly sure which way to turn. He made himself slow down long enough to read the wall symbols, oriented himself, and took off again.

There was a single Jaffa on guard at the door of the ring chamber. Danyel didn't pause, fired once as he came around the corner and the man collapsed in a heap of armor. Danyel closed the door behind him, scanning the controls. It looked as though everything was working, and he punched in the coordinates, hoping the pyramid was clear. But anything would be better than being trapped on the mothership, and he stepped up onto the platform. The system hummed, the rings gathering above him, and the door slid back, revealing a startled-looking Jaffa.

Danyel fired at him, missed, and ducked low himself as the Jaffa brought up his staff weapon. And then the rings slammed down, and he was suddenly in the pyramid's dim light. He rolled hastily away from the platform, and a woman's voice called softly, "Over here!"

It was Vala, and his other self, crouched in the mouth of a corridor. Danyel picked himself up and trotted toward them.

"Good to see you."

"Maybe," his other self said. "We're not exactly out of the woods."

"There are Jaffa between us and the main entrance," Vala

said. "And another group near the Stargate entrance."

"In fact," Daniel said, with a certain perverse satisfaction, "we're kind of trapped between them."

"It's better than being on the ha'tak," Danyel answered, and hoped it was true.

Teal'c dragged Ra's body back to the controls, draped him over the panels as though he'd fallen there when Danyel shot him.

"In the side," Egeria said. "We must keep him confined to the sarcophagus until we can leave the ship."

Teal'c nodded, lined up the shot, and fired. The blast seared skin and flesh, blistered the casing of the control platform, and Egeria gave a nod of satisfaction.

"Nean'tac! Nean'tac, where are you?"

Armored feet sounded in the corridor, and Teal'c lifted his hands, his staff weapon carefully uncharged. Nean'tac shouldered past his men, took in the scene at a glance. "My lord! What happened here?"

"He needs the sarcophagus," Egeria said sharply. "At once."

Nean'tac gestured to the nearest men, who moved to obey. "It shall be done. But—how did this happen?"

"The Tau'ri," Egeria said. "Somehow he must have freed himself, and overcome the others. They are sly and tricksters, the Tau'ri, especially when the Ancients aid them."

"But you are not harmed, my Lady," Nean'tac said.

"I was not here," Egeria answered. "Nor Teal'c. We heard shots fired, and then the alarms, and found this." She took a breath. "And I order this, as a goddess and loyal subject of your god. Our first duty is to our lord! Recall the gliders! We must bring him safe to Abydos."

There was a moment of hesitation, and Teal'c braced himself. If there was a fight, somehow he must win. And then Nean'tac relaxed, bowing, and motioned for his men to take up stations.

"At once, my Lady. It shall be done."

Egeria turned, took her place beside Ra's throne, one hand resting on its arm. A clever claim, Teal'c thought, and delicately done. "Abandon this filthy world to its fate, Nean'tac. They will pay in due time."

"Yes, my Lady," Nean'tac answered. The ha'tak rose, lights flaring as stressed systems fought to compensate, and more warnings sounded as the gliders came on board. In the screen, the sky darkened from blue to indigo to black, and the stars blazed around them. They had done it, Teal'c thought. Somehow they had done it. He slanted a glance at Aset and saw the same surprise in her eyes. And then it was gone, hidden behind Egeria's mask, but he had seen, and knew they had all three survived.

The tractor beams cut out, and the jumper rocked wildly. Jack swore, grappling with the controls, static nipping at his fingers. "Sam!"

There was another yelp from the back, and the fat snap of a bigger spark, but then the jumper steadied. "What happened?" she called.

"The tractor shut down."

"That's good, right?"

"Yeah." Jack knew he sounded doubtful. He felt doubtful, as though he knew Ra was going to try something different, something worse. But the ha'tak was moving, its shadow retreating — the ha'tak was lifting away into the sky, the gliders scrambling to catch up. "Ai! Do you see that?"

"He is running, O'Neill." Ai's voice sounded caught between laughter and tears. "He is gone."

"Shut this down, Sam." The jumper was starting to tremble under his hands. No, the trembling was becoming a full-scale shaking, rattling his teeth in his head. "Shut it down!"

"I'm working on it! You can't just turn it off like flipping a switch —"

But even as she spoke, the shaking eased, the thick blue

light fading. The thread that had tied them to the wormhole thinned and vanished, and the Stargate stood untouched, the event horizon rippling blue within its circle. Jack brought the jumper gently down onto the beaten ground, and Sam came forward to join him. Her hands were covered with tiny red flecks where sparks had stung her, and her hair was matted to her head. He certainly didn't look any better, Jack thought, but he couldn't help smiling at her.

"We made it," he said, and she leaned against his shoulder.

"We made it," she agreed. In the gate, the wormhole winked out. He could hear distant shouts, Basa and Teal'c moving in to mop up what was left of the Jaffa, and on the tac screen the other jumpers were circling, decloaking as they came in to land. He would deal with that, get everything organized and taken care of, but just for the moment he rested, his head against Sam's ribs. Someday his luck would run out, but it wasn't today.

CHAPTER THIRTY-FOUR

"YOU HANGING in there, Carter?" Cam asked, crouching down beside the low bed. Carter's pants leg had been cut to just above the knee, and Daniel was checking the dressing.

"I'm good," Carter said, trying to force a smile, though it hurt like hell. It wasn't the first time she'd been hit with a staff weapon, and it wasn't the worst by a long shot.

Ai, the fourth person in the room, frowned. "Is there nothing you can give her to ease the pain?"

"I don't want to be out cold," Carter demurred. She looked up at Cam. "And besides, we're leaving soon. Right, Cam?"

"Yeah." Cam patted her shoulder. "One last round up, and then we're gone. We're going to take the stolen puddle jumper back where it belongs. Home."

"And will you also let me go home?" Ai asked, her brows rising.

"Yes," Daniel said firmly, looking at Cam.

"It might change the timeline if she doesn't," Carter said. "Imagine what would happen if everything she does for the rest of her life didn't happen. We have no idea what that would change! And what about her descendants just winking out of existence? I mean, what if someone like Miko Kusinagi didn't exist? The whole Atlantis expedition might have been lost four years ago."

Cam nodded. "OK, that makes sense." He stood up. "Let's get this show on the road then. What do we need to do before we close up?"

"A bunch of things," Daniel said. "O'Neill's bringing Marik, for one, and says he wants him gone —"

"So let's do them." Cam looked down at her. "You hang in

there. We'll make it as fast as possible."

"I'm OK," Carter said, and watched them head out the door.

Ai shook her head. "I don't understand. Who is this person you speak of?" She sat down on the other side of the bed.

"Dr. Miko Kusinagi," Carter said. "She's a scientist, a fine engineer like you. And like you she has the ATA gene. She comes from Hokkaido, from Mishihase. Who knows? Maybe she's your great a thousand times granddaughter. But she's on the Atlantis Expedition."

"She's been to the City?" Ai's voice was hushed.

Carter nodded. "She lives there now. I saw her there a few months ago."

"You've been to the City?"

Carter nodded, closing her eyes and seeing again the soaring ceiling of the gateroom, the spires of Atlantis against the morning over a soft tropical sea. "I've been to Atlantis. I was there for a year."

Ai's voice hitched. "My grandmother did not remember it," she said quietly. "She was a baby, an orphan from one of the colonies that fell. She was not yet two years old when she was carried through the gate in the final evacuation, carried by a stranger to a new world and a new home. She didn't remember the City at all. She could tell me no stories."

"And that's how the stories were lost," Carter said quietly. "That's how we forgot." She opened her eyes and took Ai's hand. "But it's still there. It's still waiting. And one day a guy named John Sheppard with the ATA gene will walk through the gate to Atlantis, and the city will come to life. Wherever he and Miko and the others with the ATA gene go, lights will come on and systems reboot and the whole city will breathe again."

Ai looked at her and there were tears in her eyes. "Tell me about Atlantis," she said.

Carter swallowed. There was no harm in that. It only fed the legend. "It's very beautiful," she began. "Even to me, and I'm only human."

"You're sure about this?" Cam looked Danyel in the eye.

"Positive." Danyel nodded solemnly and offered Cam his hand. "Do me a favor and look after my team, OK?"

Cam shook it. "I'll take good care of them. Don't you worry about a thing."

"I won't," Danyel said. "Tell Jack... Tell Jack I've got Abydos back."

"I'll tell him," Cam said, and let go. "Y'all take care of yourselves."

"We will," Danyel promised clear-eyed, just as if there weren't a whole world full of prehistoric dangers waiting for them.

O'Neill and Sam came out from the house, Sam with a sunshade over her shoulder and a spattering of red marks across her face and arms where the sparks from the jumper had burned her. O'Neill looked tired still, but more relaxed than Cam had ever seen his counterpart. Danyel looked over his shoulder, his mouth quirking into a wry smile.

"It's still weird not having Teal'c here."

"Indeed it must be." Their own Teal'c came around the back of the jumper, supporting Carter, whose leg had been thoroughly bandaged, linen wrappings over the field dressing. Marik was already on board, sitting uncomfortably on one of the rear seats, his hands securely tied behind him, and Carolyn was waiting in the opening to get Carter settled.

Daniel came around the back of the jumper. "So. I don't suppose you've changed your mind?"

Danyel shook his head, and Cam straightened.

"I know I've asked before, and I know you've said no, but—this is the last chance I can give you. Are you sure you're not coming back with us?"

"It would be really weird," O'Neill said.

Sam smiled. "Thank you, but—we're staying."

"Ready to go?" Daniel asked, his voice a little too bright.

"Yeah," Cam said. "As soon as Carolyn has Carter settled."

Behind them there was the sound of pickaxes at work, Hor-Aha's men burying the stargate for once and for all. "Ai's already headed out for Mishihase. She says she'll never say a word about what happened."

Daniel looked at him keenly. "And you believe her?"

Cam shrugged sheepishly. "If she does tell anybody... I guess it will turn into one of those wild stories about gods and heroes who had battles in the sky a long time ago."

"I suppose it will," Daniel said, and he put his hand on Cam's shoulder. "You know, you've learned a lot about how culture and oral transmission work."

"I'm not actually stupid, Daniel."

"I never thought you were." Daniel said. "It's just, you know..."

"O'Neill left some big shoes to fill. I know." Cam shrugged again.

"You're really different from Jack," Daniel said. "And that's a good thing. He was exactly the man the program needed then, and you're exactly the one it needs now."

"Which just leaves us the question of what happens when Carter gets the *Hammond*," Cam said. "Breaking up the band again."

"I expect we'll muddle through," Daniel said with an ironic twist of his eyebrow. "And it's time." There were shouts out where the men were burying the Stargate, the sounds of workmen calling to one another. Daniel looked toward the sound. "Someday," he said quietly. "Someday a little girl named Catherine Langford will watch her father dig that up. She'll watch them raise it from the sands and she'll wonder what it does. She'll spend her whole life wondering. And one day when she's old she'll come and find me and we'll open a gate to another world." He looked at Danyel. "To Abydos."

Danyel offered Daniel his hand. "I hope you find your way home."

Daniel nodded slowly. "I hope I do too."

Carolyn looked up from beside Carter. "We're ready."

"Good luck," Sam said softly, and Cam nodded.

"Thanks."

She and O'Neill took a few steps back, Danyel following more slowly, and abruptly O'Neill drew himself up into a parade-ground salute. It should have looked ridiculous, from a man in linen shorts and a gold chain and nothing else, but Cam felt a sudden lump in his throat.

"Godspeed, SG-1."

Cam returned the salute, knowing there weren't words, and started up the ramp into the jumper. Carter was watching, and he had to clear his throat before he could speak. "You OK?"

"I'll keep until we get home," she said with a smile. "It's all good."

"Then let's get this show on the road," Cam said.

They took off into a crystal clear Egyptian morning, skies without a hint of smog or industrial pollution. All of that was centuries in the future, along with antibiotics and ice cream. Carolyn leveled the jumper out neatly at 5,000 feet, following the course of the Nile northward over the green fingers of the Delta, toward the cerulean waters of the Mediterranean, Cam riding shotgun in the second seat. Carolyn was getting a lot more confident flying, and besides the jumper liked her. In the back, Vala and Teal'c were watching Marik.

"I kind of wish we could have a look around while we're here," Daniel said from behind Cam. "Cloaked, of course. But it would be really nice to just take a quick side trip over to Mesopotamia. Or Troy. The first city built on Hisarlik was begun about now. Also this is the First Harappan Period in the Indus Valley, and very little is known about it..." He stopped, his voice trailing off, and then began again in a different tone. "And Myrddin's people are building Stonehenge, and some other grandchildren of the Ancients are founding Caral..."

"Daniel," Carter said gently, reaching across the aisle to touch his shoulder. "Let it be."

"I know." Daniel squared his shoulders. "I got into this because I wanted answers to the mysteries. But the answers aren't here on Earth. They never were." He looked at Carter and shook his head. "Ai doesn't have them. The children of the Ancients never did. The answers to our questions about the Ancients, about who we are and why, about what they chose and what they did and what happened to destroy them—those answers are all out there."

"Where we're going," Carter said and squeezed his shoulder. "That's where we're going, Daniel."

Cam looked at Carolyn, for once in perfect agreement. "But I suppose there's no harm in a little low altitude flyby of the Yucatan. After all, it's right on the way."

Cheyenne Mountain
2008 AD

Hank Landry stood up and headed for the coffeepot to pour himself another cup.

"I don't think you've got time for that," Jack O'Neill said. He was still lounging in the visitor chair, his casual pose belying the tension in his face.

Hank looked around. "Why not?"

"Because SG-1 has been gone four hours." O'Neill got to his feet. "And four hours is the safety parameter built into Janus' puddle jumper. It can't arrive within four hours of its own departure."

Hank blinked. He swore O'Neill looked smug. "How the hell do you know that?"

"Carter told me." O'Neill picked up his cover. "Come on. Let's go up to the parking lot."

"The parking lot?"

"Why risk making the transition back to our time in the Mountain?" O'Neill asked. "Lots of wide open skies up there. Come on."

The elevator seemed to take forever. Every sentence he could think to begin started with 'If Carolyn.' But he couldn't think that way. He couldn't start that.

Out through the security checkpoints, everyone hitting the wall for two generals. O'Neill didn't look worried at all. Hank hoped he didn't. But Carolyn...

Out through the tunnel, out past the sentries on duty, saluting as they passed.

"And there we go," O'Neill said, looking up at the sky with satisfaction. There was nothing to see. And then he felt it, a breath of wind from the wrong direction, a sudden downdraft. The air shimmered. The stubby familiar form of the puddle jumper decloaked right in the priority carpool lane, settling to the ground as smoothly as a Harrier.

He could see Carolyn through the windscreen, her face calm with concentration, shutting down the board as Mitchell leaned over her shoulder, and Hank clamped his jaw shut to keep from making a sound.

The back gate came down. "Welcome home, SG-1," said Jack O'Neill.

Egypt
2492 BC

An ibis started up, rising in a flurry of white wings, its reflection mirrored in the waters of the Nile beneath. Jack O'Neill sat on the end of his dock, fishing. It was sunset and there were a lot of mosquitoes, but there were a lot worse ways to finish the day. He batted one away from the baby on his lap. "See there?" Jack said quietly. "See those little rings on the water? That's the fish coming up to the surface to eat bugs."

Ellie watched the circles solemnly. Who knew whether she understood or not, or how much she'd remember, but it was worth saying anyway. Eastward, where night gathered, the first bright stars were appearing, Venus rising like a beacon in the clear sky.

"Starlight, star bright, first star I see tonight," Jack said to

Ellie. "That's what you say to make a wish." He wondered what she'd wish for. Probably dinner.

"I wish I may, I wish I might," Daniel said, coming down the dock.

"Have the wish I wish tonight," Sam said. "Didn't you hear us calling you for dinner?"

"Sorry," Jack said. "I didn't hear. And you didn't finish the wish."

"I don't know what to wish for," Sam said.

Jack looked at her over his shoulder. "You don't wish we'd gone?"

"No." Sam reached down and scooped up Ellie. "Not a bit. But I do wish..." Her voice trailed off.

"What?"

"That they'd left a big bag of chocolate." She grinned at him. "Now come on."

Jack got up, turning to follow her down the dock, and then stopped. Daniel was standing still, looking out across the river. "What are you doing?"

"Finishing the wish," Daniel said. "I wish that Teal'c will have a long and happy life."

"I wish that too," Sam said, coming to put an arm around his waist, Ellie in the other arm.

"Me too," Jack said, his arm around her shoulders on the other side. They stood for a long moment on the end of the dock while the stars came out and the river flowed toward the sea.

Approaching Abydos
2492 BC

The Goa'uld mothership voyaged through hyperspace, traversing stellar distances in a matter of days. Outside the blur of its hyperspace envelope, the universe went about its business as usual. Within, Ra slept in his sarcophagus.

In the best guest quarters assigned to a Goa'uld queen, Aset stood beside the window looking out at the meaningless patterns of shifted stars as though somehow she would see something of worth there. Her hair was braided with gold, and a hand device encased her fingers. Emerald silk, diaphanous as clouds, clothed her. Her sandals were set with jewels.

Her First Prime came and stood behind her, inclining his head solemnly. "What is it that you see?" he asked.

Aset turned, and it was she who looked out from painted eyes. "Only that I am homesick." Teal'c put his arms about her waist, his forehead dipping to her shoulder. "It is a small thing."

"Not to you," he said.

"It is," Aset said. "When by all rights I should be dead, and so should you. So should she, Egeria. This is better." She lifted her head, her eyes on the window where their shared reflection was caught in the angle of glass. "We stand at the beginning of a great story, my friend. What tales there might be of the centuries to come! You and I will see and do so many things, and we will light a flame that will never be extinguished!"

"And when I am gone, you will outlive me by centuries," Teal'c said calmly. "And Egeria will remember us long after you and I are dust." He tightened his hand about her waist. "It is fitting."

Her tone shifted, Egeria as well as Aset. "But for now," she said, "there is joy. We will live and love."

Teal'c closed his eyes, and could not in that moment find the words to gainsay her.

Area 51
2009 AD

Sam had never met the Secretary of State, though of course she'd seen her on TV for years. She'd been the First Lady when Sam was assigned to the Pentagon, a shiny new lieutenant twenty five years old. But Sam hadn't exactly gotten White House invitations in those days. Now the Secretary had come to Area 51 to launch the *George Hammond*.

There was a reviewing stand built of hastily painted timber beside the *Hammond*'s bow, bunting flapping in the stiff wind.

Probably Walter had seen to that. He was the one who always seemed to remember the bunting. Jack never did.

Jack was talking to the Secretary easily, impeccable in his beribboned blues, Mitchell standing politely a step behind him. The rest of SG-1 were clustered a little distance away, amid the strange mixture of dignitaries and construction crew waiting for the official launch, set apart from the flight suited crew of the *Hammond*.

Sam wore the flight suit, the new ship patch heavy on the sleeve. Over her heart was the other one — Col. Samantha Carter. Jack had grinned at that, tweaked it with one finger. "As a matter of fact, it does say colonel on your uniform."

"I made sure of that," Sam had said.

Now he looked up and gestured her over, turning to the Secretary. "I'd like you to meet Colonel Carter."

The Secretary was tiny. That was the thing that was so surprising. Sam was used to being taller than a lot of women, but the Secretary always seemed to loom so huge that it was odd to look down half a foot at her. She wore a bright yellow jacket, bright as a caution pennant in the brisk desert wind, and her hair was dyed the color of wheat, but her age showed around her eyes, sixty something and hard as nails. "Colonel Carter." There was warmth in her voice. "I've heard a great deal about you."

There was never a good answer to that, one that didn't make you either sound smug or like a smart ass. Sam settled for saying, "It's a pleasure to meet you, ma'am."

"I believe it was June of '98," the Secretary said. "When Apophis was attacking Earth. I was evacuated from the White House. But SG-1 came through." She glanced up at Jack.

"All in a day's work," Jack said.

"Apparently," the Secretary said dryly. She offered Sam her hand and shook it firmly. "Congratulations on your post, Colonel Carter. I trust you'll keep it from being too much of a boys' club out there."

"I'll do my best, ma'am," Sam said, and she couldn't help but smile.

"The *George Hammond*," the Secretary said. "He was a fine man, and I regret that he's not here today."

"If he were, we wouldn't be naming the ship after him," Jack said, his mouth tightening, getting flip when something mattered.

The Secretary glanced up at him again, then nodded gravely. "This is a fitting way to honor his memory."

Sam looked away, blinking against the glare of the desert sun on the *Hammond*'s hull. She couldn't help but hope that in some sense he was here, that he saw what he had wrought. *Thank you*, she said in the quiet of her mind. *Thank you so much.*

"If you'll do the honors," Jack said, putting a champagne bottle into the Secretary's hand.

"By all means." Everyone quieted as the Secretary stepped up to the microphone on the platform beside the bow. "It is both an honor and a pleasure to be with you today..." she began.

Sam came to parade rest without thinking about it, her expression attentive and bland as the Secretary began her speech. Her eyes roved over the smooth lines of the *Hammond*'s bow, over the crew assembled in perfect order, Major Franklin barbered within an inch of his life, his flight suit ironed to sharp creases, Lieutenants Chandler and Wright, Davies and Ikram, and behind them with the Marine detachment a flash of red-gold, Captain Cadman's hair severely coiled beneath her beret. Her new team.

She'd come full circle. She was forty-one, the colonel who'd seen it all and done it all, all the way around the circle until she stood in Jack's shoes, ready to begin again. The universe has symmetry, if only you can stand far enough back to see it.

The Secretary finished her speech and broke the champagne bottle across the bow with a practiced hand. Everyone cheered. Other bottles were opened more conventionally and the military band started playing. *Off we go, into the wild blue yonder...*

Her mind supplied the words unsung.

Daniel was at her elbow. "Here you go," he said. "Breaking up the band."

There wasn't anything to say to that, so she just hugged him, feeling his startlement for a moment before he relaxed. "You be careful," he whispered in her ear.

"I always am."

"Break a leg!" Vala said chipperly. "I mean that in a good way."

"I hope I'm done with broken legs for a while," Sam said.

"Good luck," Cam said. "And remember, if you need us, just holler."

"Indeed," Teal'c said, and put his arms around her, tight and solid. "We will never be far away."

"I know." Her voice sounded odd, and it shouldn't. She was the captain now.

Teal'c stepped back, inclining his head formally.

And there was Jack. He didn't offer her his hand, but his eyes were warm. "Carter."

"Sir." Everything they had to say had already been said.

"We'll see you in a couple of months."

Sam took a deep breath and turned away. The *Hammond*'s crew was waiting by the ramp, Cadman looking to her for her signal. "Yes, sir." She raised her voice. "Let's do this."

They went aboard, the whole ship humming with life, the crew hurrying eagerly to their duty stations. The bridge buzzed with activity, and Sam waited a moment before she sat down, her hand on the back of her chair. Out the forward windows she could see the corner of the reviewing stand, the Secretary's yellow jacket and Jack in his blues beside her, Daniel and Teal'c behind him, looking up.

"All systems are green," Major Franklin said from the forward seat.

"Confirmed," Wright said. "All green."

She had words prepared, but they deserted her. Instead she came around the chair and sat down, lifted her chin. "OK. Take her up at your discretion, Lieutenant Chandler."

There was no sense of motion, just the whipping of wind around the reviewing stand, Jack reaching up to hold on to his cover, the Secretary shading her eyes.

The *Hammond* lifted into the cloudless summer sky.

Authors' Note

As always, we are grateful to the pre readers who have given us so many helpful suggestions in the process of writing Moebius Squared, especially Amy Griswold, our partner in crime for the Stargate Atlantis Legacy series. We'd also like to thank Gretchen Brinckerhoff, Lena Sheng, and Lena Strid for their keen eyes and enthusiasm. We'd also like to thank our editor, Sally Malcolm, for allowing us to take SG-1 out for an adventure! It's been amazing fun!

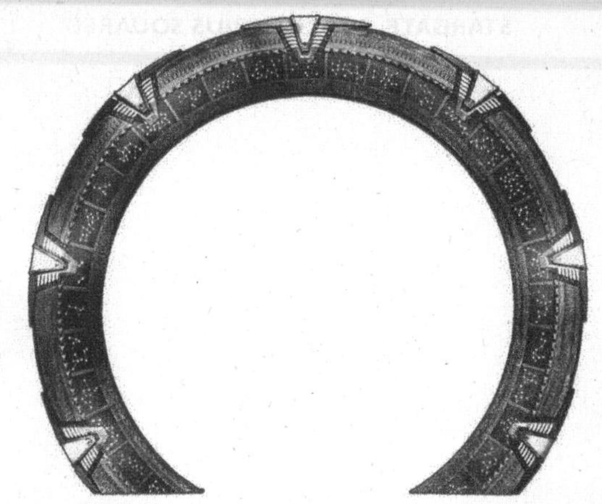